Abou

Julia Kite trained as a social scientist in London and New York, and holds degrees in policy and urban planning from the London School of Economics and Columbia University. She is an alumna of quiz shows *The Chase USA* (which she won) and *Jeopardy* (which she did not). She lives in Manhattan with her fiancé and their parrot. *The Hope and Anchor* is her first novel.

THE HOPE AND ANCHOR

THE HOPE AND ANCHOR

JULIA KITE

Unbound Digital

This edition first published in 2018

Unbound

6th Floor Mutual House, 70 Conduit Street, London W1S 2GF

www.unbound.com

ISBN (eBook): 978-1911586975

ISBN (Paperback): 978-1911586968

Design by Mecob

Cover images:

© Shutterstock.com
© Textures.com

Author photograph: Charles Chessler

Printed in Great Britain by Clays Ltd, St Ives Plc

For my family

Dear Reader,

The book you are holding came about in a rather different way to most others. It was funded directly by readers through a new website: Unbound.

Unbound is the creation of three writers. We started the company because we believed there had to be a better deal for both writers and readers. On the Unbound website, authors share the ideas for the books they want to write directly with readers. If enough of you support the book by pledging for it in advance, we produce a beautifully bound special subscribers' edition and distribute a regular edition and e-book wherever books are sold, in shops and online.

This new way of publishing is actually a very old idea (Samuel Johnson funded his dictionary this way). We're just using the internet to build each writer a network of patrons. Here, at the back of this book, you'll find the names of all the people who made it happen.

Publishing in this way means readers are no longer just passive consumers of the books they buy, and authors are free to write the books they really want. They get a much fairer return too – half the profits their books generate, rather than a tiny percentage of the cover price.

If you're not yet a subscriber, we hope that you'll want to join our publishing revolution and have your name listed in one of our books in the future. To get you started, here is a £5 discount on your first pledge. Just visit unbound.com, make your pledge and type NEELY18 in the promo code box when you check out.

Thank you for your support,

Dan, Justin and John
Founders, Unbound

Super Patrons

John Alexander
Moné Alvarez
Matthew Ames
Mark Ashenden
Annie Berke
Diane Berman
Sally Blue
Jason Bradford
Candace Brakewood
James Brolley
Jack Burger
Charles Chessler
Sharon Chin
Louisa Cilenti
Jorge Concha
MaryHelen Crispo
Michael Drinkard
Michel Estefan
William Jacob Farrell
Ann Feldman
Peter Field
Nate Field
Art & Lynn Freedman
Edna Freeman
Let Gammon
Rachel Gilman
Steph Gladstein
David Gulley
Vlad Gutman-Britten
Hayk Gyuzalyan
Kieran Healy
Richard Hensley

Peter Hicks
Paul Holbrook
Will Hughes
Jonathan Hull
Marlon Hungriano
Sumeet J
Wendy Jacob
Patricia Jacobs
Mary Johnston
Meghann Jones
Andrei Kopelevich
Debbie Kahn
Warwick Kelly
Melisa Kenslea
Robin Ketro
Dan Kieran
Dolores Kite
David Kite
Cathy Kite
Steven Kite
Jennifer Kitses
Kayley Kravitz
Harold Laidlaw
Andy Larsen
Kristen Lepionka
Warren Malone & Janna Levin
Bruce Levine
Zach Lorden
Linda B. Lubell
Kevin Lucas
Laurie MacDougall
Gautam Malkani
Susan & Marc Marcus
James Masente
Eric McClure
Sean McGhee

John McLaughlin
Ritamary McMahon
Bridget McNulty
PJ Mead
Harley Metcalfe
Lee Millward
John Mitchinson
Andrew Montgomery
Veronica de la Mora
Sam Nair
Aaron Naparstek
Rob Newland
Matthew Nguyen
Noreen O'Donnell
Kwaku Osei-Afrifa
Raza Panjwani
Yolanda Perez-Shulman
Laura Pinzur
Justin Pollard
Alexandra Reisner
Lynn LeDinh Rouse
Cassidy Rouse
Alison Ryan
Dianne Schweiger
Pauly Silver
Christina Smolen
Piers Stanger
Alex & Judi Stein
Basia Surož
Marcelle Thiebaux
Christopolis Tiberius
Andrew Ward
Mary Grace White
Lianna Willson
Margaret Winslow
Lois Wolff-Friend

Jack Wranovics
Robert Wright
Tricia Zion

The one constant in every city is change. While the settings in this book are real places, years have shifted the specific details. This book is a work of fiction.

With grateful thanks to Will Hughes, who helped make this book happen.

Deconstruction

One

'Neels.'

'Yeah?'

'Neels.'

'What?'

'You smell of salt and cigarettes and love.'

She wanted to shake her head, and then shake him. Mentally she searched for the one perfect word to describe the way he spoke to her, the way he always spoke to her when he was out of excuses but couldn't stand the silence. It was on the tip of her tongue, but that was firmly wedged behind her teeth. The name of this little pocket of London, the borough, the name of this chunk of the city made into a verb and put into the past tense – that would work. That would suffice.

It was half seven in the morning in *Hackney*, and Sam had his nose buried in her hair.

Neely sighed, louder than strictly necessary, and regretted it immediately. She knew Sam read far too much into every action. In that quick release of breath he would sense his own inadequacy. Or perhaps, Neely thought, spotting the empty can of lager lying on the carpet, *I'm* the one reading too much into this, and he honestly doesn't give a shit what you do and never has and never will, and that's why nowadays he's shagging a big-nosed bitch from Bristol and not you.

Hackneyed, Neely thought, shivering against the couch cushions. *You and him and everything about this flat.*

'Neels.'

He did that often – used her name, pointlessly shortened by a mere syllable but no letters, as a statement and not a question.

'Neels.'

'What?'

'Stop doing that.'

'Stop doing *what*?'

'Being so fucking far away.'

3

She remembered to breathe normally this time, and not deflate too obviously. 'I'm only in Westbourne Park.'

'Far away.'

'No it's not. It's nothing on the Tube. Get on the Overground.'

'Neely. Move in here. I'll take care of you.'

He knows exactly how beautiful he is, she thought, *and that's why he gets what he wants. He always gets precisely what he wants. Even when he's not sure what he wants.*

'I don't want taking care of.'

'You should. You'd like it.' He raised her chin with one finger and locked in the stare. 'You and me.'

'Can't happen. You're not giving *her* up so quickly. And you know it.'

'It could. I might. Just be like…'

'Like what?'

'Fuck it.'

Sam set his drink down on the carpet, crossed the lounge in three strides, and crouched in front of the wall of records.

'What do you want to hear, Neels?'

'Anything. You pick.'

'Let's have some Leonard Cohen. Yeah?'

'Oh god, no. Leonard Cohen's depressing.'

'You're depressing.'

'Your mum's depressing.'

'My mum's lovely. She still gets all the men in Manchester.'

He tried, and that's why she couldn't hate him. He tried. He'd repeated more times than anybody needed to hear, over the phone and to her face, in letters and in sounds, *I'm not some cunt. I'm not like that.* And she had believed him, because she had been silly enough to think he had been trying to convince her of that fact, rather than himself.

'Neels.'

'What?'

'You're not drinking.'

'Of course I'm not. It's not even eight in the fucking morning.'

'It's nice. It's a Cuba Libre. It'll wake you up.'

'I'll have a cup of tea if you're offering.'

'You're so boring.' But he plodded off to the kitchen regardless, and Neely scanned his wall of vinyl while he made the brew. He has every single thing the Smiths have ever released, she thought to herself. Even both versions of 'How Soon is Now?'. Nobody's that thorough. And they all fit on one shelf. Imagine having your entire life's work so neat and tidy and portable. Imagine making yourself into a boxed set, and imagine what would happen if at the last minute you realised the lid didn't fit.

'Here. Drink up.' He crouched in front of Neely, knees poking through yesterday's slashed denim.

'It's too hot.'

'It's supposed to be hot. It's tea.'

'Yeah, well, I'm not gonna burn myself. Is that how Sophia drinks hers?'

'Hey. Be nice. Please.'

Neely dropped her head, brushing Sam's face with her ponytail. He smelled of nothing when she rested her forehead against the ridge of his collarbone. He does not smell like anything at all, she thought. He doesn't even smell of booze and that's two pints of lager and a rum and Coke, more rum than Coke, he's had since I woke up.

'Neely.'

'What?'

They stared.

'Kiss me.'

Hackneyed. But she did, and then returned to her place on the sharp edge beneath his neck.

She closed her eyes so that she could better hear what she thought, then knew, she heard: the heart, frantic this time, battering itself silly against his bones. We are too close, Neely thought. What, two inches? Well, that's if you start at my face, the skin, the senses. From my brain there's more of a distance. But not too much. If he thinks Hackney to Westbourne Park is a voyage then what must he think of me here, now, with so little space between us, just thin fabric and thin skin and bones I forgot were quite so delicate. She held her breath and listened to that bassline telling death to fuck off for now. Hollow muscle banging away at its assembly-line tasks. And I say *my* job is dull, Neely thought to herself. How much faith we put on nothing more than a metronome of low notes. She shifted and heard the tentative pattering of new rain on Sam's windows. They had sung together when they were drunk, with Neely on the harmonies because when she drank she never managed to down as much as he did. Well, usually not. And last night was not usual.

'I'm really happy with her, Neels. Don't hate me for being happy.'

She sighed and didn't care who heard. 'Sam, I've got to go.'

'Don't be like that.'

'No, really, I promised Angela we'd go to lunch. And I'm disgusting and I need a wash and I'm knackered.'

'Just call her and tell her you'll be late. She doesn't have to work at that fucking swimming pool today?'

Angela. She shut her eyes, clamped them tight enough to start the clouds of colour dancing behind the lids, and an image of her girlfriend appeared from the dark swirls of the prisoner's cinema. The mess of brittle blonde curls wrapped around long fingers, the legs dangling over the edge of the sofa on the other side of the city. *Go on,* she had told Neely last night, her voice betraying the tiredness she said was keeping her in for the night. *Go on, have a blast, give him my love.* Presumably she hadn't meant for that to be taken literally.

Neely frowned, pretending to consider the proposition. 'No. I've got to go.'

'Ten minutes?'

A sigh, a nod. He pulled her down, gently this time, so that they both lay on the carpet, and he held her close again. It's what you wanted, the girl thought to herself. It's what you wanted and you can't even enjoy yourself, you miserable cow.

'This is fucking uncomfortable.'

'Bed?' he grinned.

'Yeah, why not?' Plenty of reasons.

It was longer than ten minutes, but he didn't have a clock, and her watch, carefully unfastened before she passed out the night before, sat at the bottom of her handbag. In days to come, she will want to remember more. She will not only regret that the previous night's alcohol fuzzed her memory, but that there was not more to remember.

In order to create a memory, something has to happen. Something significant. The general rule holds that there must be an action, a reaction, a stimulus, some noise. Something to remember. And despite their best efforts, her actions didn't inspire the result they both desired.

Of course nothing happened. Two cans of lager and god knows how much rum. *Hackneyed*. Hiding her disappointment behind a blackout curtain of hair, Neely rearranged Sam's jeans and left the zip at half mast.

'Neels?'

'Yeah?'

'You can't go.'

'I have to.'

'No, Neels… I mean, you really can't go.'

'What's up?'

Sam sighed, the colour draining from his face as he stared at the ceiling. 'I've… I've just taken some Viagra. Only it hasn't kicked in yet. I thought, you know, because… we could…'

Christ, she thought. *You're only thirtysomething. I've only got a girlfriend.*

'Sam, I'm going.'

'Please, Neels.'

'I'm going.'

'Neels.'

'I'm sorry.' She wasn't.

At the door, she turned and looked back through to the man in his bedroom, atop the sheetless mattress. *Is it his face in his hands or his hands in his face?* Neely wondered, then made her feet cross the threshold. Jesus Christ, girl, she muttered to herself as the door clicked shut. If you turn into a pillar of salt, there's no way you're making it home through all that fucking rain.

She changed trains at Highbury & Islington, then King's Cross. The free papers were telling Londoners not to count on a white Christmas. Inside her mittens, Neely rubbed her fingers to keep the blood moving. Despite herself, she smiled. Angela would piss herself laughing when she heard what happened. Of course, Neely wouldn't tell the whole story, just the bits they could have and hold and try not to giggle about in Sam's future company. Just what would make Angela smile, none the wiser. She'd put the kettle on and bring Neely a brew and they'd sit down and laugh until they couldn't breathe. Neely knew she would be able to look back on this shitstorm and giggle soon enough. It would be okay. Angela would be there.

Neely Sharpe was an office manager. She hadn't planned for it, but life had chucked those circumstances at her and she never swatted them away. Nowadays she went to the office, and she managed, and she made it to the weekend, and through the weekend, and back into the ballet of routine.

She fumbled in her handbag, the black patent-leather satchel from Topshop already starting to tear at cheaply stitched seams, her mittened hands too clumsy to find her keys quickly amidst all the assorted junk. Once inside, she spotted the post lying on the floor. She picked out the envelopes for Flat C and nudged the others aside. It wasn't her job to look after the other tenants. It was only her job to comply with the landlord's misspelled sign on the back of the door: PLEASE CLOSE SECURLY. SAFETEY IS EVERYBODY'S RESPONSABILITY. Tidying up after Flats A and B was not her *responsability*. Neely scampered up the narrow stairs, feeling her way around the curve in the dark the way she had done since the light had burnt out two months ago. By now she could fit her key into the lock completely blind.

'Angela! Angela, you're not going to believe this. I got so shitfaced with Sam last night, I woke up on his couch. I didn't mean to. I got way too pissed.'

The flat felt not nearly as warm as it should have been. Shame. She had been looking forward to the blast of heat in her face, the coziness of windows so fogged up that she couldn't even see the shops across the street. The red-and-white stripes of Khan Halal Meats blurred to a fuzz of pink; the windows of the flats above, flats presumably similar to her own, just dark gaps floating in a grey day. But Angela hadn't turned on the radiators.

'Angela? You in?'

Obviously not. Angela Archer wasn't the type to put on another jumper when she owned a perfectly well-functioning electric fan heater. Some things are luxuries, she had once said, and this ain't one of them. I'm not going to freeze like I'm too skint to put on the heat in December. So what if it's another fiver? I'm not that poor.

'Aaaaangela.'

Nobody home. Nobody had been home.

Neely sighed. She shrugged out of her coat and switched on the fan heater, crouching to warm her whole body at once. After a few minutes basking in the heat, no longer focusing on the chill in her lungs and the nipping of her ears, she noticed the hunger. There hadn't been anything to eat at Sam's. Well, nothing worth eating. His new woman had left a bunch of bananas on the table, dangling from a little wooden banana-stand-tree-whatchamacallit that apparently made them ripen better than just leaving them on the countertop for free. Sophia was the kind of woman who cared about the right way to ripen bananas, who *could* care about bananas, Neely thought to herself. *What a fucking lovely human being. What a perfect specimen of contemporary aspirational womanhood. What can I offer compared to that? I am insensitive to fruit and their needs.* And there had been plenty of booze in his flat in Hackney, but that would have only lightened her head instead of filling her stomach, and she didn't believe the hair of the dog should go anywhere near a human mouth. That's how she knew she wasn't too far gone, not yet, even if she had a hangover, even if she had promised herself she wouldn't get one this time, again.

She walked to the kitchen and, with one freshly thawed hand, reached for her mobile. She could ring Angela without looking: speed-dial number two. Number one was her brother, a chemist in Cambridge. With the other hand, she pulled a nearly full box of Frosties from the cupboard. A superior cereal. She and Angela agreed on that. But they had to be actual Frosties. No Sainsbury's own, No Tesco Value Frosted Flakes. There was a difference, and they could both taste it, even if all those variations on a satisfying crunchy and sweet theme came off the exact same production lines. More of Angela's philosophy: if you're going to pinch pence shopping, buy the cheap pasta or a crap cut of meat, but blow the budget on breakfast.

Don't start the day off by reminding yourself what you can't afford. Save that for later, when your work and the world and everything in it have done a grand old job making you miserable and a little extra degradation won't matter.

She pinned the phone between her ear and shoulder as she shook the Frosties into a clean bowl and emptied the last of the milk onto them. After a few rings, the recorded voice of her girlfriend informed her that she couldn't answer right now, but if Neely left a message, Angela would get back to her soon, thanks, bye. 'Angela. It's me. Wake up, sleepychops. Wherever you are, pull up your knickers and come home because I've got a story for you. All I'm going to say now is: Sam. Love you. Bye.'

She should have asked Angela to pick up more milk. No bother. Neely could just run to the Costcutter on the corner. Harrow Road had a reputation for dullness, but she couldn't agree. Harrow Road had everything she needed. For the things she wanted, she could simply hop onto the 18 bus or jump onto the Tube and find them quickly enough. A proper boozer across the street and a few doors down. A library, the swimming pool where Angela worked, about a million restaurants, all within a brisk walk. And Neely always walked quickly. Three stops on the Tube to the new shopping centre in Shepherd's Bush. Two stops in the other direction to Paddington. Neely thought practically, and Harrow Road was an overwhelmingly practical place. Not flashy, not at all, but far from soul-destroyingly, condemnably bland. Dull, she thought, is just lazy shorthand, the acceptable way to say you think the shops are beneath you, and you think you're too good to live above them. Lytton Way, Stevenage – now *that* was a bona fide boring stretch of street, nothing going for it but the train station tempting her out. Half an hour to King's Cross. She had spent too many half hours to and from King's Cross as a teenager, and she intended to spend as few as possible in the future.

Neely tapped the face of her phone to redial. Angela Archer, the screen read, displaying a photo of the girl taken in warmer days. Not as if she needed to remind herself what Angela looked like. It was simply how she preferred to see her: Angela at a midsummer gig in Hyde Park, leaning back on her elbows in a patch of grass made even more lush and green by a phone app's filter. Black vest, black hat – fedora? trilby? Neely couldn't remember what it was called. Red fingernails against a Heineken bottle. Half-smile. Serene, her gentle edges pink with sunburn. The kind of Angela who Neely liked to see in December. She smiled despite herself, and then heard the voicemail introduction again.

'Angela. Where is yer arse? Bring it back to the mothership A-S-A-P. Oi. Answer your phone.'

Must have been on the Tube. Or she'd put it on silent and hadn't felt it buzzing. She could be dozy like that sometimes, usually when her epilepsy tablets had been tweaked and she hadn't had enough time to get used to how they made her feel. But that would only last a few days. No big deal. Angela insisted it was no big deal. She didn't want anybody making a fuss over her or treating her differently just because she had fits now and then. 'I'm not special,' she insisted. 'And even if I was, I'd want it to be because I did something amazing, not because my brain's wired wrong. You know that woman in the States who smashes empty beer cans with her tits? The one from *Rude Tube*? I swear, honest to God, I would rather have people picture something as daft as that when they said my name rather than think of some spacker shaking on the floor.' Angela had told Neely this relatively early in their relationship, and Neely found it telling: who Angela was, and how her life had moulded her into the cheeky young woman she had fallen in love with so completely and so easily. Angela had made it very easy. Most people couldn't be loved by everybody. Some people couldn't be loved by anybody. Angela Archer struck Neely as the kind of person who could be loved damn near close to universally, because you started talking to her about the meaning of pity, about the suffering she'd had in her life, and then she reminded you there's a woman in the States who smashes tins with her tits.

And Angela knew Harrow Road. She was from here. As in actually, really and truly grew up kicking-distance away, just over the canal. Nobody else Neely knew was actually from London, *real* London, not *Kingston*, not *Epsom*, not *fucking Watford*, but a part of London that had always been London for as long as anybody who mattered knew. Angela Archer was a West Londoner, born and bred. Maybe she would never be able to afford to buy a house in her childhood postcode but, in Neely's eyes, London already belonged to Angela Archer. She walked down Harrow Road like she had memorised every crack in the pavement and had an explanation for how they got there. When she nodded at shopkeepers, they nodded back, except for the one miserable bastard their age at the newsagents. If all relationships were, at their very heart, built on exchange, then Neely thought she had done well for herself. With Angela Archer, she had a home beyond the walls of their flat.

Neely devoured the Frosties and tipped the sugared milk into her mouth, trying not to remind herself that last night – this morning – she had behaved like somebody doing her best to smash up that happy home. She hadn't meant it. She never did. She never planned to get that plastered. The hangover tap-danced lightly around the orbits of her eyes. *You fucking idiot.* She thought about a mug of tea, but not very seriously. She checked the kitchen clock: just past eleven. She hadn't lied to Sam. Angela had indeed suggested they grab lunch and hit Westfield for some last-minute Christmas shopping. She just hadn't specified when. Surely if she wasn't answering her phone then she wouldn't be home and ready to head out again for quite some time.

Neely Sharpe shivered, yawned. Now able to concentrate on sensations other than the cold in her bones, she suddenly became aware that she smelled. Not majorly, and not disgusting. Like Sam had said, salt and cigarettes. She didn't think love had a particular smell, not a universally definable one at least, so she couldn't comment on that. But definitely salt and cigarettes. She rinsed out her bowl under the kitchen tap, then plodded through to the shower to turn it on and let the steam fill the room. Once she felt warm enough to strip off, she shut the door and immersed herself beneath the hot cascade. Black hair fell over her face, parted for her nose. Any evidence of last night swirled down the plughole with citrus-scented suds from a bottle that promised to wake her up with the power of ten lemons, like it was really that easy.

She tried to clear her mind under the shower head, hoping that flushing out the superfluous crap would make room for what she really wanted to remember: last night. She recalled saying goodbye to Angela and hopping onto the Tube at Westbourne Park. Change at King's Cross. Change at Highbury & Islington. Hackney was overrated. Took ages to get there, and for what? Well, Sam made it worth it. They'd watched the band where he knew the bassist, then moved elsewhere to see the band where he knew the singer. He had been buying the drinks, so she drank. This in itself had been a momentous occasion. Sam never had cash to spare. 'Where's Angela?' he had asked, and Neely explained that she hadn't felt up to it, said the batteries were low, she was going to take it easy. Sam seemed to accept the excuse. After they wobbled up to the Babble Jar, where Sam had known the entire damn band, the sound guy and the ginger bartender with the peacock-blue stars tattooed up her neck, Neely's memory dimmed and flickered before burning out completely.

I shouldn't fucking drink, she thought. *And I really shouldn't drink like men twice my size. By twenty-seven, you should know these things. You should grow up. Fuck. Moron.* Neely wrapped her hair in a towel and wrung it out like she held a grudge. She couldn't be arsed drying it.

I'll just take a nap, she thought. *Clear my head. Rearrange my thoughts, or rather let my thoughts rearrange themselves. That's their job and they're not half bad at it. I can spare the time. And when I wake up, Angela will be here. She'll know what I should do. She'll be here.*

Later, final hints of hangover chased away with Nurofen, Neely drifted into the lounge: to the hi-fi, and all that its sound waves could touch. She crouched before the bookcase, which held nearly as many albums as books, almost all hers. Most of the CDs never left their cases nowadays, but she held onto them like medallions, like antiques. She had inadvertently arranged them by season, and winter was for those voices dead before either she or Angela had been born, or those voices that sounded like they wanted to be.

Neely touched each case, deliberating, remembering the verdicts Angela had pronounced on them: Lou Reed, unlistenable. Tom Waits gave her the fear. Oh, but Tim Buckley was alright, Angela had liked him. She'd asked Neely if he was touring any time soon, unaware they were several decades too late. Now Neely smiled to herself at this recollection. She remembered watching Angela. She remembered smiling then, and folding her arms tightly in front of her, pulling the fabric of her cardigan taut even though she knew it was no use, that all of Harrow Road could probably hear the chiming in her chest like the electric carillon of the parish church in Stevenage, that grey tram-shed of worship in the centre of her hometown, its tower rising against the gardens and the council blocks and the never-ending traffic heading somewhere else. She couldn't muffle that noise in her heart no matter how hard she tried. Angela had been sprawled out on the carpet, listening to Neely's albums, completely deaf to everything but the stereo.

She remembered something else, too; something Angela had asked. 'Doesn't this sad bastard stuff bring you down?'

'You can still make beauty out of ugliness,' Neely had sniffed. *Like you*, she had wanted to say. *When you're coming round from a fit and you're out of it and your face gets stuck like you're chewing a wasp. And then it's all soft and you sleep and a smile you don't even know about spreads across your face. And I watch you until I'm sure you're not going to decide to quit breathing. Like that.*

Like how Sam's eyes did not quite focus when he was drunk, which was most of the time. But last night he'd pinned her against the shut-up butchers in Ridley Road Market for the kiss and while she was trying to figure out which eye she should look into, the one drifting ever so slightly up or the one making its way almost imperceptibly to the left, he had whispered in whisky fumes, *I've been wanting to do this for fucking ages, Neels*, and there had been no appropriate response for her to give as he moved his lips down to her neck and slid his fingers under the waist of her skirt besides, *Me too.*

Now Neely abandoned the task of picking an album and stared out the window. Lights had begun to pop alive in the rooms of other flats, teasing her with the question of who might live within, and what they might be doing that Neely was not. In the flat opposite a youngish man, Arab as far as Neely could tell, lit a cigarette. He was chatting and laughing to somebody who had his back to the window, his hands clasped behind his head, elbows pointed out, perfectly framed. On the pavement below, headscarved women – Somali, Neely guessed – scurried through the cold, faces down, strides determined. *How cruel*, she thought. *You come all the way from Mogadishu or God knows where because you're starving or running for your life or whatever, and you end up in a winter like this.* She walked to the kitchen to put the kettle on.

They would move, she knew. As soon as Neely got a pay rise. Angela wasn't going to be earning any more money any time soon, but Neely didn't mind paying extra. It's what you did when you were in love, she figured. You quit counting every penny. You let little things go. They could move up from Harrow Road, maybe Queen's Park or Kensal Green, a flat in a lovely carved-up Victorian house instead of above a high-street shop. And why couldn't Neely dream of such things? They had been together more than a year – and together was the best way she could think of describing the two of them. *Girlfriend* sounded silly, trite. *Partner* was too stuffy. But Neely and Angela, Angela and Neely, they were together. It wasn't a lie. It was simple, it was true. And the simplest explanation, she knew, was almost always correct.

Making tea required no thought whatsoever. She could do it drunk or in a daydream or both. Sometimes she longed for complication, for a puzzle behind the minutiae of everyday life to remind her that there was plenty of brain desperate to be challenged, but not today. Not after last night. Her hands moved without her to manipulate the electric kettle, but as she reached for the sugar, she suddenly stopped. She felt that the little heat in the kitchen had rushed out, as if a gust from outside had blown open the door and all the windows, and the tiny hairs on her outstretched right arm stood upright. Still sitting where they had always sat, portioned out in their case labelled with every day of the week, every time of the day: Angela's tablets.

Two

Evening, almost. December, dark before it had any right to be, street lights on long before the clock hit five. Their glow fell upon the short girl moving along the pavement in her woolly hat, jaundicing her face as she returned to the front door to 490 Harrow Road. *I must be the only person in London still using this damn thing*, Neely thought to herself as she stomped back up to Flat C with the phone book. She'd had to go all the way down to the bike shop, the one right where the postcodes of Harrow Road changed, to find anybody who had a copy. The old couple at the newsagents couldn't speak English; Neely had mimed clumsily, plucking at her shirt for the colour, then simultaneously speaking on a telephone and flipping imaginary pages. 'Phone book? Do you have? Telephone book?' Blank stares all round, washed with a touch of pity: the girl was probably a bit wrong in the head. Had to be. Would have said so in their own language the minute she left.

She stared at the pillbox, doubting her perfect eyesight, willing the little SATURDAY's contents to vanish like they should have done first thing that morning, like Friday's had done before them. She had already run out of convenient words to shoot at it, run out of *fuck fuck fuck* and *oh shit* looping ad infinitum, and the phrases that rushed in to fill their newly vacated void in her head were Angela's own: 'I'm not special. I don't want any fuss. I don't want people to worry about me.'

She took the thick book into the front room, dropped it onto a carpet that still bore the faint impression of Angela's elbows and feet, then retrieved her mobile. Too many Archers in London. She knew Angela's sister was called Andrea – 'A' names, alliteration very big in that family, the brother called Alex or Adam or something like that – but there were no Andrea Archers on the page. Neely liked names, liked rolling the letters around on her tongue and in her brain, deconstructing the syllables, tracing the roots. Maybe it's why me and Angela get on so well, she'd thought on many nights as she fought the noise from Harrow Road for sleep, and lost. Archer and Sharpe. Too stupid to be coincidence.

Angela had always laughed at that. Angela, always Angela. Nobody called her Angie, not even her family. Angie Archer was too sing-song, too cutesy, she'd explained, but Angela Archer rolled, it swayed and swelled and pitched back and forth, rocking upon the waves. She made Neely dizzy. Always did, from the first time they talked at the Porchester Centre swimming pool. Well, the first time they had said more than the necessary few words essential to transaction. Neely had taken to swimming after her last break-up, and Angela, perched atop her stool at the front desk, had taken her money for the day passes.

Initially, Neely hadn't paid much heed to the smiling blonde girl behind the till during her period of mourning for her life with Ruby Sullivan. Easily the most gorgeous girl Neely had known during her three years at Goldsmiths College, Ruby possessed an easygoing sexuality as integral to her presence as green eyes and size five feet. Predictably, she had no problem blagging her way into any gig from Dalston to Hammersmith. In these cellars and glorified pubs, with Ruby and the affected airheadedness the girl had carefully cultivated via expensive education, Neely danced and drank and forgot her disappointments. Namely one massive disappointment: the aborted doctorate, the three further years at King's slogging away at *Homes Fit for Whom? A History of Public Morality and Social Housing Allocation in Inner London, 1919-Present*, three years of work that had left her qualified to be nothing more than an office manager. All through the transition from promising young academic to mediocre young administrator, Neely had been lucky enough to find herself the one Ruby came home to after long nights of rejecting men who went stupid at the sight of her, too stupid to realise she wasn't interested in anything other than the booze they could buy her. Unluckily for Neely, Ruby also came with a fuse so tiny it could be easily mistaken for an errant fingernail clipping. And one day, for no discernible reason, Neely had flicked that clipping straight into the fire. She couldn't even remember precisely what she had said or done. But she remembered what Ruby had said: get out. And Ruby had also said: everything is your fault. And: you can stay a fucking office drone for the next forty years. You just don't want anything more. You don't know who you are or what you want and even if you did, you wouldn't fucking want it enough, and that's your problem. You don't want anything enough. Including me. So enjoy your dull, shit life.

Without Ruby's approval, Neely thought she would never feel interesting again, never feel worthy of curiosity. So when the girl at the Porchester Centre finally asked her a question, her head jerked up so quickly that she assumed the questioner could hear the cracking of her neck.

'How did you get the name Neely?'

'What?'

The blonde girl had blushed, as if she had just found a schoolgirl error in her sums. 'I've never met any Neelys before. Is it an old name in your family or something?'

'Nah.' And then it was Neely's turn to redden slightly, though not for the first time since she had spotted Angela behind the desk, months back, wearing the name tag that told her Angela was Angela. 'It's stupid.'

'Go on.'

The fiery feeling had spread up her neck, bloomed across her cheeks. 'I was supposed to be a boy,' she had mumbled. 'And my parents were going to call me Neil. I'd had an Uncle Neil, my dad's brother, and he died right before I was born. Somebody cocked up doing the scans and told them, Mrs Sharpe, Mr Sharpe, you're having a baby boy. Didn't go exactly to plan.'

And Angela had laughed – not impolitely, but that pealing, teeth-apart laugh that felt like complete approval, like a benediction. 'Didn't go entirely perfect for me, neither. I was supposed to be a total angel.' And Neely had laughed back, noticing for the first time how fake her own sounded. *I want her to teach me that laugh*, she had thought. *I want to do that to people. Make them feel perfect even if they're talking shite. I want to have that kind of light, even if her teeth are not quite straight, even if she really does need to bleach her roots.*

Neely returned to the present day, took her felt-tip, and struck through all the Archers that couldn't be Angela's dad: the women, the people with postcodes far from West London. Then, sucking her teeth,

19

she started down the column of who remained. No answer at the first one, a Ben in Chiswick. Told off by the second, D in Hanwell: there's no Angela here and didn't she know it was his day off and couldn't she leave him alone? No joy in Ruislip, Hounslow, or Hammersmith, but J in Acton answered on the second ring.

'Hello?'

'Hi, sorry, my name's Neely Sharpe?' Her voice always took on that apologetic, vaguely Antipodean rising inflection whenever she was nervous. Angela teased her for it, hummed the theme tune from *Neighbours* or shot off a Kylie Minogue medley until Neely got a grip. 'I was wondering? Is Angela there?'

'I'm sorry... Ellie?'

'No. Neely. Angela's flatmate.'

'Nee-lee?'

'Yes.' Going deaf, she assumed. Decades of squealing rails, driving the Tube.

'You live with Angela?'

Christ, she thought. *He doesn't know.*

'Yeah. Yes. Are you her dad?'

'I've a daughter called Angela, yes. She didn't say anything about a flatmate.'

'Your daughter, she's kind of tall, got really curly blonde hair, works at the Porchester Centre?'

'That's Angela.'

'It's just, I'm trying to find her. We were supposed to go to lunch today, I can't reach her on her mobile, and I'm just wondering, she didn't say she was going away or anything, so I thought maybe she'd gone home?'

A pause at the other end. 'How do you spell your name?'

'N-E-E-L-Y. Neely Sharpe, Sharpe with an E.'

He doesn't know who I am. She never mentioned me.

Neely shifted her weight on the carpet, and caught a glint of light off the CD balanced atop her hi-fi. She saw Angela staring, unblinking, into the spinning disc that night when Tim Buckley had reminded them how they didn't know what to say, they didn't know what to do. The plaintive ghost-voice, dead before either of them were born, promised that he knew them better than they knew themselves. A soft smile, the slight nod. Angela had been listening.

'Neely?'

And I don't know him, either. Angela made sure I didn't. Her heart sped up and caught in her throat.

Neely killed the call. Pressed the red dot and watched her phone's background reappear: the skyline as seen from the lounge where she sat, but in sunnier days when everything had felt as certain and solid as brick and concrete and limestone. The phone felt hot now, pulsing at her fingers. She dropped it on the floor and pushed the phone book underneath the hi-fi cabinet with her feet. Her movements scrubbed Angela clean off the carpet.

If Angela was not in, then it made sense to Neely that she must be out. Basic logic, common sense. Any idiot could figure that out, and Neely had always thought herself more than a scratch above any idiot. So she locked the door and hit the pavement in the evening chill. She did the Harrow Road door to door, a tour of the pubs and their yellow-lit insides. Why might Angela be in the pub? Again, logic: she might be in the pub because she was definitely not in the flat, and if she was not in the pub, then that would be one less place left to look afterward. Simple as.

A peek in the Barlby Arms: no Angela. Not on either side of the wraparound bar, which split the pub evenly down the centre and gave it the only bit of charm to be found within its walls. She was not sitting by the old men watching the cricket highlights, nor was she among the tracksuited wasters around the snooker table. The Windsor Castle: no sign of Angela Archer. No sign of anybody in particular, because the clientele at that moment certainly counted as nobodies. Neely recognised them. The gingery one with the broken nose and the fingers shakily looking for something to scratch was called Rob, a fitting name for someone whose only useful skill seemed to be thieving. His girlfriend, Gina, sat across from him. Her lips were split again. Rob wasn't responsible for that. He'd have a go, and usually an ill-advised one that left him the worse off, at anybody except his girlfriend. He'd go especially mental on anybody who looked at her sideways. Neely knew this. She'd seen it happen before on the corner of Harrow Road and Elgin Avenue just around kicking-out time. Gina had spoken three words to Neely in all her life: 'Black don't crack,' with a cackle, when she saw Neely staring at a scrape on her cheek one night during a pub quiz. *But it just did*, Neely had thought back, smiling only to be polite. Rob and Gina hadn't been playing that night. They never did.

Rob and Gina always migrated pub to pub, wispily, like Neely was doing now, and as she leaned her full weight into the door of the Hope and Anchor and grunted it open, the heat and the noise rushed to meet her. Melanie the barmaid's eyes did, too. Her face registered relief for a split second before she covered it with an asinine grin. On nights like this, she served as quizmaster and ringmaster of a human circus with far too many coked-up amateur clowns and no safety net beneath the trapeze. Mel was in fact younger than Neely, but her overall appearance was that of a once-stunning outfit that had been put through the wash twice as often as recommended, and on a turbo spin cycle at that. She had both faded and sagged considerably since she and Angela Archer had shared a classroom at Sion–Manning School. Her ankles were too big for her high heels, which were too high for any practical purpose and made her wobble on the carpet. The thick, inexpertly applied highlights in hair pulled tight against her skull gave the impression her head had been burnished by a sculptor who had quickly lost interest and moved onto the next project before finishing the first. The overall effect screamed, from every curve: I will grow old here and I will die here and when that happens I will be doing the exact same thing I am doing now. And right now, she was verbally wrangling a speeding skinhead who had greeted Neely's arrival with nothing less than the facial equivalent of a raging hard-on.

'Is that the stripper? Told you, we should have a stripper in here, not a fucking quiz.'

'Shut up. No, it's the encyclopaedia. We'll ask her. Her decision is final, OK?'

'Could still be the stripper if she's up for it.'

'Fuck off! Her missus will poison you for that.'

'Her missus! Girl-on-girl? You're sitting on a goldmine here, Mel!'

The barmaid-turned-emcee snorted and turned to the newcomer. 'Neely. Question. Settle this for us: is Pluto a planet now or not?'

From the same stubble-ringed mouth, on the same tirade: 'Why can't we just fucking Google it?'

'I said no phones! Neely?'

She glanced from the man to the barmaid and back. 'Well, that's the thing, it was, and then they got rid of it, and maybe they'll bring it back, but not yet.' And then she gave them what they had asked for: 'No.'

'Ha!' Mel hollered. 'Sit down, Jim, Brainbox says I'm right, Pluto's not a planet any more. The correct answer is that Venus is the smallest planet around. Goddess of beauty. Small but perfectly formed. Like this girl here. You're wrong, you're wrong.'

'It's Mercury, though,' Neely blurted, unaware her time to contribute was up.

'You what?'

'Mercury's the smallest planet, not Venus.'

The room breathed; first, a silent inhalation before a burst of laughter.

'Change of plans, Mel! Let Shorty here run the quiz and you go get your kit off, get on top of the bar!'

'Fuck you. OK, that question is a freebie. Everybody gets a point. So that means... alright, the standings are, it's Great Western Wasters with 6 points, Doctor How with 7, and both Quizlamic Jihad and I Wish This Microphone was Jim Newlands' Cock with 8. Happy now?'

'Happier now you've finally admitted it!' the Jim in question yelled, and the room hooted as if they hadn't heard this play out every week since time immemorial.

'OK, five minutes, everybody go have a piss – in the actual toilet this time, Martin! – and then it's the picture round,' Mel snapped, dismissing her audience before turning to Neely. 'Alright, Neely? The shitshow's in full force tonight. Ignore Jim. He's pissed but he's harmless.'

Neely straightened her face. 'I'm alright. It's just, has Angela been in today?'

'Nah. Haven't seen her. Everything alright?'

'Can't find her. She's not answering her phone.'

'Ooh. No, haven't seen her since yesterday. You two fall out?'

'No. Why? Why was she in here yesterday? When?'

Mel leaned back dramatically. 'Jesus, cool your boots. Just saying, she was alone yesterday, and you're alone now. Well, she wasn't alone yesterday, it's just that *you* weren't with her. Haven't seen that since before the two of youse were together.'

'Who was she with?'

'Nobody. Well, Rob. She talked to Rob a bit, before Gina came in. Then Gina started giving her evils so she backed off. How thick would you have to be to think Angela wants anything to do with him? Fucksake.'

'Did you hear what they were talking about, then? Angela and Rob?'

Mel's patience depleted faster than the average pint of beer on this particularly wet weekend night. 'Neely, I have better things to do than stick my nose in the business of every single person who comes in for a drink, yeah? Leave it out. She was here, you were elsewhere, you both have your own lives. If you two are having problems, I'm not getting involved.'

'We're not having problems. I just... I'm sorry. I'm just worried about her. This isn't like her.'

'Maybe her phone's broken. Maybe she just needs a little time on her own. Relax.'

'Sorry.'

'For what it's worth, she looked like she was having a good time. Let her tell you about it. Just don't smother her. She's been smothered her whole life by people worried about her. Alright?'

'Cheers,' Neely said, with no conviction and even less gratitude.

'Neely?'

'Yeah?'

'Sure everything else is alright? The two of you really didn't fall out? You look like you've seen a ghost. One who's stripping on the bar like Jim said.'

Of course everything's not alright, she thought. *I just told you. I can't find Angela. How do you think that's alright? In what solar system would that be alright?* But she held her tongue to retain an ally, no matter how tentative. Laughed at herself. 'Yeah. Everything else is fine.'

'I swear I'll send her to you quick-style if she shows up.'

'Great. Great.' Lying was easier than she expected. Neely didn't bother to look around, to survey the scene for herself. She took the startled face and the body to which it was conveniently attached, turned, and faced Harrow Road once again.

It took Neely a moment to register that it wasn't the cold making her eyes sting. At her back, she could hear the men hollering in the Hope and Anchor, with Mel's strident local voice shouting them down, and her body shook with shivers. A bit of her stomach had dropped out and she was not entirely sure how to stuff it back in, and all she could concentrate on was her sudden need to be back indoors, alone, somewhere quiet and safe. She shut her eyes as she waited for the traffic light to change, and Angela was there behind the heavy lids, curled up on the sofa, paging through this week's *Heat* and absently wrapping blonde curls around a painted fingernail, waiting for Neely to come home and not the other way around. *Put the stereo on*, she'd say. *Come on, play some of your misery music and tell me about last night.* And snuggled up next to Angela, Neely would feel like the most interesting woman in the world, not an office manager but a storyteller, the one tasked with passing along wisdom on a planet of disposable idiocy, someone who'll change one world and that one world belonged to a lucky Miss Angela Marie Archer of London W9. And that would be enough. And the boiler would hum and the radiator would blaze and the pills in the little compartment marked SATURDAY would be gone, with their bellies full and their little hearts beating with tidy, unthreatening love. But then Neely remembered the smell of blood and bleach outside the butchers in Ridley Road the night before, the foreign words painted above the shut-up market stalls blurring together, and the whisper's rush of air into her ear as she let Sam's fingers touch her waist, then lower.

Guilt prickled up and tickled Neely's back as its buzzing wings tried to poke their way through. She opened her eyes and waited for the green man and hated herself a little more.

In certain situations, Neely could turn back time quite easily. She pressed the button at the last pedestrian crossing before her flat, and a decade dropped away.

Then:

There is a slit in Neely Sharpe's trousers, the ones she wears to school. She has five identical pairs hanging in her wardrobe but these are different because these have got the slit. A bit smaller than her little finger, which, like the rest of her, is stubby and not entirely straight. Right on top of her left thigh, closer to the knee than the hip. A slip of the scissors trying to hack open the packaging of a new pair of headphones – why do they always make it so impossible to cut? – and through the stretch black polyester the blade had skidded, taking a thin path of skin with it. Neely had watched the tiny blood beads rise from the inch-long scratch, purely out of curiosity; she had pressed her finger over the blood when the specks had stopped growing, wiping them away only to watch them reappear seconds later. It is not clear to Neely, a fortnight later when the scab is gone and the line of fresh skin it left behind invisible to everybody but herself – because at fifteen, there is nobody looking at the goldish curve of her thigh except herself – that she had no idea what she had expected to achieve. Realistically, she could not have expected anything to change at the level of basic biology. Neely understands this on a theoretical level. She's good at science. She understands the importance of methods, of testing hypotheses and making sure she has eliminated all realistic alternative explanations before she dares claim causality.

On the empirical level, she remembers what her uncle Roger had once said, some throwaway quote from a scientist or a comedian, one of those quotes dull people repeat in the hope of sounding slightly less dull, but which always backfires because every other dullard in your postcode is saying the exact same thing: Madness is doing the same thing over and over again and expecting different results. Neely knows that it isn't madness at all. It is bullet-proofing. She hadn't the heart to say that to Uncle Roger, though. Ruin the humour he found in feeling clever, or the cleverness he felt in getting a laugh – however forced – from the people around him who still had lives more exciting than middle management and a mediocre Sunday roast, a halfway (but only halfway) competent football club (Luton Town; he'd made himself useful teaching Neely the offside rule), a wife who wasn't a munter but also (let's face it) not one winning any prizes in the oil painting division of an amateur art show held in a nondescript community centre on a day when it might rain or it might not, and everybody browsing this display of average, the middle of Middle England, can speak of little else other than whether the weather will indeed be nice for ducks.

Little Neely has higher hopes.

Little Neely also has plans. They are nothing all that earth shattering, but she knows they are less dull than most because she is sharper than most. Neely knows that the reason most plans fail is because nobody ever tells the planners they are wrong. No, you are not going to be the next Pamela Anderson. Not because you're ugly (even if you are) and not because one of your fake tits is bigger than the other (though it is, though, it is), but because of simple maths. Probability, specifically. It is simple for Neely as maths is her speciality. Say there are 2,000 young women in Stevenage alone who aspire to be paid on a regular basis for getting their tits out on demand. Now, the population of Stevenage is approximately 84,000 (she Googled it once). One in forty-two residents wants the job. The population of England – only England – is a touch over fifty-three million (ditto). Approximately half are women. Maybe lop one-third off that to account for kids, really old dears, and puritans. That leaves 17,666,666 women of the appropriate age (she does it in her head). Set up the fractions and solve for X and you get 420,635 souls (ditto). Meaning, one aspiring glamour supermodel sitting in history class at Fenlands Comprehensive has up to 420,634 potential competitors for the fame, and the odds of that dream coming true look pretty fucking dire indeed. Boob jobs, Neely concludes, are just another form of an idiot tax. Uncle Roger is always calling the National Lottery the idiot tax, which he finds hysterical but, because Neely is brighter than most, she recognises the subtle differences. You can play the lottery and lose nothing more than a few pounds. Fake tits, at their cheapest, are several thousand quid, and it's not like buying pasta where the value brand is essentially the same as Extra Finest. Bad fake tits are subject to leakage, to infection, and to a curious phenomenon called breadloafing in which the implants migrate toward the centre of the chest, forming one shelf-like protrusion known colloquially as the uniboob. Neely has Googled this extensively, and, as with most of her forays into the obscure and clinical and slightly bloody, she is unable to explain why exactly she did so.

Curiously, considering predilections which have been clear to Neely for quite some time, the sight of these galleries of flesh-gone-wrong (and, more importantly, gone right) evoke little to no reaction in her, whether emotional, visceral, or otherwise. Neely does not know why this is the case. She is satisfied enough with her own breasts and has no objections to those of others. But she feels no revulsion upon viewing clinical photographs of unfortunate instances of encapsulation, where the body rejects its silicone additions and, unable to kick them to the kerb, reacts by forming a rock-hard enclosure around the intruder, thus passive-aggressively (but more aggressively) forcing those who introduced the implant to come back and take it the fuck out and make amends. To Neely, these pictures are no worse than those of meat, and she dutifully eats her auntie's Sunday roast with no objection whenever she's invited over. (Uncle Roger will die in a pile-up on the M1 while Neely is at university and, at his funeral, she will feel bad for paying so much attention to how fat his children, her cousins, have become since the days when they played garden football in their green enough, pleasant enough, corner of the Home Counties. And then she will feel bad about not feeling worse.)

Neely feels no arousal, either, at the site of the more-perfect-than-perfect specimens, the good made better through the wonders of science. In theory, Neely should like pneumatic tits because she likes what they're attached to, as does her brother, who has pictures of Katie Price on his wall and stuffed under the mattress alongside the by-products of his appreciation for those tits and the woman attached to them. But Neely is largely indifferent. At this age, she attributes this feeling, or lack thereof, again to the fact that she has plans. Practical plans. Ones that are not only realistic, but also likely. Neely will go to university. This is a given. She has made the right plans and with those plans she will achieve Something Of Note. Those plans include relocation to London at the earliest possible opportunity. Stevenage, though a decent-sized town, has felt too small for some time. After all, a big fish in a small pond gets caught and deep-fried and eaten. Neely longs to get lost.

But at this moment, Neely is bored. She sits in a history lesson much like all other history lessons held since the occurrence of the historic events. The last notes in her jotter were put down ten minutes ago, sometime in the late seventeenth century, elsewhere on this island. With more concentration than necessary for a girl who is brighter than most, she is deeply absorbed in the matter of turning goldish skin blue. Through that small razor cut in the fabric of her trousers, she colours in the space where scabs once sat. There is, of course, the small matter of the trousers being black and her biro blue, but in the light below the desk nobody could tell the difference even if they wanted to look, and they don't. What matters is that it is good enough. Neely, typically one to rail against simply being good enough, is perfectly content with this one slip, this one secret lowering of standards. It feels subversive and almost dirty. She moves the tip of the pen in cross-hatch motion, covering and re-covering the same bit of her ground. Just for good measure, she prods the edges of the split fabric, colours in beyond their borders, makes sure all possible views are covered. She's looking, she sees. That's all she needs.

'Neely Sharpe? What did I just say?'

A jerk of the head, an apologetic face. 'I dunno, Miss. Sorry.'

'Pay attention, or at least pretend to.'

She chooses the latter option. In her head, Neely is imagining music. Gigs in London. Places she only knows from between the covers of *NME*: Brixton Academy, Hammersmith Apollo, Shepherd's Bush Empire, The Garage on Holloway Road. She imagines all the people she'll see, the songs she'll sing along to, songs she hasn't yet heard, by bands that have yet to form and slog and send off demos. There's a life outside Stevenage, she reminds herself, and not for the first time this day. The five words live as a constant hum in her head, somewhere between maths and English.

But before that life, there is PE. There are laps to be run around the flat playing fields of Fenlands Comp, efforts to beat the clock just for the sake of beating it. Neely doesn't understand why she should put in the effort: there are no prizes. The clock doesn't give a shit what she does with it, but it has never done anything to hurt Neely and so she is disinclined to flog it half to death. She feels more offended by the landscape offered to her as a defining feature of her adolescence. On her mother's side there is a bit of India; on her father's, Italy. Having never actually been to either, Neely imagines them as lands with drama neatly built into their bedrock, and life has dealt her the relative flatness of Hertfordshire. As breeze pulls errant black strands from her ponytail, she imagines the grass beneath her trainers as something with greater stakes. A hillside, a heath, a pockmarked bit of earth she can share with somebody else, somebody who wants to be close enough to touch her, and not just because they're looking at her exam paper for the correct answers. Somebody to trace the legs, the thighs, that one specific curve. And she thinks of that photo in her brother's *Melody Maker* with PJ Harvey wearing nothing but her guitar and black knickers and the black T-shirt that commands Neely, or any other viewer, to lick her legs, and Neely thinks, it really is that easy. You go to London and you ask and then you get. She who dares, does. Then in the changing rooms afterward, swapping the regulation black jogging bottoms for the regulation black uniform trousers which are just like any of the others except for the little mistake she sliced into them, she lets the others see too much. *Jesus Christ, Neely, what did you do to your leg?*

The girl looks down at the smear of blue, the smudge that has strayed from its course. It has become the kind of stain that needs an explanation. It doesn't become her at all.

She shrugs. 'I fell.'

In Harrow Road, lights were blazing in every window of buildings virtually identical to her own. She could see people in one where rainbow-coloured fairy lights blinked and twinkled at the margins. A girl standing in front of it flipped back her hair and laughed, open-mouthed and silent. Neely frowned. It wasn't supposed to be like this, she thought. She should be that happy, she should be burning bright. And maybe it was Angela and maybe it was something else – whatever she wanted to use Angela as an excuse to do, or not do.

A number 18 bus stopped in front of Harrow Road Police Station at the same time Neely reached its steps. Of course it did, that was the stop: *Harrow Road Police Station*, that calm lady's voice on the recording always announced, always jolting Neely out of her daydreams just in time to kick her arse out the door whenever she rode. Neely paused now, and the driver thought it was for him. 'You getting on, then?' he barked, and she didn't hear him, so he shut the door in a huff and cursed her under his breath. Neely looked up at the building, with its red brick and ornamental mouldings gently illuminated, and she thought about how the lady on the bus announcements wasn't even from London, she was from Manchester, she just got the list of all the places and their pronunciation and did the recordings, and rumour was if you made a Freedom of Information Act request to Transport for London, they would give you a CD with every single sound file on it, more than fifteen thousand of them, all the announcements and stops and destinations, all the snippets of noise from the route numbers to the emergency instructions to the apologies while you are being held momentarily to regulate service. Why? Because you might want them someday.

She thought of Angela's voice wrapping itself around all the local words, the push-and-pull of short and long vowels whenever she said Harrow Road. Where do you live? *Harrow Road.* Where did you live before? *Kensal Town.* Anything more you'd like to say about that, or there? *No.* Sometimes people pried. They wanted more out of her. Neely didn't. The sound of the words was enough. She tried to give Angela what she wanted: no fuss, no worry. But now, as the wind kicked up and sent her hair flying around her face, Neely had doubts. And she hated those doubts. And she thought, if I'm supposed to be brighter than most, then why the hell can I not see any hint of a path before me, why do I not have the slightest idea what I should do next?

The problem was place and the problem was history. She thought, if she were anywhere else, were anybody else, would she walk through those police station doors and say, to anybody paid to care, *My girlfriend is missing?* Because she knew that the instant she went inside Harrow Road Police Station, the minute she talked to the police, she would be crashing Angela's past – those people Neely didn't know, those doors she'd never unlocked, those stories to which she'd never been privy because they were probably none of her bloody business – into her own present, and she knew too little of the former to have the faintest idea whether this was wise. And Neely didn't like to be wrong. Not in school and not in things that actually mattered. She'd rarely been wrong, but if she ended up being wrong now, making her nice little middle-class fuss in this less-than-nice street, then she might as well pack her bags for Stevenage. She could hear it in Mel's voice, the accent as local as the black water slogging through the Grand Union Canal: *Leave it out, get a life, cool your boots. Don't fuck it up. Not for Angela and not for us.*

Neely shivered and made her frozen feet walk on again, onward from Harrow Road Police Station and its red bricks. Nothing special. No fuss, no worry.

And when Neely crossed the street and reached number 490, where the lights were still off in Flat C, she kept walking.

Three

She couldn't go home on a Saturday night. If she had wanted to spend her weekends tucked up in front of the television then she might as well have stayed in Stevenage and saved on the rent. But where to go? Dalston? Tube, another Tube, then the Overground, and then what? Try to finish what she'd started with Sam?

Fuck, Angela, where would you go? When you hadn't the foggiest idea what to do, when life and everything in it hit the fan, where would you go?

The canal. Of course. Its surface at night was a rippling binbag big enough for any scenario Neely could imagine. It was right there, waiting for her to walk alone at night for no good reason. *But I've got a reason*, Neely thought, feeling the stabs of cold in her toes. *So long as I'm out here, there's a chance she could come back there, back home, and I just won't know it yet.* Compared to the solid logic that had played through her mind when she had left the flat, this rationale felt like grasping at straws. Worse, grasping at a particularly greasy pole, dancing around it on the off-chance somebody might stuff a fiver in her pants. A losing game by any definition, yet she might as well play. But she'd need more than just the coat she'd stepped out in to canvass the pubs; wind over the water and whatever she might find beside it called for the full winter armour, the hat, the gloves, a scarf to bury her nose. Trying to look as inconspicuous as possible for the few people on the Harrow Road, she stopped, turned, and walked back towards number 490.

She didn't expect the three figures sitting outside her front door, and she couldn't recall them having been there just a few minutes earlier – but then again, she hadn't been looking down at the door, only up at the dark gape of the window. From across the street, in the dim sodium light Neely could discern a tall man at the centre, horrifically underdressed for the weather. He wore nothing at all above the waist. He was flanked by two women in puffer jackets, a black and an electric pink. The former carried a small electric torch, and she was making the weak beam dance on the brass numbers screaming out Neely's address. The other seemed engrossed in trying to peer through the flap of the letterbox, though Neely knew there was no chance of her seeing anything but more darkness. Neely waited for a few cars to pass, and then crossed straight to them, the details sharpening into focus. The man's skinniness had crossed the line into the realm of the pathological. Even sitting, he looked comically stretched, with a loop of black plastic carrier bag handles emphasising the thin wrist. Across his ribs, somebody had painted in block capitals distorted by the ripples of bones: FUCK ME. Neely blinked and wondered what she could possibly want to do less than that.

She breathed deep and let the cold stun her lungs. 'What are you doing?'

The man in the middle shivered and the women huddled in close to him. Now Neely was near enough to see the loop of tinsel atop his head, the pound-shop silver halo stark and bright against the mess of hair that vanished against the dirty, dark door. 'I'm the baby Jesus. Everybody who lives here is protected. Wish me a happy birthday for next week?'

'He's lying,' snapped the girl in pink.

'Erm, alright,' Neely replied tentatively.

'It *is* his birthday, though. Today.'

'Happy birthday.'

'But his name is Brian.'

Neely snorted. 'Oh, and let me guess, he's not the messiah, he's a very naughty boy.'

The pink girl's face curled into a question. 'Yer wha?'

'Never mind. Why are you looking in the letterbox?'

The makeshift messiah spoke for himself. 'My name is Brian, really.'

'I believe you.'

'You could be nice and tell us yours.'

'It's Neely.'

'Neil?'

'Neely. Nee-lee.'

'And what the fuck are you doing out here tonight, Neely?'

'Trying to get into my flat. Could you move, please?'

The girls both jumped to the side, but Brian stayed put, his facial features curving into a question, as if Neely's request and her reason for it were both completely foreign.

'Could you move?' Neely repeated, hoping no quaver of nerves had made it into her voice.

'You're coming home already?' he asked. 'It's early.'

Within her handbag, she slid a key between two fingers. 'Yes. I am. It is. Can you just move, please?'

He groaned, grabbed onto the black-coated arm beside him, and hoisted himself to standing. Neely thought she heard the crack of joints like icicles snapping. 'Why aren't you going out?' he asked.

'Went out last night.'

'That was last night. Go out again. It's the weekend.'

'Nah. Not feeling it. Just needed a walk.'

Brian scoffed. 'You're so boring,' he yelled in her face, and Neely recoiled. Second time she'd heard that off a man that day.

The girl in the black coat swatted at him and stared at Neely. 'I know you. What do I know you from?'

Neely shrugged. 'You live around here too?' The girl shook her head, looking not interested enough in particulars to pursue them.

'What are you called, again?'

'Neely.' She paused with her keys in mid-air.

'Tasha. That's Michelle. And the fuckwit over there, he's already been introduced.'

She slid her key into the lock, but didn't turn it. It was the shiver that suddenly caught Brian – contorting his arms, jerking his neck, rustling the carrier bag – that made her stop. Made her think. *Angela. Those tablets.* 'Erm… can I ask you something?'

'I hate when people ask permission to ask questions,' the fuckwit over there blurted. 'It's pointless! You're *already* asking a question. Why are you asking if you can do what you're already doing? And what happens if we say no? You're just going to be quiet? Of course you're not. That's fucking pre… *presumptuous*, that is.'

'Mother of God. Shut up,' Tasha hollered; her voice, all Yorkshire vowels, echoed around the increasingly empty street. She turned to Neely. 'Go ahead.'

'Where are the rest of his clothes?'

The Michelle one burst into laughter. 'Back in Harlesden!'

Tasha shrugged. 'It seemed like a good idea. House party, yeah? But there was no fucking heat in there and the electricity's about to go. You can either plug in the sound system or plug in the heaters and you can't have a party without music, can you? We were cold, like, so we went back into the garden and pinned his shirt and his coat to the washing line and lit them up. It was gorgeous. It was brilliant.'

'I hate you. Good coat, that was.'

'Old piece of shit with a hole in the armpit, you grotty bastard,' Michelle snorted. 'And that was the stupidest shirt I've ever seen in my entire life. Face it, you're better off.' Suddenly re-registering Neely's presence, she continued: 'And he was moaning and moaning about it and we thought he needed some cheering up so we went about advertising that he's open for business.' She jabbed at the words on his skin.

'Did it work?'

'*Obviously* not.'

'So what are you doing now?'

Small, dim lights flickered on behind all three pairs of eyes, bringing them suddenly in line with their surroundings. Michelle spoke first. 'Fuck. Don't know. We just figured we'd find something. He's from around here, he knows where things are. Yeah, Brian?'

'Kensal Town. We'll go to Kensal Town. I know some people.'

'You passed it, though,' Neely piped up tentatively. 'If you came from Harlesden.'

'Did we? Eh. Must not be anything going on if I didn't notice.'

You can't not notice, Neely thought. *Kensal Town is the Trellick Tower and Meanwhile Gardens; you can reach out and touch them from here. I do, all the time. And Angela, she knows every blade of grass, every crack in the pavement, every floor of the high-rise. How could you miss Kensal Town?* She watched her breath condense into white wisps in the black chill all around and above her head, then sucked it deep. 'Listen, do you want to come in?'

The puffs of fog hung in front of her mouth in the night before breeze swept them to death. They didn't sound like her words. Sure, they had her tone of voice, her timbre, but it wasn't the kind of question Neely Sharpe would ask, not here and not now. No, they were Angela's words.

Neely stared at Brian, who stared at an indeterminate point somewhere above her head. The Tasha one looked blank, but the Michelle one considered the invitation with a bite of her lip.

'Are you a serial killer or a cult leader or something?'

'Would I tell you if I was?'

'Ooh, this one's clever,' Brian cackled, snapping out of his trance. 'Is it your own place or do you share?'

'My flatmate's gone.'

'Gone where?'

'Just gone. So do you want to come in? Warm up?'

Neely wondered if this trio considered their own propensity for bad decisions, and what even qualified as bad in their book. Burning clothes good, coming back to a stranger's flat bad?

The Michelle one nodded. 'Alright, then.'

'Thanks,' the Tasha one added.

'I'm starving,' Brian moaned. 'We should make some food. What you got?'

Michelle elbowed him bluntly through the fluff of her coat. 'What? You can't make food. You can't even make sense. Look, I'm the designated thinker here. It is my job to think for you. And you too, Tash. I'm the designated thinker and my thoughts say we should get a KFC and bring it back up to this nice girl's – fuck, sorry, what's your name again?'

'Neely.'

'Neely,' Michelle repeated. 'We should bring a big KFC bucket up and share it, cos that's just the right thing to do, innit?' She barely paused for confirmation. 'Yeah, that's a plan. That's a good chill-out. See, Tash, we've met someone cool, yeah? Brian's good for something. He found this place. You're cool, Neely.'

'I'm fucking cold,' Brian yelled. 'Can we at least go inside?'

'It's warmer in KFC. The fryers and that,' said Michelle.

'Then why the fuck aren't we in there? Why weren't we there all along?'

His breath stank. He spun away, and there was something familiar about the jut of his shoulder blades through the taut skin of his back: stubs, little wings poking their way through. Neely pushed down her own uncertainty, the feeling that kept prickling her there, threatening to burst out altogether and lift her away from this place. She pointed up the Harrow Road in the direction Brian had already begun to walk: 'That way.'

'No shirt, get out,' the manager yelled at Brian, who retreated to the street with Tasha's dark bulk hanging off his arm. The remaining two took their places at the counter. 'Yes, may I take your order? Late nights. Crazy people, yes?'

Michelle stared blankly. 'Crazy people. Yes. Can I get a big bottle of Coke and whatever red wine is cheapest?'

'You want off-licence, not chicken.'

'Well I want a Family Feast, too. Ten pieces.'

Neely shrugged apologetically from over Michelle's shoulder. *Stupid wasted white girls, yeah?* she would have mouthed, but there was no way anybody could have lip-read through the grease on the perspex partition.

'One Family Feast. Anything else? Off-licence is Great Western Road. Hurry, closing soon.'

Michelle spun around to face Neely. 'Check that out. People are so *nice* here.'

'As opposed to where?'

'Dunno. Everywhere else.'

'Where are you from?'

'Around. Like way back? North Herts.'

'You're joking! I'm from Stevenage.'

'Baldock! Where did you go to school?'

'£16.99, miss,' came from behind the partition.

'Yeah, yeah, wait a second. Neely, can you get cash from the others? You don't pay. It's your house. But tell them I need a tenner.'

Invigorated by this small gesture of acceptance, Neely tapped the glass door and Brian jumped out of his clinch with Tasha, a purely utilitarian pose using her parka-clad body as a shield from the cold. *Money*, she mouthed. Two blank faces. She pushed open the door, leaning her entire body into the metal frame. 'Money. Michelle needs a tenner.'

'Give me ten quid,' Michelle hollered from two feet over her shoulder, translating from a language Neely didn't realise she was speaking.

'Heard you both,' Brian growled. 'And I don't have any money.'

Tasha swatted him out of the way, purple paper held aloft: 'I've got a twenty.'

'Fuck! Where was that twenty when Matt went to score?'

Now Tasha's swat became a punch. 'Shut up, you spacker. Didn't your mum ever teach you indoor voices?'

'I don't have an indoor voice because does it look like I'm FUCKING INDOORS RIGHT NOW, TASH?'

Neely snatched the note and let the door close, gently pushing the cold back into its natural habitat and away from the bright lights and fried chicken. She passed it into Michelle's small, frozen palm. The girl slid it under the partition and pocketed the change.

'It was a fantastic party, really,' Michelle said, picking up a conversation that had not yet begun. 'Started last night. Would still be going on if they hadn't been raided.'

'Who's they?'

'Whoever's house it was.'

'In Harlesden? You don't know whose party it was?'

'Does it matter? When you go to house parties do you show up with personalised gifts or summat?'

Neely shrugged. She did, sometimes.

'Anyway. You're from Stevenage, yeah? So what the fuck are you doing living around here?'

'Just ended up here after uni.'

Michelle whistled through her teeth, stopping just short of a sneer. 'Ah, yeah.' Through the glass, Brian pulled a face; all bulging eyes and bared teeth, he slid his palms down the glass. A hard edge inside his carrier bag clunked against it. Michelle lifted both red middle fingers. Tasha laughed, open-mouthed and silent on the other side of the barrier. Neely looked away. The laugh, the mouth behind it, they weren't like Angela's at all.

'Family Feast, ten pieces, Coca-Cola,' called the man behind the counter, though there was nobody else whose order it could have been. Neely took the initiative, scooping the steaming carrier bags into her arms and mouthing a vague apology. Michelle held open the door and the pack charged forward into the night, onward, westward down the Harrow Road.

Nobody spoke until Neely, just before the junction with the Great Western Road. 'Michelle? You wanted wine?'

'I want tequila now.'

'Whatever. There's an offy on the corner.' A few steps took the group to its long-locked and night-darkened door. 'Well, shit.'

Michelle grimaced. 'Don't you have anything at home?'

'My girl— er, my flatmate doesn't drink much.'

'So neither do you?' barked Brian, as if Neely stood thirty feet away rather than one foot down.

Neely shrugged. 'Not a lot.'

'You're so boring,' he boomed, even louder.

'Shut the fuck up, Brian,' Michelle growled, reassuming the responsibilities of the Designated Thinker. 'People are sleeping.'

'Not here they're not.'

Michelle pointed: up, around, in front, behind. All the windows over Harrow Road. Some lit, most not.

'Wake them up, then. It's too early to be asleep. West London is so boring. If you want to sleep then go to... Dorset. I don't know. Why did we even come here?'

Neely, puzzled: 'I thought you lived around here?'

'I *used* to. I live in Dalston now. Things *happen* in Dalston. Not fucking... *sleeping*.'

'Wait,' Neely remembered. 'There's whisky. I have some whisky. Is that OK?'

Her three new companions laughed. 'Is it the kind with alcohol in it?' Michelle squeaked through her giggles. 'Yes. Fuck. Of course it is.'

'You're so sweet, Neely,' Tasha cooed. 'Listen to this girl. "Is whisky okay with you?" Has anybody actually told you it wasn't?'

'I've never asked.'

Michelle, sensing the momentum of attention shifting away from her, piped up, 'We were talking, y'know, when you two retards were waiting outside, and Neely and I were practically neighbours, y'know? She's from Stevenage, yeah?' Nobody cared enough to respond; Neely, uncomfortable in the subsequent silence, reached into her handbag for the keys, desperate for something to jingle. She stopped her group in front of the door to 490, brass numbers dull in the street light.

'You really live here?' Brian asked, stepping back to crane his neck for a better look at all four storeys: the shop, the maisonette in the middle, the one-bedroom flat at the top with the windows dark. Neely thought he looked slightly confused, but she didn't know him well enough – at all – to discern whether that was a departure from the norm, a regression from the mean.

'Yeah, why?'

'Funny place to live.'

'No it's not, it's just regular. Watch out, there's no lights on the stairs.'

The group bumped silently up the three flights, Tasha pulling out the tiny torch to illuminate a path. Neely prayed, silently: *Let her be waiting. Don't let it be three against one. Let me have an ally. Let me have a laugh. Let me open the door and there she'll be, just having a doze with the lights off, ready to make everything better, and she won't even have to try.*

She turned the key and opened the door to a dark and silent room.

'Fuck,' Michelle breathed, breaking the silence as Neely flipped the light switch. 'This looks nicer than I thought it would. From outside, like. This street's a shithole. No offence or nothing. But you've got a really nice place.' Tasha slowly wandered the perimeter of the lounge, hand tentatively smoothing its way across pale painted wall and bookshelves, hi-fi and picture frame. 'Really nice. It's… tidy.'

Neely plopped the bags of chicken onto the coffee table. 'I'll get some plates.'

'Whisky?'

Right. They were promised whisky. 'Yeah, let me get it out. It's way back in the cupboard. I only use it for cooking.'

'Cooking?' Tasha squawked. She shimmied out of her parka, a doughy roll of belly protruding below an elaborately crocheted and seasonally inappropriate halter-back. 'Like what, you put it in soup?'

'No, no, more like baking, really. That's what I meant. Cakes and that.'

'You bake cakes?'

'Sometimes. Why?'

Tasha shrugged. 'Nobody's got time for that.'

'Well, my hours at work aren't that bad. That's the only reason why I don't quit. I'm an office manager. It's boring.'

'What does the office manager do?'

'Manage the office.'

Can't say fairer than that, read three faces, and Neely decided not to make polite conversation about their work, or lack thereof. She didn't want to know, she didn't care, and she didn't want to have to care. She only wanted a bit of company on a Saturday night. She only wanted to do what Angela might.

She dragged a kitchen chair to underneath the cupboards, then climbed on top and dug behind the electric mixer, unused since summer, until she uncovered the remains of Johnnie Walker. 'Brian? Is it actually your birthday?'

'Yesterday.'

'Here you go, then. Happy birthday.' She passed the bottle down to him. 'How old?'

'It's rude to ask,' he snapped, unscrewing the cap. 'Wahey, this is nice. Thanks.'

'Don't mention it.'

'Just did. Do you have glasses?'

Neely leaned through space to grab at a distant cupboard handle, and deftly passed down four juice glasses. 'These are the only ones we've got. They'll have to do.'

'I'm not complaining,' Michelle laughed, having wrestled the bottle out of Brian's grasp. She poured four even half-glasses, quadruple measures. 'Cheers. This is really nice of you, yeah? Fuck. There's still good people in the world.'

Neely smiled. She hadn't done anything wrong. Bad decisions were one thing, but only bad consequences mattered, and she didn't see any of those hanging around the gaff right now, getting underfoot, sticking to the kitchen countertops or rattling the window frames. And at least nobody was laughing at her. The four raised their glasses; Brian downed his drink in one go, wincing slightly. 'Not bad for an old cunt,' he congratulated himself, though he couldn't have had more years behind him than Neely did herself. The two companions laughed, and Neely joined in because she felt absolutely certain it had nothing whatsoever to do with her.

The wince faded slowly as Brian thawed and became aware of something other than the cold. 'Er, Neela, can I use your toilet?'

'It's *Neely*. And no.'

'What?' Any goodwill drained from his face; even Michelle raised an eyebrow.

'I'd rather you didn't.'

'What do you want me to do, piss out the window?' Brian whined, and Neely spluttered a quick giggle despite herself; that would be a scene. One night with Angela out of the house and already she had let it descend into anarchy. 'You can't just invite somebody into your home and then say the toilet's off limits. Come on.'

'Sounds like that's exactly what she's doing, idiot,' Tasha laughed. Neely wasn't terribly concerned with his bladder. She surreptitiously scanned his arms. No holes, no sores, no scabs, just the crease from that black bag still cutting into the skin. Safe enough, but she was not surreptitious enough. The man scowled.

'Oh. *OK*. I'm not going to snort anything off your toilet seat, if that's the problem.'

'It's not – '

'If I had anything, I'd do it right here in front of you, and I'd share it, because I'm nice like that, you know? Hospitality. Hos-pee-tal-ee-tee. The most underrated of virtues.'

'Brian,' Michelle growled. 'You had the entire fucking canal out there for taking a piss. Why didn't you do that?'

'I was too cold! You can't piss when you're freezing. It's a scientific fact, innit.'

Neely sighed, then pointed. 'Fine. It's just to the right.'

With all the grace of a cat and similar manners, Brian ran to the toilet. His two companions looked at each other passively. Neely's insides writhed in the silence and she figured she could actually feel them: a stomach nudging a liver knowingly, lungs and heart conspiring quietly, spleen having a grumble to itself, *can you believe this mess?* Her brain, on the other hand, was curiously quiet. She spoke to shut everything up. 'Don't get me wrong, it's not that I care what people do. It's just not for me. Coke, smack, all of that, you know it came into the country up someone's arse.'

From the faces of her guests, Neely could tell this was news, and she didn't know whether to feel proud of herself or exceptionally stupid for letting their kind in. She poured herself another measure and retreated to the lounge. Soon she heard the toilet flush.

'There. I didn't piss on your curtains,' Brian announced as he re-entered the room.

'There's no curtains in there.'

'So I didn't piss on them. Didn't spunk in your towels, neither.'

'Good.'

'I spunked on your nice purple feathery whatsit.'

She believed him for a moment, recalling hanging the boa, the Christmas party staple on the hook at the back of the door, and her face showed it. Brian cracked up. 'I didn't. God! Go check if you like.' He flopped down on the couch in between Tasha and Michelle, who clinked their empty glasses and swiftly set about fixing that deficiency.

Under halogen lights, Neely could see her company and the damage done: the bas-relief topography of eczema winding its way along Tasha's pale jaw, angry red chilblains and scabby hangnails decorating Michelle's fingers, the grease in all their hair. And then there was Brian, his tinsel halo lost somewhere along the Harrow Road, and his proportions even more curious fully illuminated: his arms reminded Neely of the gibbons at the London Zoo, minus the coating of thick hair. She and Angela had gone during the summer and had been thoroughly wanked at by one energetic male who had the same long, rubber-jointed limbs as the man now sitting in her lounge. And there was another body conspicuous in its absence from the couch, from the flat, from their sacred stretch of the canal where Angela had told Neely, in warmer days: Look. This place. Look.

My amazing Angela, she's somewhere that's not here, and strangers are sitting in her space, each one of them in need of a good scrub. This is what she'd do, isn't it? She'd smile and just try to make everybody happy, yeah?

'Brian.' She had noticed the shivers, those tiny fasciculations rippling under the skin. It was rude to stare.

'What?'

'Are you cold?'

'Yeah. Isn't the heat on?'

'Full blast.'

'Can I borrow a top?'

The Michelle one laughed. 'She's half your height, idiot.'

'My flatmate's stuff might fit you. She's taller than me.'

'Serves her right for fucking off.'

'She didn't "fuck off", she's just gone out,' Neely sighed, willing it true. 'Wash off that paint or she'll kill me.'

The two girls grabbed his skinny arms and dragged him into the kitchen – Michelle looking defeated, Tasha gleeful. One turned on the tap full blast as Neely cautiously entered the bedroom. It was warmer behind the closed door, her and Angela's combined hoard of fabric in bedding and cheap clothes insulating the brick box. And most nights, they'd be insulating each other.

Neely chose a work shirt, a shapeless blue polo that usually dangled from Angela's shoulders, showing off her collarbones until her boss made her button it to the top. PORCHESTER CENTRE, the embroidery read in red, a dull approximation of the glowing neon sign that lit up the building at night.

'Christ! Fuck! That's cold. You bitch,' Neely heard coming from the kitchen.

'It's steaming. Shut up,' Michelle admonished him, and the tap stopped.

Quietly, as if the three in the kitchen could hear her, Neely stepped toward the bed, looking in vain to see if she could find an outline or an indentation or any evidence of Angela's presence. A shed blonde strand clung to the pillow, and Neely thought she could see it move just the slightest bit with her breath, or the draught from the window frames. Windows with their chipped paint and their soot, with their splinters and their shiny glass, keeping Neely in, keeping everyone else out, except for the ones Neely let in through the fucking front door.

Neely returned with the shirt. The girls were scrubbing Brian with kitchen roll, dropping the paint-soaked results back in the basin. Neely squinted; they didn't seem to be making much of a difference on his skin, but the girls didn't seem bothered.

'I look like a sausage. I look like dog food. Stop that.'

'Almost done,' Michelle snapped with little conviction. 'Stop your moaning.' Grey water trickled down his legs, dripping ghostly piss-pools at his feet. That better not stain, Neely thought, and then admonished herself.

You let this shower of idiots into your flat and your biggest concern is the state of the lino? They could be anybody. He could be a rapist, they could be brainwashed, this could be *folie-à-trois* and any minute now you'll be offered the chance to make it *quatre*. And with the decisions you've been making around men lately, you'll probably say yes.

The girls continued to mop; the words stayed staining even as the wet wads of kitchen roll grew dark. Tasha noticed Neely staring. She smiled. 'Permanent marker underneath,' she said, stabbing a chubby finger into his sunken chest. 'We thought ahead.'

'That was my idea, actually,' Michelle piped up. 'Designated Thinker, like. I thought of it.' She jabbed him as well, her chipped gold-glitter fingernail sparkling.

'Stop touching me. You're like doctors. Worse,' Brian grumbled. Neely tentatively offered him the shirt, which he took and promptly used as a towel.

'I thought you wanted something to *wear*.'

'S'alright, s'alright.' To prove it, he slipped the damp fabric over his head, emerging from the neck-hole looking mildly dazed. Neely followed his line of sight to the refrigerator. He was staring at the photos taped, blu-tacked, and magneted onto it: Neely and Angela in the scorched grass, the concert in Hyde Park. Neely and Angela, canalside; the former pointing and shooting her finger-gun at the photographer's eyes, the latter affecting theatrical boredom. Neely and Angela, side by side in the Hope and Anchor's back booth – Waster's Corner – with Sam's ear and elbow and greasy fringe just poking into frame. Bonfire Night: Neely's hair swallowed completely by the blackness around them, and Angela's popping peroxide-blonde in the camera flash. Neely and Angela all.

'Is that your flatmate?' he asked, voice clearer, honed and alert.

'Ooh, let me see.' Tasha walked over and squinted into the glossy snapshots. 'She's beautiful.' She looked to Brian for approval, but he nodded blankly, his eyes flickering from face to face.

Neely spoke, softer than before. 'I don't know where she's gone.'

Tasha kept staring. 'Bri. She looks like Twitch. Don't you think?'

'I don't know a Twitch.' He absent-mindedly picked at the embroidery on the damp top. Neely noticed someone had varnished the nails on his left hand black, and the chips in the lacquer spread mountain landscapes across his fingers.

'Yes you do. Twitch! *Twitch* Twitch.'

'Shut up about your imaginary friends, Tash. Have a drink.'

Brian's eyes had glazed over slightly, and Neely was reminded of Angela's usual absences, the fits that were barely fits, the times her brain seemed to invisibly drop out of her body for a few moments and then slipped back in as if nothing had happened, though for the life of her she couldn't explain where it had gone. *Petit mal*, they were called. Just a little bit bad.

Part of Brian was gone, too; Neely looked at him and saw the lights were off but somebody was still at home, huddled around the last candle left, hands cupped around the flame, desperately willing the wick higher. Long gone, beyond sense or redemption.

'You alright?'

Brian shook his head violently as if dislodging a fragment of sleep, a bit of shrapnel behind the eyes. 'Need your toilet again. Feeling a bit sick.'

'Oh, fuck, are you going to chuck a whitey?' Tasha yelled. 'Worse house guest ever, you.'

He vanished. Neely began to gnaw on her fingernails as the women unwrapped their meal at the table in the lounge. She looked into Angela's eyes in one of the photographs. There was happiness there, and not even the forced kind. Neely knew Angela didn't have it in her to deceive anybody, even in that benign a manner. It was completely beyond her. If she'd been unhappy, Neely would have known.

Brian reemerged quickly, eyes watery but no redder. 'False alarm. Right. Chicken?'

'Bring the bottle,' called Michelle, who had already begun to dig into her Family Feast and wanted something to wash it down.

Brian and Neely left the kitchen and the latter perched herself next to Michelle on the couch. But Brian lingered by the hi-fi on his way to join them. He perused the CDs, gently touching each as if they were rare volumes in a library vault. His movements had grown slower and more deliberate, Neely noticed. Gone was the frenetic, shaky tension of only minutes earlier, as if during those few minutes in the toilet his brain had sat his nerves down on the naughty step for a firm but fair talking-to and an agreement to get a fucking grip. That, or he'd taken something else.

'Pick some music, Brian!' Tasha screeched. 'Neely, is that OK?'

Neely nodded through a mouthful of hot chips, but Brian looked decidedly unimpressed at the selection and began to narrate his decision process. 'Hmm... No... Not that... Jesus. Nobody actually listens to Lou Reed. Why do you have Lou Reed? Nobody –'

'Yeah, yeah, she heard you the first time, nobody listens to Lou Reed,' Michelle moaned at him. 'Don't you ever have anything nice to say?'

'All your music,' Brian began, an accusatory finger stabbing toward Neely, 'All your music, see, your music is the kind of music that makes people want to hang themselves.'

'Be nice,' Michelle growled half-heartedly through her teeth and her chicken wing.

He ignored her once more. 'I'm only saying, it's... argh.' And Brian flung himself backward against a bare scrap of wall, eyes clamped shut, fingers kneading a headache at his temples. He slid slowly to the floor. 'It's just so *heavy* in here. You're one of those heavy ones. Maybe that's why your flatmate left?'

'You're a right cruel bastard sometimes,' Michelle muttered and kicked him in the ribs with no real malice and even less effort.

'God, this room's gone mad,' he moaned, but he smiled with his words. 'Hold still. Make it hold still.'

'It is still,' Neely said.

'I'm sailing, I'm sailing,' he giggled. 'On the Grand Union Canal.'

'You what?'

A hand shot out and caught her wrist, pulling her down to his level. Neely winced as her knees hit hardness; Sam's floor this morning had been carpeted and hers was wood. Downstairs would complain about the noise. Downstairs complained about everything. Downstairs especially complained whenever she and Angela came home late together, four feet up stairs, two voices giggling. This was double worse.

'Look, seriously, are you alright? What exactly did you take?' She took a moment to notice he was holding her hand to his chest, splaying out her fingers. I look grey, she thought, staring at her skin. Maybe it's the lighting in here or maybe it's me, but he looks white and I look grey. FUC M, his skin read with hers in the way.

'My heart's fucked.'

She didn't know how to respond to that. It felt like Sam's had. Or Angela's. It felt like everybody's she had ever felt.

Michelle shook her head. 'He's fine. He's just a sad bastard.'

Tasha giggled. 'Yeah. He gets like this. Is it your bedtime, Bri? Do you need to be tucked in tight and kissed goodnight?' But then she, too, yawned. 'God. Chicken. A bit of grease, and I fall right asleep.' She said this with the Johnnie Walker bottle held delicately between two fingers, the other hand poised to unscrew the cap. Nobody replied.

A wave of yawns dominoed around the room. Neely wished somebody had put a record on. Any record. She wished somebody would make any noise. She wished it until she knew wishing would do no good.

'Do you want to sleep here?' she asked, high-pitched. Pathetically. Plaintively.

'I don't think we'll make it down the stairs, really.' Tasha slurred. 'Thanks. We'll kip here, on the couch, yeah?'

Brian had already nodded off. Neely watched his foot jerk against the scratched wood floor. His plastic bag made a makeshift pillow.

'He's dreaming,' Michelle murmured, a slight smile creeping at the corners of her mouth, suffusing her face with a hint of mischief. 'He's out cold. Thank god for that.'

Neely paused. 'Who's this Twitch, Tasha?'

'God,' groaned Michelle. 'I think she's one of the sad little Shoreditch hipsters he sells Es to for twice the price as anybody else because they're really that clueless. Or maybe that's another girl. He's got a whole harem of gorgeous fuck-ups he's in love with, and he's obsessed with this one because she's the only one who won't shag him.'

'Pretty much,' Tasha shrugged, nibbling on a fingernail. 'I can't keep them straight.'

'What's her real name?'

'Fucked if I know. They all have their names like that, yeah? One-Shot gets drunk off wine gums. Branson's still a virgin. But Brian never shuts up about Twitch. He never shuts up, end of. You're witnessing magic here, right now. He's out cold.' Tasha and Michelle shared a half-second of eye contact, blank and passive.

Neely poured herself the end of the bottle. She didn't even like how it tasted. She didn't even like how it made her feel.

'Look, don't let us keep you up. You've been... really nice, yeah? Really nice. To us.' Michelle suddenly looked about sixteen years old, peering at Neely through heavy-lidded eyes, her fingers drifting up to her mouth even as she talked. 'People don't do stuff like this for me, for us, know what I mean? You're just a good person. Cheers, yeah?'

'I'm... yeah, I'm going to go to bed.' Neely stumbled slightly as she stood up from the sleeping man's side, and reached for a napkin to wipe the grease from her fingers. 'Look, if you want anything else to eat or drink or whatever, just take it, yeah? It's not a problem. Is it warm enough in here for you? I don't have any extra blankets, I'm sorry, but do you think you'll be alright?'

Both women nodded like dashboard toy dogs.

'Wait!' she heard as she retreated toward her bedroom. 'Hold on a sec!'

Neely turned back. 'Yes?'

'I know now. I know how I know you. I remember.' Michelle smiled again, her eyes shut. 'Pub quiz. You and her in the photo. Second place.'

'Goodnight,' Neely nodded, and didn't look back.

'And a perfect score for the music round.'

Neely didn't bother with her face or teeth. From behind the bedroom door she listened to Michelle and Tasha mumbling among themselves. Neely strained to hear anything coherent, to make out any sense or substance, but they were too quiet. She shrugged off her clothes and kicked them into a corner, then pulled the duvet tight up over her head so that nobody would hear her cry.

She awoke with a mouth full of fuzz and a skull that felt too small for her brain. The second morning of this in a row: well, that was why the weekend lasted more than one day. When the room stopped spinning around her hungover head, Neely stood slowly and stumbled out the bedroom. She didn't like how her hand shook as she guided herself along the wall. She didn't like herself very much and she didn't like the scene in the front room. First, she saw the front door: chain off. The couch, vacated. The space Brian had covered on the floor was bare now, without even a mark to prove he had been there. Were it not for a tidy pile of empty chicken buckets and oily paper wrappings, she might have shaken off her last memories as a particularly pathetic dream.

No strangers and no Angela. No Angela on a Sunday morning.
SUNDAY.

They'd told her that he sold pills to girls who didn't know any better, and never shut up about the one who wouldn't love him for it. She would have found this beautiful, years ago. She would have wanted to draw out the story, flesh out the characters, dangle their dreams from the ceiling lights. But there were years between then and today.

Neely dashed into the kitchen and shoved aside the kettle. There they were, the days of the week in plastic boxes: unbothered, unstolen, each tablet in its little compartment. Topiramate 200mg, little yellow circles prescribed in the name of Angela M Archer, who had now missed two days. She sighed, then brought her hands up to each side of her head and squeezed. Bad decisions and good company.

She poured a glass of water from the tap and stumbled into the lounge. Slowly, shakily, she began to gather the rubbish, replaying what she could remember from last night. Whisky all round, Tasha saying Angela was beautiful – well, she was, wasn't she? Of course Angela was beautiful. Anybody could see that, even Angela herself. Maybe she had decided she was too beautiful for Neely, and taken that beauty somewhere else. Somewhere off the Harrow Road, all Costcutters and KFCs, no-name junk shops and no-name people from a blur of elsewheres. It was as good an explanation as anything else, and all else she knew was nothing. Neely picked up her mobile and dialled that speed-dial: voicemail again, without a single ring.

Strangers didn't call Neely beautiful unless they were whistling from a building site. They called her clever, but right now she didn't feel particularly clever. It wasn't clever to take strangers into your home. Strangers didn't call Neely beautiful, but Angela did. And Neely just wanted to feel beautiful, and more importantly, to feel interesting. To be the one someone actually wanted to come home to in the evening. There was nothing wrong with that, she told herself, rationalising the previous night. Nothing wrong with an honest experiment. But she had woken up in the same flat in which she had laid down her head the night before, and she was still alone.

Time for the police. Definitely. But first she needed a plan, she needed to know what she was doing before she laced up her shoes and threw on her coat and walked into Harrow Road Police Station as if she knew anything she needed to know. She needed some noise. She'd put on a tune and gather her thoughts and it would be better than it was before. Of course it would; it always was.

The hi-fi was exactly where she had left it. Of course it was; she hadn't expected it to sprout legs and toddle out of her flat, down the dark stairs, and out onto the Harrow Road. No, there was nothing amiss there. It was the shelf below it that stood starkly, brutally bare. All her CDs, the row of plastic cases and paper booklets and little metal circles, were gone. *Her* music. All the songs she had loved and all the singers Neely had dreamed alive even when they were decades dead and gone. All the bands she had seen at Brixton Academy, Hammersmith Apollo, Shepherd's Bush Empire, The Garage in Holloway Road, carrying her from her Stevenage bedroom to the heart of London, or at least to somewhere around a blackened lung. On the arm of the couch sat the borrowed phone book and along its side, crookedly inscribed on the compressed paper, someone had left Neely the only explanation she had seen in days.

Done you a favour, the note read, the black marker used to write it lying uncapped between the gravy and the burnt chips.

Four

'Where are you from?'

The truth is London and the truth is too complicated for most people. Barely anybody in London actually comes from London, or at least none of a certain kind of person, the kind of people Angela has a feeling she is supposed to know. When she wants to sound posh, she says Notting Hill. When she wants to sound hard, she says Shepherd's Bush. When she feels like telling the truth, she says it's round about North Kensington around Kensal Town, sort of, W10, know what I mean?

The truth is tricky, it is sticky, it is treacle. She doesn't have time to explain the intricacies of West London human geography to everybody who asks and, quite frankly, Angela gets the impression that nobody who asks *really* wants to know. They want the one- or two-word answer, so that's what she gives them. She is quite skilled with customer service. Her boss even says so; nobody ever complains. She gives them exactly what they want, when they want it. Notting Hill. Shepherd's Bush. North Ken. On the topiramate she becomes so dozy that sometimes she forgets within minutes which answer she's just given. Notting Hill, Shepherd's Bush, North Ken. Alright? Yeah, alright, that's wicked, OK.

It isn't OK, and it hasn't been for a long time. If there is a continuum of human happiness on which OK is dead centre, then things have been bouncing about in the space below that point for years, to the extent where OK now looks pretty damn wonderful. Angela Archer was aged nine when she had her first fit, twelve when her mother died, sixteen when three boys from her neighbourhood took her behind the railway depot and took turns teaching her not to be such a frigid bitch. Shortly afterward, what remained of her family moved from Ladbroke Grove down the road to East Acton and she finally realised it was not the trauma that put her off boys but rather the recognition of a more permanent preference. Angela Archer had been recalibrated.

At this specific point in time, a time long before Neely Sharpe comes home to an empty flat, it has been only a year – her eighteenth on this planet – since Angela made that realisation. And for the year since she had that realisation, Angela has been taking her bicycle deeper and deeper into West London during her free hours. *I haven't understood myself and I've been living in this head all these years,* she thinks. *Imagine how much I don't understand about this city.* She waits for flashes of brilliance to pop into her head every time she goes winding along the Grand Union Canal towpath, the one that starts at Paddington and takes her all the way through to Greenford before it becomes impassable. She has been waiting quite some time.

There is a bend early on the route, one where the towpath hugs the Westway and flirts with it a bit before shifting away from Westbourne Park. Angela has watched the graffiti on the concrete walls under this part of the motorway morph for months, but has never laid eyes on the people responsible. They don't want to be seen. Obvious reasons. But still, it's a bit noble of them, Angela thinks. Yeah, they tag their work and all, but nobody actually *sees* them. It ain't like being on television and showing off for the cameras and having everybody stare at you and want to shag you. These people are what they make. No back-story. No explanation. They do their thing and then they disappear and it is what it is. Maybe they know something the people on *Big Brother* don't when it comes to making your name. Well, everybody knows something the people on *Big Brother* don't. They're a load of thick shits.

Impulsively, she grimaces as she speeds by the Ladbroke Grove Sainsbury's. Angela spends more time at this Sainsbury's than she likes: it's a weekend job on the tills. She'd been in hospital that day so many Octobers ago when, just on the other side of the supermarket, fireballs tore through the morning and the Sainsbury's car park filled with the dead, dying and miraculously spared. 'There's been a rail crash at Ladbroke Grove,' she remembers her mum telling her, the gentle voice coming to her as she lay among impossibly fluffy pillows in an impossibly uncool hospital gown. 'Two trains hit each other and then caught fire.' It was the simplest, most gentle way to explain to a child, bewildered by her own brain, what had happened to her neighbourhood on one of the few occasions she wasn't in it. The stench of diesel fuel and all it had burnt lingered over the Archers' corner of West London for days, and her mother quit going to that Sainsbury's altogether, driving two miles to another one to avoid any reminders. 'Turn it off,' she barked whenever the crash came up on the television news. 'I've had enough. We know enough. It's nothing to do with us.' Mr Archer would always protest feebly before conceding every time.

Like most things prohibited by parents, the disaster's allure only increased in Angela's imagination. Something terrible had happened where she lived, and she'd missed it. All of it. Her mother wouldn't even let her go hang out with Jenny Wedmore, because she lived in Kensal House, a crap modernist monstrosity of a block that offered a perfect view of the railway from Jenny's bedroom. Deprived of first-hand knowledge, Angela had had to obtain what she could, where she could.

'They haven't got all the bodies out, y'know,' her big sister, in the middle of a half-hearted teenage goth phase and resentful at having to babysit, told her a few nights later. 'Some of them got trapped when the carriages got all torn up. They can't get to them until the big cranes come out and lift up everything. It could be a week that they're just lying there dead. Not joking.' Nightmares inevitably ensued. When Angela finally confessed to her mother why she kept waking up screaming, her sister got a smack in the face with Mrs Archer's sovereign-clad hand. In retrospect, Angela felt guilty about the punishment. Poor Andy hadn't told any lies. It wasn't a crime to not make the truth palatable.

But enough of the past. Or at least that part of it. Strange to recall one incident, the sudden compression of deaths into one date and time, when right across the canal from that Sainsbury's is a veritable city of the notable dead. Isambard Kingdom Brunel is buried here in Kensal Green Cemetery, the engineer entombed within spitting distance of the railway he built. The storytellers: Trollope and Thackeray. A famous tightrope walker called Blondin, who has a little orchard named after him somewhere in Ealing, one Angela will never know exists because Ealing, the next borough over from the one where her father has just bought a house riddled with dry rot but free from history, may as well be on the moon. Angela doesn't know who GK Chesterton is, he's not on the school reading list, but it is safe to assume she would have looked upon his lines about this place with a nod of the head, a tacit acceptance: *For there is good news yet to hear and fine things to be seen; Before we go to Paradise by way of Kensal Green.* And then she would have laughed long and hard at the idea of Kensal Green as a celestial motorway service station. Be sure to scan your Nectar Card at Sainsbury's and start collecting karma points today. The Afterlife is accessible via the northern edge of the car park during normal trading hours. Closed Sundays.

The next leg of the route is Angela's favourite, though she fears it would be dull to admit it. For the mile-and-a-bit from Scrubs Lane to Stonebridge Park, she pedals through a place that is somewhere between the city and the country, the present and the past. Here, industrial estates hug both sides of the canal, relics from when the boats on the water were meant for something other than leisure. Nowadays, Park Royal is home to those businesses where Angela suspects the overwhelmingly average are in charge. Used cars. Small scale import-export. Lots of food. An industrial recycler screams its name in block letters across the top of its warehouse, P O W E R D A Y, as if passing traffic like Angela might be tempted to stop by for a quick browse. Amidst all the hard, thankless, decidedly unglamorous slog, nature has been reinstalled: elm and lime and London plane, great big weeping willows, all shade the cyclists. Angela listens to the hum and creak of machinery, punctuated by the odd crack or crush, and knows that the city is working. She doesn't care about football, but there's the Wembley Arch in the distance, a signpost, marking space and her place in it. A nature reserve, maintained by nobody in particular, juts off to one side, filling a gap between the towpath and the railways. It's good for birds, this bit. Families of swans paddle by, the young ones starting as awkward grey balls of fluff that grow up to armour their faces with the first moult, heading towards where Angela just left. Earlier this spring, caught in a sudden storm, she waited out the rain underneath these brick bridges, watching mist descend like history. And she's seen homeless men washing their clothes here, hanging them up on the brick walls to dry in whatever sun they can get, and the memory of it causes her to suddenly become extremely fixated on the path directly in front of her. The ground beneath her wheels feels flat enough, but when the path emerges from the trees just before the old Harlesden Lock, she has risen; now, she rides two storeys above the North Circular Road. Of course she *thinks* she has risen. It is incomprehensible to imagine something as massive as the North Circular lowering itself for the likes of her.

Past Stonebridge Park, slabs of council estates soon to be cleared – *regenerated*: this is Metroland. Angela rings her bike bell frenetically as she rounds a ninety-degree curve on the narrowing path, stray twigs and vines whipping her outside leg. Fewer factories and more bungalows and semi-detached houses. Even another Sainsbury's. On the opposite bank of the canal, two mutts play-fight in the grass beside their owner's narrowboat as the long-haired, shirtless man tends a barbecue. Angela rings her bell again; he waves. He's strange but he's safe for her, stuck on the opposite bank with no crossing nearby, and that's why Angela likes him. He has moored his boat a sufficient distance from the golf course so as to not attract attention. Nobody is playing today, and if she weren't watching the path in front of her in preparation for another bend, Angela would see the flags on the pins lazily flapping in a slight summer breeze. And then the strangest thing: the landscape ripples. Across the canal, hills rise out of Horsenden Park. This looks like a proper bit of countryside, not the token nod to greenery found in most of the city parks Angela knows. She sees an exit from the towpath, and takes it. Ignores the older couple strolling, ignores another happy couple with kids. Ignores the grass and then the pavement and zips into the street as if nobody else would ever need it. Right now, they don't.

She lifts her feet off the pedals and sticks her legs out straight in front of her, one on each side of the blur of a front wheel as she picks up speed going ever-so-slightly downhill in Greenford Road. *Wheeeee*, she calls out despite herself. There's nobody in the street to hear her. This far out is where cars are the rule, not the exception or the foolish purchase of a boy racer who then curses the hours wasted trying to find a place to park the fucking thing. Angela will never drive a car (not allowed; imagine having a fit behind the wheel and taking out a dozen other drivers when all you wanted was a quick trip to the shops) and quite frankly she has no business on a bike (similar reasons, but potential carnage most likely limited to only herself and the emotional health of anybody witnessing the sight), but it doesn't stop her loving the thrill of acceleration however she can get it. *Fucking wheeeeeeeeeeeee*, she speeds past the retail park – all the usual suspects: Next, Carphone Warehouse, Costa Coffee, names recognisable whether you were brought up in Shepherd's Bush or in Sandringham – and underneath the railway bridge, where the Underground is no longer underground. She's going downhill fast, which Angela regards as preferable to nowhere fast because at least the scenery changes. She passes Uneeda Drive and makes a mental note to remember the most stupid street name she has ever seen in a lifetime of noticing the names of places. Uneeda Drive, Uneeda Walk More Often You Lazy Fuck, Uneeda Life, Uneeda Chicken Cottage or Something Out Here Because I Can't See Any Place People Just Go to Hang Out. It's all houses down Greenford Road. All semis with brownish and reddish roofs, all a variation on the same Middlesexual theme. This is where they write Middlesex on their post even though Middlesex doesn't even exist any more, Angela remembers. Christ. Wow. *Wheeeeeeeeeeeee.*

She reaches Western Avenue. She knows Western Avenue. The A40. It's what the Westway becomes once you're, well, west. It starts on the edge of Shepherd's Bush, just past the White City Estate, and presumably goes further west than anywhere she's ever been before. Angela shifts from the road to the pavement at the traffic light. Looks left, taps her heels against the bicycle's sturdy frame: *There's no place like home. There's no place like home. Follow the greyish shit road.* But instead she turns right. Northolt, a sign informs her, lies ahead. And Yeading, and Ruislip. She's never even heard of Yeading. But Ruislip, *West Ruislip*, is the place the Central Line ends, the dead end of the Tube's big fat red artery that bisects a map she knows so well. Her dad drives the Circle Line. When she was small he snuck her into his cab and they orbited the heart of the city and he called out a fact at each stop: this is Farringdon, see the cattle ramps left over from when Smithfield Market sold things people actually needed. This is Moorgate, site of the worst crash in the history of the Tube. This is Tower Hill, which used to be just down the road until they moved it. Remember which year that one closed? *Angela, pay attention.* She doesn't pay attention too well and she doesn't know how much of that is her fault and how much can be blamed on the lamotrigine, on the carbamazepine, on whatever else they're trying on her this year. Attention must be rationed, so she has tried to get to know the world around her to the best of her ability in the hope that, should her attention be depleted altogether, small signals and familiar signposts will be enough to carry her home.

Knowing she is still within grabbing distance of that long red Central life-Line, the one that will safely deposit her a short walk from home no matter how long it takes, she leans forward and pedals harder. She takes a moment to inspect the Polish War Memorial, sitting on its own island smack bang in the middle of the road. Big fuck-off bronze eagle up top. Angela scans the names, looking for one she has a chance of pronouncing correctly, and there it is, in between Milewski and Minkiewicz: SGT. J. J. MINGE. Angela laughs, then feels guilty even though there is nobody nearby to hear. Then onward she goes, climbing northwest. The A40 curves but the pavement stays straight, and Angela finds herself deposited into another suburban street. Across waste ground and back gardens, she can see rows upon rows of semi-detached, all in the Middlesex style, some with sheds, some with children's toys, some with laundry lazily waving from lines and racks. *Who lives in a place like this?* she thinks and, at that moment, Angela Archer decides to get lost.

She turns when she wants. Here, a shopping parade of mock-Tudor two-storey buildings, the structures nicer than the ones she knows but holding the same crap newsagents, the same post office, the chippy that does a little Chinese, the off-licence. But the skies look brighter here. The roads are wider. Or maybe they just have fewer irate motorists honking and parking two-deep and spouting threats. She turns, and turns, and turns again. The frequency of green slits between buildings increases, then decreases again as houses compress back into terraces. *Where are all the people?* she wonders. A postman, a middle-ager walking his dog. Some sort of terrier she can't name. Not a Staffordshire like the ones in her street. And everywhere, sky. She's not wearing a watch but, even if she was, she would not have bothered checking how much time she wastes threading through the streets of Hillingdon, of Hayes and Northolt and Yeading, switching her legs to autopilot whilst wide eyes take in every suburban detail. The kind of details people living here stopped noticing ages ago are what imprint onto Angela's mind: benches outside shops, a distinct lack of dog shit and graffiti, and that the trees planted along pavements here are not the trees planted where she's from, originally. These trees are thick-trunked and aspirational, erect, daring the heavens to rain down on them. And they don't, of course they don't. *Fucking hell. How many places like this have I never, ever been?*

She rides blind. No maps, no compass, no knowledge of what goes where. Yet the invisible tether hooked onto her clunky third-hand Raleigh pulls her back to Western Avenue. She's not ready to go home. It's going to be a long ride back there. Her temporary salvation comes just a few hundred metres away: a park unlike any of the others she's discovered today. In fact, she's never seen a park like this anywhere, not even in books illustrated or otherwise. Four perfect grassy half-domes, increasing in size, rise up beside the road. They could be the burial mounds of her prehistoric ancestors on this island. A family, from biggest to smallest. Or maybe a Druid tribute to tits. She rubs her eyes and blinks hard but the four hills still sit beside the road, and she knows precisely why they send that tiny bit of fear shooting up from her feet: they're too perfect.

She speeds into the grass and circles lazily, sizing up what lies in front of her. She drops the bike and approaches the highest of the hills. Angela doesn't have to look around her to see if there is somebody who could steal; there is nobody nearby except for the stream of drivers, and they aren't going to veer off the motorway to snatch that piece of crap. Though her legs feel like jelly and her arse is nearly numb from the bike saddle, she feels seized by a need to climb, because today she is Angela the Conqueror, she is somebody who found a new land and explored it and would have planted a flag if she'd had one, and there was morning, and there was mid-afternoon, and it was good.

Angela sees the flies before she sees the fox. Two greenbottles, cavorting in mid-air. Maybe an intentional dance, or maybe pure utility. The sun catches their iridescence, and that's what catches Angela's eye. Angela doesn't know a thing about insects and she doesn't want to know. They land almost simultaneously upon the red-brown fur lying atop the summit of this impossibly symmetric mound of earth. The animal's face is not frozen in the peaceful sleep recognisable as death's sibling. Rather, she died with a grimace, with canine teeth protruding from a black rim of lip. Angela freezes but the flies still move. She was a she, and a mother at that: lying on her side, her two rows of teats are now utterly useless, a complete waste, no good to anyone or anything that may come across them. A breeze, one Angela didn't notice pushing or pulling her bicycle as she circled the streets below, catches the fox's fur, and ripples it gently. Only Angela's eyes shoot into motion. She looks for a wound, a gash, a bullet, any explanation. There has to be one. That's how life, and in turn death, work: there is always a reason you can figure out if you're clever enough. And when she finds nothing, she thinks that's her fault.

And now she is running, running faster than she ever has done in her life even though there is nobody chasing after her. Halfway down the hill, she trips and shrieks and it is the first sound out of her mouth in hours; a smear of mud, darker than she expected and with garish green blades of grass embedded within, stains her tracksuit bottoms. She's on her bike within seconds and speeding away from the green and onto the grey pavement. Her wheels leave black skids on it as she points her bike east. Clinging to Western Avenue, and only stopping to avoid the inevitability of being flattened at the Hangar Lane Gyratory had she not, she barrels down toward London, London proper, London and all she's ever known. Once home, she throws her bicycle down onto the paved-over bit of front garden, narrowly missing the car that she can't drive and never will, and she's inside before the rear wheel can stop its lazy mid-air spin.

'Angela? That you?' she hears her father call from the lounge, but she doesn't reply, and he is used to this. He knows it is his younger daughter because seconds after his unanswered enquiry, a bedroom door slams and two shoes thunk against the floor. Angela lies in her bed and stares at the ceiling, but she does not cry. She catches her breath. And she fails spectacularly at trying not to think.

Everybody said her mother was so young when it happened. Too young, and not that old by today's standards. At seventeen, Angela's mid-twenties feel like eons away. She has the gift of still being so young that she doesn't appreciate how blissfully, foolishly young she really is. She hasn't thought much about it, but she assumes that by twenty-four she will be gone from West London altogether. At the closest – the absolute very closest – she'll consider Camden Town. Get a bunch of friends and rent a flat together and really live it up. They'll have jobs that pay enough for that, somehow. Or East London. Hackney is where everybody with anything interesting in their head goes now. Whatever. But probably, maybe, most likely not West London. Her best mate just moved to Wood Green with her family. A straightforward trip on two Tube lines, it's only zone 3, but she might as well have emigrated. She actually got out. She took that step, she's on her way to living before she dies. Angela works at Sainsbury's and doesn't even know how to look up the scan code for instructions how to do likewise.

The sweat dries on her brow. She rolls over and stares out her window at the street below. It's quieter here than Kensal Town was and there's nothing to catch her eye, so she shifts focus to the windowsill. Clock radio, lipstick (Lilac Lustre, £3.99 from Superdrug), more lipstick (an obscene pink called Girl About Town, packaged in a little bullet that reminded her of a matt black tampon, stolen from House of Fraser), tissues both used and clean, pens both dry and full, and the blank book. It's a chunky brick of a journal, odd for an impulse purchase. Why did I buy that? Angela thinks. I can't remember. I'm not that good at drawing and I don't need to drop twelve quid on fancy crap like that. Twelve quid is the money I saved not paying for that lipstick and instead I went and pissed it away on some posh paper. Oh, but the cover's lovely, it is, all thin vertical stripes in every colour. Not just the ones you think of, the blue and the purple and the red, but the ones with names you have to think about. Fuchsia, magenta, lilac, indigo. It's fun, it is. Fun but not childish. It looks like what I'd want to carry places where people would see it. I could write in it on the bus or the Tube, if I wrote. I could write. I can draw. That's it. I'll write, I'll draw.

The third pen she tries actually has ink in it. Baffled at how to begin, she starts with what she knows: ANGELA MARIE ARCHER she prints in block capitals on the first page. Can't argue with that. So far, no foul. Underneath those letters: the date. Underneath those numbers: she doesn't know, so she begins to sketch a cycling silhouette. On the next page, she tries to capture in light biro strokes the face of the fox, the fallen animal, the vanquished queen lying alone atop her hill. But it's not quite right. It's flat, it's not right at all. Angela tries another approach: *I took my bike way out west and oh my days everything was absolutely ridiculous,* she writes, then crosses out her words with one black gouge. Silly. Worse than silly – stupid. What's the word? Trite. That's it, trite. And boring. I'm boring. I'll come back to it, Angela thinks. I'll fix it, I'll keep at it. I'll do more later. I have to do more later because there's a lot of ground to cover, a lot of London I have to figure out. And no guarantee I've got plenty of time to do it.

Seven years later, Angela Archer does not live in Camden Town or Hackney or anywhere within walking distance of the two. She lives a stone's throw from her old North Ken home, on a main road where her mother barely ever took her shopping as a kid because it didn't have what they wanted and only some of what they needed. She remembers, when she was little, what her mother always said when on one of her rants about the state of where they lived and what ought to be done about it and what they ought to do for themselves because nobody in this damn world was going to do it for them: Harrow Road makes you feel poor and foreign.

But her mother is long gone and Angela has grown tall. And she stays in West London long after her sister and brother have shot off, and she finds a flat in the Harrow Road and she finds a short girl from Stevenage with a job so boring Angela sometimes forgets what it is. They do every pub quiz within a stone's throw of that little flat, and come top three in each and every one, because there's something about this short girl from Stevenage, a lot of brain hidden under the painfully tight ponytail that shows off those high cheekbones, that highlights that face which has something of a history about it. Angela doesn't feel like the strange one, the exotic one, when she's around Neely Sharpe, though she'll never admit it, because she knows that in Neely's eyes – those nearly-black eyes, eyes that she knows how to use to melt Angela every fucking time – she's the most interesting person in the world by dint of her postcode alone, and that's a tough act to maintain. But Angela will try. Angela A-for-Effort Archer. She may not be clever and she may not be revealing the secrets of life and death through either painstaking method or blessed serendipity but nobody will ever say she doesn't try.

Years later, she tried to keep her explanation simple; tried to keep things succinct for the girl who seemed to have so many words for the simplest things. This is the greatest place in the world, she told Neely, as they walked arm-in-arm on the canal towpath at Little Venice on an early autumn weekend afternoon before the desperate cold blew in. Neely wanted a coffee from the little café barge, and so they got one each and made them last half an hour as they tossed biscuit crumbs at the birds. They could have stopped in one of the canalside pubs and avoided the chill that nipped at their fingers when they set down their warm drinks, but they'd already had their fill: at the Hope and Anchor in Harrow Road, where Angela had a shandy and Neely her pint of Newcastle Brown, and a packet of salt and vinegar between them. Neely had once admitted to Angela she had been confused her first time inside their local. It shared a name with another pub, in Islington, where her brother had once snuck her into a gig underage. When she had been fifteen, that had been the most glamorous place on the planet, and London the home of her dreams, and then years later she had landed in Harrow Road. The two buildings had nothing in common but their name, but Neely didn't mind: the pair of nouns fitted no matter what corner of the city she chose. Angela had smiled at tiny Neely coming back to the table from the bar, a pint in each hand dwarfing her bony fingers, crisps clamped between her teeth. And Neely had smiled back, making the crisp packet crinkle. And Angela had laughed, and so had Neely, and the junkie couple permanently installed in the corner had wanted to know just what was so funny, what the fuck was so very funny?

After the coffee, they set off on foot along Angela's old route: west.

Along the motorway, the graffiti still screamed all bloody and neon among the grey. There was a bit of fluff, provenance unknown, stuck in the shorter girl's high black ponytail. Angela granted it reprieve. For now, it could stay. The two women passed underneath a footbridge, walking just slightly faster than a swan and a small flock of mallards swam. Laughter rose from the little restaurant on the opposite bank and joined the thin smoke from its fireplace chimney. Late lunchtime wine and conversation were flowing between the good-looking, well-off new locals who probably wouldn't believe Angela if they asked her where she was from and she replied *London* without the slightest hesitation.

Neely, she began. *Neely. Look. This place is sacred. Look.*

Five

In the snapshot that accompanied the memo shot out from Harrow Road Police Station on Monday morning, Angela had been caught off guard by Sam's point-and-shoot. It captured her face in a split-second of naive serenity before laughter and a playful swat. Neely had been ready. Neely had posed and pursed her lips into the perfect duck face. Neely had wrapped an arm, hidden from view, around her girlfriend's back, displaying her to eventual viewers as a prize to be claimed and cherished. But half a year later, Neely had stood in their kitchen, pulled the photo from its magnet on the refrigerator, and snipped herself out of the summer scene. Without Neely, Angela leaned slightly into a nothingness to her left. Her gold-looking hoops dangled, garishly yellow, in front of newly bleached curls. She could have been anybody, and that was the point: she made an easy memory.

Neely knew that nobody at the police station had believed her when she said, *Angela has no family.* There was always family. They may have been reluctant family, possibly even dead family, but they existed in the pages of history, the most boring pages, the phone books and electoral rolls and civil registers, the ones skipped over to get to the good stuff. They would still show up in the index at the very back, if someone bothered to look.

As outer London slept and inner London stumbled into taxis and onto night buses and through puddles of spew and rain, the report hit every station from Heathrow to Havering: *Angela Archer, last seen on 18 December, is 24 years old, five foot nine inches tall and of proportionate build, with green eyes. She has dyed blonde hair with brown roots. She has lived in West London her entire life. She failed to return to her flat in Harrow Road after finishing her shift at the Porchester Centre and her flatmate has reported her missing. Her disappearance was completely out of character.*

At the last time she was seen, Angela was wearing a long black coat and distinctive red ankle boots and carrying a black leather-look handbag believed to contain her wallet and mobile phone. No other personal effects have been reported missing from her residence or place of work. She suffers from epilepsy and there is reason to believe that she does not have any medication with her. Without this, she is vulnerable to fits which sometimes leave her confused and disoriented.

Due to her medical condition and the cold weather, Miss Archer's disappearance should be considered a matter of priority.

An hour later, hair fixed, lipstick and mascara perfunctorily applied, clad in her most nondescript dress and black leggings, Neely left for work. She would only be half an hour late, and if she shrugged and said *doctor's appointment*, nobody would ask for any further explanation. The last thing she wanted was an office conversation that went anywhere remotely near her private life. Nobody there needed to know she had a girlfriend, let alone one who had seemingly fucked off without warning. The office was already half empty for Christmas, anyway. People with places to go had begun to go there, and barring any major disasters – exploding photocopiers, say, the kind that took out half the graduate scheme cohort – Neely figured nobody would particularly care where she had gone.

Westbourne Park to Great Portland Street, her train trundled on as she read a discarded freesheet. Slow news week for everybody else in the city, it seemed. She walked the few minutes to her office with her head down, butting into the wind, and took her seat in silence once inside. She swivelled in her desk chair. Sipped her tea and wished she'd added another sugar. Reloaded the *Guardian* website for the fifth, sixth time. It was a paper she never read on actual paper. She looked at the clock – 12:02 – and tried to think of the last time she'd bought a real newspaper, the last time she'd slid some shrapnel over the counter at the newsagents and ruined a white top with smudges of ink. She checked the time when she finally gave up: 12:06. Oh well.

She clicked the little black X in the corner of the web browser and killed the *Guardian*, then promptly frowned at the empty desktop and double-clicked again to revive it. She had woken up on the wrong side of the bed, and a cold bed at that. The meter had run out in the middle of the night and, with no time to top up her card at the newsagents before work, Neely had shuffled around the lonely flat wrapped in her duvet, spilling the new carton of milk down her front and coming dangerously close to crying over it. And thanks to those three on Saturday night, there hadn't even been any music to take the edge off. She thought that she shouldn't be in a flat with the gas and electricity on a meter. That was for people in Mike Leigh plays set before she was born. Hopeless people and cautionary tales. Not Neely Sharpes.

Once she had exhausted everything interesting on the *Guardian*, she switched to the *Independent* and read the same news. There was nothing else to do. Nothing of importance. Nothing to justify the years of study and a perpetually pathetic bank balance, and nothing to indicate that here, in this office, sat somebody brighter than most, feeling herself growing ever dimmer.

Angela never read the news. At another time, this would have turned off Neely only marginally less than if Angela had confessed a penchant for eyeball-licking or crushing bugs with stilettos or any of the other fetishes the internet had handily informed her both existed and paid reasonably well if one was female, at least mildly attractive, and willing to perform on camera. But that was back when journalism was aspirational and admirable, just like how that doctorate had been a sure thing and a solid plan. That was before Ruby Sullivan had showed her just how easy everything could be, if you knew the right people – and how utterly impossible if you didn't.

No, Angela wasn't one for the *Guardian*. On rare occasions she'd drop a quid on *Hill and Rise*, the local rag for local people, blushing and admitting she only wanted to see if anybody she'd grown up with had been nicked. The crime pages were all low-level stuff that wouldn't make the *Evening Standard*: Local kids torch local Scouts hut. Local granny mugged outside local Sainsbury's Local. Still, the local reader never failed to become engrossed in those pages, and Neely had admired Angela from across the lounge in those moments, the sunset tinging her girlfriend's hair gold, real gold, as she read, slowly and deliberately. Very slowly.

And there were *those* times, Neely admitted to herself in the computer screen's glow, hating herself for it. Those times her gaze at Angela went on long enough to make her eyeballs glaze and, Neely realised, *she's been on that one page for ages.* The girl close to top of her year at Fenlands Comp, shacked up with a girl who rarely read anything more demanding than *Heat.* It wasn't a matter of what was wrong with Angela – what was wrong with *Neely?* She couldn't help but remind herself that half the point of university, as far as her parents were concerned, was to enter into the right crowds, circulate in the right spaces, meet the right person. It had worked for them at the North London Poly, after all. Rita Mangal and Tony Sharpe had met first thing on the first day of Freshers' Week, for God's sake, possibly the only two people in the history of British education to take starting as they meant to go on quite that seriously. They'd told that story when they'd come down to London over the summer and insisted on taking Neely and Angela to dinner. Neely had tried not to redden over the moussaka at some Finsbury Park Greek restaurant that was older than her parents' degrees; she tried not to cringe as they recalled their months of stealing its bog roll after their grants had run out, or the story about that time Rita had been called a Paki by *some subnormals off the Andover Estate who probably couldn't have pointed to India on the map if a year of dole cheques had depended on it.* Their poverty had been nothing but a phase, something with a sell-by date. If they had kept it around too long, it would have smelled off. Neely had nudged Angela sympathetically – no, apologetically – under the table, but the girl had played along, laughing at the right moments, asking the right inoffensive questions, giving nothing away.

Your flatmate is so nice, they had relayed to Neely over the phone the next day. *She's a bit quiet, isn't she? Bit shy? Oh, but she's so nice.* Yes, Neely's flatmate. Rita and Tony didn't have to know it was only a one-bedroom flat.

Now here in December, Neely couldn't help but ask herself the question she was sure her parents would have done, if they'd known the truth: *Three years at Goldsmiths, almost three years at King's, and the best you can do is the girl who takes the cash at the Porchester Centre? Who didn't know where Copenhagen was back during Eurovision? Who paused a bit when you asked her to divide that cake recipe in half?* Get a girl instead of a guy, and generally speaking, right-on Rita and Tony probably wouldn't care. But get Kim Nice-But-Dim and it would certainly be

A Bit of a Concern. Every time this thought tried to surface in her consciousness, she pushed it down, buried it, poured concrete directly over anywhere it might try to hide, but it still had its way of wriggling itself free.

No, Neely chastised herself. *No. Not now. Leave it out. It's not the time.* She rubbed her eyes and rubbed away the thought. It wasn't important now: she loved Angela, Angela was missing, and the wave of self-loathing would just have to wait at the door, quietly and politely, for its turn.

'Any word on the copier, Sharpe?'

They called her Sharpe here. She didn't particularly feel it.

'RICOH says tomorrow.'

'It's only going to break again. Every time we repair it, it just breaks again.'

'Oh, well, now that you mention that extra information, let me get out the tin of fairy dust I've got stashed in my desk drawer and let me fetch my magic wand from where it fell behind the filing cabinet and I'll cast a spell that makes office equipment never break, because I've had that ability all along, I was just waiting for you to validate my existence.' *Fuck you.*

'You alright, Sharpe?'

Neely smiled sweetly. 'Course I am. It's Christmas.'

'So, tomorrow?'

She breathed. Deep this time.

'RICOH says tomorrow.'

The budget for this month had been settled. All the employee assessments were scheduled for the new year, that post-hangover valley of winter. The junk mail had been dispatched to the recycling bin. Tea well-stocked. Once they came back from Christmas and New Year, it would be time to dip into the petty cash stash and buy two bottles of red, four bottles of white, and a crate of lager for the all-staff meeting. Neely got to choose those. She disappointed herself for a moment thinking about how this was joy for her now, whether to pick French or Californian, chardonnay or sauvignon blanc. Had to decide which paired better with ripe bullshit. And if someone else was paying, there was certainly something about the Portuguese rosé.

She slipped into the toilets, clutching her mobile phone. Tap, Sam Wylie, tap. She knew he'd be asleep, dead to the world until at least noon, but she rang him anyway, listened through the empty rings and through the beep of his answerphone. 'Sam. Angela's gone. I haven't seen her since Friday and her phone's off.' She paused, and heard her breath fuzz in the receiver. 'Call me back, yeah?' And she tapped again to kill the one-way conversation before slinking out, head down, as if caught in an act – any act, anything that she could be called upon to answer for, because at least then she might have an answer. But nobody was looking and nobody cared.

She returned to Google, to the computer and to the free rocket-speed internet connection that was one of the few perks of the job. During last week's longest spell of time-wasting, Neely had followed a link from a news story about somebody who tried to climb Everest unprepared and promptly died well below the summit, and she had ended up learning that the most-worn paths up that mountain were essentially graveyards of Western hubris. Well, not exactly graveyards, because in graveyards, bodies were hidden from sight and it was assumed they would eventually decay. Not so in the Himalayas. The cold preserved the corpses so that years, decades even, after death, the fallen climbers still had flesh on their faces. It was too dangerous to bring them down. People climbing that high barely had enough oxygen to haul themselves back from the summit and they couldn't add a body's weight to their load. If climbers saw other people dying that far up the slope, they left them, or else they would end up in the same boat. Or cave. Crevasse. Whatever. Helicopters couldn't land, either. The air was too thin. So the dead just lay where they fell. They became signposts.

Neely looked back in the web browser's history and picked up where she had left off last week. There was Green Boots. Got his name because he was wearing green boots, which must have been fashionable in the nineties and were now preserved for all time, Neely thought. There was an American flag and a teddy covering one woman who couldn't be brought down. There was her hand: picture taken eight years after the fact and it still had all its skin. It was there on the internet for Neely to click and enlarge and wince at slightly before moving on to the next victim. Even an explorer from the 1920s. He was there, his skin was there, his jumper and socks and hobnail boots were there along with a bit of broken rope that said all anybody needed to know about how he ended up lying there for so long. And far more recently, there was a man called David Sharp. Sharp without an E, but Neely flinched regardless. She speed-read enough to learn that all indications seemed to be he had suffered. He was found by a camera crew filming a Kiwi double amputee scaling the mountain. Bit of an indignity to be shown up like that by a man with no legs, thought Neely, and then promptly hated herself for it. There was a film clip. Another click, another link. David Sharp was sitting in a cave, nearly frozen. He moved his head. Some Antipodean voices made excuses. David Sharp was sitting in a cave, dead. In London, Neely Sharpe clicked the back button on her browser and tried to look busy. Nobody would believe she was sitting so transfixed at a budget sheet, would they? They couldn't be *that* thick. She tried another path, and went back to the woman with the teddy and the flag and the perfectly preserved hand. Her name was Francys. The first woman to make it to the top without bottled oxygen, Wikipedia told Neely. And then she died on the way down. Neely was not impressed. Apparently she fulfilled a lifelong dream, making it up the mountain without oxygen. Neely sighed. *You died for your dream and I'm going to die waiting on mine. Who's the moron here?*

This browsing wasn't morbid to Neely. It was life, and some unusual ends to it. And at least these people, from their green boots to their plush teddies, had ends. Because everybody had a beginning, of course. It was how they managed to tidily wrap everything up before shuffling off the side of the Earth that made them matter. And of course they mattered. Here they were, on the internet, and whatever's on the internet lasts forever. But they died dreaming and they died alone.

She spun in her chair and stretched out her back, staring at the ceiling, thinking: There are some people who, upon hearing somebody else has managed to walk on water, will insist on learning to walk on air. And that's just fine, so long as that walking has a practical destination. Maybe you're trying to kill a spider up on the ceiling and you don't fancy waiting for it to drop down on its bit of silk. That's useful. But if you're walking on air for the sake of walking on air then maybe you deserve to put your foot in the wrong place and take a thorough tumble to where the mortals can't reach you and retrieve your carcass.

They're sad, but you're bitter. You've become bitter and it doesn't become you at all. London was supposed to make you happy, and it did for a while, didn't it? If you stepped off the train from Stevenage right now, and met the likes of yourself, you'd turn right back around.

She thought of Angela bringing her sunflowers, sunflowers she had picked up from Somerfield. She knew where they had come from because Angela hadn't bothered removing the packaging, hadn't scratched away the label that showed their price had been reduced 50% to clear. That was love to Neely. Angela knew Neely liked bright yellow blooms and knew Neely worried about Angela's bank balance. That, that was what Neely wanted. Perhaps it wasn't necessarily love, but it was at least the opposite of ridicule. And it was what she wanted. Her dream was Angela Archer, all five feet nine inches tall and brown roots and God knows how many years until a promotion. And her dream could be out there, now, lying alone.

That's it. Fuck babysitting the graduate scheme. She cleared her browser history and put on her coat. She was going to find Angela Archer.

She walked miles along the canal from Paddington to Ladbroke Grove and the cemetery, largely alone: anybody who might have been out for pleasure could find their pleasures somewhere else in this cold, in this run-up to Christmas. Neely honestly didn't expect to peer over a fence or through a garden and spot her girlfriend but, in the absence of any real idea where Angela may have gone, this made the most sense. The canal was both wild and domestic, serene and foreboding, a home and a way away from it – all it took to flip from one to another was a shift of light. If worlds had to collide, if trouble had to sneak up on anybody, it would happen here.

At Ladbroke Grove she climbed the stairs back up to the street, shook the thoughts from her head, and concentrated on the concrete. The Angela Archer Neely had photocopied onto posters at the library could have been loads of women, and that was the point. Best to cast a wide net. Neely did the casting down the Harrow Road and its tributaries, armed with grip tape. In and out of the newsagents and off-licences she darted, meekly asking if she could stick an Angela in the window. 'She's my flatmate and she's missing. She lives down the road, she's not well, we need to find her,' Neely would mumble until she got the requisite shrug of a reply. And so the blonde girl looked out on the street from among the adverts for the best-rate phonecards to Eastern Europe and Africa, the rooms offered and the rooms desired, and one particularly ubiquitous card eagerly offering the services of Princess, Thick XXL Goddess for All Your Dreams Call Now. Angela Archer, face wan and washed-out by the photocopier, had a difficult time competing with her.

MISSING – ANGELA ARCHER – 24 YEARS OLD – 5'9″ TALL, BLONDE HAIR, GREEN EYES, FROM HARROW ROAD. WEARING LONG BLACK COAT, SHORT RED BOOTS, BLACK HANDBAG. DISAPPEARANCE OUT OF CHARACTER. Neely found that last line curious: the need to distinguish that for some people, disappearing was perfectly normal, part of who they were.

Angela was at the top of the stairs at Westbourne Park Station, gazing silently at the waves of travellers passing her by. Now and then there would be a girl from Sion–Manning School oblivious to how the passive face and its goldish hoops belonged to somebody who had also once worn the purple cardigan and sat in the headmistress' office scrubbing off the weekend's nail varnish. Dozens of identical Angelas lined the shopfronts of Harrow Road, from where the tourists first disappear to where Westminster gives way to Brent and its silent cemeteries.

There was no Angela Archer at the newsagents. They must think I'm mad, Neely thought, recalling her desperation with the phone book. She gestured at the photocopied face to the tired shop owner, probably Pakistani but just as possibly Indian for all Neely knew. And she hated not knowing, a hate tinged with shame. *Your own nan's Indian, you should know. Not being able to tell one brown person from another is such a* Daily Mail *thing. You should know better.*

'This woman is missing. She's my friend. Can I stick this in your window?'

His headshake was confusion, not outright refusal. Neely slowed down and brought out the rising inflection again. 'See her? She lives three doors down? She disappeared and nobody knows where she is? So if I could put this in the window, in case somebody has seen her? Is that OK?'

A voice from behind her, in a language Neely wished she could properly identify. She and the man both turned. The speaker looked vaguely mid-twenties and vaguely disgruntled, and Neely surmised it was a son; obviously unhappy to be working in this tip for his dad when all of London stood outside the door that beeped a little too loudly for every entrance.

'Sorry, can I help you?' He smiled. Seemed friendly enough. The older man turned back to his newspaper. Urdu, Neely noticed. It's Urdu. That's Urdu script. It looks like Arabic, but it's not. I was bored at work and read about the differences on Wikipedia. Small, but there. They're Pakistani. Got it.

'Hi, yeah, sorry,' Neely began again, temporarily thrown. 'I was just saying, I was wondering if I could put up one of these signs in the window, because my girlfriend's gone missing and maybe someone's seen her?' *Girlfriend* came spinning out of her mouth reflexively; she hadn't been thinking to edit the word. She held up one of her photocopies as if to prove her intention, as if to emphasise that no, she was not planning to paste up porn.

The man narrowed his eyes at the printed Angela's wide, blank ones. 'Erm, I'm sorry, we don't let people put up posters. Sorry, just a shop policy.'

'I saw you've got cards up, though. It doesn't have to be right in everyone's face. Off to the side would be great.'

He shook his head, the friendly welcome gone. 'I can't, sorry. If we let one person do it, we'd have to let everybody.'

'But you've got one for Winter Wonderland.' Neely knew she was flailing at a losing game. 'Please, it's for a good cause.'

'No. My dad doesn't want it. Can't do it.'

'Alright,' Neely growled, and stomped out. Fuck you and fuck your annoying doorbell, she thought to herself as the latter beeped behind her. It was the word, it was definitely the word. Of course they don't want Harrow Road becoming some sort of lesbian Mecca. OK, Mecca probably isn't the right word, either, all things considered. But still. Let one lesbian think you're her pal and suddenly they're all moving in and displacing your grannies from these shit, damp flats, and turning your crap shops into, dunno, whatever we're supposed to like.

It was only once she'd heard the door shut behind her that she realised she had forgotten to top up her card for the gas and electric meter.

Neely hadn't been sure what she had expected from the police that morning. The TV shows about them she liked, the procedurals and the dramas, mostly American, always crammed full of a decisive morality largely matching hers in the end, conveniently omitted the paperwork except to have a character moan about it now and then. So when, instead of being whisked into an interview room, Neely had been handed a form to complete, she'd approached it with curiosity more than anything else, dutifully starting at the top and following the directions: *Please fill this out to the best of your ability. Write down as many details as possible.* It seemed silly – borderline insulting – that she was being told to do her best; if she were going to do a half-arsed job of trying to find Angela, Neely thought, then she wouldn't even have bothered coming to the police in the first place. But the questions were, by and large, simple. *Angela Marie Archer, 490 Harrow Road, Flat C, London W9. Blonde hair (dyed), curly, long,* she wrote. *Green eyes.* Maybe *5 foot 9 inches tall.* Not fat, not skinny. *Medium build.* She is *white, English.*

Does the missing person suffer from any medical condition, including mental health conditions? Do they need medication for this and do they have it with them? *She has EPILEPSY and left her tablets at home. She WILL HAVE BAD FITS without them. Doesn't know where she is when she comes round.* Neely had dug in on the capital letters as if this urgency might make Angela jump the queue for attention.

It was the final question that gave her the fear, started those prickles of unease popping under her skin again: the circumstances of the person's disappearance and when they were last seen. *I don't fucking know*, Neely thought. *If I knew, I would not be sitting in a police station. Who asks a question like this, one I can only ever get wrong?*

'What do I do while I'm waiting?'

'I would advise you to talk to as many people as you can. All of Angela's friends who you know. People she worked with. Ask them about anything they remember her saying or doing. No matter how silly it may seem, no matter how insignificant.'

'I thought that's what the police do.' Neely hadn't known how to say it without sounding ungrateful.

'Oh, and we will. We will explore all lines of enquiry, we will put all her details in a computer – a national computer. But it always helps to talk. Jog people's memories.'

Neely had nodded. 'Alright. But what do I do if there's nothing?'

'I'm sorry?'

'What do I do if you can't find her? If nobody knows anything?'

'Miss Sharpe, we'll do everything we can.'

It hadn't been much of an answer, but at least they'd seemed to take her seriously.

There was now only one place in Harrow Road that made sense. She leaned her full weight into the door of the Hope and Anchor and relished the blast of heat on her face.

'Mel. I still can't find her.'

'Fuck. Not even a phone call?'

'I went to the police this morning.' She waited and watched the barmaid's face, searching for any judgment, any endorsement or condemnation – either would validate her decision. But Mel stayed as blank as she ever got.

'They tell you anything?'

'No, why would they?'

Mel shrugged. 'Dunno. They always think they've got answers, don't they? I still think you've nothing to worry about. She's in one of her moods. But I'm up for anything that wastes cop time.'

'Mel. You saw her that Friday. Are you absolutely sure there was nothing weird?'

She rolled her eyes. 'Nothing weirder than usual. She was happy,

Neely. So if you're thinking she topped herself, forget it. If she were going to do that she would have done it a long time ago.'

'That's a horrible thing to say.'

'You're upset that I said Angela *wouldn't* kill herself? Jesus. You're twisted.'

Neely sighed. 'You know what I mean.'

'Whatever. What I mean is, and what I've only tried to tell you a million times, is that Angela's stronger than you think, and she always has been.' Mel smiled wryly, then dropped her voice despite the absence of any eavesdroppers. 'You know, she made Rob cry. That Friday. She did.'

'What?'

'Don't ask me why, I had better things to do than pay attention. But right after she left, I remember, he was crying. Actual tears and all. Ugly.'

'Mel, fuck, you didn't say anything?'

'Why the fuck would I? Do you think it's my job to be everybody's shrink? Just because I serve them doesn't mean I want anything to do with them.'

'Well, where can I find him?'

'Rob? Hang around in here a while and he'll turn up. Fuck knows where he lives now. Like I said, he's not my problem. Unless he overdoses in the bogs. And then I still wouldn't touch him without gloves. Drink, Neely?'

'No, I gotta go. I'm just going to go to the toilet.' She slid over the carpet, freshly and futilely hoovered, thinking, *either I'm going mad or everybody else is, and the odds aren't on my side.* Inside she turned the taps on full blast and bent herself backward to face the ceiling, so that her own gathering tears would stay exactly where they were. A barely perceptible stain of damp marked the ceiling, starting in one corner and creeping outward, where it fanned into a faint bloom.

She had seen that blossom before – not in her flat, not in Stevenage, certainly not in Ruby Sullivan's immaculate home or Sam's hole in Hackney. Neely momentarily shoved aside her sadness and remembered the place, the space. It was in North London. It was in Angela's other world.

A Saturday night in September, the first chilly one of the season. House party. Angela had carried the bottle of wine under one arm, a Spanish red against the black wool. Neely had been dropping hints: 'Why don't you introduce me to some of your mates from around here?' Shortly afterward the birthday invitation was extended her way.

More specifically, it was Marianthi Adamou's birthday and, before Neely Sharpe, there had been Marianthi Adamou. Not that the two were interchangeable – Neely served functions Marianthi simply could not – but even though human love is not quantifiable, on a practical level it cannot be infinite, and before Angela invested hers in Neely, she spent disproportionate time with another impressively swotty girl. They'd grown up with each other: Angela had stood little more than three feet tall when they met at Barlby Primary, and now she was *five foot nine inches tall and of proportionate build*, in *size six red ankle boots* she just grabbed at New Look when they caught her eye from the window. Archer always followed Adamou on the school register, although in matters non-academic, influence usually flowed in the opposite direction. Angela taught Marianthi what music she should listen to, and how to shoplift it from HMV. Crucially, during awkward and low-budget teenage years, when both girls felt cursed by their similarly curly hair, they swapped beauty advice. Whereas Angela was blonde, albeit chemically, Marianthi Adamou's wild mane grew jet-black and sat proudly piled about her head, demanding space for itself and its bearer. They used to experiment in front of a shared bathroom mirror, splitting a bottle of Frizz-Ease, testing all manner of electric implements in an ultimately fruitless quest for the secret to easy, effortless moisture and shine. Angela was more willing and able to sacrifice hours to the straighteners and the balms as she had neither three sisters waiting for the toilet, nor a pair of parents constantly on her back to revise, revise, revise because her father didn't leave sunny Limassol to run a greasy café in a rainy country so that his children could be mediocre.

They never fell out, Angela and Marianthi; they just gradually wandered into different camps of adolescence for a while, pitched their tents and resigned themselves to figuring out how to keep out the rain. This was largely down to necessity: Marianthi needed the long hours behind her books, and Angela needed the few pounds an hour she could get working. And so one had her photo printed in the local paper in full colour holding her A-level results, which still would have been good enough to study medicine even if she hadn't had the excuse of coming from a mess of a school; the other sold the old dearies that same paper at Ladbroke Grove Sainsbury's. But years later, only just pre-Neely, they had both gravitated back to under the Westway on Bonfire Night to watch a heap of broken doors and park benches go up in community-sanctioned, police-supervised flames. From across the shimmering heat one spotted the other. It didn't matter whether Adamou first saw Archer or Archer spotted Adamou, but as the fire licked the concrete motorway above them, they nattered on like four years apart had never happened.

And so on this night, with Neely on her arm, Angela barrelled into the Wood Green house without knocking, 'MAAAAAAAZ!' announcing her arrival before the room could even see her face. 'AN-GEL-A!' the birthday girl replied, a foghorn over the fey indie rock boys singing out from speakers attached to her newish-looking laptop. For a second there was no Neely: the two embraced, grinning like idiots, because Westbourne Park rarely came to Wood Green and vice versa. Then: *This is Neely, my girlfriend.* And Angela could call Neely her girlfriend because Marianthi already knew the preference if not the girl herself. In fact, she was the first person to whom Angela made the rite-of-passage confession in plain language, and Maz's reaction, Angela silently acknowledged, was probably the reason why she found it so easy to approach girls like Neely Sharpe, girls with tight ponytails and wise eyes, girls who took the world and themselves very seriously indeed. It was because Marianthi had shrugged, smiled and announced that she had figured as much for a while but she didn't want to say anything. *You don't fancy me, do you, Archy? Joke. Do you want a drink or are you still on those tablets? Well, there's Coke if you want it, NO NOT THAT KIND, I'd rather have you rot your teeth than your nose because I'm always looking out for you, Archy. You got me. And you know it. No matter what, we're alright.*

Tonight, Neely took comfort in how her girlfriend seemed to know just as few other guests as she herself did. The two stuck to Marianthi, if not limpet-like then at least developing a few rudimentary suckers. Invitations to the house party had been extended casually and, as Marianthi got to know the friends of friends of hangers-on who had come to her home to drink her booze and smoke her fags and eat her heaps of her mum's loukoumades, Angela and Neely took their front-row seats.

'So you're a doctor?' a young American asked, trying to split his eyes between Marianthi, sitting against a wall, and her blonde friend casually observing the action from a few feet away.

'Yeah.' Not really. She was only twenty-five as of that morning, and still training.

'That's awesome.'

'Suppose so.'

'What kind of doctor?'

'Gastroenterology,' Marianthi replied, as if this was the most natural thing in the world for a café owner's daughter from the Kensal Town Estate to do with her life. 'I deal with people's guts.'

'Cool.'

'Well, my mum and dad have a restaurant,' she said, more to herself, as if an imaginary interviewer had asked her why she didn't choose paediatrics or gynaecology like most of the women she'd known at university.

'That's awesome.'

'Not really.' For all her careful cultivation, Marianthi couldn't hide the trait so common among those clever people who lack the cut-throat Machiavellian ambition for business but who have far too many social skills to bury themselves among computers and data, among figures and facts. She had a complete and utter inability to take a compliment.

From a safe distance away, Angela leaned into Neely's ear. 'Maz is loving this. The girl is absolutely *loving* this.'

The American took the cue to shift topics. 'So, Marianthi... Mary-ANN-fee. That's such a cool name.'

'Cheers.'

'Where are you from?'

'West London. Place called Kensal Town.'

'No, like, where are you from originally?'

'Oh, like where I was born?'

'Yeah.'

'St Mary's in Paddington.'

Angela was squeaking now, trying to stifle her laughter. Neely jabbed her with one elbow, but she was equally eager to see the play being scripted in front of her. She just knew how to hide her amusement.

'But... your ancestors and stuff like that? What country were they from?'

'Oh! Well, my dad's from Cyprus and my mum's from Enfield, so I guess you could say I'm Greek.'

'Greek. That's cool.'

'Yeah. I'm proper hairy and all.' Marianthi wiggled her legs, bound in opaque black tights, as if she needed to elaborate.

'Your hair's awesome. It's huge. Is it a weave?'

'Fuck off! "Is it a weave?" I'm not Amy fucking Winehouse. Nah, it's real, all of it.' She shook her head in the young man's direction. 'Here. Touch it. It won't eat you.' And he obliged, and it didn't. 'Here, you want to touch some sexy hair, look at Angela. Angela, come here. Angela Archer has the most fantastic hair in the world. Pure sex hair. It's fucking, fucking angora bunny rabbit stuff, even with all the kinks. Angela! Let him touch your hair. Just for a sec. Come on.'

Angela giggled. She left Neely's side and crouched beside her old friend, pulled the elastic from her ponytail, and tilted her head forward so that her curls nearly touched the floor. Marianthi quickly raked her hands through Angela's hair, separating out the strands. Angela helped herself to Marianthi's wine glass, taking a cheeky gulp underneath the curtain of curls hiding her face.

'Touch that,' Marianthi ordered. 'Amazing, innit?'

'Oh, yeah,' the American dutifully replied, looking slightly less stoned, a slowly waking befuddlement crawling across his face.

'Angela has got wicked hair,' Marianthi cackled. 'Y'know, her mum's black!'

'No she isn't,' Angela barked back, aiming a mock punch at Marianthi's shoulder. The birthday girl stuck out her tongue, visibly pleased with herself. Neely watched the exchange like a dutiful student, but the lesson was being held in an altogether foreign language. She couldn't follow the details, and wasn't entirely sure she had correctly interpreted the main idea. Angela drained the wine. 'Nah, my mum's – what's your name, anyway?'

'Brandon,' the American replied, the upward inflection not at all too different from Neely's own tendency, only this time giving him the unfortunate impression that he wasn't entirely sure he had given the correct answer.

'Alright, Brandon. Just saying, no, Maz here is taking the piss. My mum ain't black.'

'What is she then, some kind of Greek too? Because that is serious hair for a white girl. Serious hair.'

Angela grinned. 'She's dead.'

For several seconds, silence but for the carefully curated soundtrack spilling from the laptop. Marianthi's face didn't move; she'd clearly set this scene before. Angela wasn't waiting to see who would blink first; she fluttered her lashes, her smile not shifting a hair's breadth.

'I'm... wow, I'm sorry about that.'

'Don't be sorry. It's not your fault. Unless you gave her the cancer. Then you can have it back. Thanks but no thanks, y'know?'

'Oh. I'm, I'm, er... I'm gonna, uh... I'll be right back, yeah?'

Marianthi nodded, eyelids at half mast. 'You do that, Brandon.'

Exit, stage left into the garden. The girls watched him rush, patting his pockets for a box of cigarettes that had never been there. Once Angela and Marianthi felt he had made it securely out of earshot, they momentarily locked eyes in a quick game of don't-you-dare-laugh-I'm-warning-you-don't-even, a game that ended in a draw because nobody, not even Neely as the closest referee, could have determined who broke first.

'Did. You. SEE. His face?' Marianthi shrieked, one arm wrapped around Angela's shoulders, the other holding her empty glass. 'Oh my days. Archy. That, that was too easy. You broke your own record. Winner and still champion, you.'

Angela's red, laughing face finally came up for air underneath its mess of curls. 'What a twat! Where do you find these, you madwoman?'

'I send out the Bat Signal. I light up the sky and they all come running. Not the Bat Signal, fuck, the Maz Signal. A great big sloppy kebab beamed over Wood Green. Fucksake, Neely, don't look like that, that's what these blokes are for!'

Neely blushed. Whatever she had been looking like, she hadn't meant it. For all her bitterness, for all her tendencies to ramble about the state of the world and particularly how she wasn't benefiting from it, she knew she could be a soft touch. That's what people told her. People like her friend Sam, Manchester Sam, Sam Wylie. His favourite hobby was pointing out all the moments her tough facade crumbled, all the times her bitch-face softened into pity. 'You think you're so tough, Neely Sharpe, but I've got you all sorted out. You're a pussycat,' he had laughed at her in the pub during that one quiz at the Hope and Anchor, but Neely had thought he'd been looking over her shoulder at Angela while he said it. And it hadn't mattered to her, it hadn't mattered one bit. He was the addition to their team that night, and with his help, they had slid into first place, for the first time, by one question: name the three women who have played bass in the Pixies. He had it, easy. Old-timers hadn't a clue. Won a thirty-quid bar tab and bragging rights. 'You got a good thing, Tiny,' one of the old ones had shouted to Neely with a wink. 'A real good thing.' She hadn't known how to respond, so she had sipped her pint.

Now Neely smiled despite herself, and let her eyes wander to Brandon, standing out in Marianthi's licked postage stamp of a garden, flicking at his lighter. She saw him throw back his head and sigh, the universal symbol of *fucking hell, man.* Always curious, always one for experimentation, Neely tried the pose from her spot on the floor. That's when she saw it: winding across one corner of the ceiling of a Wood Green terraced house, a water stain that could have been a creeping vine as easily as it could have been a snake. Or, Neely thought, feeling the wine ever so slightly, it could have been nothing at all. She squinted at what she thought she saw, and then she knew she had seen it because it dropped down and splattered on the tip of her nose: one tiny teardrop of water. On the first floor, somebody had spewed ouzo and a considerably solid dinner into pre-war plumbing and now the house was fighting back. Mutiny. But Neely didn't know that yet. She wiped the drip from her face, wiped the hand on her skirt, and leaned back to watch the show unfolding around her: the remnants of Angela's life before there was a Neely Sharpe in London, a Neely Sharpe in 490 Harrow Road.

'Easy,' she called to Angela as she saw her refilling a wine glass, but she was too quiet for anybody to hear. Her voice got lost in the music, louder now, the basslines rumbling into the floor and snaking up her girlfriend's hips. Side to side, swinging, not a care in the world.

In Harrow Road, Neely blew her nose into a square of toilet roll and tucked her hair back under her hat. She had covered their neighbourhood, slathered it in images and details. Even if kids pulled down half the posters, everybody would still know: this is Angela and this is what she's like and this is where she is not, even though this is where she belongs. Neely looked at the remaining posters, into the Angelas staring at the sky, and wondered how, exactly, she had come to make that last assumption. She hated being wrong, and there was someone in Angela's world who could tell her whether she was right.

If I were Rob, she thought, *then where would I go? If I were Angela, where would I look for him?*

But she wasn't Angela, and her last attempt to do what she thought Angela would do had been a shambles. She winced as she remembered the crude command inked across the man's chest, and the pillowy coats the women wore as they spread out on the sofa, her sofa, *their* sofa, marking the space where Angela could not be.

She began to retrace her earlier steps, checking to make sure each and every paper Angela still stuck to its proper place. Something comforted Neely as she followed Harrow Road to the Halfpenny Steps, over the canal, through the Kensal Town Estate, with all those Angela eyes on her. She kept a lookout for a broken nose and a general air of desperation, but Rob evaded her.

If she went home, Neely thought, she would want nothing more than to hear those block-heeled boots stomp up the dark stairs, barge through the door, and demand to know *why the fuck are you plastering up my photo everywhere, why couldn't you at least choose one where I'd done my make-up decently?*

There was a chance, sure, maybe Angela would be angry at Neely. Angry at the fuss. Maybe she'd be embarrassed. Humiliated. Not ready to have to explain to everybody who'd seen the posters just what had happened after all. Maybe she would come back and then want to keep away for a while, blow off steam. Maybe she would want nothing to do with Neely for a while. Or maybe for longer than a while.

Maybe she'd gone home somewhere else.

Six

Her shoes left soggy grey footprints as she slammed the door, crossed the lounge, and retrieved the white pages from the floor. ARCHER J, W12 – that had been the one. It was easy now, with computers. Those few details were enough, with a few clicks around Google, to tell her the full address of John Archer, whose household also likely included an Alexander Archer but no women to speak of. *Fuck privacy, God bless the Electoral Roll and our electronic overlords,* Neely thought, and put her gloves back on.

On her way to the Tube station, she spotted all the posters still taped in place, not yet fallen victim to wind or rain or children with the tendency to draw spurting cocks on whatever surface they deemed fit. *East Acton,* she thought. *That's only a few stops. How come Angela never went to visit? Or if she did, why not take me?* Without knowing those things, she didn't know whether to feel hurt. But she did know that even if her dad lived in East Acton now, most of Angela's childhood had taken place closer to the Harrow Road, just across the canal on the Kensal Town Estate. Neely could walk to Kensal Town – and indeed she often did, crossing on the footbridge to Meanwhile Gardens, that odd name for a patch of grass in the shadow of the Trellick Tower. She had been back today, stretching her girlfriend's face over lamp posts and community noticeboards, wondering if today's Angela bore enough resemblance to her as a child, or if – in a city where the only constant was movement and change – enough people would recognise the name.

'Do you still have friends on the estate?' Neely had once asked, innocently, shortly after moving in with Angela. 'Should we have them over? Flat-warming, like?'

'I've got you,' Angela had replied. 'Everyone I know from back then is a waster. Don't need them.'

'Why do you still live here, then?'

'I won't forever.'

Neely had followed her girlfriend's lead and let the tiniest of sly smiles spread across her face. 'Where would you want to go?'

'Haven't thought about it much.'

'Oh, sure you have! Come on. If money's no object, where are you headed?'

Angela had revealed those not-quite-straight teeth, and she let herself giggle. 'Camden Town. When I was a teenager and I didn't realise that even the smallest place is millions, I thought I would move there. Even though everybody says it's past it now. Definitely Camden Town. You?'

'Dalston,' Neely had replied without a nanosecond of hesitation. 'I love it there.'

'Dalston!' Angela hooted, only half incredulous. 'No way. Dalston's scummier than here!'

'Ah, but it's fun, though. There's always something going on.'

'You and your skinny indie boys.'

'I am *done* with skinny indie boys. Done for good.'

'Moved on to plain West London girls?'

'Just the one. And you're not plain.'

Angela had smiled shyly, and shrugged. 'I didn't say plain was a bad thing.'

'It's not a good or a bad thing, it's just a thing. But you're not plain. You're gorgeous, Angela.'

'Fat lot of good it's done me, yeah?'

'Don't be like that.'

She laughed. 'Well, got to look on the bright side. I could get discovered tomorrow, yeah? Some scout could decide to go for a swim and pluck me out of the Porchester Centre and into superstardom. I mean, Kate Moss was from Croydon, yeah? So stranger things have happened.'

Neely hadn't known what to say, what to do. Any well-meaning lie would have sounded just like that, a lie. But what kind of girlfriend would she be if she couldn't make Angela feel better?

It had occurred to Neely, as the months since leaving King's turned into years since leaving King's, that the only skill she had managed to cultivate to a level of mastery was self-pity. It disgusted her, but not enough to spur her to get out of it, mostly because she didn't know how. And living with Angela only made her feel bad about not feeling worse. Sure, Angela kept her cards close to her chest when it came to talk of the past, but her upbringing had undoubtedly thrown a few more challenges her way than Neely's – safe and sound in Stevenage – had done. That was Neely's assumption, but she knew it was true. The epilepsy, her mother dying – those alone were enough to make Angela the kind of person who could teach Neely a bit about resilience. But Neely, so used to having the answers, so used to being asked for them, didn't know how to ask somebody else for help.

How did you do it? Neely thought. *How did you become the kind of person who could love me?*

Not long after her mother's death, around the time she had learned how to set her face and numb her heart to any slights, Angela had thought she might have had an ally, or at least a kindred spirit by way of diagnosis, in Carleen Ward, alias Electrogirl. Everybody around Kensal Town knew Carleen. She was the girl who had come back from the dead and had the long scars winding, like fiddlehead ferns or fossilised primordial leaves, across her body to prove it. Age ten, playing on the open expanse of Wormwood Scrubs with her little brothers when a fast-moving summer storm unfurled over West London, she had been struck by lightning. In the absence of any trees nearby, Mother Nature had taken a leaf out of Mother Ward's book and picked on the biggest child.

Carleen had died for a solid three minutes and they'd brought her back. She got in the *Evening Standard* saying she'd heard voices telling her to walk into the light but she'd told them to piss off and, next thing she knew, she was back. She'd lived, and now, several years after the fact, she lived with fits, too. Epilepsy and constant headaches and a rotten temper and a right eye that seemed almost paralysed in her head; the lid never closed entirely and she couldn't look at anybody, friend or foe (but usually foe), with quite the right amount of attention. In her frequent rages she'd go after the boys who had been spared that day, the ones who had run to the prison gates to tell any grown-up who would listen that their sister had been flung into the air and had landed twenty feet away from her shoes. And if the brothers weren't available, she would go after whoever was convenient.

'Archer,' Carleen had barked at the bus stop, her purple school cardigan a misshapen and washed-out copy of Angela's. 'When's your sister going to stop getting pregnant by refugees for benefits?'

'She's not pregnant,' Angela had muttered.

'Well, she's not pregnant *right now*. Didn't she kill it because she only wanted a flat, not a black baby to go with it?'

'At least she's got her own flat,' Angela had shot back, swelling with pride at the memory of Andy's last visit to the estate: she had taken her time walking down Hazelwood Crescent in those new high-heeled boots so that everybody could have a look. Her hair had just been cut and dyed into a glossy auburn wedge that covered one eye and left the other scanning the street, like a CCTV camera with a vengeful streak, daring anybody to stare back. Andy had looked good, and Angela knew it. And maybe Carleen, watching from her family's home in the shabbier end of the road, crammed with dogs and whichever boyfriend her mother had this week, had known it too.

Angela had watched as Carleen considered the statement. 'Right, she does,' Carleen had conceded. 'But you won't. They won't let you live alone, the way you are.' And then it had been laughter all round from the other girls at the bus stop, similarly purple-clad girls who would sit by Angela in school as if nothing had ever been said or done, because secretly they were just relieved it was Angela Archer being knocked down a peg or two by the strange and violent girl who had come back from the dead, and not them. It didn't matter that Carleen, with her hair-trigger temper and budding enthusiasm for cheap vodka on top of epilepsy, was even less likely to successfully negotiate independent living; even if the hand dealt to her was far worse than Angela's, she had excelled where it mattered to teenage girls. She'd made herself the bitch to be feared.

'We're in this together, you know,' Angela had told Carleen just barely above a whisper as she passed by on the way to the last available bus seat.

'Oh, *fuck* no,' had been the older girl's reply. 'I have an excuse. You were just born retarded.'

Angela had opened her mouth to explain that she wasn't stupid, she was doing just fine in school, and she had been normal until she was nine. Then she reconsidered, and shut it. She knew people thought her thick, but the truth was the world simply made more sense when she was quiet. It didn't matter. Carleen had moved on to find another victim.

Last Angela had heard, Carleen was banged up in Holloway for stabbing her boyfriend, missing a major artery by a centimetre and thoroughly fucking up some very expensive tattoos. That had made the *Evening Standard*, too: 'It's his fault, he knew I was mad when he moved in,' she'd said in her defence. If somehow fourteen-year-old Angela could have known this would happen years later, it would have made little difference; teenagers don't think in the long term unless they're considering how they will never, ever, *ever* live down whatever slights have been inflicted upon them at this very moment. Especially when those slights are public and have the very real chance of getting around the adolescent gossip grapevine to whoever it is you have your sights on impressing.

Generally speaking, Angela wasn't interested in boys, but she was interested in a certain Brian Powell for the same reason she had considered begging for an alliance with Carleen Ward: he, too, was a freak. And in a way he was worse off than Angela, because at least during the 99% of the time when her synapses were firing just fine, she didn't seem strange, she didn't seem off. Brian was stuck in his genetically fucked body twenty-four hours a day, seven days a week, for his entire life – which, as he told it, would probably not be terribly long. 'Either my heart will give out by the time I'm forty or I'll bleed out from a burst artery. That's what happens,' he told her, matter-of-factly, sitting in Meanwhile Gardens, the two of them half-heartedly aiming rocks at passing narrowboats and landing nowhere near their targets. The prognosis didn't stop him smoking, and Angela had helped himself to a cigarette from his pack, which he lit with spidery fingers before demonstrating how he could bend them backward grotesquely until they were nearly parallel to his forearms.

'Doesn't hurt,' he had shrugged.

She didn't find him attractive in the colloquial sense. Not physically, certainly not sexually. (She was curious, though – purely from a scientific standpoint – whether his comically elongated limbs, usually hidden under multiple layers of sweatshirts cushioning the sharp angles of bone, had any bearing on the size of his cock.) Rather, Angela had found Brian magnetically alluring. He thought about death. He probably wouldn't run off if she told him about her own experiences around it. *He would make a decent confidant,* she thought. *He won't run away if I say what I think. He's not supposed to run at all. Gets to sit out PE.*

'So, are you on any good drugs for your fits?'

She had spluttered a short laugh. 'No. They just make me dozy and stupid.'

'You're not stupid.'

'Cheers.' She had chucked another rock, narrowly avoiding a mallard, and tried to appear deeply interested in it. *Don't let him try to kiss me. Oh my god, that would be beyond embarrassing. I'd have to pretend. I'd feel so bad for him. What if he's a virgin and he dies that way?*

'It's the truth, though.'

'What about you?' She had only shifted attention away from herself because she couldn't hoist it up and chuck it into the canal altogether. 'Anything fun?'

'Nah. Boring shit old people take for blood pressure, that's all. But dozy sounds good. Dozy can be fun. Can you get me some?'

'Dunno. I'm a mess if I skip them.'

'Er, forget it.'

'Maybe I could pretend to lose a box, yeah? The doctor will have to write me a new prescription. What's he going to do, say no?'

Brian had nodded, half-interested. 'It's a plan.'

A few days later Angela went to the Porchester Library and looked up Marfan syndrome. Holy shit, she thought. Jesus Tesco Value Christ, Brian is head-to-toe *fucked,* for *real.* Someone worse off than her: a reassurance, some promise. Then she had walked down Queensway to Boots, handed over her new prescription for another thirty Lamictal, and slipped a lipstick up her jacket sleeve as she waited for it to be filled.

She had delivered the tablets to Brian in a carrier bag with a packet of cheese and onion crisps and a Coke. She figured it was the least she could do; the boy was doomed. But she couldn't lose pills more than once, so once Brian had finished her pack, she had siphoned off her own supply. She tried to be judicious: two a week. That was how many she could skip and remain reasonably fine. And she didn't give something for nothing. Brian arrived in Meanwhile Gardens for one of their transactions with quality hash packed into a tube of Smarties, all for her. It was a cut above – no, a massive axe-hack above the crap Andy sometimes shared.

Sometimes they'd walk back to his together for hot knives or a go on his remarkably normal older brother's bucket bong. The Powells lived in St Ervan's Road, in one of the marginally – only marginally – nicer terraces. His mother wasn't much for housekeeping, but Angela had liked the dustiness and the cat hair, the way the clutter felt like a warm cloud as she and Brian sat and laughed and got high and never, ever touched. And they talked. Mostly, they talked. They spoke about subjects that weren't allowed outdoors in the light of day, those topics which only felt safe in the space between his single bed and the tiny joke of a kitchenette.

'How did your mum tell people she was going to die?'

'She didn't. She said she had cancer and they figured it out themselves. How do you tell people *you're* going to die?'

'I wait for them to ask.'

'Do they?'

'Do you ever see anybody talking to me?'

'I talk to you.'

'True.'

'So. Tell me you're going to die.'

'I'm going to die.'

'See? Wasn't so bad.'

And they had laughed.

'If I make it to twenty-five,' he had told her, casually but deliberately, 'I'm going to fucking burn this estate down. It'll be my birthday present. Because if I'm still around then, I definitely won't have enough time left for it to be worth their while throwing me in jail. It'll be a party. Like Bonfire Night.'

'Well, don't bother inviting me, because there's no way in hell I'll still be kicking around here in ten years. I'll kill myself quicker.'

'I want a soul transplant. Trade in my body for a new version but keep my brain and all.'

'No such thing as souls,' Angela had shrugged.

'What do you think happened to your mum, then?'

She had been caught off guard by that one. 'No idea. I try not to think about her. I think, like, the only bit of her that still exists is memory, and I've got that, and my sister and my brother and my dad have got that, so it's like she's split up and become parts of other people. And we're all gonna go round like that, like some big immortal recycling scheme. You don't know it, because you're not you any more, but a bit of you becomes someone else.'

You couldn't just become somebody else in Kensal Town. Camden and Hackney were full of people reinventing themselves as easily as they bought chicken and chips, wearing out their identities like their box-fresh jackets, but not here. Not this place. This wasn't the part of London with enough of the right kind of newcomers to make it easy to become somebody new. Sure, Angela had Jenny Wedmore and she had Marianthi Adamou, she had her sad and beautiful sister as an unwavering ally, but she wanted a different self. The closest she could get to the privilege that young recent arrivals all over London had was to find somebody new enough to her.

As Neely Sharpe, reading history at Goldsmiths, was sitting her first-year exams, Angela Archer was sitting in Meanwhile Gardens with a can of orange Tango sufficiently diluted with vodka. There's no way of proving it, not in this world with these laws of physics, but there is a chance – the slightest chance – that at the exact moment that Neely put down her pen, slumped in her hard institutional chair, and sighed with the knowledge she had done all she could humanly do to secure a future, Angela had been reclining in the rough grass, lighting a cigarette, and wondering who would shuffle off this mortal coil first: Marfan Boy or Twitchy Retard. The Freak and the Twitch.

Neely keyed the address into her phone, shoved it in her pocket, and started her walk to the Central Line. Mr Archer drove a Tube train, that's all she knew. Angela had told her once that he'd been on duty the day of the bombing, and even though his train wasn't hit, he'd been offered time off for stress. He'd refused. Didn't want to set a bad example for his kids: if you can work, then work, because somebody's got to do it and there's no good reason why that shouldn't be you. Angela had started at Sainsbury's at sixteen, shelf-stacking at Homebase at eighteen, tickets at the Electric Cinema a year later, then the Porchester Centre, and never signed on.

Neely wasn't working, not in the strict sense of the word. Alongside commuters and tourists, she maintained the code of urban silence from Queensway to East Acton, looking out the Tube carriage window at her fuzzy reflection as if there was something to see, touching her Oyster card to the ticket barrier and pulling tight the scarf she had hopefully, naively loosened in the brief warmth of her journey. The Tube spat her out onto a semi-suburban street: no shops except for a minuscule newsagents-cum-fruit stand tucked beside the railway embankment. She knew she wasn't far from the canal, *their* canal, the one she and Angela walked when it was sunny and when it was not. It was just behind her, just over Wormwood Scrubs. Neely checked the address on her phone again. A five-minute walk, at most. She tucked her nose into her scarf, her hat over her eyebrows, and walked.

Nobody walked beside her. Whoever lived around here was working, or minding their own business, or both. Looking closer, she saw the shabbiness of the homes, their missing roof shingles, decades of grime blending into brown brick as if it belonged there. Here and there, a lazy patchwork job on a wall, the bricks not quite the right shade. But despite this, there was a pride in these homes, that peculiar bucolic British air on the edge of inner London. No graffiti decorated those patched walls. Mattresses didn't sprout from the pavement like fungal eruptions, and barnacles of rubbish didn't decorate front gardens, as small as they were. This corner of East Acton had just enough aspiration to never let down anybody who had it framed as their goal. And it must have seemed a solid goal, for people like the Archers.

Neely stared dumbly at a terrace of houses with steep hipped roofs, their walls all covered in pale blueish-greenish stucco. The end house had an old-fashioned street sign, the kind that still said *Borough of Hammersmith*. No, Angela could not have grown up in this place. She was transplanted in as a teenager, Neely knew, for a few short years between leaving school and finding her own flat on the Harrow Road.

Down the road and around two corners, she followed the map on her phone, finding herself in front of the magic number before she realised it. Before even approaching the door she knew nobody was home in the brown brick semi behind the tidy hedge. No lights on behind the net curtains, no car at the kerb. Neely rang the bell anyway, knocked for good measure. Behind those still and silent nets she saw the basics of domestic life: a sofa and pair of stuffed chairs like any others, ornaments on a mantelpiece, the entire scene remarkable for its utter lack of distinctiveness. Neely didn't know what she had been expecting instead. Some sign of vibrancy, some clue that the man who could make Angela Archer had some part of a personality he passed down to her.

She walked around to the side of the house, stepping apologetically over the bit of grass. Neely tried the gate, a basic wooden gate like thousands of others in West London: locked, naturally. She peered into the side window, but this time the glass was frosted over, like the panes in her own bathroom, like a *fuck off*, it was none of her business.

Maybe she doesn't want me to find her, Neely suddenly thought, and felt the chill creep up the back of her neck with the weather. *Maybe there's a bloody good reason she got lost. And maybe that reason's you. You remember, you had Ruby, and you had fellas back at Goldsmiths who you thought were into you, whose surnames you were already trying on for size even though all they wanted was a regular and inconsequential fuck, and you waited and waited for them to call and they never did and you wondered if they'd been knocked down by a bus or if they were suffering from amnesia after a particularly hard crack on the head obtained against a bedpost whilst shagging somebody else. You waited for a call, a text, whatever, and it never came, and nor did the replies to yours, even though they were alive and existing just fine, just not wanting to exist with you. They didn't need you, and neither does Angela. Maybe that's what you've got. Maybe that's all*

you're going to get. Maybe she figured that fucking off was the only way you'd
get the message. Maybe she's more than you think.

A bus had pulled up to the stop in front of the next house over. Neely
watched as a girl with the same high, tight ponytail as her own, but
with a face hardened to make her look older than anybody wearing
her school uniform had any right to be, passed in front of the Archers'
home. The girl glanced over at Neely, who couldn't break the stare in
time.

'What the fuck are you doing?' the girl called.

'I, erm...' There was no quick way to explain the chain of events
that had put her there.

'Creep.' She sneered, not breaking her stride, and continued down
the road.

Neely hastily scanned the street for any other passers-by, anybody
who may have seen her, but nobody else had got off the bus. She stole a
glance in the direction of the schoolgirl. No sign of her, mere seconds
later: vanished.

She tiptoed back to the front door and pulled another photocopy
from her bag. She slid it halfway beneath the doormat, leaving Angela
staring at the sky. Then Neely ran, but not in the direction she had
come. She sped south, to the Westway and across it, down the
downmarket roads, to Uxbridge Road – as close to a copy of Harrow
Road as she could get, another high street of lowbrow shops, named
for a suburb, in the city – to another train.

Last-minute Christmas shoppers piled on board at Wood Lane, arms
laden with carrier bags. Neely envied the younger girls. Teenagers
overdressed for the task. Students with elsewhere accents, comparing
their plans, talking about home. She stood to dutifully yield her seat
to an old man and his walking stick, and wedged herself beside the
train door. The tower blocks around Latimer Road moved into focus.
Neely squinted to look for lives going on inside them, but couldn't see
anything clearly defined.

The train continued its curve, sliding in to meet the Westway. Now
Neely had cars to follow, all bright lights and darkened interiors, as the
Hammersmith & City trundled into Ladbroke Grove. More shoppers.
More voices from elsewhere. Somebody trod on Neely's foot and

offered no apology. In the distance, she spotted the tower blocks of the Warwick Estate sprouting from the endless night of their corner of West London. At Westbourne Park, she exhaled and popped out from the carriage, feeling herself expand as she walked across the platform to the exit. The *Exit, Sortie, Ausgang*, as the sign on the wall detailed. Neely had never seen the foreign languages at any other station. They were only here, she assumed, for that one weekend, that one weekend in fifty-two when every white person suddenly loved black people in West London and everybody suddenly forgot that white people in West London can't dance. That was Angela's line. She could say things like that and not sound bitter. Those words were the reason Neely had never bothered trying to get a prime viewing spot for the Notting Hill Carnival. No, she and Angela didn't bother with the crush of crowds all looking for the *Exit, Sortie, Ausgang* when the end of August rolled around and their neighbourhood became somewhere people actually wanted to see. They just went to the pub.

She walked under the Westway, over the canal, past the Grand Union Bar where she felt too uncool to drink and the Somali restaurant where she felt too plain to eat. Then she turned into the Harrow Road: the Hope and Anchor, *her* local. Number 490, *her* home.

'Neely?'

Standing slightly pigeon toed in an expensive-looking pair of ankle boots several steps above anything New Look churned out, Ruby Sullivan kept a respectful distance from *her* ex-girlfriend.

'Ruby. Hi.' Neely felt too tired to register surprise. 'Are you alright?'

'Yeah, yeah, I'm great,' she smiled, visibly relieved. 'Listen, sorry, I've seen those signs up. I didn't put two and two together before now. I just went on Facebook and figured it out. The missing girl, she's your girlfriend?'

'Mmm-hmm.' Normally, Neely would have polished her trophy, the Angela Archer on her arm, flesh and blood and beauty. It's just that the photocopy was less to boast about.

'I'm so sorry. How long has she been gone?'

Read the poster, you cow. 'Since Friday.'

'God, that's horrible. Any clues?'

Neely pointed at one of the posters in her hand. Had Ruby always been this thick? She seemed to recall feeling the tables being turned when they were together. Not that Neely had been thick – no, not at all. She knew she was brighter than most and Ruby knew it too. Ruby just hadn't liked it, and Ruby had been blessed with the rich kid's inability to tolerate doing nothing about a situation she could change.

'Look, Neely, I came by because, well, I'm going to tell the police, but I wanted to tell you first. It's about Angela.'

'What about her?'

'I saw her. In the pub.'

'When? Which pub?'

'It was last week. Wednesday afternoon.'

'I saw her Thursday. So you don't need to tell the police.'

'There's a bit more than that. And I only need to tell you. Listen, Neely, can we go inside?'

'I'd rather not. What is it?'

'Well, that's the thing, like. I'd seen her before. A few months ago. You weren't with her.' Neely racked her brain, flipped through a mental Filofax to place herself in time. September? Her mum's birthday. She'd gone up to Stevenage for the weekend. 'Around here. I had stuff to do at Westbourne Studios, you know what I mean?' Neely didn't. 'And then I went for a drink with some of the band, and she was there. We... well, she came back to mine. I'm still in Wellington Road. We went back to my flat. And, erm, I needed to tell you. I wanted to tell you.'

'Went back to your flat and then what?'

'It didn't mean anything, Neely. I didn't know who she was, let alone you two were together then. I was looking for you. I really was. She recognised me from a photo you had. She said so. A photo on your phone. She was drunk. She was really, really pissed. It was right there in that horrible shithole...' Ruby pointed down the road at the Hope and Anchor, its interior lights dim through dirty windows. '...and I shouldn't have done anything with her, but I was off my face...'

'So how do you know it was really Angela? Could have been anybody if you were drunk. Could have been any hot blonde London lesbian. You've had a few.'

'Neely. I know you don't want to hear it. But it's the truth. That's why I'm telling you. And I'm sorry.'

'Quit saying you're sorry. You did what you did and I never knew. And that's that.'

'But she had this, she had this kind of fit – I thought it was nothing, I didn't know she was epileptic till I saw those posters. I thought she'd taken a bad pill. And she woke up and she was fine after a bit, yeah? I thought it was nothing, she'd just taken something dodgy.'

'Well, she didn't. She doesn't swallow everything dangled in front of her face, Ruby. Not like you.' In her past life, this would have been the point where Neely ducked to avoid the pint glass rocketing bottom-first at her face and run out of the flat, down the stairs, and over the road just in time to avoid Ruby shrieking that she was a stupid mess who didn't deserve a girl who could have anybody in London if she wanted.

'Neely, she was off her face. She was all matey with this creepy pisshead dealer, this total freak, they were old pals, he was giving her freebies…'

'Rob?'

'Who's Rob?'

'Funny-looking nose, kind of short? Scabby?'

'No. Funny-looking all over. Tall. Angela was well out of it. She didn't know what she was doing. It was my fault, not hers. I wouldn't have done it if I'd known you two were that close. She didn't say. I thought you two, you were just mates, that's all. She was all like, "Neely Sharpe, my mate Neely," know what I mean?'

'Yeah.'

'Neely, please. Don't be like this.'

'Ruby. I don't care. I'm not being "like" anything. I don't care about any of that. I don't even know why you're fucking telling me. What's your point? You just want to feel better? Angela is missing and that's all I care about.'

Ruby shifted her weight, searching for anything in the streetscape to focus on besides Neely's stare. 'You know… give me some of those flyers. I can make more copies, put them up all around, yeah? I'm off to Westfield, I haven't even done my Christmas shopping. It's gotta be heaving with people, maybe someone's seen her?'

Neely sniffled. 'Thanks.' *This is the part where you're supposed to swallow your pride and belch out diplomacy, maybe ask if she wants to come inside after all,* she thought. *Make her a cup of tea, let her warm up.* But just as the words were trembling on the tip of her tongue, a gust of wind down the Harrow Road lifted the edge of her scarf and licked the bare skin of her neck. Neely shivered violently, involuntarily, and turned away from home. To the pub.

Seven

'No sign of her?'

Mel the barmaid was drying glasses when Neely came into the Hope and Anchor, taking in the rare lull between the day drinkers losing the last of their money and the night shift storming through the doors.

The short girl shook her head and plonked herself onto a stool. 'No idea. She still won't answer her phone. God knows if the police are even going to do anything.'

'I'm so sorry, love. I swear, if I hear anyone saying they've seen her, I'll…'

'I know. Cheers, Mel.'

'Sure you didn't have a row?'

'I think I'd remember if we had.' She remembered a lumpy couch, the smell of damp in Hackney. A mind-splitting hangover and Sam's way of avoiding one. She remembered reaching for her keys in the cold and believing, knowing, that however monumentally she had fucked up her day or her week or her life, Angela would make her feel better.

Mel shrugged. 'Hey, bad news about your new best pal.'

Neely shot up straighter. Who, Sam? How would they know each other? 'What do you mean?'

'Rob, yeah?'

'Fuck off, I haven't found him yet.'

'He's having lady troubles, I heard.'

'Hmm?'

'He might be on the market before you know it. Him and Gina, rough patch. Forking each other now, I heard.'

'Mel. That's typically a good thing in relationships. Perfectly normal.'

'No, you heard me wrong. *Forking*. Just heard Gina stuck a fork in him.'

'Oh my god.'

'Yeah. I mean, I knew she was mental, but that's *mental*.'

Neely shuddered, and considered that he probably deserved it. 'Hope she missed his tattoos.' Quietly, entirely inside, she enjoyed this shift in topic, the opportunity to observe a disaster that had nothing to do with herself.

'Oh, no worries about that. He's only got tattoos on his arms.'

'What?'

'She stuck the fork in his face.'

Neely winced.

'Hey, who knows, maybe she knocked his nose back in place. Don't look like that! Look on the bright side, yeah?'

'You're telling me to look on the bright side when it's Christmas in a few days and I can't even get my girlfriend on the phone. I don't have a clue what she's doing or where she might be.' Neely blew into her cupped hands, still white and stiff with cold. 'Look, what's up with Angela's family?'

Melanie raised an eyebrow and Neely spotted the tiniest hint of disdain on her face. 'She's your girlfriend. Why are you asking me?'

'Erm, well, you're from here, right? And you knew her growing up? And I just figured, because she never really said much, I mean, I don't know how much...'

'Her mum's dead. You know that?'

'Yeah. Of course. And her dad's a Tube driver and she's got a sister and a brother somewhere else.'

'OK, so what more do you need to know? What do you mean, "what's up" with them?'

Neely felt her fingers curling, the slight defensiveness rising in her nerves – for her girlfriend, for herself. 'I dunno, I just don't really know what they're like or anything, whether they got on or whatever. I've never met them.'

'You never, y'know, talked to her about that? Bit fucking weird that, yeah?'

She sighed. 'Forget it. I just thought maybe she might be with one of them.'

'Nah. They moved away, she stayed. If Angela wanted to be with her family for any amount of time, then she wouldn't be living around here, yeah? And she doesn't want much to do with them, I guarantee it. Her dad's a miseryguts type. Nice, yeah, but I think he never got over her mum. I think her little brother's in Scotland now, student. Quiet kid. Weird arty type. And, oh god, her sister. I haven't seen her in years, but Andy was… a fucking trip. When we were kids, yeah? Anyway. You don't have to worry about any of them stealing away Angela and throwing her in Straight Camp or whatever, if that's what you're thinking. Angela's the normal one in her family. Anyway. Are you drinking? What can I get you?'

'Diet Coke, please.'

'Nothing in it?'

'Nah.'

Mel, sounding like she had found her stride, kept talking. 'You're a lightweight, aren't you? Little and large, you and Angela. She'll have twice as much as you and you'll be twice as pissed.'

'Angela doesn't drink that much.'

'Oh, Neely, love. She does. Just not around you. Since we're talking about things that it's weird you don't know. I've known her for ages. She gets so pissed she can barely stand sometimes.'

'Fuck off, Mel. You know she's epileptic. She can't drink that much.'

'And you think I haven't cleaned up after her when she's had a fit and pissed herself? Neely, she only gets falling-down wrecked when you're not around. She even said so. She told me, you're good for her, you know? I never mentioned it. I figured that whatever was going on, the two of you had it sorted, you were alright. Letting her cut loose sometimes. Giving each other space, innit. Not living in each other's pockets all the time. I thought that was sound, really. But if she's gone and fucked off now and left you on your lonesome then you deserve to know what she gets up to.'

'Was it so sound that you kept giving her booze when you know what she's like?'

'She's an adult, Neely. She can do what she likes.'

'Yeah, well, look where that's got her now, yeah?'

'I don't know where it's got her. Neither do you.'

'Then do you know why the fuck I'm the only one who seems worried about that?'

Melanie sighed and smacked the top of the bar with her towel.

'Neely. Jesus Christ, you need to chill out. Just saying, maybe Angela needs a little space.'

'Look, she didn't take her tablets. She wouldn't go away without them.'

'And you told the cops, yeah? That's all you can do. If they don't think she was kidnapped then neither should you. Fuck knows why you expect them to do anything.'

'Why aren't you worried? It's the medication. If she doesn't take her tablets, she'll have fits.'

'Christ, Neely, she had fits even when she did take them, when we were kids.'

'That's different. There are new drugs. She's been on new ones for months.'

'Neely. She can look after herself. She's always wanted to. People don't give her the chance because they think she's a fragile little retard. Don't be one of those people. Don't be a reason for her to not come back.'

'She *is* fragile.'

'But not a retard. She knows what she's doing. I think she knows her epilepsy better than any of us do because she's only been living with it her whole fucking life. Be furious with her when she comes back, yeah, but in the meantime don't give yourself a heart attack. I have enough people to worry about, yeah? Don't make me add you to the list.'

'Is Angela on it?'

'She's not. Because Angela is going to be just fine. She's testing you. Probably waiting to see if you're going to chill out and not treat her like she's a fire hazard. No, here's number one – oh god, and number two – on my worry list.' She gestured toward the opening door, where Gina slipped a protective arm around her boyfriend, apparently having had a major change of heart. Neely spotted the bandage under Rob's chin and across his jawline, the stickiness of the tape beginning to peel from his skin and threatening to expose Gina's handiwork. 'Oi! How many stitches did you get?' Mel hollered.

'None, they just taped me up at St Mary's,' Rob yelled back, and Gina gave her the Vs.

'Let's see, then.' Mel bounded over from behind the bar, glass and towel still in hand, and gingerly peeled back a corner of grubby adhesive. Neely winced and resolved to drink her beer from bottles from now on. Melanie scrunched up her nose. 'Ooh yeah, I see. Christ. That's going to scar.'

'Don't touch it.'

'Don't want to. Don't want your bugs. What did you do to deserve it?'

'Fuck off and mind your own business,' Gina muttered.

'Get out of my fucking pub, then. You're the one who came in. It's a business, not the public library.'

'It was an accident,' Rob sighed, sounding distant and unconvinced of his own words. Neely was considering whether he meant the stabbing, or his actions provoking it, when she realised other eyes were upon her own.

'Oi. Why are you always staring?'

Neely impulsively jerked her head back. 'Sorry?'

'Angela's girl,' Gina continued. 'I see you around. And you're always staring. Don't you ever talk to anybody but her?'

'She talks to me,' Mel shot back, but nobody listened.

'It's rude to stare.'

'Sorry.'

'Nah, come here. Talk to us.'

'Buy them a drink, they mean,' Mel scoffed.

'Wouldn't say no to a pint,' Rob shrugged. 'I've got a pain to dull.'

Mel was on a roll. 'Oh, and I don't suppose you could *possibly* have anything for that round your gaff. Nope. Absolutely nothing on you with painkilling properties. Alcohol's the only anaesthetic you can imagine. Beer, at that. You're so fragile.'

That word again, Neely thought. She knew it was sarcasm in the barmaid's voice, but still, that word. Funny definition of fragile these people had. And didn't have. She slowly stood and crossed to their table. 'Alright, what are you drinking?'

'I want a *pint* of whisky,' Rob cackled, displaying a row of neat and even, though slightly yellow, teeth. 'One each for me and the lady.'

'You're both getting watered-down piss,' Mel snapped, and trudged back behind the bar. 'And you'll like it.'

'Lovely hospitality,' Gina replied. 'A pub in this country closes every day, and you wonder why.'

'I know why. It's because there's no money in it. Because certain wasters think alcohol grows on the magical booze tree out in my garden. And it does, but I have to pay for a shitload of fertiliser.'

Gina snorted. 'Local charm,' she muttered quietly, then shifted her attention to Neely. 'So. Tell us about yourself. Your name's Neely.'

Got it in one, Neely thought.

'You think we're gonna bite or something?'

'What?'

'Seems like that must be the reason you've never said hello and you stay so far away from us.'

In the split second that Neely tried to think of a suitable reply, Gina began to laugh.

'I'm joking, I'm joking. Christ. So, what do you do when you're not with Angela and not in here, Neely?'

'I'm an office manager.'

'What does that mean?'

'I manage an office.'

'Oh, right, that explains everything. And you've been with Angela how long?'

'Year-ish. How d'you know her?'

'We know everybody. I know Rob, Rob knows everybody.'

The man spoke for himself. 'I'm from here. She's from here. Known her since we were kids.'

'Where does her sister live now?'

'*Angela's* sister?' Rob asked, as if there could be another. 'Andy fucking Archer. She's ancient history. I think she got married, that's why she moved away. God, Andy Archer, what I'd do to see her today. She's got to be a mess. We called her Nails, yeah, because she had this thing, yeah, where if she was fighting a girl with really long ones, she'd sit on her and snap them off.'

'Nobody cares,' grunted Mel, but not very insistently.

'Just grab their hands and snap! Snap! Snap! Fucking hell. They don't make psychos like Andy any more. So she was mental, yeah, but she was alright, and she was always good for a bit of fun, or at least that's...'

'Southall,' Mel answered, rolling her eyes at the back of Rob's head. 'And her dad's in East Acton.'

'I was just about to say that,' Rob growled. 'Fucksake.' Gina rolled her eyes.

'Well, Rob, if you know everybody, perhaps you can tell me something.'

'What?'

'Why the fuck am I the only one worried about her?'

They laughed, the couple, and not like Angela's laugh when Neely had met her at the Porchester pool. She might as well have asked them how to spell her own name.

Rob tapped his fingernails on the tabletop, dirty brown on dirty brown. 'Neely. Listen. I see you around here all the time, yeah, but you're not from here, you don't know what we do about what's gone on. She's hard as nails. Always has been. She just doesn't show it. Angela's a superhero. Master of disguise. Mistress of disguise? Fuck, whatever. The Angela you're so worried about, that's not who we know. That's not who she is.'

Don't you fucking tell me who Angela Archer is.

'What did she do to you, then?'

'What?'

'What did she do to make you cry?'

Gina spluttered out a laugh.

'Friday night. When you last saw her. Mel...' Neely dropped her voice and already regretted what she'd given away. 'Mel said she upset you. You were crying. What happened? You've got to tell me. Please.'

He shot a glare, almost imperceptibly, in the general direction of the bar. 'Haven't the foggiest what you're talking about.'

'Rob, please please please do not bullshit me. I need to know where she's gone.'

'Love, I can't remember this morning. Don't ask me to remember Friday.'

Neely turned to Gina. 'Do you remember?'

Gina narrowed her eyes. 'Someone's been telling you porkies.' She sneered in Mel's direction. 'Stupid cow.'

'I'm serious, please, anything. I don't have any idea where Angela's gone. I can't sleep. Even if she's just gone away a while, like Mel said. She left her tablets at home. If you've got epilepsy, and you go off those tablets, you could have a fit, and you can die of that, right? People die from fits. If they're really bad.'

Rob sucked his teeth. 'Yeah, but she hasn't been taking those tablets for ages.'

'Yes she has. She's not taking carbamazepine any more, she's off those, but she's on topiramate now.'

'Are topiramate the little pale yellow round ones?'

'Yeah.'

'She's not taking those.'

'Shut up. I see her take them. She's got a little box with the days of the week on them, and every day she empties one.'

'Well, then she's faking. Or she's got two prescriptions. Because she's been giving them to me and Gina. She didn't tell you?'

'The *fuck?*'

'Nah, she wouldn't tell you, would she.'

'You're not epileptic.'

'Well, I don't think she is any more, either. She got better or whatever. Because she said she doesn't need them any more. You ever taken one of those for fun? Not even once?'

'God, no, why would I?'

'Nah, you wouldn't, would you?'

'Stop talking like that and tell me what the hell you're on about. Giving you her tablets?'

'We were, y'know... Gina and I, would have been, dunno, two months back? Yeah. We thought we'd do it properly, you know, get clean. Angela said topiramate made her want to sleep all day and she hated it but she thought they might help us get through the worst. She was thinking of us.'

'It didn't really work,' Gina admitted. 'Not that well. You know. But they are good if you want to sleep. Blotto. Quiets your brain right down. God knows what her head must have felt like on them every bloody day.'

'And no use in them going to waste,' Rob added. 'Cos she said she was done with them.'

'She wasn't done with them.'

'She said she had to get off them. Because they make kids into mongs or whatever it is. So she must have told you.'

'What?'

He shrugged. 'At first I was surprised you two decided to, y'know, let her carry it. But, y'know, it makes sense, cos you've got the better job and all. You keep working and she'll have the kid.'

'*What?*' Junkies. Neely shook her head, the slightest paroxysm, as if convinced a stray cobweb somewhere in her earhole was responsible for what she had just heard.

'It just makes sense. Eco... economically, yeah. And I meant to ask her, like, is your brother going to be the dad? So at least it's kind of like you? Please tell me he's at least taller than you are.'

'You're not funny, Rob.'

'Not trying to be.'

'Then what are you on about?'

He raised an eyebrow; Neely thought she heard the creak of wheels starting to turn. 'Angela told me the two of you wanted a kid. That you couldn't wait. Just a little longer until you told everybody.'

'Then she lied to you.'

'She's got no reason to lie to me. We go back. Me and her. Way back.' Pointlessly, Rob gestured over his shoulder to a point in time before Neely Sharpe, possibly even before Neely Sharpe dreamed of London. But Neely preferred to take the signal literally, and stared at the wall behind him.

'A *baby*? What kind of shit is this?' she asked nobody in particular.

'Fucking hell,' Gina giggled, which set off Rob as well. 'You can drop the act now, Neely. We know. Congratulations, yeah?' The two of them shared whatever joke was in it with their eyes, then their hands. In their corner of the Hope and Anchor in Harrow Road, an invisible curtain came down between them and the rest of the patrons, and they fixated on each other with a singlemindedness typically reserved for their substances of choice.

Neely froze. If Rob wasn't lying, then the only explanation was that she had been wrong. Clueless, almost criminally thick. And she wasn't used to that. She didn't know how to react. She didn't know how to be wrong, not about Angela Archer. If anybody knew Angela, Neely assumed, if anybody knew the secret facets, it had to be the woman Angela came home to every night until last Friday. She figured that, sure, Mel might have met Angela years before she did, they may have come from the same postcode and the same schools, but she didn't know Angela the same way – not just pissed, but vulnerable and scared and a fully fledged woman. Naked and honest and feeling miles away from rumours that swirled around their front door, laughing and moaning and begging Neely not to stop doing whatever she was doing because it made her so, so fucking happy in a place full of more sadness than anybody deserved. Because Neely loved her. Just did.

'Fuck.'

'Neely, are you serious? You're telling me you didn't know?' Rob seemed more in focus now, his movements more deliberate, his voice stronger.

'No. I didn't.'

'How couldn't you know?'

'If I knew how I couldn't know, then I WOULD KNOW, wouldn't I?' Neely saw Gina wrinkle her nose, spoiling her face. 'Fuck this,' Neely growled and popped off the bar stool, leaving a half-full drink.

Mel rolled her eyes. 'Neely, come on.'

Neely ignored her and stepped onto the street before putting on her coat. She had an entire night before her, too many questions and, brewing somewhere in her belly, from the fear and worry and uncertainty all mixed together, was enough rage to power a small borough.

Up the dark stair: she stumbled and punched the wall. Punched it again and didn't care if Flat B complained. *Fuck, fuck, fuck.* Shaking fingers dropped her keys. Through the door on the second attempt: *fuck, fuck, fuck.* Her fist hurt, so she kicked the closet door, then the sofa. She was supposed to be the clever one. And they were laughing at her in the pub now, surely, just like someone had always laughed at her, no different here from Stevenage.

No way in hell could Angela have wanted a child. For one, she never spoke about it. Never, other than a few noncommittal comments about the sweet dispositions of her sister's two. The vague *maybe someday*, much like Neely's own. Neely scoured her brain for any of the slightest clues missed, and came back blank. It was impossible. Definitely not now. And definitely not without Neely. Unless she had been completely oblivious, so wrapped up in her own head that she had only made a mirror of the woman she loved. Unless she had been completely and utterly wrong about everything.

Who was laughing at her harder now – them at the pub, or Angela Archer?

Neely paused at the window and stared down at Harrow Road. She yanked the curtain shut, and screamed. Fell into the sofa and screamed again, into the cushions this time. Flat B could call the police if they cared.

Fuck the places they'd been and the places they'd planned to go. Fuck the life they'd built together and the one they planned to pursue, the secrets shared and the secrets made, the double bed and the double life: *My girlfriend got pregnant and didn't bother to tell me. And I was too stupid to figure it out.*

She stormed into the kitchen as if the place had personally wronged her. It had: she snatched up the little case with all the tablets and chucked it into a drawer. The plastic compartments burst open and SATURDAY and SUNDAY scattered, pinballing against wooden corners, coming to rest against corkscrew and oven glove and matchbook and cheese grater. From the cabinet below that drawer, she retrieved the bottle of Rioja, the one she hadn't shared with the accidental house guests because it was special, it was for Christmas. Well, there wouldn't be Christmas this year. Neely wrenched off the screw top and the bottle slipped from her trembling fingers. She watched it fall, her reflexes too shot to stop it. The glass exploded on contact; a burgundy chrysanthemum bloomed over the white of her socks and spat on the hems of her jeans. She watched the wine wick through the fabric, pool like inkblots on the lino, glistening shards in wreathes around her feet.

Neely caught her breath at the sight of this strange and sudden bloodbath with herself in the centre of it. This mess wasn't like her – this life wasn't like her. She wouldn't cry over spilled wine. She wouldn't cry over whatever story anybody wanted to tell her about Angela, because they couldn't prove it, they couldn't do a damn thing until Angela came back and said those words herself. No, she decided, she would hold it together for now, until she could be sure. Until she heard it all from Angela. Then, if she had to, she would rage, she would scream, she would self-pity like she had never self-pitied before. But for now, she would hold it together.

She reached for the kitchen roll and pulled long sheets, letting them drape down to the floor. The dustpan wasn't in its expected cupboard. Tiptoeing amidst the broken glass, Neely made it to the bathroom and began to search the cupboard beneath the sink there. Behind the white bottle of toilet cleaner and the dark blue Domestos, a rainbow flashed. Neely pulled it out, into the light: a small hardback book, a journal maybe, its spine worn, its edges smudged graphite grey.

She couldn't recall ever having seen it before. It wasn't her purchase and hadn't been her gift. And even if it had been hers, what was it doing behind the tampons and extra bog roll? Nobody would absent-mindedly leave a book there. Not her and not Angela. And if it wasn't hers, then it had to be Angela's, hidden away from Neely's eyes.

Neely knew at that moment that to open the book would be to cross a line that she alone had just drawn out of paranoia, or fear, or just plain magical thinking. There was no such thing as un-learning. Whatever lay within the book, whatever was written, she would read and know and possibly never forget, whether she wanted to or not. All she knew was that Angela didn't want her even touching this, even knowing of its existence.

Fuck it. There was nothing else she could do. And there most certainly was a pit, a dark and growing space, opening in Neely's stomach: the old stabbing loneliness. As a child, it had come from too many evenings spent devoted to schoolwork rather than any semblance of a social life; later, it was whenever she'd hit a dead end in her studies that led her to scan the same page ten times and comprehend none of the words, or whenever Ruby had stormed out. She needed a friend. She needed a good book. More importantly, she needed to know where the hell her girlfriend had gone, and if there was even a shadow of a shadow of a hint in whatever those pages contained, then she needed to read it.

She would start at the beginning. It was logical, and – she figured – only good things could come from logic. From a corner of the sofa, the corner in which one curled-up Neely Sharpe could fit very comfortably indeed, she opened to the first page.

ANGELA MARIE ARCHER

So far, so good. Uneventful was good. Uneventful was guiltless.

A line drawing – also unremarkable. A bicycle. Nobody could argue with a bicycle. Nobody, unless they'd been hit by a cyclist, or had their bike stolen, or otherwise been wronged by someone on two wheels. It was a decent drawing, Neely had to admit. She herself couldn't draw for toffee; even images she could picture in high-resolution detail once she shut her eyes – Angela, awake and asleep – could never translate from her brain to her hand. It was strictly stick figures from the pen of Neely Sharpe. But no, the bicycle was a perfectly fine bicycle. The dead fox on the next page – also perfectly fine in terms of technique, even if it was obviously not fine for the fox in question. The only words on the first four pages were snips, not sentences: *Thru park. Right at Western Av. Polish War Memorial. Past the airfield.*

Neely skimmed over sketches of buildings – vaguely familiar – and Tube trains moving through a cityscape – very familiar indeed – until she found the first block of true text. It was written in a green shimmery gel which, as far as she knew, had never crossed their threshold.

I CAN DRINK ON KEPPRA! I mean YES I'm not supposed to, but there's nothing about the tablets that would make things worse if I did. Fuck you carbamazepine! No more zombie no-fun Angela. Just no getting pregnant hahahaha.

She pulled out her phone and Googled the pharmaceutically foreign words. Anti-epileptics, of course. No surprises. On the following pages, drawings took over again: portraits mainly. She recognised Andrea instantly. And the dark-haired brother. A woman drawn from memory, repeatedly, in profile and from the front, the minor details subject to revision but one constant: *1963-2002* in looping calligraphic script around her neck. Landscapes Neely couldn't identify, couldn't pin down as captured from life or conjured from imagination.

'These are fantastic,' Neely breathed, though there was nobody to hear. She flipped ahead through the dates, years passing beneath her fingers, until she found a portrait of a woman in profile with a long black ponytail tied atop her head. A mark of the moment she had entered Angela Archer's life.

Madly, stupidly, ridiculously in lust. FINALLY. Was starting to think something was wrong with me, but NOPE, here I am in full working order! She's teeny tiny. Kind of Italian or Spanish looking maybe? Didn't think I'd go for that but she's adorable. Not a student because she didn't ask for the discount. I'm guessing middle class and so embarrassed about it! Wouldn't be the first. Got Tony to let me look at the CCTV so I'll remember what she looks like when she comes back. I know she'll come back.

She knew nobody was watching, but Neely tried to hold back tears anyway. Her eyes shifted to her work shoes, discarded by the front door: boring black pumps she didn't wear between any Friday night and Monday morning. They blurred into black blobs as the tear spilled. *I meant something,* she thought. *I mattered.*

Her finger skipped and a chunk of pages flipped over to a new block of text. The tone had changed, the handwriting hadn't:

If this ground is poisoned then you find a new ground. Where am I going to go? If there's no way up then there's only down below. I am not in hell. I am not going to hell. I don't believe in hell. It's a big city. Where am I going to find a place?

Neely winced. That didn't sound like Angela at all, but it was in her hand, in black letters now. She agreed with the cryptic message, or at least the bit of it she could parse: yes, it was a big city, sure. But people could still have small minds, and that would be true no matter where they lived. She had the nagging suspicion that time was more important than space. Part of the appeal of leaving Stevenage had been the knowledge that Neely's past could be her past, and could be conveniently packaged and left where it belonged. Archived, and only referenced when needed. Angela may have lived in London, but she didn't have the anonymity that drew so many other people, her own girlfriend included, to the city. Neely bit her lip. What Angela had needed, she thought, was to draw a clear line between her childhood and who she became. Weed her life story. Fashion it the way she wanted. Neely had long wanted to tell that to her girlfriend, but it seemed rude, intrusive. Poking her nose in where it didn't belong, just like Ruby had always told her. Coming in as a visitor and acting like she owned the place. So she had kept her mouth shut.

What I think can't hurt her, Neely thought to herself. *Not if it's the truth.*

The journal entry still didn't make sense to Neely. Angela had never spoken like this. And Neely felt a creeping coming up her hands – a sensation that she was trespassing, that she had wandered into something to which she had no right whatsoever. Well, she *was* trespassing. It was a bloody massive invasion of privacy. Angela had trusted her. But Angela wasn't around to answer questions, so how else was Neely supposed to learn anything?

Her entire life, Neely had taught herself everything that was important to know. She had always been a reader, a researcher. And now the life of Angela Archer, and what had become of it, was her subject. But it was the fear again, sizzling small currents down her hair, that here again she would fail. Just when it mattered, when it was no longer Dead White Males or Higher Maths on the pages in front of her, then that so-called bright mind of hers wouldn't come up with anything worth writing down. If she couldn't figure out Angela Archer from the words of Angela Archer, then what good could she be, to her dead girlfriend or to anybody else?

She lay the book's spine flat on the couch and let the pages fan out like a sunrise. Where they split, closest to the centre, Neely peeked.

I can't feel angry and I can't feel sad. Over them. I don't understand. Andy drinks anger with her tea and spits it all out but I can't be like that even when I try. Why can't I feel anything when this is supposed to be the worst feeling of them all? I'm wrecked. Everywhere I go, it's ruined ground.

Neely shook her head, though nobody was around to see. The tablets, she assumed. They made Angela dozy, they sucked out her emotions, but that was simply the price for getting rid of the fits. Brains were difficult; even people without epilepsy had trouble reaching that perfect equilibrium. Somebody should have told Angela. How come nobody had told Angela what to expect?

She flipped the page.

I wonder if I am stupid because I let it happen, I let them do what they did to me. I didn't fight back because I was thinking that would only give them a rush. I've read that some people freeze when this kind of thing happens, like it's neither fight nor flight but something else completely, but that wasn't me. I knew what I was doing. I just wanted to lie there on the ground and it was the best ground in the world but I ruined it.

There was no further commentary on that page, no elaboration. Of course not, Neely thought. Angela was writing for herself, not for the *Times*. She wouldn't have to explain anything. Neely flipped the page: a drawing. Neely thought it looked familiar. A bridge. Nothing special, nothing unique. Not any of the iconic London landmarks known around the world to people far less invested in the city than Neely was. Crisscrosses of metal, shading that might have been rust or might have been thoughtless scratches of the pencil. Neely thought it looked vaguely familiar, but she couldn't pull any details from memory. She focused instead on what she knew for sure: Angela's hand, scrawling a frame around the margins, *ruined ground ruined ground ruined ground.*

Neely gently closed the covers of the book. This wasn't the voice of the woman she loved – a voice so calm and collected and sweet, the light laughter breaking ever so gently through the gates of her teeth, the ribbon of her lips. A voice that could suggest to Neely that maybe she just shouldn't dream, and not sound bitter or vengeful, brutal or cruel. The advice had sounded so practical coming from Angela: if the problem is your dreams then get rid of the problem. But either somebody had got rid of Angela or Angela had got rid of herself, and that's why she wasn't here right now to tell Neely she'd done an awful thing, violating her privacy like this; that she should have left well enough alone.

She dropped the book as if burnt. Paranoia rose like bile and she had to remind herself she hadn't been drinking, not at all. Denial was the only option Neely could see. Denial and subterfuge. She picked up the book and took it through to their bedroom. The wardrobe door held back a plethora of Angela's discards: flimsy vests fallen from their hangers, handbags for warmer seasons, jeans she simply couldn't have been bothered to hang up. Neely dug into the mounds of fabric and dropped the book within them. If – when – Angela came back, then it would merely look misplaced. Maybe, Neely figured, hating herself for it, she could convince Angela that she'd never seen the book at all, that Angela was merely confused. *Maybe you moved it after you had a fit and forgot? Never seen it before, Angela. Don't know what you're on about.*

It could work. Or maybe it would just be insult on top of invasion of privacy. So much for trust. *Why did you have to do that? What do you honestly think you just achieved?* Neely berated herself. *And who the fuck is the Angela who could write these things?*

In the kitchen, the wine had begun to leave a stain on the lino. Neely gingerly picked up the largest pieces of glass then mopped next-to-uselessly with the already sodden kitchen roll. It smelled like a crap night out. She returned to the bathroom, stripped out of her sweat-soaked clothes, and ran the bath: hot this time. The sound of the gushing taps filled her ears, and she shut her eyes, imagining it as the roar of the Underground taking her somewhere with purpose, with a definite reason, continuing the exchange of life moving in and out, on its way into the city.

Neely stretched out in the bath until the water went cold. She didn't bother washing her hair; she'd take a sickie tomorrow. She drained the bath, donned the fluffy bathrobe, and made herself a cup of tea, daring herself to avoid looking at that accusingly bare shelf in her front room. She lost.

Then she shot the remote control at the TV, bringing back to life the same BBC News she had watched last night.

Two minutes later, she turned off the television. Nothing she wanted to watch.

She looked in the refrigerator. Nothing she wanted to eat.

She rang Sam. Answerphone.

She pressed the button on her laptop and waited for it to come alive. Once she got the web browser open, she headed straight for Facebook, onto Angela's profile, onto the roll-call of past acquaintances and distant memories all summed up by the convenient label *friends*. She clicked onto the search box and typed in *Archer*, returning a blank.

Andy, she tried, getting a bald man in Barnet, and *Andrea*, nobody at all. She hit the back button and set about browsing through the photos, but each and every one was unremarkable. Angela Archer had a past, Neely knew. The problem was that whatever she knew of it wouldn't be enough. And as far as she knew, that's what Angela wanted.

She walked back to the kitchen on tiptoe, as if there were somebody who could hear an apology. She pulled the second bottle of Christmas wine from its hiding spot and opened it carefully this time. Then she opened the drawer and collected the tablets, dropping them into her palm before returning each one to its proper compartment. She snapped the tiny lids shut and slid the case back to its spot beside the electric kettle. Dustpan in hand, she swept up the splinters of glass from the kitchen floor.

'Sorry,' Neely whispered.

Eight

Hangover. Asleep, awake, sweating through the bed, cotton wool in her head. She reached for the phone and squinted. *Sorry didn't reply earlier. Come round*, the text begged her, its neat and even font nothing like its writer. *It'll be OK. Promise. Never lied to you yet. SW. xx.*

Westbourne Park. Change at King's Cross. Change at Highbury & Islington. Dalston Junction. Neely deleted the text before she spotted him already inside the café. Against her better judgment, she believed him. It was always against her better judgment. So much so, she wondered if she could really call it better, and what kind of judgment it was at all.

'I rang her again this morning,' Sam whispered from across the café table. 'Mailbox full.'

'Oh, Sam.'

'But it's still got her greeting and all. "Hi, this is Angela, I'll get back to you when I can" and that. I knew she wasn't going to pick up for me if she didn't pick up for you, like. I just wanted to hear her voice.'

If Angela carried her postcode everywhere she went, then Sam was her perfect counterpart because he had no history, none that Neely knew of, from before he arrived in London several years back. He was from elsewhere, that was for sure. Manchester. No wonder the two had gravitated toward each other after Neely's introduction and stayed stuck. He must have seemed such a clean slate, the lackadaisical young man hiding behind his deliberately dirty hair, trying to make sense of the life that suddenly lay before him. Enter Angela Archer, who knew the city, and he had his very own position in an unholy trinity, a guaranteed floor on which to crash after late nights in West London.

'What are we going to do, Neels?' Sam mumbled. 'I feel like I should be out there walking around and calling her name and that, but where do you start? I mean, what do you...' he trailed off, waving his hands around his head. Neely understood. Big, messy, mad city. Too big, too messy. And mad. They could start at Centre Point and circle, circle, circle ever-wider, spiralling out until the flats and terraces became semis, and the houses became green belt. But what if they found nothing? What if, between the two of them, there was just too much to sift through and see?

'The police are looking. That's what matters,' Neely tried to reassure him, not believing a word of it herself. 'They've got loads of people.'

'Missing White Woman Syndrome. Never thought I'd be so grateful for it. Aye, but not really the right white woman, y'know?'

'She's not a criminal. And she's not got five kids by seven men.'

'Well, yeah, but that photo of her. On the posters. I hate it. They make her look like a chav, don't they?'

Neely wasn't bothered. So Angela looked like a bit of a chav. It was a picture of Angela and it looked like Angela.

'Could be worse, Sam. If she was butch, she'd be totally ignored. Or worse. If you're going to disappear, you have to be pretty. She won the lottery on that one. People remember seeing someone like her.'

He shrugged. 'Thank Christ for you lipstick lezzers, y'know what I mean?' Neely couldn't help but giggle. 'Sorry,' Sam muttered.

'No, no. It's fine. It's just, something Angela used to say. She'd go, "God, Neely, you're not a lipstick lesbian. You're a manicure-and-full-face-of-slap bisexual." Trust me, I was flattered.'

Sam smiled, his lips tightly together. A frog face. He glanced out the window, caught his reflection. Decided he didn't fancy the look on his face and promptly wiped it back to blankness.

'She'll show up any minute and we'll all be laughing at this fuss.'

'Mmmm.'

'Well, the police won't be laughing, but they're just doing their job, innit.'

'Mmmm.'

'And then we'll take turns smacking her for putting us through this.'

'Yeah.'

Neely fought his silence. This was no time or place to be contemplative. 'Sam, what's wrong?'

'Other than the obvious? Fucksake.'

'Sorry, sorry.'

'No, sorry. It's just…'

'A lot to think about?'

'Bit of an understatement.'

She reached for one of her cigarettes. And she'd been doing so well. Neely had thought the stress would make her light up more often, but in fact the opposite had happened. She had lost her cravings for nicotine as the gnawing deep in her belly had continued to grow. I only smoke around Sam, Neely realised. He brings out that feeling.

She had decided on the Tube not to say a word about what she'd learned the day before. Sam didn't need to know. She swallowed the secret, letting it roll into a tight ball down her throat. This much she would keep from him, as it had been kept from her. This much she could have for her very own.

'She must have known about Friday night, Sam. She knew about you and me and she left. I can't think of anything else.'

Sam rolled his eyes. 'Don't be daft. You said she was already gone when you got home. How could she have known anything?'

Neely shrugged.

'And don't be so overdramatic. *You* and *me* didn't *do* anything.'

'Really? So I take it you've told Sophia?'

He snorted. 'No.'

'Why not, if it's nothing?'

'Because I'm trying really, really hard to not fuck things up with her, if you haven't noticed.'

'I haven't, actually,' she shot back bitchily.

Sam let out something halfway between a sigh and a groan. 'Look, Neels, I'm not perfect. I never said I was. You and me... this isn't the time for a post-mortem, yeah? Not now.'

She shrugged again and added another sugar to her tea, vowing not to apologise to Sam before she had a chance to apologise to Angela.

'Anyway. I wanted to tell you. I had a dream about Angela last night.' Sam pushed his glasses up the bridge of his nose. Neely thought their plastic frames ridiculous, but never said so, because she knew Sam owned mirrors just as functional as her own, and therefore doing so couldn't possibly tell him anything that he, deep down, did not already know was true. 'You were in it, too.'

Neely sat up straighter. 'What was happening?'

Sam picked at the edge of a sugar packet, lazy fingers tormenting the thin paper. 'You two came round to mine, yeah? And Angela had my guitar for some reason. She sat down on the couch and took it out the case and went, "I did you a favour. I restrung it for you."'

'She actually said, "I did you a favour"?'

'Yeah. What about it?' Sam noticed the downturned corners of Neely's mouth, the curve between lips threatening to drag the rest of her face down with it. Neely thought of letters on a phone book that wasn't hers, on a shelf suddenly lightened by strangers, but she just shrugged.

'Nothing. Go on.'

'Anyway, Angela takes out my guitar, tells me she's done me a favour and restrung it. And I look, and all the strings are made of barbed wire. From a thin little razory one to a big thick bastard. And she just picks it up and starts to play.'

'She doesn't play guitar.'

'Fucking hell, Neels, it was just a dream. It was bananas, OK? Angela's sitting on my couch playing this barbed-wire guitar and it's just the worst noise I've ever heard in my entire life, it's these... like noises straight out of hell. Or somewhere just down the road from it. Groans and shrieks and everything. It's not like a guitar at all. And her fingers are getting all sliced up by the wires, shredded up, she's bleeding all over the fucking gaff, and I'm telling her to stop and she's just laughing at laughing, all over these pure mental nightmare screams.'

Neely shuddered. 'Jesus Christ. Then what?'

'She just kept playing.'

'Was it a song at all?'

'Nah. Just that noise. Like someone or something getting torn apart.'

'Well, what was I doing?'

Sam shrugged, and Neely nearly recoiled from the gut-punch of her own irrelevance, even in the night-time neural fiction of somebody else's brain. 'You were in the kitchen.'

'Making the bloody tea.'

'Something like that.'

'So then you woke up in a cold sweat and decided to take your monthly bath?'

'Ha ha. No. I was yelling at Angela to stop, and she wouldn't, so I tried to grab the guitar away from her and my hands got cut up, too.' He stared down at the pair of them, as if reassuring himself that the pain and the blood and the metal had never really touched him, but should they ever decide to, then he would be ready, he would know.

Neely snorted. 'Well, don't grab barbed wire next time.'

'Shut up, Neels. It was a dream. I know you *routinely* dream of being the filling in a Nick Cave and PJ Harvey sandwich even though that would never happen, not without copious drugs for them and about thirty felonies committed by you, so shut up and let me tell my *stupid fucking story*, alright?'

'Have not,' she muttered, and sat back.

'So my hands are bleeding and her hands are bleeding and she just keeps laughing her head off like it's the most hilarious shit to have happened since the time you two made me dance to Adam Ant down the Dolphin. She's laughing, really laughing, even though she's a bigger mess than I am. Our blood is getting all mixed together, yeah? I can't tell how much is hers and how much is mine. And it's staining the couch and the wall and everything because we're starting to fight, like really physically fight, and I'm telling her I don't want her hurting herself and all she's doing is laughing at me.'

'Sure she was laughing at you?'

'Of course she was.'

'Not laughing at herself? Or just the situation?'

'No way.'

'And I was ignoring all this?'

'I don't remember what you were doing. You'd gone away. You were in the kitchen. You didn't notice.'

'Whatever. What happened next?'

'That was... er, not much, really. We were hitting each other. Slapping each other and that. She wouldn't stop trying to play the damn thing and I couldn't stand it and, y'know, I remember I put a hand over her mouth, because she kept laughing – it was horrible all mixed in with those screams and our blood all over each other. I tried to shut her up.'

'What, did dream-you suffocate her? Strangle her?'

'No!' he answered, too quickly and far too loud. 'No,' Sam repeated, returning to his usual tone of voice. 'That's when I woke up. Swimming in sweat. And I did have a bath, if you must know, thank you very much.'

'Christ.'

The waitress arrived with Neely's scampi special, the peas in a tidy mound, a slice of anaemic tomato atop a stingy portion of lettuce that Neely had no intention of touching anyway. Then she refilled Sam's coffee, letting a few drops slosh over the side. It seemed more careless than intentional, but Sam curled his lip in contempt regardless. Neely, engrossed in the ritual of tipping just the right amount of salt over each station of the plate – the breaded fish, the glistening golden chips, that scrap of salad, those neon peas – didn't notice.

'So what's it all supposed to mean, Doctor Brainiac?'

Neely shook her head and reached for the vinegar. 'Absolutely nothing. Dreams are just knit-together old shit that's kept in separate cages during the day. For good reason. When you fall asleep they break out and have wild sex and the resulting brain-gonorrhoea gives you nightmares about guitars with fucking barbed wire for strings. Forget it.'

'Brain-gonorrhoea? What's up with you?'

She sighed. 'The barbed wire is you beating yourself up over how she's gone even though it's nothing to do with you. Some kind of misplaced guilt because you're OK and you worry she's not. You were fighting with her because you think you left things on bad terms with her. Maybe.'

'I didn't. We were fine. And see, it does mean something.'

'I'm making this shit up, Sam. What do you want me to say? My head's all over the place.'

'It doesn't matter,' Sam sighed, taking the kind of long scratches through his hair that Neely instinctively found repulsive, morning bath or no morning bath. 'Whatever it is, it's bad.'

They sat in silence, Neely chewing, Sam spending more time flicking the screen on his phone than attending to his coffee.

'This scampi's disgusting.'

Sam reached out and popped one into his mouth, grimacing in agreement. 'Minging. Don't know how you can eat this stuff, anyway.'

'Says the person not eating at all.'

'On a bit of a cleanse, really. Flushing out all the bad stuff.'

'Well, I guess alcohol's a disinfectant.'

'Shut it.'

'On the organic vodka again?'

'Only the finest. No pesticides in my belly.'

'Hope it's fair trade. Karma's going to get you if some poor Russian child is being whipped in the distillery.'

'Ah, but the tears add that clean finish.'

'Is that what Sophia said last night?'

'She's still in Bristol. God, you're just a dreamboat, aren't you?'

We've got the banter, Neely thought. Whatever the hell else we have between us, lying in wait and ticking like the countdown of a bomb wired up to our hearts, at least we can talk to each other. Christ, the two of us, we can talk. The world, at least our little corner of it, is falling apart, but at least we can talk.

'Come on, let's get a move on, then.'

A half-eaten plate of food, a half-empty mug.

Neely had made new flyers at the library that morning, four to a page of A4, chopped into tidy quarters. Each flyer bore the same photograph as yesterday's posters, but harsher-looking shrunken down in black-and-white. *It's like she's dead already*, Neely thought, then cursed herself for even allowing in the thought.

'So, what do you think? Do we skip everyone who definitely doesn't speak English?'

'You can't really tell though, can you?'

'Like the old Turkish grannies. Or anybody fresh off the plane. Suppose they could recognise her face. But then how would they tell anybody?'

'I dunno. It doesn't matter, Sam. Fuck it, just give them to anybody you like.'

Lack of supply turned out to not be a problem. 'Have you seen this woman? Have? You? Seen this woman?' At Ridley Road, a respectful distance away from the first market traders and smack in the middle of foot traffic, Neely thrust her fliers at passers-by and received similar ignorance from both the potentials – the young, the ones in ironically poor dress, the ones with empty eyeglass frames perched atop noses, and the women in intentionally tragic jumpers and the men in trousers of testicle-strangling tightness, the ones like she and Ruby had been – and the abso-fucking-lutely nots. 'This is Angela? She's missing? Have you seen her?' Neely's voice, pulled askew by that peculiar rising inflection, sounded uncertain, as if she were still learning her lines.

Across the street, outside the Overground station, Sam tried a more personalised tactic. 'Hello, sorry to bother you, but this is Angela Archer, she's…' And footsteps would quicken, eyes would dart down to the pavement, and he would lose his target. Hands thrust deep into pockets or occupied by suddenly urgent mobile phone matters had no use for a scrap of paper that explained, at the reader's own convenience, that This Woman is five foot nine inches tall with blonde hair and the small matter of epilepsy and no medication. A few he chased half-heartedly for a few feet, perhaps not so much oblivious to their lack of interest as eternally optimistic.

Across the street, perhaps because she was not burning her energy moving her feet like Sam, Neely's frustration rose toward her neck, travelled down her arms, starting to tingle at her fingertips. What the fuck is wrong with you bastards, she thought. OK, granted, it's not the same as hearing screams in the dead of night and instead of actually doing something you roll over and go back to sleep because you can't be arsed getting involved. But it's just as rotten to the core, not giving a shit. It's two seconds out of your day to take the fucking piece of paper. Three if you bother looking at it, and fewer than ten if you actually bother to read it. And that's too much to ask. No, you're off to go do whatever it is that's so much more important than life and death and Angela Archer. Off to buy another pair of deliberately ugly trainers. Off to pay ten quid for a shit drink while you listen to shit attempts at jazz because somebody told you that's what you're supposed to do to look cool and you were thick enough to believe them.

Jesus, she thought. If Angela could hear me! She hated hearing me bitch about work – she'd listen, yeah, she was good like that, but she hated it, really, Neely recalled. Reminded her too much of her sister, once I got on a roll, once I got on a real bitter stewed-black-coffee-in-a-three-day-old-pot rant. *Don't be like that,* she'd say. *You're sounding like Andy. My sister could be beautiful if she didn't bring a tornado into your head every time you ask her how her day's going. I don't want you like that. You're better than that, Neely.*

A queue of raging drivers sent up a crescendo of horns, making Neely jump back from the street onto the pavement and into the moment. Maybe, she thought to herself, it's because you're becoming a fucking Londoner. And she warned you all about this. She did.

Sam waved from across the road. Shrugged his shoulders. Neely glared, then crossed the street, waiting for the signal this time.

'Fucking pointless, innit.' Sam stared down at the face on the top paper and traced the contour of one cheek. 'What are we gonna do, Neels?'

'Dunno.'

'You're supposed to know something. You're the clever one.'

'Fuck off.'

'Should I come back with you? To yours?'

'Nah, I'm alright.'

'You sure?'

'Yeah. I want some time alone. No offence.'

They walked together to Dalston Junction, Neely reaching for her Oyster card, Sam searching for his words.

'Chin up, Neels.'

'Same to you.'

A drop of drizzle landed on her hairline and she retreated with a step backward to the safety of the platform awning. The ammonia tang of stale piss hit her directly in the nostrils. She wanted to be home, right there and right then. It was where whatever was left of her dreams still had an incubator, however tiny, even if the heat and light had faded to barely a burn.

The train pulled up to the platform, the concrete darkening with the first of the rain, and Neely stepped aboard.

The rain sublimated into snow as Neely rode west. Cold weather warnings poured forth from computer screen and *Evening Standard*. On her walk home from the Tube station, her eyes fell on Londoners huddled in their coats, shivering in bus shelters.

But the summer after Angela had turned sixteen had brought parties. One of Marianthi Adamou's sisters had got engaged to somebody who had never seen the slightest smudge of trouble even a single day of his life: a cause for celebration. The family had invited half of Kensal Town to their garden in the shadow of the Trellick Tower, and when it couldn't hold more than the barbecue and the extended family, the festivities had spilled into Adair Road.

When Angela walked up the street, she spotted Marianthi seated on the low wall next to Jenny Wedmore. Maz wasn't called Maz then; she was still Marianthi Adamou, the mouthful of a name, her black hair – short back then – frizzed up like the halo in a burnt image of a saint, if girls from North Kensington ever made it to the level of painted icons. Jenny was wearing her brother's chunky watch; Marianthi, another big sister's denim skirt.

'There's your man,' Jenny had giggled, jerking her head toward a group of boys where Brian towered above the next-tallest. Angela blushed and muttered the usual about how they hadn't done anything, they were just mates, that's all. It was the first time she had seen him in a crowd, just talking and laughing like one of the lads. And she didn't feel pleased, but she did feel proud. *He's alright, Brian. He'll be OK, he'll weather the storms. And I will, too.* She had accepted a can of Strongbow from Marianthi and opened it with a satisfying crack. To her surprise, Marianthi had pushed a second into her hand.

'Go on, go give him one. Dare you. Oh shit! He's coming over, shut up, shut up.'

'Alright, Archy?' *Archy.* She liked that. Nobody called her Angie, she hated being called Angie, but Archy would do just fine.

'Alright.'

Her friends had smiled and discreetly slid away, arm in arm. Jenny had looked over her shoulder and nodded encouragingly. *Go on, girl.*

'Having a good time?'

Angela had shrugged. 'It's… busy. I didn't know you were pals with them over there.'

'Not really.'

Trying her best to feign cool disinterest, Angela had hoisted herself onto the wall, sitting in the spot her friends had vacated. 'Smile, youse,' called out big Eleni Adamou, who didn't know any better. She hoisted her camera. Angela and Brian both froze. 'And look alive!' Angela had smiled, lips tightly closed, and perched an elbow on the boy's arm. A click and they sprang apart; Eleni laughed and moved on.

'Marianthi's your best mate, isn't she?'

'She and Jenny, yeah. Known them forever.'

Silence. Thirty quiet seconds between teenagers has been clinically proven to last longer than for fully grown adults in full control of their minds and bodies.

'Archy. Let's go, yeah?'

'Where?'

'Wanna show you something.'

Angela peered into the garden; Marianthi was dancing with her sister's fiancé to 'Fill Me In' by Craig David, shaking her hair, making the little kids laugh. The song had been buzzing out from every car stereo on the estate for weeks. There was no reason to think this rendition would be any different from the hundred previous.

'Where?'

'Down on the canal.'

He extended an arachnid hand.

Sexuality, officially, did not exist at Sion–Manning School. It was never discussed, debated, or even acknowledged in an open arena. Of course, its shadows were suggested in those illicit spaces: in the toilets, in puffs of cigarette smoke aimed up at the air vents; in the changing rooms before and after PE, pejoratively to the girls who had what others wanted and presumptively by girls who feared they would never follow suit. Angela kept her mouth shut and didn't deliberately court attention in these matters. She'd once had a fit and pissed herself during assembly and from that point on she had focused on remaining as invisible as possible, or at least as invisible as an undeniably pretty teenage girl could. Mumblings and fumblings about sexual interests and actions were for, and about, other girls. And that suited Angela just fine. She had heard the rumours about Genevieve Paderewska, who cut her hair militarily short and had never been seen wearing as much as a smudge of lipgloss, but Angela and half her peers had ruled it was the doing of fanatical Polish Catholic parents who not-so-secretly hoped she would take the vows instead of getting pregnant by English boys like all her sisters promptly had done after leaving school. And then there was Anne-Marie Laverty, whose exploits could make the editor of any men's mag not only blush but flat-out run away in need of a sit-down and some sugary tea, but she had an excuse: she was mental, truly mental, sectioned before her sixteenth birthday.

Of course, there were people Angela fancied. She fancied Chioma Acholonu, head girl in her year, who sat in front of her in school now that Marianthi's parents had sent her somewhere decidedly not Catholic. Angela was in love with the precision of Chioma's accent, with the curve of her impossible neck, the sheen of flawless skin and her flawless schoolwork. She watched Chioma in class when she should have been watching the front of the room; she felt pale and spotty and unfinished, a rough draft not yet cast in metal or fired to the permanence of stone. No, she was still the clay, the putty, the wan wax model. Chioma, one of the only people who could look amazing in school uniform because she looked amazing in everything, most of all her own skin, was as remarkable to Angela for what she didn't do as for what she did: eternally unfazed and unruffled, Chioma approached school and all those in it with a single-mindedness of purpose. She never fought or answered back. Any disparaging comments sent her way were ignored, soaked up and diluted in the pages of her books, shattered to pieces against the armour of her purple blazer. But unlike the impenetrable shell that Angela had watched form around Andy, Chioma's exterior retained that softness, that approachability, a certain sweetness, even. Life rolled over her as inconsequentially as breeze.

And Angela fancied Bex Burton, one of her sister's few remaining friends. Bex was a tornado: loud, irrepressible, her hair plaited and wrapped into two horns of ginger pigtails. She'd worked behind the bar at the Hope and Anchor for a while, where her quick wit was welcome but her two-year-old was not. With the loss of that position came the loss of precious time for reading on the job all those books for the Open University course she was taking. So she took a job stacking shelves at Sainsbury's instead, stole whatever she could get away with, and taught herself cooking with recipes off the internet. Angela's favourite evenings were those spent in Andy's flat, Baby Rebecca underfoot, Bex making fun of Andy's ample stocks of Pot Noodle as she sautéed and braised and marinated impossible creations that had been smuggled out as their individual ingredients under her work fleece mere hours earlier. All that chopping and grating and slicing and she never, ever chipped her nails, which were always glittering perfection, always bold colours: aubergine, mustard, blood. Sod the OU, Bex said, she was going to become a chef. She could work nights, take care of Rebecca during the day. Angela loved the idea of packing so much into a life, filling it to bursting, and never looking the slightest bit bothered. As far as Angela knew, Baby Rebecca didn't have a father. She didn't need one.

Now Angela's head buzzed with cider and anticipation. It didn't matter that she didn't fancy Brian; he was going somewhere and taking her along for the walk. Specifically, he was going west along the canal towpath from Meanwhile Gardens. Just past the Sainsbury's, he took her hand. Despite herself, Angela smiled, and Brian followed, and then the giggles came.

'You're alright, Archy.'

'You're alright, too. Yeah?'

This isn't bad, she thought. *This can't be bad. It feels fine. I never thought this would feel fine. Fantastic to feel fine. If we're both freaks then neither of us are. Fantastic to feel wanted.* Her cheeks burned, but not with shame; if anybody had passed them walking the other direction on the path, Angela would have sworn they could have seen her aglow.

They passed the gasometers and the cemeteries: Kensal Green and St Mary's. Habitually, she waved and smiled at a pair of old dears on a houseboat, then smiled wider when her efforts were returned. Soon they had walked the width of W10. Angela's palms began to sweat in the warm evening.

'Brian, come on, alright, what is it you want to show me?'

'Won't be a surprise if I tell.' And he smiled, cheeky and toothy.

'How far out is it?'

'Not much more. Here, let's go up.' He pointed to the steps leading to Scrubs Lane and they dropped hands as they walked up to rusty Mitre Bridge.

Angela paused to orient herself, even though she had taken this route hundreds of times before, mainly on her bike. She loved Scrubs Lane above the canal: it barely felt like London around here. Just past the warehouses and the railway, both sides of the road were walled in greenery. Her sister had called it the post-apocalyptic garden path. Angela had called it her own.

'This is the best place in West London,' she breathed, reaching out to run long fingers over the carpet of ivy that poured over a fence. 'It's like being wrapped up warm. Wormwood Scrubs. It's my favourite park. Nowhere's got anything on it.' She knew she sounded strange, uncharacteristically romantic about a scrap of street. She didn't care. If anybody was going to know what she meant, it would be this boy.

'Here,' Brian called from a few paces behind her, pointing across the street at a gap where a well-trodden path began. 'Let's go in.'

On paper, the Archers were Catholic; in reality, they lived in West London and wanted decent schools for their children. Angela wasn't sure if she believed in a god, but she knew that every time she stepped into a lung of London, a canalside or a park or anywhere vaguely green and quieter than from where she had come, she felt something like deliverance. Walking in front of Brian, she raised her face to the canopy overhead. She shut her eyes for a moment as she walked, inhaling the sharp summer scent. Her father had taught her the names of different trees, how to identify them by leaf, where they all grew and why. He had said it was important, crucial, to learn everything she could about the earth on which she stood. Wormwood Scrubs was a bit of nature reserve wedged between railway and prison, hospital and A-road, but under the arbour, Angela thought she had reached paradise, by way of Kensal Green Cemetery and Sainsbury's.

'I know a place,' Angela breathed, 'Just a bit further in. Not too many people go there, but I know it.'

'You'll be showing us the way, then.'

It wasn't Brian's voice. Angela stopped suddenly and heard no footsteps following her. She spun round. Where Brian had been one, there were now three. She knew the others; she'd seen them on Adair Road, with Brian then, with Brian now. Charlie Edwards from the other end of the estate and Mo Zubairi from just over the canal, just off Harrow Road. Boys she'd seen, boys she knew when they passed in the street and boys she knew to let go on their way without acknowledgement or comment. Boys who looked at her like there was something they wanted, and she felt stupid for not knowing how to tell them they couldn't have it. Her sister was better at doing that. Andy was always the one screaming *fuck off* and *go crawl back up your mum's vag, you sad cunt*. Boys thought Andy was mad, and she wore the assumption like armour, so they left her alone. Mad meant trouble. But they thought Angela was stupid. Stupid meant easy.

'Oi. Dozy bitch. I'm talking to you.'

'What?' she tried to shoot back, all stabs at bravado dead on arrival. 'What?'

Mo silently walked around to behind her back. Charlie chuckled and shook his head. 'Alright, Bri. That was simple, yeah? Knew you could do it.' Brian said nothing.

'What?' she snarled.

'God, you're so fucking stupid,' Charlie laughed again.

She looked back toward the road, at the sandals that were useless for running, then at the boy who'd brought her there. 'Brian, what?' His face didn't shift a millimetre; he didn't say a word. '*What?*'

'You shouldn't ask stupid questions.'

Instinctively she yelped when Mo wrenched her arms behind her back and the other two held her legs. It didn't particularly hurt, but she screamed because that was the protocol. That was the right thing to do, she figured – you're attacked, you scream. But the instructions went right out the window when Charlie sent a fist, deceptively heavy, smack into the centre of her face. This time it *did* particularly hurt, and her vision blurred with a stream of tears following the stream of blood from her nose, but she stopped her shrieking.

Angela tried to get her footing, tried to find enough leverage to kick, but her sandals skidded in the mud and then her mouth joined them. The earth upon which she had stood, and now lay, tasted bitter and cold. 'You're not going anywhere, sunshine,' Charlie told one ear as he yanked back her hair.

'Brian!' she screamed, willing him to not be complicit in the act even as he took a starring role. He said nothing in response. He always looked so frail, so disproportionately and grotesquely fleshless as he towered over everybody in his path, but he was still heavy enough to pin Angela down in the dirt. And those double-jointed fingers – well, he could hold on to her wrists no matter how hard she struggled. But once Charlie had managed to dispatch her tights and skirt, she quit struggling, and by the time he had finished and Mo took his turn, Angela could have easily been mistaken for catatonic.

She had lain still and kept her brain busy.

Think of everything you've learned, she thought. Think of elm and lime and London plane from here to the canal and all along as far as it goes, of the difference between beech and oak, and everything that makes a poplar not an alder and vice versa. Because this is how you survive. It's a game, Angela. You learn through games. You're not as thick as people think. And you like games. Every second you don't fight back, you really win a little. Don't let them know you're hurt, and you've practically got victory sewn up. You get points for everything you can take without giving them anything in return. And you're doing fine. You're good at this. It's not that bad. It could be worse. You've felt worse. That time you had a bad fit and hit the sideboard on the way down and got that little scar below your chin. At least that's what Andy told you, that's what she said when you woke up. There was blood on the carpet but it looked worse than it felt, it looked far worse than it really was. These things always look worse than they really are. Your sister scrubbed at the blood and it came right out; well, it took a while, but what matters is that it came out, it was fine in the end, it was as if nothing had ever happened in your little house in Kensal Town. You lived. A girl called Andy and a boy called Alex and you right in the middle, you're fine with being in the middle of things, you're fine and well, you're doing great. You're winning this one. You'll live.

Mo came with a low groan, the kind Angela had never heard in films or in person, and she scared herself by smiling. It was poor taste to celebrate victories while still on the pitch, in front of the away end, so she straightened her face even though there was nobody to see it pressed against the grass, the blades tickling the corners of her mouth. The boy pulled himself out of her and the one who had brought her here eased his elbows off her back, released his hands from her arms.

'She's fucking bleeding.'

'Are you gonna have a go or not?'

'You joking?' For a second, she found solace in Brian's astonished reply. But he kept talking. 'God no. Wouldn't touch her with yours, not like that.'

'All this trouble and you don't want to have a go?'

'Nah. Nasty.'

'Clean yourself up, you slag.'

'Fucksake, you dead?'

Angela rolled herself over, wincing at the unusual brightness of a pale grey sky between the overhead leaves.

'Brian,' she stated. And that's what it was, a statement. Neither a request nor a plea. Just a label, the name of the one who *wouldn't touch her with his*. 'Brian.'

Finally, he spoke to her. 'What you looking at me like that for, you fucking retard?' But he didn't hold the stare.

She watched Charlie reach into his jacket and she knew what for: he'd bragged about it, she'd heard all she needed to around the estate about his knife and what – whom – he had allegedly done with it.

'See this? Not a word. Not *one fucking word*.'

But Angela heard the fear in his voice. Of course he was scared. Scared of her. Because nobody looked at him and his blade and remained so utterly, blankly passive. They fought or they flew, and that was that. But it all made perfect sense to her. She wasn't afraid of him, of it. If he had wanted to do anything more, after having his way, then he would have done it. But here he was, respecting the rules of the game. She had won, and he had that good grace, he had that sportsmanship. Respect.

He broke off their stare first, folding the blade and shoving it back down into his pocket. 'You really are a fucking window-licker.' Then he turned and joined his friends, who were walking back the way they had come as if they had gone to the Scrubs for a simple game of football. Brian was now one of the lads. He could be trusted. He'd delivered the goods. Angela stayed on the ground, blank-faced and doing her worst subject, mental maths – *eleven elevens are one hundred and twenty-one, twelve twelves are one hundred and forty-four, thirteen thirteens are oh shit three times thirteen is thirty-nine now bring down a zero and one times thirteen is thirteen and that's one hundred and thirty plus the thirty-nine makes one hundred and sixty-nine, fuck yeah, fourteen fourteens are –* until their three shapes disappeared off the Scrubs altogether, off toward home. She massaged blades of grass between her fingers, giving them an experimental squeeze in all their damp, earthy thickness. And she smiled, cleaning herself off with a few handfuls of leaves. Elm and lime and London plane.

In a spasm, she laughed long and loud, knowing nobody was going to hear her, the same way nobody heard her when she had taken the trouble and bothered to scream. She grimaced through the pain as she stood and ground her blood into the soil and moss. She tried her best to walk straight as she followed the path the boys had taken, on their way home after proving they were men and that's all they would ever be. Angela had the upper hand on them there, too. Because *I am fucking invisible and invincible. Maybe I'm an angel. I am already a ghost.*

She crouched on the lip of the canal and saw her reflection ripple. A moulted goose feather floated over her water-eyes, and she smiled. Angela wiggled out of her sandals and gingerly lowered a foot into the water, wincing at the cold. It was summer; she expected to feel something like heavy air closing in to grip her, maybe something like a bath. But she knew that was silly – there was nothing cleansing about the canal. Marianthi, who had already begun to read medical textbooks at the Porchester Library, had told her about the diseases people could get if they took a swim – rat-piss viruses, flesh-eating bacteria – but that was Marianthi's world now, and Marianthi was already on her way out of West London. Angela knew right then she wasn't going to follow. She was in the soil now. And she was in the water. And she didn't want to be cleansed, she didn't want to disappear. She wanted to stay right here.

She sat on the bank and dangled both legs. In this light, with this muck, she could see down only to mid-calf. Her feet didn't touch bottom, but they didn't touch anything else, either. She squinted at what she thought she saw beyond leg-depth, the reflections of the sky and shadows underneath. How deep could it be? Deeper than a swimming pool, shallower than the sea. If she jumped in completely, then maybe she could find out. But maybe, still, she would never know. Maybe she would flail and flail blindly down there and not touch the ground. And even if she did find the bottom, Angela thought, what would be the bloody point? *Ding ding*, a family on their bicycles sped behind her back. *Behind you!* one cheery voice called, though it might as well have belonged to the whole world.

Nine

In Harrow Road the 23rd of December begins with a creak, a groan from the city and everything in it. A brief stab of sunlight finds Neely Sharpe wrapped in a duvet, her blackout curtain of hair fanned across her pillow and over one eye. In the absence of her girlfriend, she cuddles up against the radiator. She has dreamed of nothing in particular since Angela went away. Every morning when she awakens she has the vague perception that something has been swimming through her unconsciousness for the past several hours, but she has not the slightest idea what. A week ago, this unknown would have unnerved her, disappointed her, left her feeling decidedly lacking in brainpower. Now she doesn't give a shit what it is, or if it's nothing at all. She checks her phone for messages that are not there. She reaches out of habit toward the space in her bed where nobody sleeps, and when her hand touches the cold sheet she remembers Mel from the pub telling her it's probably nothing and Neely realises she is right, there is nothing there for her at all.

In Dalston, Sam sleeps on the couch where Neely last passed out. The couch, because he couldn't make it the last final steps to his bed. He stumbled home only a couple of hours earlier after a couple of drinks turned into eight. It often does, but his body refuses to get used to it. His body is sick of giving him these warnings, these extra chances, and is contemplating a mutiny, but not quite yet. He lost a guitar pedal last night. He just doesn't know it yet. He also lost fifty quid and his Oyster card to a particularly discreet pickpocket. He doesn't know that either.

There. Blink and you'll miss it. Light flickers upon the still faces lying upstairs in the last squat left in Errington Road, W9. It doesn't get much sun, this room, and neither do Rob and Gina, asleep in their coats. The arm she didn't fling around him still holds what remains of last night's cigarette. Burnt a decent chunk of skin out of two fingers but mercifully it spared the bed linens, the mattress, the rotting plaster of the walls, and their lives. And the girl didn't feel a thing. She will soon, though, she will: they will awaken swirling-headed and aching, with shivers that have little to do with the cold. But for now, they sleep. Behind twitching eyelids, Gina rides a black horse through the streets of Nottingham. At the kerb, in rapt attention, stand crowds of eager-eyed students from the university and her friends from school and her cousins who haven't lost the island accents that embarrass her so much, and that scrawny white boy guitarist with the heart and teeth of gold who first shot her up, all watching this ragged Lady Godiva's parade. *Marry me*, any one of a hundred says. *I can't*, she replies, *I'm on my way out*. Rob breathes so shallowly he looks still. In his dreams, he is sailing, he is sailing on the Grand Union Canal. The sunshine takes its moment, then takes its leave.

The day begins in West London and Angela Archer is still missing.

Angela Archer is still.

Neely didn't know it, but in the Missing Persons Team, an informal pool had formed: who would find the body, when and where. Ten quid to enter. Closest to correct on all three wins the whole pot. It wasn't cruel, it was coping. Nearly everybody guessed a dog walker, except for one Detective Inspector Grey who was convinced it would be an old couple out for a stroll.

But there were no dogs, and the hysterical phone call came from a twenty-four-year-old who looked closer to fourteen. Acted it, too. Riding her bike along the Grand Union Canal, she'd spotted the mosaic embedded into the dirt along the towpath, the one asking her to Please Keep Our Nature Reserve Tidy. Head firmly embedded in the clouds, she'd wandered into the expanse of spindly trees between the canal and the railways, searching for birds. They were easy to see in a leafless December, up against a dull grey sky: little flashes of blue and orange, a red breast here, a gold cap there. And not more than ten metres from where she had dropped her bicycle, the wool the colour of the canal.

Angela Archer lay nude under the long coat that had been thrown over her body. The handbag lay under her head, its strap digging into the purple cheek where blood had quit fighting gravity and come to rest. New Look ankle boots, reddish and size six, might have fallen off, might have been thrown. 'Don't touch it!' the first officer at the scene screamed at the daft girl when she picked one up from beneath a tree. 'Don't touch a thing!'

In the distance, a train: going, not coming. Then a radio, crackling, relaying just the facts back to Harrow Road Police Station. A little speculation couldn't hurt Angela Archer now, but this new reverence, the kind she'd never had a chance to experience when it could have mattered, wasn't helping much, either. The landscape around her came alive with uniforms in their black and white and all those greys, the wide and sad eyes. Looking at the dead and waiting on the living.

Neely stood in Iceland, studying hors d'oeuvres. There were prawns on skewers and egg rolls and tiny chicken satays. So much choice for so cheap, she thought. Of course it was not going to taste orgasmic on anybody's tongue for two pounds a box, but food's food, food will fill you up, it will do exactly what it says on the tin or the box or whatever and if you can't find something you like with all these choices then it's your own bloody fault for being such a snotty so-and-so. Think about it, you can have all your party nibbles without the fuss of a party. It's brilliant, she thought. When you think about it.

Christmas had never been much of a big deal in the Sharpe house, and this year her parents had said sod it altogether and decamped to the Caribbean. One-week cruise. Enjoying retirement before they got too old to have any fun. Neely's London had emptied, and the people she knew had gone back to where they came from, none of those places being London. *I bet even Ruby packed up and hopped on a train to Cheltenham,* Neely thought. *And she'll love every minute of it, no matter how much she used to whinge about her family and that lovely old town.* The expats were left within the M25, the Aussies and the Kiwis, but none of them were close enough friends to invite Neely over to eat their turkey and drink their booze. *It's OK,* she reassured herself. *It's not sad to be eating Iceland snacks on your lonesome. You had a plan. A good one. A bright one for when the early nights draw in. As far as you're concerned, you will still be spending Christmas with your girlfriend. And you don't know, she might even show up.*

She stood in the queue, crawling forward at a pace the average garden snail might have found a bit tedious. A basket of frozen food on the floor, slowly thawing underfoot. Hands that barely felt like her own, inserting her card and punching in the PIN. The worker at the till might have wished her a good day, might not have – Neely didn't hear, didn't care.

As she walked down the Harrow Road, back down the straightforward street to her flat, the chill in the air caught her hair. A breeze sent it dancing into her face, stuck strands to her lipgloss. Neely turned her head to pull them free and caught sight of the Halfpenny Steps, the pathway over the canal. Invisible strings pulled at her legs and sent her across the street towards them. It was cold enough outside to spare her purchases for a few extra minutes.

Every time Neely walked the Grand Union Canal, she felt she was crossing some line – not exactly between the real and the sublime, nothing as pretentious as that. Rather, on the canal, footsteps pattering down the path, peering over walls and fences at the new-build flats with their promise, and the cemetery plots in all their permanence, she could be *within* the city, but not a *part* of it. That's what Angela had told her: the canal may have run alongside the real world, the Harrow Road and all who lived in it, but it was a different place entirely. The usual rules didn't apply here. Anything could happen all along the water. She was just an observer. Nothing here could possibly be her fault.

What *was* her fault? Neely thought, sliding her carrier bags from her hands to her wrists and tucking her hair beneath her hat. What, if she was called at that moment to atone for her sins, could she claim? Well, there were the obvious things: the memory of her hangover headache on a sofa in Hackney smacked her right behind the eyes. She had her petty moments like anybody else, her clutched grudges. But nothing irredeemable. Whatever she had done, Angela would forgive her. Wherever Angela had gone, for whatever reason – they would forgive each other. Neely stared up at the sky, at its uniform grey, with static bursting bright throughout her field of vision. Not for the first time that day, she tried to avoid crying.

The canal was a magical place, Angela had said. And so Neely let herself do some magical thinking. *She is gone because I haven't wanted her here enough. She left because I didn't keep her close enough. She vanished because I did not love her enough as she was.* The self-centredness disgusted her, in a way – as if she could possibly be so powerful to have moved Angela through this world, when she didn't even know where Angela was, or why she was there – but it also put her in control; it gave her somebody to flay. Somebody to blame.

She took the bend by the nature reserve, the grinding of machinery from the recycling plants white-noising her brain clear, and nearly walked into the tape. Blue and white: POLICE, as if she wouldn't have been able to guess. Ahead of her, a mess of hi-viz jackets and uniforms. Two were setting up a tent.

'Miss, stay back!'

She squinted into the middle distance, beyond the uniform. 'What's going on?'

'You need to go back the way you came. Please.'

Those words waved a red rag in front of Neely's eyes; a matching mist descended. 'What?' Since when was going back – to anyone, or anything – an option for her? Since when would anybody tell her which path to take, and in which direction? No, she made her own ways, she made her own mistakes, she got herself in this situation and she would bloody well decide when it was time to leave the canal and go back to the Harrow Road, go back to hating herself and hating her job and hating the knowledge of what could have, should have been; go back to her empty flat and its gaping space where her missing girlfriend should be. And isn't that what Mel in the pub said was exactly what Angela wanted – the right to fuck up her life however she wanted?

As the rhetorical questions sped through Neely's head, the heat of her anger exited abruptly with those thoughts, replaced by an icy creep. It started behind her eyes and spread, cold and crystalline, down to her fingertips. If she moved, she might crack. She knew. *Angela is here, because I thought her here.*

'Miss. I have to ask you to turn back now. This is an active investigation.'

'What's happened?' she asked, too quietly to be heard the first time. 'What's happened?'

'This is an active investigation.'

'What does she look like?'

'Pardon?'

'You've found a body? Here?'

'Miss, I cannot comment on…'

Neely's hand shot to her pocket, to her mobile, fury and fear leaving her shaking too hard to type in her passcode properly. 'The woman,' she spluttered, tapping the screen maniacally. She went into her contacts, to the very first name: Angela Archer. Hitting *call* sent up the background photo to the full screen: summer. Hyde Park. Black vest, black hat, red nails. Neely craned her neck around the policeman, looking for black coat, red boots. 'Is this what she looks like?'

'I'm not going to warn you again. This is an active investigation and you need to leave…'

Behind him, one of the hi-vizes jumped, recoiling as if bitten by a snake that had been hiding in the very typical, very English undergrowth beside the canal towpath. 'Fucksake!' Neely heard him yell. 'Scared the shite out of me. It's just a mobile buzzing. Bag, please!'

The uniform looked to his colleague, to Neely, and to the smiling face on the screen as it flickered to black. 'Wait here.'

But Neely would not be told.

The Grand Union Canal blurred on Neely's way back into the world she hadn't truly left, not really; greens and greys from the cemetery and the trees, the living and the dead, enveloped her. She tripped on the towpath and found her footing again without thinking, and kept running without a pause. She couldn't remember how she got across the Halfpenny Steps or across any of the junctions, only that she moved without stopping, and so the rest of the city must have stopped moving for her. She tripped again up the steps of Harrow Road Police Station, skinning her palms on concrete, and lay panting before the door. Lungs that could ache. A throat that could still feel raw, could still feel. She hadn't the breath to explain herself at reception but there was no need. Strangers had found out before she had. Strangers were ushering her to a chair, telling her to wait, leaving Neely with her roaring blood and weeping hands. Strangers shut the door of the room but didn't lock it, and Neely let herself out, to peer around corners and wander corridors, knowing that asking for an answer would be the one thing least likely to get her one. She watched clocks, uniformly institutional, registering nothing but their movement, the steady ticking forward of hands so agonisingly slower than her own pulse. Time passed and so did Neely, unseen moving through doors, unnoticed lingering by the incident room as the strangers shifted their focus to a strange new pair. She saw the woman and knew the green eyes in a different face; she heard the man and remembered the voice from over the phone. But she couldn't remember their names to call out. And what would she say? They'd never known each other before.

She said nothing. She thought little more, magical or otherwise, as she returned to the room and sat forgotten, watching time move. Adrenaline couldn't surge forever, as much as Neely willed it, and at its first subsidence she collapsed into sobs – long, bawling, sure to be heard outside her little institutional cubicle of wood and glass – as if every string holding her had been sliced, simultaneously, with a single clean snip. And when she had cried out all her energy, she slept, upright at the table, mind wiped blank.

She didn't know when she awoke, or how long she had slept, and whether anybody had told her what she already knew. She couldn't remember how she made her way into yet another room – white this time – with its table of microphones. The sister with the green eyes stood between two uniforms. Neely watched one tap the microphone tentatively, as if there could be nothing worse than making a false start when confirming a final end.

'This morning, the 23rd of December, a cyclist on the towpath of the Grand Union Canal found the body of a young woman in an area of nature reserve near Old Oak Lane. We have confirmed the body is that of Angela Marie Archer, who was reported missing from her home in Harrow Road, W9, on the 19th of December. The conclusion has been reached that Miss Archer was the victim of a murder. Her sister, Mrs Andrea Ormiston, has prepared a statement on behalf of Angela's family, which she will read now.'

'Thank you.' The woman bit her lip and scanned the faces of the first row. 'Erm, my family and I want to thank everybody who helped look for Angela. The Metropolitan Police and everyone else involved. And I'd like to say thank you to the person who found my sister's body, even though I haven't been told who you are. God knows you didn't need to see that before Christmas. I hope you will be OK. Thank you for helping us stop waiting and worrying. And another thing, it's just, thank you for coming today. I'm surprised there's not more of you here. I know it's the holidays but I really wonder, if she hadn't been… if she'd been somebody else, maybe somebody would have found her sooner. Nobody told me she was missing because nobody cared. Maybe somebody would have cared if she'd been different. If she'd been clever or rich or both. And now I'd just like to say that my family and I would like to be left alone. Not just the newspapers, but in all other ways. No priests, no shrinks, no flowers. We want to bury Angela and then deal with everything our own way in time. If you would like to do something in tribute then please make a donation to a charity. Epilepsy Society or whatever you like. Just, we'd like to be left alone. That's it. Don't mind us, go on with your lives, enjoy your holiday with your family and friends because we certainly can't and never will again and we have to figure out a way to deal with it by ourselves. I intend to spend Christmas getting shit-faced enough to forget that some bastard caved in my little sister's head and crushed her throat and dumped her on that fucking canal.'

Someone cut her microphone.

'It's going to be difficult but we have a lot of really good whisky. That's all. Thanks.' The woman pushed back her chair and left, the proper prepared statement fluttering to the floor in her wake.

Reconstruction

Ten

'Sit on her, Andy. She's going to hurt herself.'

The early days of epilepsy. Andy did as she was told, throwing herself over her little sister and pinning down her jerking arms. Alex, as small as he was, tried to hold down her legs. The adults busied themselves doing what they thought responsible: calling doctors, fetching pillows, reviewing the protocol. Andy would grit her teeth and hold on for dear life; Angela was never so strong as she was when she had no idea what she was doing.

Back then Andy noticed that when Angela had a fit, she lost a decade. An otherwise unremarkable ten-year-old would, in a matter of seconds, be transformed back to an infant: all unintelligible cries and grunts and gasps, the stares into nowhere. The helplessly flexed elbows and wrists like chicken wings. Punches stripped of malice, directed at everything and nobody. The complete inability of Andy, or anybody else, to get through to her. *She's gone into space, be right back,* they'd sometimes joke, because they had to laugh lest they do any manner of worse things. Easier to imagine Angela's brain taking her somewhere precious, special, where her actions might have meaning in context. But then the babyish, dreamy nowhere face would collapse as she came back to this planet. She'd look directly through her family, directly through the walls of their flat. Andy couldn't be sure, but it looked like shame contorting her features as her eyes began to focus again: the crumpled brow, the face buried in her hands, the knowledge this would be her life and there was nothing she could do about it. The doctors had warned them she might cry – or laugh hysterically – right after fits, but she wouldn't be in pain, it wouldn't be real. Like everything else, it was just her brain trying to make sense of the world, and missing the mark. *It's OK, it's OK, it's OK,* Andy would repeat as her sister came round, rocking her gently, knowing it was a lie, knowing it was just her job to try to help.

'Angela, love, can you hear me?'

'Mmmm.'

'Do you know where you are?'

The blank eyes would flutter from carpet to ceiling. 'Home.'

Andy had stroked her sister's cheek, smoothed the furrows in her forehead. 'Yep. Got it in one.'

'I'm sorry.'

'Don't be daft. What year is it?'

'Mmm.'

'What's your address?'

'What?'

'Angela. Address.'

'I'm sorry.'

'Shush. What's my name?'

'Andrea Karen Archer.'

'I love you.' She had held her sister close and waited for her to come back to Earth.

There had always been the nagging worry in Andy's mind that someday her little sister might not come back after all. People died from epilepsy, she knew. Not as many as used to, but still some. Lots got on the right tablets, followed doctor's orders, and lived to grow as old and dull and boring as anybody else, but for a long time the standard rules hadn't applied to Angela and the girl hadn't bothered even trying to follow them, so who knew?

When the police first showed up to her father's house, her father's house where she was cooking him his tea, her father's house lined with her father's photographs of Andy and Angela and their brother, but never their mother, that's what Andy had thought: Angela hadn't come back. She'd fallen on her way down, hit her head on concrete, done. She'd had a bad one in her sleep and never woke up from it. When the words finally started making sense, when she heard *missing* and *flatmate hasn't seen her* and *not answering her phone*, Andy couldn't comprehend. She couldn't consider the possibility.

The last hours of normality in Andy's life, now permanently burnt into her memory, were so bland and domestic she felt embarrassed for her younger self, who was all piss and vinegar, salt and chips, fights and fingernails sharpened into points, the girl who thought, *you will never make me what you want. I'm leaving and nobody will ever drag me back here.* In the last minutes before Andy heard the crash and clatter, the metallic sounds of her world and all its foundations and its once-undoubted firmament falling down all at once, she had been listening to Radio 1.

In Andy's head, the scene replayed itself in a never-ending loop, like the first Walkman she'd ever bought with her pocket money, the one that turned the tape over for her again and again so that it never, ever had to end. In Southall she sprang open her ironing board, then turned on Radio 1. The former was self-explanatory for a married mother of two, but she hadn't a clue why she almost reflexively put on the radio every time, and why it always had to be that damn station. She didn't even like what it played. Her husband knew this. 'You're looking fantastic for eighteen, Andy,' he joked whenever he heard the charts hum from the hi-fi, and she always laughed even though he was not that funny and she was not particularly fond of thinking back to her life in the years when she was the target audience. For Andrea Archer, the girl called Andy, age eighteen wasn't about festivals and the charts or what you imagined would be playing in the background when you finally snogged whoever it was you'd had your eye on for ages. And how disappointed you'd feel, the first of many disappointments, when it was all a bit rubbish and your lips were sore and he was rubbing an obvious erection where you would rather he didn't. For Andy Archer, because she was still Archer then, age eighteen was about being a dozen storeys up in Freston Road, with a view of the motorway and the screech of the Tube, cupboards full of Pot Noodle, over on that edge of Notting Hill that nobody would ever put in a film starring Her with the Huge Mouth and Him with the Posh Cunt Hairdo, the kind of people who lived in some London that only existed for the likes of them, but which the whole damn world thought was par for the course for her postcode. When she was eighteen, Andy Archer thought the entire world was obsessed with reminding her what she couldn't have. All those things she could never have even though they were so close that she could have hit them with one strategically aimed rock thrown from her perch in Crossway House. And hitting them would have felt good.

It was her flat, Number 44 Crossway House, hers alone – she didn't own it, of course, but it had her name on the tenancy. She'd gone homeless. Couldn't stay. That's the explanation she gave most people, and given the choice Andy would have stopped right there, but it was never enough, you had to sing for your supper and when a council flat in the *Royal* Borough of Kensington and Chelsea is what's being served in the canteen tonight then you better be belting out one epic opera of your sorrows. The Royal Borough of Kensington and Chelsea. It was written all over the street signs. *Royal my fat fucking arse*, Andy Archer spat to herself and, as there's no real place for spit to go if not out, she usually ended up swallowing her contempt for the borough, the city, the world, and everybody in it. Her mother was exempt from the shit-list by virtue of having left the borough, the city, the world, and everybody in it. The Royal Marsden Hospital, in the Royal Borough of Kensington and Chelsea, that's where she'd died, tidily disintegrating, dropping all dignity, in the fucking *Royal* Marsden.

My mum's just died, Andy had told the housing support officer. She hadn't expected it to work. She hadn't expected much of anything, but still she tried: I've been sofa-surfing with anybody who will still put up with me because my mum's just died, and my dad can't stand the sight of me because I look just like her when she was young and happy and well, and my little sister has fits and my little brother is only seven and I can't fucking deal with a kid right now and on top of that, I'm fucking pregnant. I can't be a mum when I really need my own right now and I can't have her. And I can't go back to that house. That house was for a happy family and they're gone and they're not coming back and if I have to go through that door I'll panic and then I'll do something stupid and get rid of my baby but I don't want to get rid of my baby, I just want to give birth somewhere that doesn't have death clawing at me from every wall.

She got the flat. She got rid of the baby. Not intentionally. Miscarriage happens more often than people expect on the first go round. The stress hadn't tilted the odds in its favour, either. And Andy called it It because that's what It was. Not a little boy or a little girl. An event. A mark on a calendar. A party missed. An end, and the means to it. She lost the baby but kept the flat. Nobody, not even the most faceless local government bureaucrat, could kick out a girl in that state, a girl who'd lost her past and her future so close together. Girl they called her, but eighteen was a woman, and from just across the motorway the BBC satellites beamed in news from places where at that age she would have already popped out a half dozen kids and buried half of them if she herself had been lucky enough to survive.

156

In her new home, Andy made the world very, very small. This was Planet Andrea. Not on any map. She didn't speak to the neighbours, mostly families from halfway around the world rather than half a mile down the road. Sometimes a smile would shoot across a corridor but nothing more. Andy didn't speak Arabic or Bengali or whatever, and she didn't want to know other people's problems – or even worse, their joys – in any language. It wasn't personal, it was survival. Sometimes Andy forgot that just around the corner there was a Tube station called Latimer Road. Not a station that showed up too often in travel guides or in *Time Out*. People from countries she couldn't pronounce would alight at Westbourne Park for the carnival, at Ladbroke Grove for the market; years later, when there was no Andy Archer any more, just Andrea Ormiston, and when It was replaced by a Little Him and a Little Her, and when all the time in the world once spent weeping at bare walls and watching the trains trundle on westward was now not nearly enough time to do the washing and hoovering and ironing in Southall, then there would be a new station near the old home, a Wood Lane, with a posh new shopping centre where the cheapest items in some shops cost more than a month's rent in Crossway House.

Around the time Andy had moved in to the high-rise, Angela had quit riding the Tube. With her father being a driver she never had to pay her fare a day in her life, but she walked no matter the weather. Andy always grilled Angela, pestered her to quit wasting time, and her sister never cared.

'I know it doesn't make sense,' Angela would shrug, lighting one of her sister's cigarettes because who could worry about cancer when your mum, who never smoked a day in her life, only went and dropped dead of it anyway? 'I just feel like going walking. Things make more sense when they're right in front of your face. It's just what I feel.'

'Well, what you feel is *fucking wrong*,' Andy would reply, momentarily satisfied living in her flat, her planet, her fortress, and its world of absolutes. And she'd light a cigarette, too, and the sisters would lie down on the floor and look for patterns in the pebbly Artex ceiling the way they used to look at summer clouds.

Those nights after the TV broke, Andy would sit in the window with a microwaved Tesco Value lasagne in its black plastic tray, watching the headlights and tail lights winding their way along the twist of the Westway.

At this part of the motorway and at this time of night, untrained eyes couldn't know for sure who was coming or going. Now and then she brought a man back to Crossway House – *I've got my own flat in North Ken* sounded so nice in theory – but they rarely got a second night to enjoy the view. Some people smoke after sex; Andy Archer panicked. She wanted them out. Do the deed and then you're done, goodbye, good luck, don't call me. Life was too fragile to give little scraps of it to everybody she barely knew and still expect enough of it left for herself. *Get out,* she always thought. *You and your entitlement, you and how you roll out of my bed and walk to my toilet like you suddenly deserve part of my existence, like you've done me some kind of favour, you need to leave.* She never said it, she just stared at the ribbons of cars as the sky grew lighter and the traffic heavier and her heartbeat quicker. *I can't take these people who think they're meant for some bigger purpose,* she thought. *This high-rise is the closest anybody should ever get to having their head in the clouds and the sooner we all realise that, the fucking better.*

That's what she had loved about Stuart when she met him. There were thousands like him coming down from their Dundees and Sunderlands and Swindons and Northamptons, armed with no particularly remarkable talents other than holding an unrelenting belief that the rules that apply today will still apply tomorrow, and should they follow those rules, their existences would be suitably comfortable. Men not groomed to be world-changers, men who believed that good enough was a triumph and not a slippery slope. They had met in the pub beside Ravenscourt Park on Bonfire Night. She'd had her bag nicked and she was fairly pissed and she told her few remaining mates to go on without her because she liked the look of him and the sound of him with the Scottish voice that wasn't Glaswegian, *what is it anyway, what's Dundee like, I've never been, why'd you come here, fer crissakes why did you come down here? Oh. You have a job. Tell me about your job.* And he'd told her about the job, junior management; and he'd told her about the Sunday football side he'd put together with some other lads he'd known at some ex-polytechnic now-university who had all come down to London; and had she seen that film that everyone else had seen, because he'd seen it twice; and he'd steadied her when she got up too quickly and too drunkenly and his mates in their button-front shirts were cheering and clapping GO ON MY SON! as they left but he told them to shut it and when she woke up in his bed the next morning, he was still asleep on the floor and her tights were in the same place she'd left them the previous night: on her legs, elastic goring her belly. And she had thought, fucking hell, I am going to fall in love with this man even though there is not one thing about him that is any different from millions of others. Because I have already made it this far.

The first time she let Stuart spend the night at hers, she woke up, padded out of bed quietly so as not to wake him, and wrenched open that twelfth-story window the few inches it would comply. One by one she flicked the dregs of leftover prescriptions onto the road below: Seroxat, Prozac, citalopram. They married at Chelsea Register Office. Her father's photographs caught her punching the air like she'd won the Cup Final. *Get in.* A year after that, the baby boy, and then a few years off before the baby girl. Jack and Ella. Not Jaiden and Chantelle, not Jordan and Chelsie – and how the *fuck* could Katie Pickering from school name her baby girl *Chelsie* when the correct spelling was right there on every street sign in the borough where you both grew up? – but Jack and Ella. Solid names for stable lives. Go up to Scotland every summer to see Nan. Go over to East Acton to see the Archers not too often. Have them over instead, to their home, the one she and Stuart had made together. Both the man and the boy quickly adopting Queens Park Rangers, with the girl in her blue-and-white scarf whenever she watched the matches on TV with Daddy. No Disney princesses for her. Strictly Daddy's little attacking midfielder. He'd stopped swearing for the kids, she'd stopped swearing and smoking and taking the odd E and getting trolleyed and belligerent at the weekends, and then together they'd found their little Metroland home.

They'd rented in Ealing for a while, convenient enough for Stuart's commute into the City on the Tube. By the time he no longer felt so enamoured with London as to demand a directional postcode – West Eleven, West Five, he'd once cared about these things – the housing bubble had burst and UB1 was looking like a good investment. They had investments now, Andy and Stuart. Decent ones. Lovely little house party once most of the boxes were unpacked. Angela had stopped by, already tipsy. Her face had gone a bit pink and splotchy, the way it tended to look whenever she was either drinking or about to have a fit, which she had done and which she did, and it was Stuart who caught her on her way down, whoopsadaisy, easy now, nobody panic, it's alright, could you get her a blanket, Andy? And when her teenage sister came back to the land of the living within a couple minutes and promptly puked White Russians and a bit of kebab onto the deep-pile carpet of their new lounge, Andy watched her husband laugh it off. *Jesus Christ,* she thought. *I never realised I deserved any of this joy. I never knew any of it could be mine.*

Andrea Ormiston, because that's who Andy Archer was now, unplugged her iron but she let the radio play. This is Radio 1, the DJ announced from somewhere inside his own world, closer to Crossway House than she hoped she would ever be, ever again. 97 to 99 FM, BBC Radio 1.

Andy relived that scene again and again over the days as *your sister has been reported missing* tipped over the abyss into *we have found a body and we need you to provide an identification* and finally *the coroner will notify you of when you may hold the funeral.* The police had abruptly ceased to be the perpetually evil bastards of her adolescence and instead had turned into the kind of people she trusted with her sister's life, and then her sister's death. It didn't make sense. How much easier it was to retreat back into the simplicity of the life she had chosen for herself when she left the Kensal Town Estate and Freston Road, that hard-fought victory disguised as domesticity. Ironing and Radio 1. Pop and circumstance.

When the riots had hit London, after a cop had shot dead a man in Tottenham, she had kept the TV off. She had wanted to shade Jack, who only knew Tottenham as a football club, from the violence unfolding on the other side of London, from the sight of lives up in flames. She'd surreptitiously shot looks at her phone to follow the looting. First Wood Green. Then Enfield. Hackney. Croydon. A man just down the road in Ealing beaten into a coma – not dead yet, but soon enough he would be. Crime necklaced the city with a crucial break in the chain: at least Angela was safe in Harrow Road. Funny, Andy had thought then. She's finally safe *there.*

It was after Jack's bedtime when she saw the pictures of all the shop owners on Southall Broadway standing guard. The Sikhs, the Hindus, the Muslims, together. Even a few white blokes, the few there were still around here. Not Stuart but that didn't matter. Stuart had kids, Stuart had her. He didn't need other people's problems and she didn't want them. But still, fresh-off-the-boat Asians and their streetwise kids protecting the England that was theirs. She'd swelled with a pride not her own, a pride found secondhand and at one hell of a discount, but still pride. Proud that she had moved somewhere where people knew how to fight but, more importantly, they knew how to pick their battles. Her teenage self could have learned something from them, but she had been too busy twelve stories up on the edge of the Westway. It wasn't fair. Life had let her look, but not live. She and Angela both. They lived in one of the planet's great cities, a magnet for all the world's wealth, and they'd spent their childhoods penned into their postcode. And by the time they were old enough to get out of there – well, who had time to make up for everything they'd lost?

She couldn't even remember if Angela had ever gone to the cops, back in Andy's high-rise days. Back when what Andy called The Inevitable happened. Andy wondered if her sister had even told this flatmate, the one Andy had never met, the one Angela had never brought to Southall for a visit. Had Angela even mentioned what happened? Andy hadn't, not to Stuart, but women were different that way, they were mirrors and not chalkboards. Or rather, had her sister tried, in whatever way she could, to bury her past on Wormwood Scrubs just as Andy had thrown away her own?

You have to know history. Not just places, but people, their dad would say. *You need to give it a fucking rest,* their mother would have shot back, if she hadn't been long gone. And Andy herself would have said, *Why do you think I have the answers to anything?*

And nobody would have noticed what Angela inevitably did about The Inevitable.

Andy thought about Neely Sharpe – she had the name from the police, that was all they had given – as her fingernail traced faint graffiti on the windows of her kitchen, leaving trails in the winter condensation. She thought about what any girl could ever want with her sister, and she drew a blank. She drew a snowman with sticks for arms. She drew a cat's face. She signed it, *&E*, and felt about twelve years old. Twelve was OK. Thirteen, she was passing around the two-litre bottle of White Lightning in the nature reserve off the canal path. Fourteen, got a taste for store-brand vodka instead. Fifteen, her own Inevitable happened, the details lost to the ages thanks to having had a good dose of that store-brand vodka in her at the time and, besides, she hadn't had time to dwell on it because her little sister had been rushed to St Mary's for the first time, shaking like the washer on a turbo spin cycle, and then she wouldn't wake up. Small matters of what inevitably happened to girls on the Kensal Town Estate when they got too drunk and too stupid around the boys paled in comparison to that pale little girl in St Mary's, dosed up on enough diazepam to put down a pit bull, making her dad cry and her mum curse the whole city.

Andy made her second cup of tea and moved into the front room under the watchful eyes of photographs: of herself, young and morose; of Angela; of Alex. She pulled back the curtain to watch the road and all those moving through it as if nothing had happened, because to the rest of West London – of course – nothing had. WASH ME IM BEGGIN U, a bored local child had rubbed into the grey grime on a white van's side panel. I WISH MY WIFE WAS THIS DIRTY, another finger had added. RICHARD PARKS IS A NONCE 145 BRADFIELD ROAD GO STRING HIM UP sat underneath it, and a crude figure of a cock and balls. She'd done that kind of thing herself when she was little, and worse. Far worse. That's what kids in Kensal Town did, and she had been a kid in Kensal Town, with her pink jelly shoes and her clip-on navel piercing, with her tight crop tops and baggy combat trousers, with her dying mother and her frightening sister, with a cheek-busting grin on her face when, after another rumour about what Andy Archer would do with any boy who wanted had spread up and down the corridors at school, she finally pinned down that nasty Kerry-Anne Reynolds and snapped off each and every one of her acrylic nails at the root.

She'd been a kid in Kensal Town, but then she had grown up and waited for her sister to do the same. But the girl had only gone around the corner and up the road, and now God knows where, which was worse than the nowhere fast she'd been headed for years. All those years Andy had tried, in her tiny way, to be an example for her little sister – proof that you could leave home and meet somebody decent and start having kids when you were ready for it with a man who was actually going to stick with you – and for what? So that Angela could hang around on the same roads and the same corners in the same shit pubs, being looked down upon by the same wasters. Andy had been rough back then, sure, but no more than anybody else, and certainly not the type who knew people who got murdered, at least not without a good reason. She felt too old to be taking on the identity of someone who did.

Andy shook her head even though nobody had asked a question. *Everything good that's ever happened to you has been because you got up off your arse and went looking for what you wanted, Andy girl.* She'd got that flat when she was pregnant. She'd spoken to that crooked-smiled Scotsman in the pub on Bonfire Night, and she'd said yes a year later when he gave her the ring still on her finger today in Southall Broadway. Back in Hazelwood Crescent, Kensal Town, mouths had always snapped shut when she passed, but then as soon as she passed, they got right back to whispering that Andy Archer had put more cocks in her mouth than hot meals and, judging by the size of her arse, she wasn't exactly starving. She still cringed at the memory, even if nobody could see her.

But she'd left. She'd got off that arse and left. And now, finally, Angela had left, too. Something else she knew from a childhood in Kensal Town is that when the universe breeds unfairness, decent sorts of human beings do their best to lighten the load. People who were a bit strange got a free pass to do their own thing. Expectations, even the already-low ones found in and around Kensal Town, had fallen with every fit Andy's sister had. Epileptic Angela and that funny boy she sometimes hung out with, a stick insect of a kid with some genetic disease – they had been the special ones. A little kindness, local people had called it when they ignored the petty mischief that sent them moaning in the case of every other kid on the estate. A bit of a break, they said with shrugs as they ignored loud music late into the night and clothes they clearly couldn't afford, and pretended not to see the alcohol waved in front of their faces. Andy had called it a fucking insult to Angela's intelligence. Mrs Archer had told her to shut her mouth. Her father had turned up the TV. She couldn't remember where their brother had been.

That strange boy was probably dead by now, another bit of history forgotten. And now Angela was dead, too. And who'd made her that way? Who had washed her from West London like she had meant less than brick or stone? She shut her eyes and ran through the old names and faces, a litany of half-remembered features. There were two other boys, a white one and an Asian one, their names long-lost, who Andy remembered in the blood from their burst noses after she had convinced Angela to admit who had done the Inevitable to her. Andy had enjoyed giving those two their comeuppance, and astounded herself with the sheer power of her bare fists to crack bone: *You even look in my sister's direction and I'll make it so you'll never fuck anybody again.* Another boy with a broken nose that wasn't Andy's fault; his sister, the pretty one, had been Angela's friend until one day she wasn't, because that was just the way girls were at that age, with their casual cruelties. But Angela had always been smiling, and that was at least part of the reason why people thought she was stupid on top of epileptic. What could someone like her have had to smile about? Andy cycled through the old estate in her head, going flat by flat, building by building, filling rooms with memories of who had lived there, until she realised it would be easier to list everybody who *wouldn't* have a conceivable reason to want to hurt Angela. Even with all the girl had gone through, who wouldn't have been viciously, absolutely *murderously* jealous of her joy?

Don't make me go back there. She traced the letters on the piece of paper the police had given her, an unfamiliar name in a far too familiar street. *Whoever you are, Neely Sharpe, and Angela too – don't make me go back home.*

Eleven

Neely Sharpe, alone at home in the Harrow Road, pulled open her window blinds from her bed. Unexpected sunshine hit her directly in the pupils and bored through all the way to the back of her skull.

'Fuck off,' she growled.

The sun did not fuck off.

She swore again.

Slept.

The phone buzzed. She had put it on silent so that she wouldn't have to hear the chimes of everybody's text message Christmas wishes bouncing into her mailbox. Mass-mailings, impersonal, sent without recognition that she, Neely Sharpe, was the girlfriend of Angela Archer, the photocopied face who would stare out at far fewer passers-by on the roads of West London today.

The phone buzzed. Again.

She picked it up, read the first line.

Wishing you a very happy Christmas and the best of

She turned it off. Flung it at the wall.

It didn't even break.

It didn't even make sense.

A double issue of the *Radio Times* on the floor by her bed, their bed. Bought when it was their bed, not just her bed. Fuck all on telly today besides the Queen's speech and *Doctor Who*.

Fuck fiction.

Back to sleep.

She woke up and she was not hungry. Went to the toilet. Stared in the mirror. Opened the cabinet behind it. Bottles and palettes and tubes that would never be used again. She unscrewed a lipstick, sniffed it. Not her colour. Chucked it. One Miracle Matte foundation in alabaster: straight into the bin. Angela would never skimp on her breakfast cereal but she wore make-up made for teenagers, makeup that turned her orange when without it she was porcelain, she was perfect. Stuff Neely quit buying as soon as she could afford better. Bin. The pale, candy-pink blush that neither Neely nor any Sharpe woman born would ever have worn: bin. It was then that the tears came, as they so often came now – over the waste. Total up the retail price of all that make-up, and it was such a waste. Bloody waste of good hard cash. Angela could have done something with that money. Put it in the bank. Saved it for a holiday. Because Angela thought she'd live to have a holiday next year. Of course she did. It's not something a normal twenty-four-year-old consciously considers: will I still be shuffling around this mortal coil nine months from now, when I fancy a week in Spain?

She glared at the brimming bin through brimming eyes, hating it and hating herself for having the capacity to hate inanimate objects, especially one which had served her so dutifully. And with these holidays the binmen wouldn't be around for days.

It was so much easier to be angry at a bin than at a murderer she didn't know. She couldn't draw a face, a body, anything in her mind. Neely had cried for her powerlessness the day before, cried at Harrow Road Police Station thinking someone would tell her something. All she had got was a pamphlet for grief counselling, which she had promptly dropped from her shaking hand at Elgin Avenue, where a gust of wind carried it down the road, away from the city. So today she cried in her home.

Everything she had ever studied, everything she had ever read, in the years before she could have ever expected it to be anything more than fiction, had told her that when people were murdered, it was usually by someone they knew. Sure, it always made the news when someone got dragged from a car park by a complete stranger, of course it did, because that was just so bloody rare in the first place. But for Neely to be rational, she had to remind herself of the gaping blank she drew at the first questions. Who did Angela even know? Angela knew her. She knew Sam, through her. And then she knew Melanie at the pub, and she knew Rob and his girlfriend, and she knew countless others just to smile at and say hello, people whose names Neely had never bothered to ask. *You should have let me know who you were, Angela. I should have asked. You would have answered.*

She opened the wardrobe door. Closed it. Opened it again and seized Angela's green wellies, the ones she had always told Angela to chuck out: *They're absolutely stinking, Angela. What's wrong with them? Just get new ones. Throw them in the bin.* But Angela never had, so now Neely did. Threw them away, along with the trainers Angela hadn't worn since the summer day she'd spoiled them in a puddle. Her girlfriend hadn't been able to keep her damn feet dry. But neither of them needed to worry about that now.

Into the kitchen. Filled the kettle. Poured it out. Went for the wine instead, the last bottle, a red she'd been saving. After all, it *was* Christmas, still. She drank a glass. And she thought: who will love you, Neely Sharpe? People like you don't just settle for whoever will put up with you and marry when the clock hits late-thirties-o'clock. People are lucky if they have one person in their life, one person in their entire damn life, who cares enough to love them. You've had yours. And now she's gone. And the odds of you having another are very, very fucking dire indeed. And anytime soon? Zero. Not even the tiniest fraction. You're alone and that's that and like everything else in your life other than deciding on what to do with this fucking kettle, there's absolutely nothing you can do about it.

She drank some more and she thought some more: what are you going to do, try the internet? Paste up a profile, throw it onto some virtual wall and see what wants to stick its fluids onto yours? Each one an interview. Imagine it: *So, what happened with your last relationship?* Funny, that. Well, remember that girl in West London they found strangled with her head bashed in beside the canal? That was my last relationship. Now tell me about *your* last bitch. Whatever horrible, unforgivable thing she did to you, she didn't die.

She drank some more so that she didn't have to think as much.

She stopped thinking and moved into the lounge. Turned on the electric fire. Turned it off. Waste of money. Only one income coming in here now. She'd have to move out. This was London; the landlord would find somebody blissfully oblivious to the story of the previous tenant, or maybe just double the rent and jam in a desperate extended family who knew little English and even less of their rights, plus all the housing benefit they could muster. And they'd take it, and they'd like it, and they'd feel lucky, because this is London, Neely thought. Lucky was being alive and being here and not there, and not being Angela Archer. Girls who may have been loved, but not loved enough. Because if somebody had really loved them enough, they wouldn't have ended up on the slab, would they? And so Neely knew she would continue to avert her eyes on the Harrow Road, to pretend she was the only person on the number 18 bus, to pointlessly try to convince herself that she wasn't as much a symbol to her neighbours as the veiled and draped foreign women were to her.

The phone again. She picked it up from the floor and leaned against the wall to read another group text of Christmas wishes. Slowly, she slumped down the wall until her arse hit the carpet. She deleted each message from her phone, and she lazily dropped it, letting it rest where it fell. Soon her eyes followed suit, and Neely returned to another hour of mercifully dreamless sleep.

She turned on her laptop. Couldn't turn it off so fast. Neely's eyes, crusts of sleep still crystallising in the corners, glazed over. The flat across the road was dark today. Funny, she didn't think they'd be the kind to celebrate Christmas. Didn't matter. Not her business. Back in the bedroom where she'd left it on the floor, her phone buzzed angrily against the skirting board. Neely didn't want to go fetch it, she didn't want to stand or move or leave this room ever again, but the computer was slow to boot.

Hey babes. Hope you're holding up. Here for you always if you need an ear. Sorry for everything. xxRuby. Actually, you're not sorry, Neely thought. And if you were, you'd only want to blog about it. A few flowery words about the tears in my eyes, about a silent dignity we both know doesn't exist. Fuck Ruby. Nobody was happier, nobody was secretly happier, to see Neely going dim. She knew that. How easy for Ruby, out in the Cotswolds and probably going for a walk after Christmas dinner with her new girlfriend and all their money and all their joy, to stab out a few words in a text.

The computer was ready. She clumsily double-clicked the web

browser, getting it right on the fourth and fifth tries. *That's the great thing about the internet*, she thought. *It doesn't close on holidays, it doesn't even observe Sunday trading hours.* There was infinite information out there, permanent insurance against boredom. She could read anything, learn anything. That's how she learned about corpses on Everest, and about an entire network of women making websites devoted to their stillbirths, and about all these white people who did yoga and wore turbans and changed their names and called themselves Sikhs. She wanted to learn, so she went forth and she figured it out, because that's what people did to become Brighter Than Most. Yet now, of all there was in cyberspace, that text message made her want to visit one site alone. She knew she shouldn't. Tried to convince herself to stay away, and that's when she knew she had already lost the battle with temptation. *Don't look, don't fucking look, nothing good will come of it, you'll only make yourself miserable, don't look. Don't be stupid. Jesus Christ, Neely, don't be an idiot.*

She clicked on the address bar and typed in those familiar letters from her ex-girlfriend. Oh, god. It wasn't even the photo from the posters, not the one specifically chosen for Angela's public face. Cow must have taken it off Neely's Facebook. She hated Ruby, but she had to admit the girl knew PR. This was an Angela who could slip in among the trendy types in Shoreditch, in Hoxton, in fucking Dalston, if she had wanted to. That trilby, those glossy burgundy nails daintily tilting her beer bottle to the camera. Neely's camera. And Christ, she was quick: *We at Ruby Bluesday are devastated to report that Angela Archer, missing from her home in West London since 19 December, has been found dead. Our thoughts are with her friends and family, who hoped for Angela's safe return before Christmas.*

Her home in West London.

Neely looked around Her Home in West London.

Angela had another home in West London. There was some of her there, for sure. But Neely had never made it past the front door, or the side window.

What more was there to search for? Happy families. They could have made one of them. It occurred to her, as she imagined proper families sitting down to their dinner in their proper houses on this day, that she herself had never made a proper Christmas dinner. She had done the veg before, parsnips and sprouts and that, doing her bit, but somebody else had always carried responsibility for the great big bird and the stuffing and whatnot. Cooking always felt like a good idea when she was down or drunk or both, and she needed a good idea. Something anodyne, unobjectionable; anything but unique to her on this day. She clicked the search bar and typed without much enthusiasm and even less urgency: *How to*

The internet, with its limitless knowledge, pulled up her past searches, naively assuming Neely would want to re-read what she had already learned. Silly, really. Neely learned things properly the first time. She was just like that.

How to make a cosmopolitan
How to make a lemon soufflé
How to make a paper plane
How to make it through London sewers

For the first time since she had stared into the sun this morning, Neely sat bolt upright. She hadn't searched for that. She couldn't have searched for that. Not even while drunk. She had no business in sewers and no desire to wade through any more shit than absolutely necessary.

She started the cascade of thoughts. The possibilities. Neely was good at thinking of possibilities, no matter how improbable. So she thought: maybe it's not an auto-complete, well, it is, but not one of *my* auto-completes, like the others; maybe the computer just pulled it up because that's what everybody else in the world is searching for and because this is the internet they can know those things. Maybe it's clickbait, and the government really is watching, thinking terrorists are going to bomb the hell out of toilets, but you get nicked only if you trip the wire of clicking on that link. Maybe one of the nights I was really drunk I turned on the computer and started typing random bollocks into Google just to see what would happen, because that sounds like something stupid I would do when I'm drunk. Maybe I'm seeing things and this isn't real and I'm dreaming. That's a good possibility. That's one I like. Maybe I'm dreaming.

'*Maybe you just shouldn't dream.*'

Neely knew she was not dreaming, but the memory of Angela's

voice giving her that suggestion suddenly seemed too real. As real as the search terms on her screen.

November. It had been the first really, truly, biting cold night of the season. She couldn't remember what she had been talking about. A complaint, surely. A complaint about her life and its disappointments.

'Maybe you just shouldn't dream.'

Neely had sat upright. 'What?'

'Not just you. In general.' Angela had played with her hair, wrapping the ends of curls around her slender fingertips. 'Maybe we put too much, y'know, what's it called. Importance? Nah. Emphasis. Too much emphasis on having dreams.'

'Don't be silly.'

'I'm not being silly, Neely. I mean it. Think about it. From the time you're little, from the time you're in school, you get told to have dreams. Not just any dreams, but really big ones. "I want to be a pop star." "I want to be Prime Minister." "I want to be a footballer." We think it's normal to do that to kids, that we're helping them and all. We're not. It's cruel, it's really fucking cruel. Adults get children's hopes up, making them believe they can do anything so long as they work hard. But they should know better, yeah? Why not tell them to have normal dreams? And be OK with that? Dream that you're going to meet somebody who doesn't knock you around. Become an estate agent. A bank manager. Own a shop. Something like that.'

'That's not normal to me, that's not enough. You have to aim for bigger.'

'Cos you think you're special, Neely Sharpe.'

'I don't think I'm special.'

'Of course you do. Everybody thinks they're special.'

'It was just, a lot was expected of me. I was the swot at school. I was supposed to go off and do big things.'

'And people like me were supposed to do small things. You were the type who could dream of setting the world on fire, yeah?'

'I didn't say that.'

'Well, you assumed you'd do bigger things than people who weren't so clever. And you are. You make more money than me.'

Neely had snorted. 'That's not an accomplishment. It's just money.'

'Neely, the only people who say "it's just money" are people who have never had to worry about money. I can guarantee that. I will gladly chop off my right tit if you can find me one person on any of these estates who thinks money is no big deal.'

Neely had ignored her. Not intentionally. She simply had momentum and it couldn't be stopped without an almighty crash and inevitable casualties. 'Things were just supposed to happen because I was clever, I am clever. I think I'm clever, unless my brain's atrophying from disuse. And things haven't fucking happened and I'm tired of waiting.'

'You're still young.'

'I'm twenty-six.'

'That's young.'

'Not getting any younger.'

'Everybody else is getting older the same as you.'

'And whatever it is they're doing right, I'm not.'

Angela sighed. 'Well then, maybe... nah.'

'What is it?'

'Nothing, I dunno.'

'No, what is it? Say it.'

'Maybe you just shouldn't dream. That's all.'

'I've got nothing if I don't dream. I don't have reality, that's for fucking certain.'

Angela had looked at her with clear, earnest green eyes. 'You've got me.'

And Neely hadn't the heart to tell her that wasn't enough. Back then, it wasn't. And now it was too much.

Twelve

Christmas Day became Boxing Day became the bridge to New Year's Eve. Time heals all wounds, Neely heard from her brother, her father, her mother, all imploring her to return to a home she had quit calling such several years previous. And each time, that lie tore them right open again. The 29th, 30th, 31st, she woke up and the life that was could no longer be. The life that had once lain there beside her as she rubbed the sleep from her eyes and stretched awake her stiff limbs had gone, departed, passed away, slid on its shoes and coat and hat and slipped out the door silently, making sure to turn out the lights and lock the door while she was dozing. It had left her on good terms, but it still had left.

The first of the year, the second, the third. All that Neely could think was that Angela had been twenty-four and dead and gone and she'd done nothing and had been nothing and if Neely followed the dead girl tomorrow then she'd be nothing, too. Just as much a nobody, only with the fun addition of student debt to strike off. Maybe Angela had loved her, needed her, but those precious achievements had vanished along with Angela's life.

Sometimes she would look at the empty spot beside her in the bed and see in her future the same shapeless space. Time stretched out before her just as it always had and, as she watched the world news on constant loop from the well-worn pocket of her sofa, she saw a world expanding and leaving her behind, tinier than ever. As the world and the city continued rolling along just fine without Angela, without Neely leaving the flat, she could only think about how twenty-seven was no longer so young, having moved from the gifted child to the promising adolescent to the excellent student to the office manager to the Harrow Road, where she felt poor and foreign, and the fact that she was really neither poor nor foreign yet still on the Harrow Road made her a failure.

Here you are, Neely Sharpe, she thought. *In bed, off work, with nothing to do with yourself other than fail. Failing at mopping up Angela's existence, and your own.* She did not know what she did not know about how to deal with the remains of a life.

The police came to collect her computer on the third. Routine procedure, they said. If Angela used it, then they needed to have a peek. Having been briefed that *this one probably watches too many cop dramas on TV,* they had assured Neely she wasn't a suspect, it was all simply routine, as if murders happened in the borough on a daily basis. They had called her in for an interview, too, apparently not having received the memo that she was useless at them. *You're not a suspect, this is just routine procedure, we just need to hear you say the last things you saw Angela doing.*

Naturally, she had figured it was a lie, and through a flurry of nerves had proceeded to tell nothing about Angela and everything about herself: where she'd been, what she remembered drinking. *I just want to sleep. And all I do now is sleep. Who the fuck would want to kill my girlfriend? I just need to sleep.* The two detectives had exchanged sympathetic looks and turned off the voice recorder after Neely asked if it was true that they got sacked if they sneezed on DNA, and told her the liaison would let her know any news.

On the fourth day of the new year, she ran out of milk. Neely tossed the plastic into the recycling bin without bothering to rinse. *At least Harrow Road's got everything I need,* she thought. *I can stay in this little strip of street between junctions forever if I like. Costcutter, right there at the corner. Everything I need.*

She plucked an assortment of coins from the mess of loose change on the windowsill and stuffed them into her pocket. It was still colder than it had any right to be, even for the end of December. She wound her scarf twice around her nose and pulled her hat as low as it would go, as low as it could go with the knob of her ponytail poking out the back. There in the closet, Angela's coats: all but the long, black, wool one. Neely's coat: short, puffy, making her look likewise. She descended the stairs blindly; the landlord, away for the holidays, still hadn't replaced the corridor light bulb, and Neely's eyes welled up when she thought of missing shoes, red, size six. Souvenirs from a life, and she couldn't even claim them. When she reached the Costcutter on the corner,

Neely lowered her eyes and kept walking. She turned right, over the canal, under the Westway, to Westbourne Park Station.

'Come in.'

Neely walked into the flat. She didn't know why she expected it to look different. Same mess, same piles of pillows scattered on the floor. The miniature cactus in the window stood proudly in its little pot of pebbles. Defiant, even. Close to an hour on a bus and the Tube had sufficiently dried her eyes.

'You holding up alright, Neels?'

'Yeah. Surprising myself.'

'Any word on the inquest?'

'Nothing whatsoever.'

Sam sighed. 'Yeah, well, there wouldn't be, would there? I'm not going to go anyway. Pointless, innit.'

He had that choice. Neely would be called as a witness. She'd have to hear all the details, everything she had already educated herself to anticipate. Hours spent on Google searches, going from one click to another, learning what would happen and what she would need to do. Because she had needed to know. Because Neely Sharpe was still brighter than most.

'I called her dad. They don't know when they can have the funeral.'

'It doesn't matter.'

She shrugged. 'It does to me.' And she watched the man stare at the wall opposite, bare but for that Underground map.

'You're looking alright, Sam.'

'Trying.'

Neely peered into the kitchen. The banana hanger had two pieces of fruit on it, heavily speckled brown. Sam continued. 'Holding it together. Thinking Angela wouldn't want me to sit around feeling bad. She'd give me a smack and tell me to sort myself out. Make something good come of all of it.'

'Mmmm. Yeah.'

'I'd like to think she'd be telling me, Sam, this is your wake-up call. No more messing. Quit being an idiot, sort yourself out, make a better life.'

'That was Angela. Knew how to fix people, she did.' Neely plopped down onto the familiar brown couch.

Sam stretched his arms above his head, his old shirt riding up over the smallest suggestion of a gut. 'Yeah. Gonna make a change. Cut down on the booze and that.'

'All clean living from now on?'

He smiled and sat beside her. 'A couple of laps round the Downs every morning, y'know. It'll do me some good.'

'I look forward to seeing you in a sweatband and sex-attacker shorts.' She caught herself and thought of apologising, then didn't bother. Sam didn't notice.

'Neely.' The statement, not the question.

'What?'

'Neely Sharpe.'

'WHAT?'

'I'm just saying your name. I like your name.'

'Sam Wylie. What's up?'

'If there's gonna be an inquest then I should tell you something first.'

'Hmm?' She sat up straight and looked at Sam, who sunk, loose-limbed, into the couch cushions. *How old is he, anyway?* she thought. *Older than me, yeah, but how much?* She thought he suddenly looked curiously young, his eyelids at half mast, his face suffused with a rare sadness.

'Me and Angela.'

'I know, Sam, I know.'

He looked away. 'Nah. You don't.'

'You what?'

At that moment Sam became very fascinated with a bit of dirt underneath his thumbnail. 'Angela told you she wanted to have a kid one day, right?'

Neely bit her lip. There was no use passing along pub gossip. 'Sort of. Eventually. Abstractly, that's all. Once she got herself all sorted out. No real plans. She'd have been a great mum someday.'

'But she wanted to have a kid.'

'I *know*. So what?'

'She would have needed a man for that.'

Neely raised an eyebrow. 'You offered, then? You said you would be the baby's father?'

He nodded.

'Oh god, Sam. I'm sorry.'

'No. You don't get it. I was *going to be* the baby's father. Angela and I... Angela was pregnant, Neels.'

Two faces in the pub flashed back at her. 'No she wasn't.'

'She was.'

'*No she fucking wasn't.* Don't be an idiot. We lived together. She was my girlfriend. If anybody was going to know she was getting it on with a turkey baster, it would have been me.'

Sam lost interest in his fingernails and stared Neely in the eyes. 'She told me. She came over and said she'd done two of the little test things, how all you do is piss on it and it either says you're pregnant or you're not. And she said she was. She really was, Neels. It'll come out in the inquest.'

'Shut up, Sam. She would have told me.'

'It's true. I'm not going to lie to you. I'm not some cunt like that, Neels. Angela was pregnant. She wasn't far gone.'

'How far?'

'Not too far.'

'Fuck you, Sam. Give me a number. When did you fuck her?'

'Two months before she disappeared,' he whispered. 'Exactly. I knew it was the eighteenth of October. The night we all went to the Dolphin.'

'The night we came back here and I crashed out with the kebab on my face?'

Sam nodded.

'You fucked Angela right here while I was sleeping?'

Another nod.

'And she got pregnant?'

'She came around and told me...'

'*When?*'

'Day before she disappeared.'

'Day before I was here and you couldn't get it up?'

'Neels.'

177

It wasn't a question, so she didn't answer. Instead, an answer began to form inside her head, all fragments and scraps, a half-baked idea slowly congealing. *Sam? He loves that Sophia. He won't shut up about that Sophia. He wants a child with her, not with a woman who doesn't love him and can't love him, can't love any man, because that's not who she is. And he's in no state to be a father. He's in no state to run a fish bowl.* Then she thought of her hours lost, those hours between the bars and clubs and their stumbles through Hackney and the moment she woke up on the sofa. Her memory of that time was gone, never even recorded, impossible to recover. But Sam, no, Sam could tank it down with no problem at all. Hours were long enough to get to West London and back and need no more than a couple of his morning cans to steady his nerves. He would have known Neely would be out cold and accounted for in his flat. Plenty of time to wreck her life however he wanted. And he knew her well enough to know exactly how to do just that.

Fuck. No. Sam, maybe nine stone soaking wet? The only other person outside Angela's childhood orbit, the only other One Who Came into her life instead of the Ones Who Stayed? *Fuck. No.* And he could lie for England and give up nothing. That's how alcoholics were, Neely knew. They had their own reality, their own facts. It was never them who were wrong. Always someone else.

'Neels, why are you looking at me like that?'

She said nothing. Stared.

'Neels, come on. I'm being honest. I told you.'

Fuck. Him.

'Neels, you've no right to be angry…'

The fragments shattered. 'I've got every right, and why the *fuck* has everybody been treating me like I'm stupid? Has there been a neon sign flashing RETARD above my head that everybody else can see but I'm too thick to notice? Because I'm sick of this, I'm sick of you and everybody being so… condescending and patronising. Like I need some kind of pity, like I'm not right in my head.'

'You mean exactly the way you treated Angela? Like a sad little feeble charity case. Some poor little mong you could come along and fix and feel good about because your fucking life hasn't acknowledged you as the genius you're *so* convinced you are. Hey, if you can't be famous, why not be the savior of the white working class? That's your plan B? What did you like more about her, that she was messed up or that she was poor?'

'Fuck you. I did *not* treat her like an idiot. I never did one horrible thing to her. I fucking *loved* her. I treated her the way I wanted to be treated.'

'Sure you did. Maybe she didn't want to be treated like you wanted, she wanted to be treated like *she* wanted. Jesus Christ! God forbid my friend be happy for me. God forbid my friend be happy for *Angela*. I don't recall *you* ever having a problem with shagging me and now you're all high and mighty because she did the same?'

'It's always about how I'm not happy enough for *you*, Sam. I don't exist to give you fucking applause every time you wipe your arse on your own.'

'Well, Angela's dead and so is my baby. My kid died with her. So excuse me if my world's not going to revolve around you.'

'I never asked it to!'

'You think you're the only person who's ever been wronged, Neely. And you're so full of shit.' He was crying now, or as close to crying as he could get; the tears hadn't spilled over the rims of his eyelids yet, but they were threatening to burst over the dams of his lashes. 'Even Angela knew it. She couldn't stand how you had so much more than she did, you have such a good life, and still you were always complaining about the world being unfair to you. If she never said it to you it's only because she was a fucking saint. So maybe she wanted to have a little fun, too. She wanted something of her own and she wanted to fuck things up for herself like anybody else. Like anybody *normal*. So I gave it to her. Yeah, I did, alright? You're so, *so* full of shit. Saying you care about everybody else, then you go whining about how you're a victim. You're always the victim. You're full of shit. You're all talk. I don't love you and I'm not going to marry you so why do you even care?'

'What did you to do her, Sam?'

'Are you fucking deaf?'

'No, I mean *what did you do to her?* What the fuck happened?'

'Oh, piss off, Neels. You're mental.'

'I don't have to listen to your bullshit,' she hissed, and snatched her handbag. 'Grow up and don't talk to me again until you've fucking sorted yourself out. Because God knows you need sorting out. And don't ever, *ever* have a kid.'

'You're all talk,' he repeated, shouting this time, as Neely slammed the door behind her. 'You're all talk!' And she waited there, just outside the threshold, as she had plenty of times before. And then she heard him sobbing.

Thirteen

Her own tears had long dried by the time Neely arrived back in Harrow Road, but her vision let her down. Everywhere she looked seemed tinged with fuzz, as if someone had, in a ham-fisted attempt at art, left everything just the slightest bit out of focus. *It might be him, it might be him,* she repeated silently in her head. *Maybe he's not what you think. Maybe he never was.*

She knew the woman the instant she came around the bend to her flat. It had to be Andy Archer standing in front of the door. It wasn't so much a physical resemblance – a wedge of auburn fringe cloaking her eyes, mumsy shoes, the kind of sturdiness born of taking enough hits that it eventually requires a steamroller over the toes to elicit a flinch; none of these things brought Angela to mind – but rather the self-possession, the silent ownership of the small corner of the world where she stood. Andy fitted into the pavement outside 490 Harrow Road because she belonged to this world, she had come from its very fabric, and she had slid back into it as easily as a pair of cotton socks.

She looked angry, Neely thought. Not angry at somebody, or something in particular, but simply as a default setting, perhaps something she lost the ability to shut off long ago, like a primordial reflex or a vestigial tail. She looked like she had been angry for a very long time without knowing exactly why, and now she was about to pick a reason.

Instinctively, Neely tensed. She figured that reason would probably be herself.

So she quit any attempt to play it cool, and stammered as she took in the image in front of her: tall like her sister, but in bolder colours, as if the suggestion of blending into the background would be a personal insult. And this woman probably never, ever laughed that laugh.

'Andrea?'

A tilt of the head, eyes peering out from under the hair. 'Andy. Neely, yeah? I should have rung but I didn't have your number.'

'I saw you, at the – '

'I just needed to come here. I need to see her home. I want – I want to bring back her stuff to my dad.' The words shot out as if they had been precisely timed, carefully rehearsed, because any failure would be too much to bear.

'Y-yeah. It's good that – it's good you're here. I, erm, here, come in.' Neely had never felt less like the urbane, detached Londoner she dreamed she would become; now she was back in the changing rooms at Fenlands Comprehensive, stumbling out of her PE kit with a smear of blue ink up her thigh. Her key slid into the front door lock on the third try, and she stumbled over the pile of post. She thought she heard Andy sigh as she pulled her phone out of her handbag to light the way up the stairs, and Neely winced: like university interviews all over again. It was how she had ruined the one she had at Cambridge – set the wrong tone at the start, came over all flustered, even forgot to shake his hand at the end. Blown completely. But that was different. She hadn't *really* wanted to go to Cambridge. She had wanted London and she had got London and she had told herself, no regrets, whether you want them or not.

'I'm sorry it's not very tidy,' Neely spluttered as she opened the door to her flat. 'How do you like your tea?'

Andy paused, scanning the walls, the floor, the bookshelves with the hi-fi and one peculiarly empty length of space. 'Same as Angela.'

It was a test, but Neely had never failed one of those. Milk, one sugar.

'Is this place just a one-bedroom?'

'Yeah.'

'Where do you sleep?'

Neely decided they could both take it, and she looked Andy in the eye. 'With your sister.' *Well, I used to,* she thought, too late.

Andy's face registered no shock and no surprise, and no humour, either. Instead, she slipped her handbag's strap off her shoulder and squinted to examine the small stack of magazines on the table beside the sofa. 'I figured. I guessed. She never said she had a girlfriend.' Neely, twisting the cap off the plastic carton of milk, tried not to recoil at the thought of not existing, even as only some abstract idea, in the minds of the other people her girlfriend loved. 'But she did mention you. Not by name. She just said she had a flatmate, and that you got on well, and that you were nice. It's the way she said it. *Nice.*'

'Well, she told me a little about you, too. And your brother and your dad.'

'Look, I know – knew – she's a lesbian. I don't care, I'm not some knuckle-dragger, I'm not some bigot. I don't think it's wrong or disgusting or anything. Me, our dad, we're not that kind of people. I just put two and two together.' Even in defence, Andy sounded like she was itching for a fight.

The spoon clinked against the porcelain mugs as Neely stirred in the sugar. She thought, but not very seriously, about just blurting it out: *I've got this theory and he lives in Hackney and he says he got her pregnant.* No, not now. It wasn't worth it. She had to be more careful than that. She had to be sure of something.

She walked slowly from the kitchenette toward where Andy had taken her seat by the lounge window. 'We met at her work,' Neely said quietly. 'And we got on really well. It was amazing. Like I had known her for ages.'

'But you didn't, though,' Andy said quietly, almost to herself, blowing on the tea and taking a tentative sip. Neely saw her squinting to read the titles on the spines of books on shelves across the opposite wall, and finally Andy stood up and crossed the room, hot mug in hand. Silently, she perused the titles, seeming to recognise none. 'Are all these yours?'

'Yeah.'

Neely tried not to stare, but she thought she noticed a softening of Andy's face. She wasn't entirely sure what she expected out of Andrea Ormiston, but she was surprised to not feel at least a bit of heat radiating off the woman from all her bottled-up anger, all the energy that must have fuelled her up the Harrow Road and into this flat. That anger seemed to have quickly dissipated with only a few sips of tea, and Neely knew her brews weren't anything special. The sublimation puzzled her. Neely didn't like mysteries, or at least she didn't like dealing with them if it felt like it might be possible to find a simple scientific explanation with only a little bit of thought.

'Did my sister read any of these?'

'Not really. I mean – not all the way through. She started a few of them but I think she got bored.'

Andy nodded. 'Sounds like Angela.'

'She liked a lot of my records, though,' Neely added, quietly, but Andrea didn't seem to hear. Silence reigned as the older woman continued to scan over her books, and Neely sensed it then for sure: the facade was not just crumbling, but flat-out falling off the front of the building, giving all passers-by a good look in at everything that she probably had bloody good reasons for keeping behind brick walls and locked doors. Angela's last home: a place with books and a girl who read them. A girl with bones like a bird, built like a child. That had been enough to capture Angela, to keep her on a dead-end life in a wide-laned street, this tiny hell disguised as West London, disguised as home. Andy bit her lip and flicked her side-swept fringe back into her eyes. Neely knew that look, the burning concentration on the tea sloshing in her mug, on the toffee-penny colour and the faint wisps of steam. She'd worn it herself those final months at King's, with the writing on the wall and the roof caving in on the future she thought she had planned: *Keep it together. You're tougher than this. As long as you're not crying, you've not yet lost.*

Andy cried anyway, the hand holding her mug trembling violently as the effort to keep her tears inside shot though her body and spilt from her eyes. Neely sat her on the sofa and ran to the toilet for tissues. 'It's alright, it's alright,' she cooed over Andy, knowing full well that it wasn't, and wondering how her own face remained unstreaked.

Andy nodded, keeping her sadness quiet enough. She placed her tea on the empty shelf.

Neely held her hand, tentatively. 'What did the police tell you?' she whispered.

'They asked me,' Andy began, slowly chewing on her words through the tears, through the snot. 'They asked me whether Angela had any enemies.'

'Yeah?'

'And I couldn't tell them.' Andy's fingers shook as she stifled more tears, so she slid one hand into her coat and used the other to tug at her hair.

Neely looked at the floor. 'She didn't. She *doesn't*. Angela's just the greatest person. Everybody loves her.'

The fingers stopped their wandering; the other hand pulled free. The women met eyes: Neely's blank to Andy's red rimmed and suddenly incredulous.

'You what?' she sniffled.

'Nobody would ever hate Angela. Nobody would ever want to hurt her.'

This time, Andy scoffed.

'What?' Neely asked, reddening at the thought that even if she objectively wasn't stupid, somebody might get a different inclination. 'What?'

'Neely, everybody's... hate-able. To somebody. I mean, you seem nice and all, but I'm sure people give you trouble. Right?'

'Well, nobody was giving Angela trouble. She'd let me know if somebody was.'

'She never let *me* know, back when she was a kid. I had to figure it out for myself.'

Neely bit her lip. 'Was she bullied a lot?'

'What do you think?'

Neely hadn't thought much about it, and the realisation made a flush of shame shoot into her face. What she thought, right there on the couch, was that *damaged* was the last word she would use to describe Angela Archer. Bullied people became bullies or they became basket cases, and Angela was just so damn *normal*. So normal that, fits aside, she could have stepped out of a place like Stevenage. She sucked in her breath. 'All I know is that for as long as I've known her, she hasn't had trouble with anybody. At least not in front of me.'

'How long have you known her?'

'Bit over a year.'

Andy shrugged and rubbed at her eyes with the tissue. 'Maybe things got better. Maybe they didn't. But Angela's not a big talker – she wasn't – you know that. If anything was wrong, she would have swallowed it and got on with her life.'

'You haven't been around here much lately, have you?'

Andy laughed, startling herself with the volume. 'Not at all. I can't remember the last time I hit Harrow Road. What's here for me now?' She blew her nose for emphasis.

'Your sister.' Neely didn't mean to sound accusatory; it was the truth.

'She came to see me out in Southall. Or we met at Dad's out in Shepherd's Bush. She never told you, "Oh, alright, I'm just going to see my dad"?'

'Yeah, but it wasn't my business…'

Andy continued like she hadn't asked a question. 'People can move, that's the great thing. All the stuff that's stuck in place? I don't care about it. None of it's for me any more. Come on, it's not like the shopping's great, is it? Costcutter and Iceland and fried chicken?'

Neely tried to smile in sympathy, in tacit agreement. Andy was right. If people mattered, and people moved, then there was no point clinging to place. But then there was the small matter of when those people didn't move, or at least didn't move until a fortnight previously. She wasn't going to mention any babies. Not now, not here. Not when she herself still needed to get her head around the idea.

'So why do you think Angela stayed here? You left, your dad left, she was bullied, so why didn't she pack up and go?'

Andy shook her head and studied the inside of her now-empty mug. 'Don't think I haven't asked myself that fucking question every time I've thought about her for the past God-knows-how-many fucking years.' She shifted her attention to her nails and the tiny smear of children's finger-paint on one pinkie. 'But, yeah… I get it. When the cops were trying to make me think maybe she had just run away. That's a load of bollocks, yeah? Because if she's stayed here so long, through everything, all the shit, then why would she suddenly leave *now*?'

'She wouldn't.'

'You swear you two didn't have a row or nothing?'

'I swear. We didn't.'

Andy sniffled and rubbed her eyes. 'Show me around this place.'

'There's not much to see,' Neely mumbled, but collected Andy's empty mug and walked it to the kitchen, the woman behind her. A dozen Angelas still beamed from the refrigerator door.

'Fucksake.'

'Sorry?'

'She looks so *happy*.'

'She was.' Neely stared again at the photos, wondering if there should have been reason to doubt. 'Here, take them.'

'No. They're yours,' Andy said a little too quickly. Neely turned to slide past her and back out into the corridor, leading toward the bedroom. Andy stopped halfway and stared up at the framed photographic print hanging on the wall: the canal basin in monochrome, Browning's Pool full of narrowboats and ducks, just down the road. 'She ever tell you about that picture?'

'No. It was up when I moved in.'

'She tell you who took it?'

'No.'

'My dad,' Andy smiled ruefully. 'I've got the same one. Only it's above the toilet.'

'I've always really liked that picture,' Neely offered, not lying but not feeling too insistent with her truth.

Andy snorted. 'Well, there's plenty where that came from. Photography's my dad's thing. Other than drinking. Angela ever tell you what he does?'

'Yeah. Tube driver? She got the free travel and that?'

'He won't be for much longer, I'd put money on it. All I'm going to say is, stay off the Circle Line when he's on duty.' Andy reached toward the bedroom door uninvited, looking up at another framed photo – a parkland scene, smaller this time – on the door itself. 'I don't have that one.'

'Wormwood Scrubs,' Neely volunteered.

'Yeah, I *know* where it is.' Andy sighed. 'I've got about two hundred of his pictures back at my house, no joke. Stupid obsession of his, going over every moment of our lives as if it matters. I go, "Dad, seriously, nobody cares," and he goes, "But I do," and then there's me going, "Well, don't you think I should have a say when you're hanging up reminders of everything I'd rather forget?" Doesn't stop him and it never will.'

Neely's ears and every hair on her neck pricked up at Andy's tone, the gush of words about a life she didn't know, and she waited with anticipation of more of the story, but it didn't come. Instead, Andy turned the doorknob and let herself into the bedroom.

Neely watched Andy's face for a reaction: perhaps a wistful smile of recognition of messy childhood habits that never died. Instead, Andy scanned the small room slowly and deliberately. Her eyes slid from one wall to another, from mirror to wardrobe to bed, over stacks of books – Neely's – and pieces of post, around the discarded costume jewelry and stray make-up, a magazine on the floor and a pair of headphones dangling from a doorknob.

Andy spoke so quietly that Neely had to ask her to say it again. 'Can I take her things back home?'

'What? Oh. Yeah. Of course.' She waved at the wardrobe, trying not to look or sound as puzzled as she felt. 'All her clothes are in there. And everything on the left side of the closet. I – I've got some bags.'

'Cheers.' Kneeling in front of the wardrobe doors, Andy picked through a heap of fabric her sister had let fall, carelessly, with the knowledge that there would be time later to pick it up. It was the abundance born of a small disposable income and a world of disposable fashion: party tops worn twice, rough-feeling jeans that had bled out half their blue in one wash, skinny-rib vests that had to be layered for basic opacity.

'Oh my god,' Andy squeaked, holding aloft a red sequinned dress with a delicacy reserved for ancient texts and baby birds. 'I bought her this. For her birthday a couple years back.' Neely feigned familiarity. She'd seen Angela wearing it maybe twice. 'Bags?' Andy hinted.

Neely jumped. 'Yeah. Sorry.' She shot through to the kitchen and grabbed a handful of old plastic carrier bags from beneath the sink. Somerfield, Sainsbury's, blank black ones from the off-licence and the market, waiting their turn to line the bin. She returned to the bedroom – *Why the hell am I tiptoeing?* – ready to apologise for only having secondhand packaging, and cheap at that, for the remains of a life.

Andy had left the wardrobe and now stood in front of the bedside table. Neely froze. The woman was holding the book with the rainbow-stripe colours. She was turning pages, faster and faster. Neely couldn't be sure, but she thought she noticed a tremble in the hand holding it up.

'That's mine,' Neely blurted out, not even knowing why, not even knowing how she thought Andy would believe her. She crossed the room, pulled it from Andy's hands, more frantic than furious, shocking herself at the lack of resistance she encountered.

'What?'

'I said it's mine. Please don't read that. It's personal.' She stumbled slightly, stepping backwards.

Andy didn't seem to care. She didn't even register any recognition of Neely, in fact. Her face had frozen with a curious blankness and her hands hovered uselessly with nothing to hold any more.

'Andrea? Are you alright?' Neely finally piped up. 'I didn't mean to…'

'Look – I'm sorry. This was a mistake. This was a big fucking mistake. I need to go.'

'What?'

'I can't – I need to go.'

'Wait. Let me give you my phone number.'

'I'll give you mine.' Andy helped herself to a pen from the bedside table and scribbled on an errant receipt that Neely had left there days earlier, her numbers scrambling across the price of milk and yoghurts and a value pack of salt and vinegar crisps. 'If you need me, call me. Not my dad. He's gone to pieces. Just – I need to go.' She sprinted for the front door and tried the handle before even realising she needed to turn the lock. Footsteps clattered heavily down the stairs, followed by Neely's lighter ones in pursuit.

'Andrea!' she shouted uselessly down the Harrow Road, watching couples and crowds part for the woman without even seeing her first. Neely saw her dart into the street, paying no attention to the car horns and shouts registering their protest at her sudden presence. By the time Andy crossed to the Great Western Road, she had disappeared into the fabric of the city.

Fourteen

It felt wrong to want to laugh. It felt like it was going to feel wrong to laugh for a long, long time. Didn't matter if it was New Year, didn't matter if the entire world had woken up to promises of renewal and repair and hopes for a future full of joy. No, it felt wrong to even consider joy, to entertain the possibility of laughter. Neely decided to feel disgusted instead.

The police had made surprisingly quick work of her laptop. Nothing to see, and not even Angela's possession, so they had returned it in a matter of days. Neely pounced upon it like a long-lost friend and soon fell way down the Google rabbit hole, right into the wide world of mortuary make-up. It was all airbrush, she learned. Regular stuff didn't work because it was designed to melt a bit with body heat. And if the Archers went with a good place, they could probably cover up everything on Angela's neck. Maybe not perfectly, but well enough. At two in the morning she finally clicked shut the blog of an undertaker's assistant, helped herself to a nip of vodka, and failed to sleep. *It's OK*, she told herself. *There's nothing wrong with curiosity. You learned something today. And this is precisely what makes you brighter than most. You seek and you find.*

Now, today, to YouTube. *Huge monster cyst explosion*, she typed into the search box. Those weren't her own words. She was only their conduit, the messenger. A monkey could, and in a lab at this very moment probably already was being trained, to do this exact job. Somebody in America, somebody she didn't and would never know, had made a deliberate decision to film said explosion and upload it onto the internet for public consumption. OK, consumption is not the best word, Neely thought, remembering how her first viewing of the five-minute home video had put her off vanilla ice cream for ages. But the point was, somebody had made this and put it up here. It was supposed to be watched, for whatever reason. And, thought Neely, I have a reason. I need to get things out of my head, I need to get Angela's face – that last time I left her – out of my head, and watching this poor bastard get nasty, infected, cheesy things out of his back is a good enough means to that end.

She hit play. As the cameraman giggled, fuzzing the picture ever so slightly, a frumpy woman with a short, frizzy perm wiped down a tiny Stanley knife with alcohol. Neely lengthened those curls, turned back years on their owner, transported her from nowhere America to Harrow Road. Angela had been standing over Neely's shoulder, eager to watch this video that her girlfriend told her she really, really, really ought to see. And Neely remembered: *OH MY GOD NEELY WHAT ARE YOU DOING?* Angela had shot backward at the forty-second mark, when the no-nonsense blade-wielder made her first incision and got hit with the first liquid spurt. *JESUS CHRIST WHY ARE YOU WATCHING THIS?* Neely cackled: she knew the best, as in the worst, was yet to come. *FUCKSAKE I AM GOING TO BE SICK.*

'Angela! Come back, it gets really nasty, just when they think they're done…'

'That is the worst thing I have ever seen. The WORST. How does it get that bad? Wouldn't you do something about that when there's only, dunno, half a pint of gunge under your skin instead of waiting until there's a bucketload?'

Neely had nodded. 'My mum said that this is only the kind of thing you'd see in the States, or here, because everywhere else in the world they know better than to make problems for themselves. This is the end of civilisation, when you think about it. Pus on the internet.'

'Wait, you showed this to your mum?'

'Yeah. She's a nurse. She's seen it all. There was one man who came in for a circumcision, yeah, because the skin was so tight that he couldn't pull it back for a wash, and she said that when they tried to cut…'

'NO. DO NOT TELL ME ABOUT THIS. You'll put me off cocks even more than I already am.'

Neely and Angela had differed little in their opinion of the male member, even though the former was willing to accept its utilitarian purpose when it suited her. The two had agreed: it's just odd. Unpleasant. Strange colours, on white guys. Minds of their own, and not particularly clever ones. 'I don't care what the magazines say, them eating pineapple does *not* make spunk taste alright,' Neely had groaned, once drunk enough to broach the topic. Angela had shrugged.

'This girl at school, Genevieve – her parents were mad, religious maniacs – she had this problem, like, obsessive-compulsive style. She was scared to death of men's cocks. They gave her the fear. And it's not like she was molested or nothing. That's what she said to me. Swore nothing like that ever happened. She just couldn't stand to look at them. She's a nun now, last I heard.'

'It's alright for some,' Neely had said, and thought about whether people first feared and then hated, or the other way round.

Neely had never really made love to a man, never in the languid and tender way she had expected would happen sooner or later, once the boys mentally grew into men. She had only fucked and been fucked. Whatever violence was in it was never serious, just implicit stage-acting, playing the roles each expected the other wanted. Only Sam had ever asked her to outright state what she wanted him to do and, so long as he hadn't drunk too much, he usually fulfilled her wishes. She knew that she had to perform for a few minutes and then she'd get the sweet release, the collapse into sweaty bodies, a few minutes of closed-eyed cuddling when she would imagine whoever it was that she preferred to have lying beside her. Sometimes a man, sometimes a woman. Sometimes an open window would let in a breeze to lick the damp skin on her back.

She and Angela, they could never keep straight faces when they were in bed. Angela was usually the one to initiate, but then always let Neely lead. They worked well together, she knew, because they were the heart and the brain, and Neely didn't have to worry about being brighter than most. She just had to be as good as the other.

She hadn't the foggiest idea why these memories, the quotidian and the meaningless, were all she could pull to the front of her brain. The video ended. Neely began to cry, not for herself and not for her dead girlfriend, but for all the idiocy in the world and the people willing to publicly display it, all collected in one place.

That had been the day Neely stopped dreaming and began lying awake. The television helped. American police procedurals punctuated by *Jeremy Kyle* and assorted *Loose Women*. She waited for anybody to come and grant her murder the ceremony she'd expected would wash up on the doorstep of any killing: A cordon at the front door, walls blackening with fingerprint dust, carpets torn out beneath her, and maybe at least a few reporters setting up their cameras, convincing somebody else to care. But nobody came, and the news bulletins that she scattered throughout her daily viewing – the world here, the national there, and always the local – remained ignorant of Angela Archer, or perhaps simply uninterested. *Here, I'm letting you into my home. Come inside,* Neely silently pleaded to the clear faces and the clearer accents. *Show me something. Tell me anything. I swear, I'll listen. I'll believe you.*

She was making tea when one finally heeded her call. The sound of the name, cutting through the stale air of her flat, made Neely spill her cup.

'Police have released CCTV footage believed to be of Angela Archer, who was found dead off the towpath of the Grand Union Canal in West London on the 23rd of December. They are asking for the public's help in identifying the individual she is seen speaking to briefly –'

She blinked the glaze off her eyes as grainy black-and-white footage flashed onscreen. Time stamp that Friday night, half nine. She and Sam would have been two drinks into their evening; at that point, she had still felt in some semblance of control. The Costcutter sign glowed, and there in its haze was Angela, alive and vital and playing with her hair, stopping to speak with somebody. The recording's resolution was too poor for Neely to make out whether her lips were moving, whether her eyes were giving anything away. But it was definitely Angela, stepping side to side in her boots, stomping away the cold. Whoever she'd been talking to had his back to the camera – and from the angle, Neely thought it had to be the one above the cash machines in Elgin Avenue. *That's somebody who doesn't want to be seen,* Neely thought. *That's somebody who knows how to stay out of sight.*

Angela and the mystery man – and it had to be a man, that much Neely could see – leaned in for a hug. She thought she saw the brush of lips on a cheek, but it could have been a word in the ear, it could have been video fuzz. The two stepped apart, and Angela slinked off back toward the Harrow Road. Seconds later, the man followed her. The news froze the frame then, and zoomed in where Neely hadn't been looking. The person who had just let Angela go was lifting one hand to scratch at a broken nose.

The number for Crimestoppers popped onscreen, but Neely didn't need it. She had memorised the one for Harrow Road Police Station.

She rang. She waited. She didn't even bother to disguise her voice. 'He's called Robert Wedmore. I don't know where he lives, but I think I can tell you where he's sitting right now.'

Fifteen

'We can't put it off any longer, Dad.'

That wasn't true, and Andy knew it. They didn't need to plan the funeral right then and there because they didn't have a body. The police hadn't released it. But she couldn't sit in Southall with all those phone calls full of apology from people she had barely remembered existed, all those offers of shoulders to cry on, knowing that she hadn't tidied up loose ends for her sister one last time. She rang Kensal Green and reserved a date for the memorial service. They'd do cremation, just like with their mum. But they wouldn't bury her ashes there, just off the Harrow Road and the canal, no. Andy wasn't having that.

She'd been very good at tidying up, Andy. Usually messes she had created herself in the first place. When she was a kid she had been brilliant at forging signatures, whether from her mother or the headmistress, to make the smaller problems disappear. When anybody picked on Angela, she could make them scatter with her mere appearance. The bigger problems took a bit more convincing but Andy could handle it.

That time Angela had cut open her chin when she fell having a fit – Andy had cleaned that up, too. Oh, and Angela had been so terrified when she came round and saw the blood on the carpet, the dark red blots spattered on the beige deep-pile. Cried harder than she usually did, probably fearing this was it, her parents were going to lock her up in the mental mong ward or whatever the other kids on the estate were scaring her with that week. Andy had swooped in with her endless kitchen roll, first to clean up her sister's face, then to see to the carpet. She remembered the can of Vanish and how she watched the foam cover up the blood. She remembered rubbing at the stain with the rag, making red lighten to pink and pink lighten to barely-there, and wondering why it couldn't be that easy to get out herself.

A fortnight later she'd found out she was pregnant.

It took six months into her new flat, her new life above the motorway, for her name to come up on the waiting list for a therapist on the NHS. Andy, with uncharacteristic clarity for that time of her life, had sat down and outlined everything she wanted to talk about in that first appointment, all she could cram into a half-hour: her mum and the ghost baby, her knack for finding all the wrong men and none of the right jobs, that creeping fear of never, ever leaving this life in Crossway House when only a half-year ago it had embodied all she had wanted. What she had ended up talking about was Angela.

'She was telling me about these boys making her life hell, and it popped into my head – it just did – that I would kill them if I had to. And I didn't care. Well, I cared a little bit, that's why I'm saying it now. But I would be OK with it. And I think it's weird that I'm okay with it. I would take a life if it made Angela's easier.' She had expected the doctor to lock the doors and dial the police, but instead she got a passive nod. She never returned for her second appointment.

That day with Neely. That little liar, calling the book of her sister's sketches, her sister's words, all her own. She had felt her hands wanting to tense into claws, sensed those old familiar rages bubbling up. So many times in her life, Andy had wasted her anger on things that didn't bloody matter – who cares who's calling you a slag, who cares who's saying you trade sex for kebabs and chips – and the one time now when she might have had a reason, she had walked away. It had been easy to sacrifice herself for Angela when they were younger, too easy to fight her battles then. So why couldn't she have pulled that scrawny little girl back by her ponytail and taken back that book with Angela's hopes and dreams and a drawing of their mother?

Why didn't you fight for your sister?

Neely threw on her parka over her pyjamas to buy a bottle of Coke and the *Mirror* at the newsagents. She stared back at the pitying eyes like a dare as the older man gave her change for a fiver. A few days earlier, she would have looked at the ground and shuffled off in shame, but not today. Not when her television had informed her that police were questioning a thirty-year-old man in relation to the Angela Archer murder. There was nobody to call, nobody to text. And nothing to celebrate, not really, not yet. But joy would come in drips from now on, she knew. She waited for the shop owner to blink.

'Mum,' she sniffled down the answerphone. 'The police arrested someone. Junkie from the estate. I helped them find him.' As if she were relaying home her exam results. As if she needed reassurance of a job well done.

'Neely, love, I really wish you'd come home. Your dad thinks you'd be safer here.'

'I am home,' she deadpanned. 'And I just said, they've got the man who did it. So unless he's planning a jailbreak just to go after me, I think I'm alright.'

'You're depressed. And you've every right to be. And I know you don't want to talk about it with me, but you should talk to someone, and I know lots of...'

Neely thought of her mother in the kitchen in Stevenage, her black hair and her flawless lipstick, her well-meaning hippie streak, her memories of a London that no longer existed. 'Mum. No offence, but I know what I need, yeah? And it's just to be left alone. I know I'm not going to magically feel better tomorrow. I know you're looking out for me. But I can do this myself.'

'You've got friends there helping out, haven't you?'

There was no use in arguing. After they hung up, Neely dragged her duvet out to the lounge and wished she could put a record on. *It's almost all over, Angela,* she thought, feeling a twinge in her face as the tears began to well. *He didn't get away with it. I got him for you. I did something useful, for real, this time. So you'll forgive me for this, because it doesn't matter any more.*

She opened the journal again, tracing over her girlfriend's name, all primary-schoolish block print, with one finger. The early pages greeted her now like old friends who neither demanded nor wanted any explanation. It was an unconditional acceptance, and unqualified love. This is who Angela had been.

Angela hadn't written much between these covers, despite the complete lack of any blank pages. Her text was disconnected, a lesser archipelago in a sea of cross-hatching and contours and long strokes. Mostly, she had drawn. Neely skipped over the rare spate of verbosity that had accompanied her entry into Angela's life. She knew who she was. She knew who she had been. She didn't have to revisit the Porchester Pool. Not now, or any time within spitting distance on the record of years. Maybe ages from now, when grief had become a distant dull ache and not this searing burn, she could walk in there again, pay for a day pass, trace her toes along the tile and remember that this was where it started. Just not now.

She stopped again at the junction, at that disjointed page: ruined ground. A time when Angela was neither happy nor sad, a time when she couldn't fight and couldn't fly. But whatever was ruined, Neely had just fixed. From right here in the Harrow Road, Neely had wiped it all clean.

You know what we should do, Angela? Neely thought, rubbing her eyes as if there was something she wanted from them. *We should go for a drink.*

Neely pushed open the door to the Hope and Anchor, and the faces swivelling to see her were missing one notable regular. She didn't stare back, only eased the door gently shut. The pub fell silent. Gina was the only one to move. She stood up from her chair in the corner and slowly walked up to meet Neely. She raised one hand and casually – as easy as opening a cupboard, or slamming a door – smacked her across the face. The crack of her hand reverberated around the room; Neely thought she saw Mel behind the bar wincing as she fell back, stunned. But Mel wasn't going to stop this, nor was anybody else. Having had no experience with this kind of confrontation, besides watching the type play out in soap operas, Neely didn't know to fight back. She didn't even know to defend herself as Gina kept coming: hands in her hair, surprisingly strong, wrapping around the knot of her ponytail. Neely heard herself shriek: a shrill, pathetic thing. Gina shoved her into the door and it hit her again on the way back to shut. Then, as calmly as she had approached, Gina stepped back.

'You fucking bitch,' she hissed. 'Couldn't keep your nose out of it. You should be locked up, not him.'

'I didn't do anything!'

'You think we're that stupid? Everybody knows.'

'That's enough, Gina,' Mel growled, but not very seriously.

Neely held the door to stand herself up, the adrenaline starting to rise with her. 'He killed Angela and you're defending him? You stupid fucking junkie, what the fuck's wrong with you?'

'With *me*? Oh, you cunt, I'll let you know what's wrong with me. You. You're the problem, you're the problem for everybody. Rob didn't kill Angela. You, though, you've just gone and ruined his life for no good reason other than you're a *mental fucking bitch* who thinks she knows everything.' She finished her speech with a gob of spit, right onto Neely's coat.

'Enough!' Mel yelled, meaning it this time. 'Neely, go home.'

The words shot from her mouth; she knew every one of them had to count, and quickly. 'Look, I wish it wasn't him, but there's DNA, there's proof.'

Gina rolled her eyes and jumped an octave. 'There's DNA, there's proof,' she mocked, in a posh voice – not Neely's, but it didn't matter. 'Are you that stupid to believe what the police tell you? They say what they like. You did their job for them, now they get to close the case, be the hero cops who everybody thinks got the piece of shit who killed poor little defenceless Angela, and go home to their families. Rob gets to rot when he did *nothing*. But nobody's going to believe a word he says. Didn't think of that? Eh? Not so clever now, are ya?'

Neely scanned the room. Instead of anger, most of the men in the pub had smiles playing at the corners of their mouths if not outright bursting through. *The fuck you looking at?* she wanted to yell at each and every one of them, get in their faces so that they could smell the hatred on her breath, but she knew it was pointless. She knew very well what they were looking at: a girl who didn't belong, among people she barely knew, up to her eyeballs in a mess of her own making.

Mel trudged out from behind the bar with a rag. With a roughness that felt deliberate, she wiped the phlegm from Neely's lapel. 'Neely, time to leave.'

'But I am telling you I…'

'And I am telling you that you have no fucking clue what you've done.' Mel's pale eyes blazed: Neely had never felt this pure an anger boring directly into her. The cheap highlights looked like battle armour now.

'Who says I even was…'

'Oh, sweetie,' Mel cut her off, something like pity mixing with disdain and spilling right off her tongue. 'We all know it was you. There's nobody else it could have been.'

Sixteen

I'm not going to drink tonight, she told herself. *If the bare minimum of self-control is now suddenly beyond my capacity, then I'm a wreck who deserves to go back to Stevenage, so I am not going to drink tonight.*

With salt and vinegar crumbs coating her fingers she scrolled through the listings on her computer. Back in uni, it had seemed like there were never enough hours in a day, days in a week, Neelys in existence, to cover every gig and show and exhibit *Time Out* flung in front of her. London had been hers, suddenly: a box-fresh gift to be broken in, like trainers, until it became a second skin. Now she just shrugged to herself: maybe, nah, maybe. That looks alright, if there's nothing better. If I can be bothered.

She chose the dress from her office Christmas party. Black, short, utterly impractical for winter, with sprays of black sequins inviting a closer look. She might want someone to take that look. Shiny tights, black, same reason. Platform shoes in case there was anything, or anyone, she'd want to see. She brushed out her hair and retied her ponytail despite the ache left by Gina's handiwork: higher, tighter. Swipe of lipstick, smudge of kohl, slices of blush making her cheekbones pop: *you bitch,* she thought, pleased with what she saw in the mirror.

Her heels clicked as she pulled the front door shut and started her walk down Harrow Road. Westbourne Park to King's Cross. King's Cross to Highbury & Islington. Hi-and-I to Dalston Junction and the Kingsland Road, where she forced her head up, opened her eyes to the option, made herself believe she could go back to some form of normal. All around Neely were the veritable step-by-step, DIY guides to exactly that. Groups travelled in convoys down the pavement, girls in their heels, girls in their duffel coats and bomber jackets and fake leopard skin. Those on their lonesome looked like they had a destination in mind and no plans to pause until they got there. For a split second she thought she saw Sam at a cash machine, shivering in his ancient leather jacket, but it was only one of his many Dalston doppelgangers.

Pick one, any one, pick a place. Dalston Superstore. She'd been there a million times, back when Ruby was her North Star on a night out. Less often with Angela. Wasn't her scene. Now Neely joined the queue to get in, leaning into the wall to make her lone status less conspicuous. The woman behind her, all crimson buzz-cut and dangerously tight jeans, frenetically tapped out a text message, en route to being something other than alone, but for the moment sharing Neely's luck.

'Hey,' Neely began, trying not to cringe at the sound of her own voice. 'Do you know what's on tonight?'

The woman grinned. 'Quiz Me Maybe.'

'Sorry?'

'Trivia. But not the boring stuff. Batshit pub quiz.'

'Cheers.' *No. Not here.* Neely came unstuck from her place on the wall and sped up the road, nearly tripping over a crack in the pavement. She stared into pub and kebab shop windows, nearly crashing into another pack of cheerful young things, as Dalston gave way to Stoke Newington. All that warmth inside, and she could have it if she wanted. She kept walking.

At Stoke Newington Church Street, she thought she heard music: distant, tinny even, but real. She let the sound pull her across the road and through the door of an unfamiliar pub, then down the stairs. The reverb of the guitar flowed through her skin, right to her lungs and into her blood, the way it always felt right. A good bassline – and this one, well, it would do nicely – never failed to wind around her, rope-like, pulling her up straight, setting a rhythm to her hips. She watched the singer, a tiny brunette in a sixties shift dress that seemed to be exploding in lime and azure flowers, wait until her moment, just the right moment, to belt. Neely could have cried in gratitude. This place wasn't home, but it had the right furnishings, it had all mod cons and a respectable address to boot.

Pure habit led her to the bar and she ordered a pint of lager, forgetting her promise until the instant her hand touched the glass. *Shit.* Oh well, it would give her something to hold. The only thing more humiliating than going out alone would be going empty-handed.

But she wasn't the only one there on her own. One other woman stood alone in the basement, past the smattering of couples and groups, and Neely did a double-take that nearly made her spill her pint. She was taller than Neely – everybody was taller than Neely – but otherwise this woman was a mirror of what Neely might have been in another time, another circumstance: black hair cropped short and spiked, the tiniest of gold studs in the same straight nose, black leather trousers and a vest too big for her petite frame. Her dark eyes loomed huge in a face bleached by a stray spotlight. A tattoo bloomed across one shoulder: a botanical scroll, all ivy and miniature blossoms in black. Like an old illustration. Like a sacred text.

'Do you want this?'

The woman stared uncertainly. Neely didn't mind; she would have done likewise if the tables were turned.

'It's Staropramen,' Neely yelled over the music. 'I forgot I'm not supposed to drink on these antibiotics. Don't want to waste it.'

The woman's face softened. 'Cheers,' she said, her fingers just overlapping Neely's as she accepted the pint glass.

She said it before she even knew she was saying it: 'I'm Neely.'

'Sorry?'

'Neely. My name's Neely.'

'I'm Nicola.'

In curious unison, they smiled awkwardly. Nicola giggled, her fingers skimming her ruby-tinted lips.

'Do you know this band?'

'Yeah. Singer used to be my flatmate.'

'Oh, yeah?'

'They've got so much better. But she's always had an amazing voice.'

'Mmm.' Neely could have sworn she saw the singer, blinking in her own meagre spotlight, smile toward the pair of them.

'I like your dress, Neely.' Nicola picked at the edge of her sleeve, making the black sequins shine. 'That's fantastic.'

'Ah, cheers.'

'You feeling alright?'

'Sorry?'

'Antibiotics,' Nicola grinned.

'Oh. Yeah, great.'

'Fancy going upstairs? Won't have to scream.'

'Will your flatmate be bothered?'

'Nah.'

Neely smiled. 'Alright. Want to get a table and I'll meet you up there? Just gonna pop to the toilet.'

Nicola's soft smile stayed in Neely's mind as she pushed through the door and stared into the smudged mirror. Her hands shook against the basin. Maybe it was the crap lighting, or maybe it was the thin film of basement sweat shining her cold-nipped face, but the reflection made Neely start. She looked so young. So far as anything about her could still be called innocent, that's what the curve of her face looked like, the blue sparkle coating her eyelids, the sheen of her cheekbones. She forced a smile, open-lipped and earnest, and she wanted to cry. She knew she didn't deserve sadness. Whatever she'd done, whatever she was yet to do, she didn't deserve to be miserable.

Maybe she would sit with Nicola, getting to know her, laughing, joking, chatting shit. That tattoo must have a meaning; maybe she would learn it. Perhaps she could lie when inevitably asked what she did: *I'm a writer. I'm between jobs. I'm thinking of opening my own shop.* Maybe they would cocoon themselves into that table upstairs talking until last orders. Who knew where Nicola lived? Maybe right here in Stoke Newington. Neely could start rewriting everything, right here, tonight.

No, she thought, and set her mouth back to solemnity in the smudges of the mirror. *Not yet. Not like this.*

Up the stairs at double speed, through the door without looking back to see where Nicola had chosen to sit. The cold stunned her on the street as she slipped through clouds of cigarette smoke, back to the High Road. She stuck out her arm for the first bus, not even noticing which one it was. It took her down to the Kingsland Road, back the way she'd come. Neely got off in Hoxton. The pavements were choked with the young and cheerful and half-cut. Looking, looking, always looking. She shifted to the side streets, searching for an empty pavement, listening to the click of her heels, remembering when this was all she had wanted – London, quite literally at her feet – and starting to feel like maybe, just maybe, she could find a way to make herself satisfied with just that again.

She stepped inside the all-night cafe off Hoxton Square for a cup of tea, and sat at a table with yesterday's discarded tabloid open to a page near the front. First Neely saw the advert for offers at Tesco: new year, same great value. Then she saw Angela. Smaller than ever, that same photograph staring up at her as if Neely were anybody. *Man held on canal murder* and two inches of text Neely could have written herself. The news told her nothing new. Angela belonged to everybody now. She closed the newspaper and covered the back-page footballers with her cup.

She thought of Nicola. It was too late to go back to her now. Neely imagined her storming out the pub in a huff and wondering, *why do I only attract the mental ones? What was wrong with that girl, anyway? Am I the problem?* And despite herself, Neely smiled. She felt that familiar spark behind her eyes: this is what it felt like to learn something.

There was a stop for the night bus right at the end of the street, but she knew she couldn't wait. She started walking. In City Road, halfway to Angel, her feet rebelled and Neely ripped off the heels, even though the pavement froze her toes, even though she knew better. *What's the worst thing that can happen?* she thought. *It already has.* She walked on westward, ignoring the catcalls, ignoring the drunks. At Great Portland Street she gave up and eased her swollen feet back into her shoes as she watched the countdown clock tick down minutes until the N18, until Harrow Road, until her home.

The radio woke Neely with news that sent her diving under the duvet once more. *Police have released a man who was arrested two days ago in relation to the murder of Angela Archer, stating that their investigation is ongoing. Miss Archer was found just before Christmas in a wooded area off the towpath of the Grand Union Canal...*

Released. The police had probably only found the tiniest bit of gear on him, but they hadn't found a reason for Angela. Whatever questions they'd asked, he'd answered. And that had been enough.

There's nobody else it could have been.

Wrong. Again. She silenced the radio with her fist and wished she'd been hung over.

She was watching *Jeremy Kyle* when her phone buzzed. Despite all the time and all the events, Neely had never deleted the contact from her phone, nor had she deleted the photo that went with it. Neat and white teeth, auburn hair spilling from under her sombrero, bright eyes in a childlike face: Ruby Sullivan.

'Fucksake,' Neely announced to nobody in particular. *I'll give her two minutes of sad platitudes and then I'm getting rid of her altogether.* 'Hello?'

'Neely. Babe. Let me in.'

'What?'

'I'm downstairs. Let me in.'

'Why are you here?'

'Neely! It's freezing. Please just let me in.'

She sighed, killed the phone, and threw her coat on over her pyjamas. She didn't bother with shoes for the two flights down to the street, where the cold came in with Ruby Sullivan.

'Neely. Oh, my god. I am *so* sorry. It's been all over the news. I can't *imagine* what this must be like. You poor thing.' The girl wrapped her in a hug that had been curiously absent from their relationship. The sensation made Neely stiffen and hold her breath: this couldn't mean anything good. But before she could decide whether to pull back, Ruby broke contact and looked at her with wrinkled nose.

'Neely. Have you been holed up for days in here?'

'What?'

'When was the last time you had a bath?'

Neely stepped back. 'It's not like I've had anywhere to go.'

'Love, you're… ponging a bit. And you should have somewhere to go. You're going to drive yourself mad if you just stay inside. A little birdy over in Dalston told me you two rowed and he's worried about you. But of course he's too much of a sad bastard to actually come and check up on you himself.'

'So he got you to do it for him.'

'*Neely*. I care about you, you know that. You know I'll always be here for you.'

'Well, cheers. But I don't need any help. Unless you know anything about… what happened.'

'Well, I don't. But I know you. And I know you need to have a hot bath and you need to go out with me for a drink. Or even just a walk down this awful road. Sorry. But you need to get out. So can I come up or not?'

Neely shrugged, ears burning. She turned and walked up the stairs, with Ruby at a respectful distance behind her.

'God, it's freezing. I got back from home yesterday but I'm taking the whole week off.' Ruby closed the door and surveyed the lounge. She gestured at Angela's journal, face down on the floor. 'Are you writing something? I always said you should write.'

Neely shook her head. 'No.' She swooped up the book and placed it on the shelf below her hi-fi.

Ruby stared and frowned. 'Where'd your record collection go? That whole thing was full up at my flat.'

'Long story.'

'Oh Neely. You're not holding up.'

'What, you expect me to be sunshine and love when my girlfriend's been murdered?'

'I don't mean it that way…'

'You don't mean anything, do you?'

Ruby appeared genuinely hurt by the barb. 'Look. Have your bath and we'll go out. I'll make you tea. Are you eating? I'll cook something. Or I'll buy you lunch. Can you at least let me do that?'

Neely grabbed the journal, not caring if she looked suspicious, and carried it with her through to the bathroom. She heard Ruby rustling through the kitchen and she stared at her face, nearly reflective with grease, in the mirror. The clink of spoons on ceramic, of the refrigerator opening and closing: small domestic noises that brought tears to her eyes as she thought, *it all could have been so easy.* She lunged to turn on the taps so that Ruby wouldn't hear her gasp back a sob.

She showered at record speed, wrung out her hair, kicked the pyjamas into a corner. A sniff of her dressing gown convinced her to opt for jeans and jumper, a pilled cable-knit fisherman's number she figured might spark some recognition from her visitor. It came from Hackney, at a time that felt like another life: clothes shopping, record shopping, gigs, drinks, frivolity, back to Sam's, cuddles on the sofa, hangovers in the morning, doing it again the next day. They had been young, or at least younger, and life had stretched out before them like that rare British summer sunset: all caramel in a candyfloss sky. Ruby could still pluck sweets from the sky if she damn well felt like it; the firmament had not fallen in on her.

In the kitchen, Ruby was deep in suds, finishing off the heaps of dirty dishes that had grown in shaky stalagmites over the past week. She'd changed her hair, Neely noticed: two white-blonde tails tightly plaited against her skull, darkening to reddish waves hanging loose down her back. Neely blinked, remembering the shake of that hair when the pair of them had felt like the only two people down in that basement god knows where in Hackney, the only two people who mattered in the wall-to-wall crowd of sweat and self-importance, singing along to the little-girl voice from the speakers telling them nothing can stop them now.

Ruby had put on weight since they'd split. Not much, but enough to round and soften her features ever so slightly. They'd both got older, perhaps wise enough to feel ashamed at what they'd been like together. 'Your tea.' Ruby jerked her head at a mug. 'Milk, one sugar?'

Neely nodded.

'They arrested somebody, Ruby.'

'Who?'

'Junkie. I know – I've seen him around, sort of.'

'So it was drugs?'

Do you want it to be? Neely wondered, trying not to let it show on her face. 'They let him go already. I dunno. Maybe they don't have enough to hang on to him? But he was on CCTV with her. Right before.'

'Did he ever give her trouble? That you saw?'

She shook her head. 'Still coming to terms with it. It's… a lot to think about.' But Neely had been thinking, and she had been thinking of that prickle down her back again. Doubt. Those police procedurals had taught her to look for the motive, but everywhere she looked down Harrow Road, everywhere she had ever seen Rob, all she could find was filthy pavement. She had tried to ring Andy, wanting to know everything about the man and who he was and what he had become, but like her sister's before her, Andy's phone was going straight to voicemail.

'How long are you signed off for?'

'I'm not.'

'What?'

'I just didn't go back after New Year. Office hasn't collapsed yet or else I would have heard.'

'Go see a doctor. Get a letter and you can stay away as long as you need. Nobody's going to deny what you're going through. You still the office manager?'

'Still the same shit.'

'Oh, Neely.'

'Stop.' She was surprised when Ruby actually listened. And she was surprised that she didn't cry. Not for herself, and not for any notion of wasted potential or lost love.

'How are the police treating you?'

'Like most other people. Forgot about me completely.'

'I haven't.'

'Ruby, this is weird. I've seen you, what, maybe three times since you were throwing plates at my head?' She watched her ex-girlfriend stiffen at the memory. 'And now it's tea and sympathy? It's fucking weird is what it is. I don't want you writing about me on your website or anything. It's too fucking… weird.' *Is she actually trying to gether way in now that I'm alone?* Neely thought. *I've wondered if she's mental, but some things are just wrong.*

'I know we were awful to each other. And I'm sorry about that. I really am. But thinking of you going through all this on your own… I couldn't stand that.'

Neely half-scoffed, half-laughed. 'Don't worry about me. I don't need that.'

'You're very worry-about-able.'

'What's that supposed to mean?'

'It means you have a good heart and you don't deserve any of this and I'm making a teeny tiny effort to cheer you up by saying I'm sorry for being a piece of work. Okay?'

Despite herself, Neely smiled.

'I mean it, Neely. You have a good heart. You'll weather the storms.'

'I know what I will and won't do. I don't need to be told I'll be fine. I know I will. Just not now. And I really don't fancy philosophy right now so don't give it to me.'

'See, you never used to talk like this when it was just us. Angela was good for you. She gave you a spine.'

'Don't patronise me.'

'Just saying. You answer back now.'

'Angela made me *happy*. It was this place that did everything else.'

Ruby craned her neck to look out at the Harrow Road. 'Glad it's good for something.' A slow smile spread across her face, softening her features. 'What will you do now?'

'I don't know.'

Ruby sipped her tea. She didn't look happy and she didn't look smug. 'Dry your hair and we'll go for a walk.'

'I don't need taking care of, Ruby.'

'Maybe I want to, OK?'

'This isn't about you. None of this is about you.'

To Neely's surprise, Ruby nodded, bright eyed and earnest. 'I know. It's about you.'

'Be honest with me. What do you want? Why are you here, really?'

'You let me in.'

'You asked.'

'Well, you answered.'

Neely sighed and retrieved her trainers. It was another fight she couldn't win.

As she gently pulled the front door shut, Neely remembered Angela's Harrow Road walk. She had never broached the topic and now it was far too late, but there had been a quirk of physiology, something that meant Angela Archer could not set foot in this street with anything but perfect posture and a gentle cloud of confidence radiating from her skin. She might have looked glum in the Great Western Road, her eyes might have been locked on the pavement in Elgin Avenue, but one step into Harrow Road and it was lights on, curtains up. Spine straight and face bright. Like she owned the place. No, like she was sizing it up to buy.

Now Ruby averted her eyes from any possible passer-by as Neely walked one step ahead. Their breath danced in white steam clouds as the two women turned into the Great Western Road. Past the off-licence, past the pizza place, past a row of carved-up terraces, and over the canal, the street sloped downhill toward Westbourne Park. The noise of traffic filled the space between them.

'Let's go this way,' Neely nodded to her right, towards Elkstone Road. 'It's alright over here.' Ruby followed wordlessly. The bit of brow bare below her hat was uncharacteristically knit, but Neely found she didn't care. They passed the Trellick Tower, laundry flapping from a few of its balconies despite the cold, pastel flags waving either hello or goodbye to the trains passing just across the road.

'Ruby. You're being really weird. What's up?'

'That one time,' Ruby began, voice wavering, 'You know, when… Angela and I…'

'It doesn't matter.'

'She spoke of you so highly.'

'She was drunk.'

'She meant it. She loved you, Neels.'

'So why'd she go with you?'

'We… Because I was a selfish bitch and in some fucked-up way it felt good to hear her say she didn't feel good enough for you? I dunno.'

Neely stopped walking. 'What the *fuck?*'

'You said it, we were drunk.'

Neely didn't have the energy to argue. They had come to the shops below the Tower, the Costcutter identical to her own and the café and the children's centre. She spotted a pub, newly boarded up, and couldn't remember its name. 'Here. Let's walk this way. Hazelwood Crescent. I like this street.'

Sideways towers stretched down the bend of the street, low rise and long. Their hallways were decks, each identical white front door visible from the road. 'Lee Hazlewood,' Ruby said softly. 'We had a good duet, didn't we? Some Velvet Morning? I miss that. I really do.'

Neely almost giggled at the memory: she'd take the low notes and Ruby would go high. It seemed too long ago that she could define herself by the music she loved, by the words of others in her mouth. This, she thought to herself, must be what it's like to be grown up.

'What happened to all your records, anyway?'

'Stolen.'

'You got burgled?'

'Sort of.'

'Only "sort of". See, you're still so nice, despite everything. Neely, promise me you'll move away somewhere better. It's awful here. You've got to be tired of the dirt and the misery all the time.'

'I can't afford my own flat in St John's Wood.'

'Neither can I.'

'Correction: *my parents* can't afford a flat for me in St John's Wood.'

'Rub it in.'

'Somebody should.'

'Ouch.' But she was smiling, showing those very whitened, very straightened teeth. 'I'm telling you, you've toughened up.'

Nah, Neely thought. *I was always like this. I just dropped the bullshit. I don't need it any more. I have nobody left to impress.*

'You know,' Ruby began, digging her fists into her pocket, 'I got such a kick out of how you'd talk about places like this years ago. Architecture. How you knew exactly when every crap block of flats went up and why. Like this street. Tell me about it.'

Neely smiled. 'That's easy. This is where Angela grew up.'

'You're joking.'

'I'm not. Hazelwood Crescent.'

'Are her family still here?'

Neely shook her head. 'Nah.'

But even in death the past had a funny way of catching up with Angela Archer, and by extension the person she had loved. At first Neely thought the noise was a dog: a sad, sudden yelp. She had to continue along the curve of the crescent to realise it was human, all too human, and coming from a doorstep three floors up. One of Angela Archer's family was, indeed, still there in Hazelwood Crescent, and was deeply engrossed in the matter of pummelling a familiar face from the Hope and Anchor.

'Not too much to say now, have ya?' Neely parsed from a distance. She had no doubt who the voice belonged to now. 'Have ya? Nothing to say then and nothing to say now, is there? Did you FUCK HER TOO?' Andy didn't give poor Rob much time to respond. He was on the ground of that open corridor, curled up and tiny compared with the woman looming above him and radiating something far beyond hatred. Hatred had been left behind on the platform several stops ago. What Andy wanted was what Andy had already got: murder.

'Jesus Christ. What's with her?' Ruby squinted up at the deck.

'Oh my god.' Neely's mouth dropped as Andy landed a solid kick in Rob's ribs. She was wearing such mumsy shoes – slip-on, mock suede – but the loathing was from another time, another life, one from Angela's stories. All the scene was missing was an awkward girl with a mess of peroxide curls and a purple cardigan, trying to disappear into the wall behind her.

'I *know*. Psycho. You really need to move, Neely. You don't belong with… people like that. *Animals* like this. You're better than that. It's not good for you to be…'

'Ruby, I know her.'

'You what?'

'I know her. That's Angela's sister.'

'Oh my god.'

As if on cue, Andy spun to face the two women on the street. Her eyes looked beyond them, elsewhere; Rob had clawed an angry red scrape down her face. 'Got a fucking problem?'

'Andrea! Stop!'

'Fuck off! Keep out of it, you nosy bitch.' But the distraction was enough for Rob to wrench himself free and bolt, stumbling, down the deck and down the stairs, falling over the last three onto the pavement. Neely's eyes were platters. She'd been an utter idiot. Of course *Rob* couldn't have killed Angela; the only things Rob physically had it in him to murder were pints and maybe bedbugs. The police had let him go. So what was Andy doing? It wasn't the time to ask.

'Run, you sick little shit. And ALL OF YOU!' Andy screamed from the deck, addressing the entire estate if not all of West London. 'You can all fuck off for what you did to her! All of you!'

Curtains began twitching on Hazelwood Crescent. Faces flashed in front of windows and instantly disappeared. They saw enough of Andy Archer to know they didn't want to see any more.

'Neely. Let's get out of here. She's mental.' Ruby had begun to shiver only in part from the cold.

'I swear, on my dead mother, on my dead sister, none of you are ever going to forget what happened,' Andy bellowed, gripping the railing hard enough for Neely to see the white in her knuckles. 'I swear to god, I will never let any of you get away from it!'

The two women turned back the way they had come, walking first, then breaking into a run. Ruby reached for Neely's hand and only got the fabric of her coat. The girl had pulled her scarf over her nose and her hat down over her eyebrows, but Neely could still see her tears.

Seventeen

Neely had felt it when Angela was doing the washing up: the slight but sharp intake of breath, the stiffening of her girlfriend's ribs when Neely slid her hands under her shirt and ran them – small, bony, never intrusive even if she had wanted to be – over Angela's skin.

'Angela. What's up?'

The sweet smile and giant eyes. They had looked not directly into Neely's, but slightly over the small shoulder, right to the tear-off-the-day calendar that had screamed MONDAY 10 NOVEMBER as if it had entire lifetimes to cram into that date. 'Really, nothing. I'm *fine*.'

Believe me, Neely heard, and she had wanted nothing more than an easy life for the woman in front of her drying plates with the tea towel. And so she had.

She picked up the empty cup Ruby had left on the windowsill several days ago, trying not to pay attention to the tremor in her hand. Neely's phone chimed from the windowsill. An unfamiliar number.

'Hello?'

'Hi, is Nee-lee there?' The voice came through a little too earnest.

'This is she.'

'Hi, Neely. My name's Rachel Martin, I'm a reporter for the *Standard*. How are you?'

'Sorry?'

'My name's Rachel…'

'How did you get my number?'

'I'm a journalist writing about Angela Archer, I…'

'Fuck off!' Neely hollered into the handset. She killed the call and threw the phone onto the sofa. She needed air, the colder the better.

Neely pedalled her bike down the Harrow Road, eastward: down the slight slope and toward the city. When the street crossed the canal, all she saw were the two council estates, the high rises and the squat brown blocks. They were the buffer zone. Behind them, on streets you had to make an effort to reach, stood the villas. Those houses, all bought but vacant half the time, were an almost-white that glowed in summer sunsets like fabric stretched over warm light bulbs. But this was winter, and everything seemed a variation on grey.

She picked Blomfield Villas to make her turn. On her left, the council blocks, 1960s explorations in the suppression of all imagination, four storeys each with concrete gardens. Ruby had been correct: she did have that gift for looking at brick and mortar and knowing a bit more than most. On her right, a terrace of white plaster and black wrought iron, a survivor of the clearances that claimed its neighbours. Lovely on the outside, the kind of thing estate agents called character, but Neely knew the interiors were carved up and crumbling, ridden with dry rot or rising damp. Ahead of her, the bridge over the canal to the streets where neither of those problems came remotely close to touching the homes. Or if they did, they were dispatched with a clinical efficiency delivered by on-call teams of men in clean white vans earning tidy livings off owner-occupiers who had already dropped four million quid on a house and weren't too fussed about parting with a few thousand more to preserve the investment. She had often wondered what it must feel like to have so much as to not notice anything missing. She wondered if Angela ever had, too, or if she had decided not to bother, to simply stay out of the heads of others altogether. Neely wasn't sure which was the easier way out.

The canal towpath could only be entered on the council estate side. She stepped off her bike and guided it slowly down to the shuttered barge where she and Angela had once shared coffees and played at being lazy, assuming they had all the time in the world. She held the handlebars like other women would guide children. No, like they would lead lovers. She sat on a bench and squinted at the sky, typically grey but glowing strangely as evening approached, a slowly dimming spotlight wrapped in filthy cotton wool.

From across the basin, a sudden burst of squawks, and a Canada goose emerged from a crowd of identical others, paddling toward her. Neely couldn't tell if the bird at the head of the group was more in a rush to leave or to arrive somewhere else, or if its companions were joining him or holding him back. They had kind faces, she thought, but they were evil bastards, always hissing and shitting and stabbing at you with those beaks.

Neely already knew from her books, but Angela had told her, too: this was Browning's Pool. School hadn't taught local girls any of his poems, but Angela must have known this was his, the basin at the junction of three waterways. And that's what she had taught Neely: how it was possible to live your entire life not only in one city, but in one hollowed-out pocket of it, and to know just enough to make sense of it in conversation to somebody who would never know it the way you did.

The goose sharply jutted its head at the sky and paused before setting off a honking alarm call. Then, in a pandemonium of wings splashing on the black water of the canal, he climbed skyward, a flock at his back.

Neely stood up and swung herself back onto the bicycle. Cold stung her face, but she pedalled west, under the Harrow Road and along the side of the Westway, past the Sainsbury's and the cemetery in the evening dimness. Almost to Wormwood Scrubs and considering turning round, she stopped and squinted. Ahead of her, she saw a light dancing. A small glow, a torch beam. It slowed, then stopped on her, on her face. In her eyes. Neely raised her arm and covered them. Moved to the side. The beam got bored and danced away.

'Hello?' she called, but not loudly enough to be serious. She walked forward some more, sure that it couldn't be somebody with foul play in mind because why would he carry enough light to show his face and risk Neely making it out alive? And that light circled the towpath twice, three times, a fourth as she approached, before its bearer aimed the beam upward at his own face, his broken nose, a pair of elsewhere eyes. One of them was blackened. Andrea Ormiston's handiwork.

'Rob?'

'What the fuck?'

'It's Neely. I'm sorry, I'm so sorry, I honestly thought…'

'I know who you are. I know you're fucking sorry. Don't blame you. We're alright.'

She could have sobbed her gratitude. 'I really don't know why…'

'Because you thought I killed her.'

'I saw you on the video and I had to say something.'

He nodded, more to himself. 'I did see her that night.'

'What did she say to you?'

'Nothing much. Nothing worth remembering. I just wanted to kiss her goodbye.'

'*Why?*'

'Didn't think it would be for real.'

Slowly, Neely crouched down beside him, and allowed herself a gentle fall into the dead leaves littering the ground.

Rob looked at her in the dim light, face blank, voice steady. 'You came to see Angela.'

'Well, she's not here,' Neely spat, instantly regretting the tone.

'I know she's not fucking here.'

'Then why… wait, wait, hold on. You're confusing me.'

'You came here to be with Angela, in the trees and in the soil and the water. You came here like I came here.' His face glistened in the torch beam.

Neely's breath caught in her throat. When, strictly speaking, had he come there? With Angela? Before her? He looked too pathetic for murder now. *Andy would have finished the job if it were really him*, she thought. *But Andy wouldn't have started it if it weren't, right?*

'Did you know her that well?'

'Fucksake. Since we were little. She and my sister Jenny. They were thick as thieves.'

'She never mentioned.'

'Of course she fucking didn't.' Neely couldn't help but think she was missing something. The plot, first of all. Several of its details. And the boat. And the boat-replacement bus service. *Be nice*, she thought. *Be a halfway sympathetic character. You can do that, can't you? This is training. This is education. Education is the one thing you ever did well.*

She sighed. Softened her voice. 'What was all that about with Andy?'

'Misunderstanding. Old business.'

'Looked like a bit more than that.'

'Wasn't.'

'Where's your missus?'

'Gina left me. She fucked off back to Nottingham. Said London was doing her head in and so was I and she doesn't want that life any more. Too many cops going to be hanging about. Shot me down.'

'I'm sorry.'

'New Year, new her and all.'

'Mmm.'

'She's getting clean. Properly. Her mum and dad are putting her in some posh rehab. They've got money. She's going to do it right this time.'

'Well, good.'

'So it's just you and me.'

'Rob, I'm sorry. I don't understand.'

'Just you and me,' he repeated, quieter. 'To figure out what she wanted. What Angela was going to do.'

'Do about what?'

'About every little damn thing.' Rob shone the torch across the canal, the beam parallel to the black water. From somewhere in the darkness came a small splashing noise: a fish, Neely assumed, wondering what survived in this canal. And she thought of another canal, in Hackney. *Hackney*. Sam's flat felt like years ago.

Neely wondered about Sam now. Probably not sitting alone in Hackney with a bottle in his hand the way she tragically painted him in her own mind. Maybe Ruby had called. No, Sam was probably with his woman, probably finding a way to feel fine. Definitely not out in the cold, crouched in dead leaves and dirt and trying to decipher the speech of the chronically out-of-it. She decided to get to the point. For one, her toes were going numb, and for two, she wasn't sure how much of the last evening light the sky would still hold for her.

'But yeah. I saw her. That last night. In the pub. She left and I followed her. She said she was going and I let her go.'

'You *were* crying. Why?'

'I told her I loved her. She said she knew. And…'

'And?'

'She said she was leaving. For good.'

'And you never told me. All the times I've seen you since she disappeared, you didn't say one thing.' She held onto the dirt and the dead leaves to stop her trying to throttle him.

'She didn't want anybody to know. I promised her. I've known her ages. I owed her more than I owe you or anybody. It was none of your bloody business then.'

'I was her girlfriend.'

'And she was my friend. If she'd wanted you to know, she would have said something.'

'What about the baby?'

He shrugged. 'Honestly thought you knew. It wasn't mine.'

Neely slowly loosened her grip on the ground. 'I'm thinking maybe you can help me figure something else out.'

'Yeah?'

'Rob. I... erm, I know I shouldn't have done this, but I've read Angela's journal. And there's weird shit in there I don't understand.'

He sniffed. Deep sniffs, snotty ones. He'd been out there for a while. 'And you think I will.'

'You know her, you know here. And you know something that Andy was yelling about, don't you?'

He shrugged. Even that looked painful. 'Alright. What did she write?'

'All this stuff about ruined ground.'

Rob nodded, slowly. 'Of course.'

'Of course *what?*'

'She was ruined. On the ground. Her ground was Wormwood Scrubs. And she got raped there. Three boys took her there and took turns.'

Neely's heart dropped to somewhere far below the ground upon which she sat. 'What? How'd you know that?'

'Everybody knew. Word got round.'

'I didn't!'

Rob shrugged. 'You weren't here then. Guess she didn't want you ruined, either.'

'She should have told me! Nobody's said a thing to me. How come everybody knew except me?' Neely held onto the ground again, bracing herself. She wanted a drink. She wanted the all-out blotto she got those times when she wanted to remember.

'Bad penny.'

'What?'

'A bad penny always keeps turning up.'

'I'm not going to keep talking to you if you're going to spout bollocks. Talk to me straight.'

Rob shrugged again. He wasn't shivering like she was, Neely noticed. 'You found me, Neely Sharpe. You came looking for me. Not the other way round.'

'I didn't come looking. I came riding my bike to clear my bloody head.'

'Well, look what you found.'

'A bad penny?'

A shrug.

'Rob, they raped her. And they didn't get caught, they didn't go to jail, nothing.'

A shrug.

'Who was it? Do they still live around here?'

'Mo Zubairi does. Brian Powell moved away. Charlie Edwards is dead. Car wreck.'

Mo, Brian, Charlie, Neely thought. Simple names. Names that could belong to anybody. 'It's too late to do anything about them. Even if there hadn't been all this time since it happened. Angela's dead, she can't prove it, so they get to go on with their lives like they never did anything.'

'What are you going to do about it, then?'

'I don't *know.*'

'Then you're fucked.'

'Oh my *god.* She must have been hurting, all this time, every time I touched her, and she couldn't even tell me. Why wouldn't she *tell* me that? I could have… I could have helped.' Neely ignored that she didn't know what she could have possibly done to help. She had never imagined there would be a need.

'Ask her. If she's talking to you. In the soil and the air and all.'

'Talk sense or shut up.'

'You don't fucking believe me.'

'I just want to know why she was wri… er, thinking about them so much. After all this time.'

223

'Didn't you listen?'

'What?'

'Listen. Now. Shush.' And he placed the torch on the ground, pointing across the canal.

Neely figured that the less she spoke, the less he would give foolish replies, and the more she kept her mouth shut, the less likely she would be to vomit. Everything inside her had churned, broken loose. Impulsively, she felt for her phone in her coat pocket. Still there, still solid. She discreetly turned her head, just the slightest bit, to look at Rob, but in the dim light she saw nothing but his silhouette against the trees. She wondered what he had dreamed of when he was little, back when Angela and his sister were thick as thieves. She wondered what adults made him believe he could do, and how old he was when he realised it was all a load of twaddle, and whether that was what made him this way. One disappointment was nothing, she figured. But too far beyond two or three, well, that was a portent of a life with a reverse Midas touch: everything you brushed against, no matter how gently, would turn to shit. Years and years of that life could make him into somebody like this. Neely shivered from the cold and from the realisation. This man next to her was a dead dream.

'It's just you and me. We're the only ones on Earth. That's who we are. Everything's up to us from now on.'

'No we're fucking not, Rob. We're nothing.'

He shook his head. *The broken nose fits him,* Neely thought. *His face should not be perfect. It has no right being perfect and he knows it and that's why he'll survive this place.*

'If we're not the first, then we're the last.'

'Or we're some of the billions in the middle.'

'Can't be,' he whispered. 'No way.'

She took a moment to consider what she might be thinking. *He* was thinking in black and white. If all life was not going to spring forth from them, then they would be the last to die. That's what he was saying. But his logic made no sense. They couldn't be the first people on earth. They couldn't, if they already knew what death was, if Angela had ever existed alongside them. *This isn't philosophy, Neely. It's not even Angela's tough love. It's junkie babble.*

'Tell me about her family. What they were like. She never told me,' Neely asked.

'Her family?'

'Yeah.'

'Andrea, Angela, Alex. Her mum and her dad. She's dead, he's a Tube driver.'

'Angela told me her dad was driving when the Tube got bombed.'

'So? There was a train crash when we were little. Ladbroke Grove.'

'Yeah. Angela said.'

'Behind my house.' He paused several seconds, then sighed. 'You know I saw everything.'

'Christ. That must have been horrific.'

'No, Neely. I saw everything.'

'I didn't say you didn't.'

'You're not *listening*.'

'I am listening. Talk sense.'

'I saw what they did to her. Charlie, Mo, Brian. I saw it. I got around. Nobody was ever looking for me but I looked for everything.'

'Why the fuck didn't you do anything?'

'One versus three. Nothing I could do. Don't fucking lecture me, don't you try. I think about her all the time so don't tell me I don't care. I care more than anybody else. More than her dad. More than her sister. More than you. Sometimes people just want somebody to give a shit. Well, I gave a shit then and I give a shit now.'

Without the option of a lecture, Neely had nothing to say. She would have offered Rob a cigarette if she'd had one, anything to make a simple show of goodwill.

'That's why I didn't say anything. This time. Because I thought she'd come back. I said nothing last time, and she stayed.' Neely was trying to parse his logic, but he kept speaking. 'Neely. She used to go underground.'

'I know she did. Free travel from her Dad.'

He snorted. 'Not the Tube. Somewhere else.'

'What?'

'This isn't the only water round here.'

She felt alarmed to notice the prickle up her spine: not cold, but annoyance. Irritation. The same way she felt about the bastards at work. A waste of her time. Someone telling her something other than exactly what she wanted to know.

Rob shone the light at Neely's feet. 'The River Westbourne runs right under us, right now. Ages ago, they made it a sewer. It goes in pipes from Hampstead to the Thames. Y'know?'

Neely nodded. Angela had told her once, told her on this very footpath.

'Her sister had a flat high up. Her brother had his university far away. And Angela and her mum and her dad, they all went underground a different way.'

'A fucking *sewer?*' Neely spat, incredulous, and angry at herself for investing in junkie babble. But then she remembered Angela's green wellies, the ruined shoes, *ruined ground.*

'Yeah, a fucking sewer. I'll show you how if you like.'

'Rob, I'm going home.'

'It's easier, it's so much easier than everybody thinks. Just a grate in the ground. You pull it up, you crawl in. I bet you walk by it every day and you just don't think about it. Angela thought about it. Nobody else did. It was all her own.'

'I don't believe you.'

'You don't have to. But how else do you think I got that book? Where did you think she kept it?'

'What book?'

'The one you were just talking about.'

'Her journal?'

'Yeah. Angela hid it. I gave it back to him.'

'Gave it back to who?'

'You know who.'

'I don't.'

'But Angela always said you're so clever.'

'*Who the fuck are you talking about?*' Her hands moved without her, and she only realised what she was doing when her fingers began to ache from squeezing his bony shoulders.

'The one who got away,' he hissed. 'Brian Powell.'

Slowly, Neely loosened her grip. And only slightly faster, the fear rose in her chest, the fear superseded by shame, her shame for assuming that in a city of millions, a simple name like that could belong to a stranger, and that she could have so easily opened the front door to one and let death right over the threshold, all the while thinking it was what Angela would have done herself.

'It's him. *Fuck*. I know him. He came to our flat. After Angela vanished. He was there, he was in our flat, he went to the toilet and he put it there. I found it behind the bleach.'

'Yeah, sorry about your records. That was payment. I'll pay you back. I got twenty for them.'

'Why?'

'Fucksake, do I need to paint you a picture…'

'Not my records, I don't care about those. Why did you give him Angela's journal?'

'He needed to know what he did to her.'

'I think he fucking knew he raped her, Rob.'

He shook his head. 'Everything after.'

'Fucking hell, Rob. Did he kill her?'

'He wouldn't. He couldn't. You know what he's like. State of him.'

'If not him, then who? The other one? Mo?'

'Nope. He wouldn't, either. And even if he would, he was working when I last saw her. After she left the pub. He sold me fags.'

'Then who?'

'If I knew, I wouldn't be sat here waiting for her to tell me.'

She didn't believe in his methods, but she sat silent nonetheless.

'She loved you, Neely Sharpe.'

'You can't stay here all night. You'll freeze.'

'She *loved* you. You were the only thing in her life that hadn't gone to shit. Nah. I'm warm. It's nothing. Angela's cold. Angela is so, so cold right now, she's so cold…'

'Goodbye, Rob.'

'But it's warm down below. Her sacred ground. She fucking loved you. What are you going to do about it?'

'I'm going to go home. Goodbye.'

'It's not enough!' he shouted, pointing the torch into her face as

227

Neely pulled her bike up from the soil and switched on the headlight. 'That's not going to be enough!'

Leave it, she thought. *Don't get the last word. You always have to get the last word, so don't get the last fucking word.* She swung one leg over the frame and leaned all her weight onto the pedals, her head spinning like her wheels, trying to sort out everything she'd heard and nowhere-near sure of how much to believe. The beam of light on her back faded as she sped eastward. If she had stopped where the gasometers kissed the edge of the towpath and looked back at where she had come, Neely would not have seen it at all.

Neely would still be asleep in the flat in Harrow Road when the ambulance passed, no sirens on because there was no rush, no rush because the canal waters don't move that fast when they reach the pool in Little Venice and the window for anybody to have intervened had slammed shut and locked itself securely several hours ago. Still, the medics would dutifully follow procedure, they would haul the corpse from the water and wait for the police to take a statement from the old dear who raised the alarm. *And they just found that poor girl down the path near the railways*, one said to the other. *Happy fucking New Year.* No obvious bullet holes, no visible stab wounds, died with all his blood in his veins and god knows what else in there as well. They wrapped the hands, bagged the body. This one, from the looks of him, couldn't have been from around here. He must have floated in from far away. Somebody else's problem. *This beautiful cursed place.*

Eighteen

Andrea knew all their names. The entire back four were Scots, and her husband was captain. At left-back, Ollie Reid, accountant, Inverness. Alongside her Stuart, David McDonald from Paisley, did something in TV, fellow father of two. The right-back, Will Fisher from Cumbernauld – a real Billy the Fish, the actual Billy the Fish from the fucking *Viz* comic playing right-back for Osterley Rovers, who could go top of Middlesex County Football League Division Two West with a win over Southall United today.

She didn't know their wives or girlfriends, if they had them. She didn't want to know. Other people's families meant other people's troubles. Surely somebody would notice them, Andrea assumed, with how Jack and Ella clapped their tiny hands and screeched for their Daddy, Sunday League Hero, whenever he made an expert clearance. Andrea slouched in the stands and smiled. She was on the temazepam now, taking them to help her sleep. Specifically, to help her sleep and not wake up in the middle of the night screaming, screaming like how she imagined her sister must have done, how she must have done before she had the breath squeezed out of her. In her dreams, like in her sister's life, nobody heard her, and she woke up choking, her hands around her own neck.

The pills gave her a solid eight hours of sleep, something she never got even before Angela died, and they left her mellow enough to yawn and not care about much in particular the rest of the time. In fact, they were becoming remarkably useful during daylight hours. She could watch a *Rastamouse* or *Peppa Pig* marathon on one of those, no problem. The world was wrapped in cotton wool and so was she. Andy couldn't help but wonder if Stuart's remarkable performance on the pitch had anything to do with her new routine. They both had a sober New Year's Eve, in bed right after the bells. *For the sake of Sunday League,* she considered, *maybe I should stay on these forever.*

There was the small matter of memory: specifically, she didn't have much of one any more. Sure, the long-ago things were still crystal clear and easily retrieved if she wanted, which she didn't, but Andy found herself forgetting the basics she had once effortlessly juggled. She dumped the washing in the machine, then wandered the house wondering where all the heaps of dirty socks had gone. 'Are you wanting chips?' she asked Stuart five minutes after apportioning a generous serving onto his plate. Where was her mobile? In the fridge. Of course it was. She'd paid its bill twice this month. She saw the concern on her husband's face, but Andy shrugged it off. In a way, it was a comfort, this slipping away of capabilities, this realisation that there was nobody to help the perpetual helper. *It's amazing I never knew until now*, she thought. *Memory doesn't have to be who I am after all.*

Two-nil to the Rovers at half time. Little Ella turned cartwheels on the touchline with a new-found friend, the kind it was so easy to make at that age, the kind it was so easy to lose. Andy wondered if she really saw what she thought she saw as the players milled about on the touchline with their bottles of water, pulling down socks, pulling them up again: the slight, knowing nods, the blink-and-you'll-miss-it moments of pity for the skipper's missus. She cast her eyes downward so that she wouldn't know and it wouldn't matter. She pulled a tenner from her handbag and handed it to Jack: beefburgers and chips from the van for everybody, and a cup of tea for herself. Her son ran off with the money and Andy turned her face to the sky, looking for any patterns in that uniform grey that hung over London from Havering to Heathrow. She didn't care who was staring. She knew nobody belonged here more than Andrea Ormiston.

It snowed that night, cushioning any Londoner's stubborn hangover with a smooth layer of white fluff. Only an inch or so, but enough to snarl buses. Naturally, the kids loved it. Two tiny snowmen sprouted in the back garden, with pebbles for facial features. Snow meant an excuse to wear wellies to the shop with Mummy. A thrilling journey, the promise of adventure, even if it was only down to Boots on the high street.

Ella is only three, Andrea reminded herself. *She is the same age Jack was when you got pregnant with her. And he turned out alright. Christ, he turned out more than alright, he's brilliant.* 'Ell, don't touch. *Ella.*' She swatted the child's hand, sticky with sugary sweet residue, away from a display of aerosol deodorants. And three years old was too young to know that her mother was purchasing a pregnancy test along with toothpaste and skin cream. She silently prayed Ella didn't notice her hesitation entering her PIN at the till. That's what happened nowadays: the sure things no longer seemed so certain.

'Mittens on, Ella.'

That was the funny thing about the temazepam. It wasn't predictable. At first it knocked her out properly, as it was meant to do, but sometimes it took its time. And in bed, if she wasn't sleeping, they were shagging. She was not sure if it was the drug itself or just a handy side effect of not having to think about much else. What Andrea did know, unequivocally, without a shadow of a shadow of a potentially counterfeit doubt, is that she craved Stuart's touch more than a mother of two in her early thirties really had any right to do. Not with the toys on the floor and the tiny dishes piling up in the kitchen. Last night she screamed, in ecstasy and not fear, and Stuart tugged her hair and hissed *shush, that'll be the kids woken up,* but Andrea didn't care. She pushed back against him, urged him on harder, harder, dug her toenails into his legs and forced him on harder, harder, told him to do it to her like the filthy bitch she was, until flashbulbs popped behind her eyes. And she fully intended to have a repeat performance tonight, tomorrow, and onwards for as long as she fucking desired to be fucked. It puzzled her a bit, why something she had been regularly practising since she was fifteen should suddenly become so interesting again when most of her hobbies from that age had long since faded away, been taken down from the walls and folded up and securely packed away with a touch of embarrassment, but she knew she loved it, needed it, would demand it from Stuart and would get it from Stuart. She was scaring him, and she knew it, and she liked it. *You don't understand, I really want it, I want you to fuck me until I can't walk straight,* Andy told him. And he looked slightly confused for a minute before he asked her how she expected to get anything done at home if she couldn't walk properly. *Fuck you,* she replied. *For that, I'm going to make you do it to me even rougher.*

I want you to hit me, she had directed him last night. He shrank back, sliding out of her and against the headboard, shaking his head. 'I'm not going to hit you,' he had told her in no uncertain terms, tone, and volume. 'I am not going to fucking hit you. I am going to call a new therapist in the morning because you are going mental. I thought those tablets were supposed to make you chill out.'

'Nothing's going to make me chill out,' she had hissed. 'I don't chill out any more. I was too chilled out all these years. I was *comatose*. And if you want me to be like that, then fuck the fuck off. Look where being chilled out has got me.'

'Where it's got you? Two lovely kids, a nice house, a man who actually *doesn't* want to hit you. Is that a bad thing all of a sudden? Is it a bad thing you're not living in that sodding damp council flat on top of the motorway, going home with any bloke who wanted?'

'You wanted.'

'Yeah. Because you *weren't* mental, you were the coolest girl I'd ever met. Angela, seriously, you need…'

'WHAT. THE. *FUCK?*'

'What is it now?'

'YOU CALLED ME ANGELA.'

'Did I? Oh, shit. God. Sorry, sorry, slip of the tongue, it's…'

'That's disgusting, Stuart. That's really… disgusting.'

'Sorry. It was an accident. We've been talking about her so much lately…'

'Jesus Christ. I'm going to be sick.'

'Andy! Don't be sick. It's late, I'm tired, it was just a slip of the tongue. Your names are so similar. It means nothing.'

She started crying then, and hated herself for crying, because she wasn't the crying kind. She'd barely cried from the pain when she had Jack, and he was huge for a baby, and back then she'd been under the stupid notion that epidurals were for women who thought themselves too posh to push but who didn't want C-section scars showing on the beach. But no, in this post-Angela world the waterworks came on for something as stupid as speaking neutrally of the dead. Luckily, the pill kicked in and she stayed silent, sleeping, for the rest of the night. Silence was the only kind of apology she was any good at giving.

Now, she wondered, would one test be enough? Might need a few. Nah. Save that for another trip. No point putting a great big tank before the horse. There was time. If she had one thing nowadays, it was time. Too much of it to measure, or to care.

Mother and child left holding hands. January: the rubbish swirled around the kerbsides of Southall Broadway on a breezy afternoon. Boots, greengrocer, home. Fetch Jack from his pal's house. All in a day's work. Southall Broadway made her feel foreign, but it made her feel alright, because she had chosen something that turned out alright. Andy looked down at her daughter: her knitted hat with the flaps, the one that looked like a cartoon penguin had come to perch upon her little blonde head. Ella was growing up only four miles down the road from where her mum once lived and her mum's mum died too young and her mum's sister was dumped like an old mattress at a tip. Four miles was enough for nobody here to know that Angela Archer, the missing woman turned murdered woman, was blood to little Ella Ormiston. Perhaps if she never spoke of her again, Andy wondered, Ella could forget. She was only three. She and Jack had been told, Auntie Angela has gone up to Heaven. You won't be seeing her again but she told me that she loved you very much.

But she and Stuart were still planning to get a sitter to watch them during the funeral, because how could she do that to her kids, how could she burden them with so much for a woman they knew so little? She couldn't. She fucking wouldn't. She wouldn't mould Ella in her image, sad and mean and drunk and lonely, the Girl From Kensal Town. Auntie Angela was deadweight in their histories. She was Andrea's burden to carry, and she wasn't going to pass it on to any tiny shoulders. She couldn't. She wouldn't. History would not be what they became.

And the next child – if it came, when it came – wouldn't need to know any of this at all. A blank slate. A West London child with no need for a past, and nothing but time for the future. Andy considered the possibility with a rush, as if she herself was being awarded a brand-new lifetime ahead of her, something she could hold and mould in her hands.

Andy tried to view the Broadway from her daughter's height: the swirls of foreign fabric on legs stomping bright holes in a winter day, the dogs seeming more human because their mouths were level with yours, the overstock of fuzzy or lumpy fruit and veg you couldn't get in Asda right in front of your eyes as the grown-ups pick from the bins above. Andy didn't remember those colours from her childhood. Her memories of that time were monochrome, mousy browns and bleached whites, punctuated with the bursts of moments: a fire on the railway, Pot Noodles all lined up in a cupboard, kohl around her eyes and her father's camera flash.

She thought of Neely Sharpe, eyes the colour of what Andy saw from the window of the night bus down Uxbridge Road: dark, of course dark, but it was the brightness that drew you in. Andy didn't ride the night bus any more. She had no reason. She had no business where it went.

After they entered Randhawa's Fresh Market she saw Ella reaching for a prickly rambutan with one mittened hand, but stopped herself stopping her. Let her touch. Let her get to know this world around her, one so bright she'd probably never be able to take it all in.

'Such a sweet child,' an older Asian woman murmured at the pair. Andy smiled gratefully, a genuine smile at this approval of her parenting, and Ella hid her face in Mummy's long coat. *Everyone's always saying that,* Andy suddenly thought, the realisation stopping her in mid-reach for an aubergine and wiping away the smile. *Everyone says she is sweet and quiet and good and all the things a little girl should be. She is too quiet. She has always been quiet. And maybe it's not a phase. Perhaps she'll grow up and still be quiet and it won't be such a wonder, and all the people who thought she was so lovely will suddenly not even notice she exists. And she'll need them, and they'll be gone, and nobody will care nearly enough. She will have a problem and be a problem. Angela was quiet. Well, relatively. But everybody was quiet compared to you. Everybody is still quiet compared to you. And you wish you'd have shut up once in a while, because one day you're going to forget the sound of your sister's voice. You're going to forget it altogether.*

'Mummy? Can we have tomatoes?' Andy shook herself out of the thought, smiled again and almost forgot to pay for her fruit and veg before heading home.

Andy slid a carrier bag from her hand to up her arm so that she could wave to Mrs Singh across the street. Southall. Nice place, with

Punjabi neighbours. Decent. The people and the whole place. Not even London, technically. It was Middlesex, which strictly speaking didn't exist any more, yet here they were. *Here you are, with your daughter and your lives ahead of you. And you're not yet too old to make another life, maybe. Once the police release the body. Once you have the funeral and all that's left of Angela really is, in your head. Once the inquest opens and shuts and gets filed away where you never have to think about it. Then, then you can begin. You have a future now, and a promise it will start relatively soon. Not everybody in this world can claim that, y'know. Not everybody gets so lucky.* She smiled to herself, knowing the truth of her thoughts. She knew that later, there would be rage. It was already building somewhere near her stomach with those strange little tablets that sometimes did the exact opposite of what they were meant to do, destroyed when they were supposed to fix. Andy knew it all too well. There would be rage, incubating and multiplying and getting ready to burst forth someday – but for today she would smile.

Ella skipped ahead, knocking snow off front gates. She squealed with delight as the solid lumps of sparkling white exploded into powder at nothing but the touch of her hand. 'Mummy, come see,' she called to Andy, but she neither stopped nor looked back. 'Mummy! Watch what I can do.' And the little girl, pink boots skidding through a city of grey, smashed all the clean and white stretches of snow she could find, all the way home to her front door. From inside her pocket, Andy's mobile phone buzzed insistently. *Wait five fucking seconds*, she thought to herself. *I'm watching my beautiful, gorgeous, perfect little do-over.*

Nineteen

There had been another party, after Ruby but just before Neely and Angela could have been considered *Neely and Angela*. Neely had found the door in a low-rise block in Kensal Road and had bought her admission with a handful of lottery tickets. The organisers would keep everything if any of them turned out to be lucky. 'You can go straight up to the roof if you want. If you're going to swap your clothes, it's the first door on the right. But you have to keep your pants on. That's the only rule.'

'Is Angela here?'

'Don't know any Angelas.'

Neely made her way up the stairs. On the rooftop she spotted a girl dressed in head-to-toe lime green, deep in concentration, punching holes in chicken nuggets and threading them onto a length of yarn. 'It's raining hen,' she said, very seriously, upon spotting Neely staring. She tied off the last knot, unspooled the string, and dangled the meat off the rooftop. Curious, Neely peered over the edge. A passer-by reached out, looked up. The girl yanked the string away. 'Say please,' she shouted to them three storeys below.

'Fuck off!'

'Close enough.' She lowered the string again. Neely watched the swearer pull a nugget free and walk away chewing, as if it were the most natural thing in the world. 'Do you want one?' the girl asked Neely, who shook her head. 'Good choice. They're a month out of date.' Neely walked on. A boy wrapped in binbags and grip tape was being carefully coated in emulsion, then rolled around the rooftop by a pair of girls who occasionally stopped to daub the paint from their hands onto the pattern he had left. They seemed to be enjoying themselves enough. *Students*, Neely thought, then turned her wrinkled nose into a smile despite herself. *Not me any more. Or ever again. Thank fuck for small mercies.*

Neely spotted Angela in a far corner, amidst a mess of mismatched deckchairs and an inflatable palm tree. She was crouched down with her chin on the parapet, carefully studying the skyline, one hand on her drink. She turned to face Neely and a smile lit her face. 'Hey. I didn't think you'd actually show.'

Neely gestured at the unorthodox painting session. 'Better than whatever's on television.'

'I'm glad you came,' Angela said, and Neely could tell she actually meant it. 'It's not my usual... type of thing. But I like it here.'

Neely crouched down to Angela's level. 'Good view, yeah.'

'I can see my old house.' Angela pointed at one of any hundreds of buildings. It didn't matter to Neely which one it was, only that it was there, and it was where Angela had begun.

The painted boy was being cut out of his binbag suit by one of his companions. A barefooted girl stepped in a wet red puddle he had left, swore, then reconsidered her situation. She began to trace semicircles with her big toe, and gestured to friends in the distance. Soon an impromptu dance party began to no music. They were swing-dancing, kicking up sprays of colour, skidding in the paint and muddling blue and green, white and red. Someone tossed the first girl into the air. She landed awkwardly, slipped, and came down with her arse in emulsion.

'I can't decide if that's cool or absolutely stupid,' Neely said to Angela.

'It's alright for some.'

'I'm boring. Criminally boring. I sit at home listening to music.'

'Nothing wrong with that. What kind of music?'

The hardest question of them all. She looked out at the Trellick Tower and scratched at her neck: nervous habit. 'All kinds of stuff. I bet you'd find something you like.'

'There's a pub quiz down the road where you're not allowed to play unless you're off your tits. That's alright. The music round is all different years.'

'Take me to that. I bet I can win it.'

'Are you good at brainy stuff or just really good at keeping yourself together?'

'Neither.'

'Bet you're both.'

'Well, we'll have to find out.'

Neely immediately became nervous when the conversation came to a lull. *Please let her talk. Please let her say something. I wasn't joking when I said I'm boring as fuck.*

'Hey, free deckchair.' They slid in together, Angela's curls tickling Neely's face.

Please let her say something else.

'Can I ask you something?'

'You just did.'

Angela had smiled. 'Can I – erm, I'm going to ask you another thing. Promise you won't laugh.'

'Promise.'

'It's going to sound ridiculous. Bonkers.'

'*Promise.*'

'You fancy moving in with me?' She paused only a moment before the words spilled out rapid-fire. 'I mean, you were saying you hate the place you're in now, since you split with your girlfriend, and you said you…'

'Of course I do,' Neely cut her off and, forgetting herself, she laughed. 'That's a *massive* relief. I thought you were going to say something terrible. Like ask me if the rumours are true that I'm a sex pest or something. But you only want to give me a place to live! Result! You're alright.'

Her stab at humour briefly didn't seem to register with Angela, but the girl took her cue from Neely and laughed along. Their wine disappeared; Angela popped up for refills and came back with an entire bottle. The chicken girl had moved onto lowering cigarettes on strings and appeared to be doing much swifter business. The dancers had taken their cue from the fall and were busy redecorating their clothes. Neely slipped an arm around Angela, glad for her warmth, grateful for her words. They lay together as darkness began rolling in. *Her perfume smells like Brighton Beach*, Neely thought. *You could do worse than that. You could do much, much worse than that.*

Angela shifted. 'I'm just going to the toilet,' she said. Neely nodded and shut her eyes, feeling for the first time in years not only content, but content with being content. It was enough. She shut her eyes and wrapped her arms tight around her jacket, warding off the first early autumn chill.

There must be something wrong with her, Neely thought. *There's probably something wrong with me.* But she pushed the thought aside and drifted into a doze. From the rooftop, in the grey and goldish sunset, she had been thrown a lifeline, and a future – unspecific, undefined, but at least existing – had been placed in front of her. *Maybe this is the place,* she thought. *Maybe here, I will belong. Me and her. It could be that easy.*

She woke to a hand on her shoulder. 'Hey.' It was cigarettes-and-chicken girl, her face ashen. 'Your pal's down in the toilets. She's not well. You better take her home. She's pissed herself.'

There was one journey Neely knew she couldn't put off much longer. She arranged the clothes in tidy stacks, paired up shoes, tied shut the plastic carrier bags Andy had forgotten. The socks and pants and bras Neely threw away. But the proper clothes, those went into a big cardboard box for Mr Archer. There was something precious about these clothes, these cheap bits of fabric anonymously cut and stitched half the world away by anonymous cutters and stitchers who had their own problems. They still smelled of Angela. That tiny bit of her, surely her family would have some use for it.

Everything went wrong from the moment she bumbled onto the Central Line to East Acton. One cardboard flap tore off in her hand. She caught one corner on the ticket barrier leaving the station and spilled those pieces of Angela all over the floor, slick with filthy slush. The red sequinned party dress, Andrea's gift, was stained dark grey. She scooped up the box and waddled the way she had come before, back when there had still been a chance of a happy ending, the possibility of laughing at her reaction at a later date over a pint and a packet of crisps. When she made it to the house, the man who opened the door stared straight over her head, then let her inside with nothing but a cursory nod.

He stank of sadness and booze. The eyes of photographs stared down at Neely from every wall in the house, shooting at her with the smell of damp: there were dozens of Angelas, young and then slightly less young but still never as old as she should have become. In a tree, on the front steps of a house that wasn't this one, on the Grand Union Canal. The Angela in her father's portraits exuded life precisely because the girl looked as if she had no concept of it ever possibly ending. Angela, staring blankly off a balcony into a sun-scorched London summer day. Angela mid-cartwheel in the Meanwhile Gardens in Kensal Town, two skinheads sitting off in the margin with their cans of strong lager, oblivious to her presence. Angela standing seriously against a door frame as a hand conveniently disembodied by the camera marked her height in pencil. She was eight years old and roughly equal to Andy at ten. Angela and her brother approximating kung fu poses at each other from opposite ends of a lounge somewhere that wasn't East Acton. Angela choosing flowers outside Harrow Road Somerfield, in a time long before Neely Sharpe. So many Angelas, like a museum, like a mausoleum.

Andy had her space, too: framed and overlooking a table where a knocked-over bottle of brown sauce had spilled and congealed, from the looks of it, a few days previous. Neely squinted at the teenage girl with black-rimmed eyes punctuating a pale, scowling face. She cradled her chin in her hands as she sat on concrete steps, barefoot in a fluffy pale gown, her hair dotted with bluebells.

Next to Andy, an older Angela was flooded with light from the kitchen window, hands busy with the washing-up and face clearly startled by the sudden awareness she was being watched and recorded. *She looks like a Vermeer,* Neely thought. *Girl with Fairy Liquid.*

Neely waited for an offer of a cup of tea that never came. Mr Archer opened what remained of the box and lifted out a few pieces of fabric with no emotion, then sighed and sank into the lounge sofa. No words, no reaction. He only moved to lift his can. Neely stood, hands folded. She knew then why Angela had never made an introduction: there was nothing for either of them in this cold and grey house in East Acton. Neely made her polite exit, walked as far as two doors down, then bolted back to the Tube.

All along the Central Line, Neely thumbed the corner of her mobile phone. Deep in her pocket, it bumped against her hip during the walk up Queensway, over the bridge above the canal, the slow trudge up the

Harrow Road. By the time she unlocked the door of number 490, she had her finger on the send button, and by the time she shut herself into Flat C, she was listening to the unexpected ringing at the other end.

'Hello?'

'Hi, Andy?'

'Who is this?' The voice Neely heard was undoubtedly Andrea Ormiston's, but sounded as if it was coming from several years in either the past or future. The dreamy, almost drunk tones didn't match the woman Neely knew, however little she actually knew her.

'It's Neely Sharpe.'

'Neely. Hi. About Monday, I'm sorry. I didn't realise it was you until you'd left.' It was a response that let Neely know there would be no invitations to Sunday dinner forthcoming, that she had dropped to the priority level of a work acquaintance, and a particularly annoying one at that. One who made voices and expected people to laugh, who ate the last biscuit from the communal tin, one who had yet to discover the miracle of deodorant, one who for the love of all things sacred would not shut up about shit that absolutely nobody cared about. That kind, and now Neely knew it.

'Look, I need to tell you something. There's no easy way of putting this. It's about Angela.' Silence on the other end of the line, silence where she would have expected a polite prompt. 'I've been looking through some of her old journals. I've figured a lot of things out. I know about the boys who raped her, and I'm sure you know too. I've figured out that...'

'Neely... don't.'

'Sorry?'

'I don't want to hear it. I'm sorry. No.'

'It's not a matter of – Andrea, this is a big deal.'

'And I am telling you I do not want to hear it. Because I know everything *already*. You've seen what I know already. And it really doesn't matter any more.'

'It does matter. It doesn't just stop mattering...'

At the other end of the connection, the sound of Andy slamming down a glass. 'Do not tell me what does and does not matter. This is my sister. I know you were in love with her, I know you were living with her and fucking her and whatever else, however you did it, but do not put on that voice and tell me what to do about what happened to her. Because maybe you thought the two of you were sorted, but I'm telling you, Angela didn't know what she wanted out of life. She hadn't fucking lived.'

'So you knew what happened to her when she was…'

'Yes. She was my *sister*. She told me those things.'

'Well then why didn't you say anything to me?'

'If Angela didn't tell you then it's not my business. Look, I did you a favour…'

Neely lost any veneer of self-control and screamed into the phone. 'Why the fuck is everybody insisting they're doing me a favour? I never asked for any favours. I never wanted any favours!' *I just wanted a life,* she thought through welling tears. *I just wanted to get a fucking life.*

In Southall, the voice came through slow and scathing. 'This isn't about you. And my family can take care of itself.'

'If that's so true then why is Angela dead?'

Either Andy didn't hear or Andy didn't care. 'If you want to help, don't remind us of any of that shit. Let it go. It's in the past. She's dead, it's dead, the end. Bit of advice, Neely, quit obsessing over the past. Burn your memories. I burned my dad's fucking photographs today, every last one of them I have, all the hundreds of little Angelas and little Andreas and little Alexes, and y'know what? I should have done it years ago. Because *none of it fucking matters.* Memory isn't who you are. It's a pair of concrete shoes. And if you want to drown yourself then fucking drown yourself but don't drag other people down there with you.'

'I just thought you should know that…'

'No. I'm sorry, Neely. Goodbye. Please do not call back.'

'Andrea–'

Too late. In Southall, Andrea Ormiston had put down her mobile, taken another look at those two red lines on the Boots plastic stick, and reached for the iron.

Twenty

She filled herself with wine, strategically, before ringing the journalist with an apology on her tongue and business on her mind. Neely figured that if she swallowed enough alcohol first, then swallowing her pride wouldn't be too difficult. Practice made perfect.

'Rachel Martin.'

'Hello. It's Neely Sharpe? From, erm, the Angela Archer case?'

'Hello.'

'I'm sorry for hanging up on you before. I was just upset. It was so much happening at once…'

'No worries, no worries.'

'But I still want to know how you got my phone number.'

'It's on your Facebook.' *Shit.* All those hours wasting time in the office and she hadn't bothered fixing her privacy settings.

'Well, how'd you get my name?'

'You're tagged in nearly all of Angela's photos. You and a Sam Wylie? He's not keen on speaking, either.'

'Hmmm.' *She doesn't need to know*, Neely thought. *That's my scoop.* 'Do you approach everyone like this after someone's been killed?'

'I was at the press conference after Angela… was found.'

'I was in the back of the room.'

'Her sister, she said something about how people didn't care about Angela because of who she was and who she loved.'

'Did you ask her?'

The journalist chuckled. 'I haven't had much luck getting in touch with her, to be honest. That's why I'm hoping you could help me. Do you know what she meant?'

'Well, "who she was": an epileptic chav who worked at a council pool. No money, no fame, no big search party leaving no stone unturned. Self-explanatory, really. And "who she loved": that would be me. Also self-explanatory. Angela was my girlfriend. We'd been together more than a year. She meant that nobody cares enough about a white-trash lesbian going missing the way they care about, you know, a cute little kid with rich parents going missing.'

A moment of silence from the other end of the phone. Just a moment, mind, but a moment that meant more than a minute.

'Oh. You and Angela, were you... committed?'

'We lived together.'

'That's interesting, it never came up.'

'No mention of any suspicious boyfriends to be interviewed and ruled out, was there?'

'Suppose not.'

'When's your article being printed? Can I see it in advance?'

'Erm, it's not quite clear, Neely. See, this is not a story, really.'

'How do you mean?' If it bleeds, it leads. Neely knew that much about journalism, from common sense and from the few days she had pondered doing it for a living before moving on to the next idea. Surely Angela's news hadn't bled out yet.

'Sorry, I should have been more clear. We haven't had any new information about Angela's... death come through. In order to write an article, there would have to be a major revelation of sorts. So until the police have anything new to tell us, we'll hold the story.'

'The police?'

'Yes?'

'Does it have to be the police?'

'Or anybody else who knows anything about her disappearance, her death.'

'Well then, I'll just have to find you a story.'

She'd never drunk an entire bottle of wine in one go before. Well, strictly speaking, there had been plenty of nights when she had swallowed three-quarters of a litre of wine, but never from a single bottle, and never on her own. Numbers were not absolute like that. A bottle's worth with friends, with howling celebration, was not a bottle's worth of pure liquid courage. She shouldn't try to keep up with men; she was too tiny. That's what everybody told her. But fuck what everybody told her, because everybody didn't have Angela Archer on their mind.

Neely shut her eyes and saw the rare golden sunlight falling on pale golden curls. Angela flopping onto the sofa, the three buttons of her work top undone. Perpetually chipped fingernails. Eyes glazing over at the crap TV she watched when she couldn't sleep. Mumblings of 'eh, nothing' whenever she was asked what she was sketching on the backs of bills. Slightly tuneless singing along to long-dead men. *Maybe you just shouldn't dream*, suggested almost like an apology.

Maybe tonight Neely could sleep without dreams.

She drained the final inches of the chardonnay and searched through the flat for the journal. She found it on the windowsill beside her bed: of course, the last place she had left it, but she couldn't remember why she had left it there. It suddenly seemed too precious to casually drop anywhere it could be seen on the outside, anywhere the sun – what sun? – could fade the ink. Neely brought the journal through to the lounge, the wine making her movements feel liquid. She'd fall asleep soon, she knew. She always fell asleep when she drank. She wasn't a cheery drunk and she wasn't a violent drunk. She was a boring drunk, because being drunk bored her and she let it show. But Neely had enough time left in her to read the final pages Angela had written.

Strictly speaking, Angela hadn't written. She had drawn. Neely instantly recognised the curve of Harrow Road, the intersections of the lines marking a motorway and the ones designating the canal. Angela had even shown the Tube station at Royal Oak. A circled hash mark sat across the Westway overpass from Westbourne Green. And Neely would have known that space on the map was Westbourne Green even if she hadn't obsessively learned local geography over the past year in an attempt to convince herself that she belonged, that she *could* belong, in this godforsaken corner of West London, because Angela Archer had labelled it, and underlined *Westbourne* with such force that her pencil point had broken, leaving a tiny burst of graphite embedded in the last page of the journal.

Frantically, sleep no longer on the agenda, Neely switched on her laptop, her hands shaking so hard it took multiple attempts to bring Google onscreen. *London Sewers River Westbourne*, she managed to type. In a blur of an hour, her eyes drank in travelogue and how-to, photo essay and polemic about the other underground, Angela's underground, the one she shared with a cadre of explorers with waist-high waders and industrial torches and half-decent cameras. Angela had owned none of those, as far as Neely knew, but as she fell further into the pages of search results, she knew she had found the right place. And she could find more for herself: over and over, the explorers explained that the sewers were hidden in plain view. They could be entered directly from the pavements millions crossed every day without a single thought about what lay beneath. It took a different type of mind to think that not every manhole and grate embedded in cement was sealed shut, and that the ones just big enough to fit a human body were meant for precisely that purpose. Perhaps not the brightest of minds, sure, but brightness was no guarantee of glory in these places sought purely for their darkness.

Neely closed her laptop and sprung off the couch, her hands and brain moving in separate directions. She grabbed the emergency torch from beneath the kitchen sink and her coat from the arm of the sofa, not noticing that, outside her window, Harrow Road was already lightly iced with powder, with more falling steadily. Lights burned in empty windows; nobody was bothering to look at Neely as she grabbed her keys but left her handbag lying on the lounge floor. She sprinted down the steps to the street and let the door slam behind her. On an abandoned Harrow Road, her footsteps left the only marks in the snow.

Past Costcutter, past fried chicken and shuttered off-licence, past Westminster Drug Recovery Options and Grace Pentecostal Church, Harrow Road Police Station and the Hope and Anchor, Neely trotted as quickly as she could without losing her footing. She crossed above the Grand Union Canal and past the tower blocks of the Warwick Estate. She turned her head from the bright lights down to the pavement and, like a mirage, there it was, and she knew before she touched the freezing metal with ungloved hands that it would somehow yield with her efforts: the grate covering the entrance to the filth that had been Angela Archer's unspoiled underground.

Looping her scarf around her face, Neely crouched on the snowy pavement, scanned the empty road, and rattled the grate. Nothing. She pulled with all her strength and felt it catch slightly before coming unstuck, pivoting open on its hinge. Rob had been right. It really was that easy. Instinctively, Neely scanned her surroundings to make sure nobody was watching before she began her descent. *What are you doing?* she thought to herself, and then pushed any concern straight out of her mind and down the hole. *It doesn't matter what you do. Clever, stupid, it doesn't matter. You're not changing the past and your future doesn't look too bright. But you're doing what you want to do, right here and right now. You wanted London. You wanted it to be a part of you. You might as well have dug this fucking hole yourself. Get in.*

Rob hadn't lied: there was heat down here. Warmth hugged her as she descended the ladder built into the side of the passage. The grate clattered back into position. She had no waders, only her wellies; fortunately, the internet had come good on its assurance that this part of the network stayed shallow in all but the worst weather. Still, Neely winced as her feet touched bottom with a slight splash, a reminder that she had reached the bowels of London.

She felt her way along a wall, down a small flight of steps, her feet shaking with the drink and the cold. Switching on her torch, Neely scanned the brick walls. *It's so clean*, she thought, gazing at the even brickwork left by the Victorians in their civic pride. Then she shone the beam downward at the slow-moving grey-brown stream. *This is it? Under London? It's just a trickle. I've seen bigger floods in Stevenage.* Then a cluster of baby wipes floated by. She jumped at the sight of a tampon string, then jumped further when she realised it wasn't a tampon string at all. It was a dead mouse's tail. Bile and wine rose in the back of her throat and she forced them back down, tipping her head to face the roof of the tunnel. Rob wouldn't lie, no. He wasn't mentally capable of it in his best state. If this was Angela's sacred ground, then redemption had to lie somewhere within this cavern. *You're alright. You're not going through hell,* Neely reminded herself. *It's warm, but it's not nearly hot enough.*

She followed the water downstream: south. Angela wouldn't have fought with the flow. For a sewer under London, Neely thought, there certainly wasn't much being flushed away. How had Angela found this place? Trial and error? Trials, sure, she'd had some. Errors, probably even more. But this one, Angela had got right: the water ran down the centre of the sewer in a small enough trickle that Neely could walk with one wellie on each side of the flow and have only the faintest suggestion of a waddle to her gait. Still, after no more than fifty feet, she began to sweat under her jumper and coat and the scarf mercifully wrapped around the lower half of her face. Through the ragged sound of her own breathing, Neely thought she could hear a rumble, a rush. She continued forward, racing another clump of wipes in the water between her legs.

The rushing noise gathered into a dull roar, less abstract, more urgent, as Neely walked toward the source. Squinting into the faint torch beam, she thought she could see a wall, a dead end; she quickened her pace. As she approached, smears of colour coalesced into the shapes of bricks, and the smaller sounds of the sewer were swallowed by the insistent static rumble. It was a fast flow of water, and Neely broke into a foolhardy trot through the muck to meet it. In daylight, she would have spotted it from far away; in torchlight, in desperation, in blind desire to find whatever world had swallowed up Angela Archer and spat her back out into Harrow Road, Neely didn't make out the junction until she stood twenty feet away. Then she saw it: the route running perpendicularly to her path, a culvert of deep and filthy and fast-flowing sewage with its stench. The websites had told her it was an interceptor, a main line. If she had been walking south, then it was racing east, toward the centre of the city like a hellish motorway. And then she saw *it*: hanging still from a peg hammered into old grout far above Neely's head, a sad denim satchel, utterly unremarkable except for its location.

Neely shuffled to the side of the tunnel, skidding slightly against the slippery bend. She reached for the bag: too short. The reek of the crossing sewer path permeated below her scarf, and she retched as she attempted a hop. No luck. Re-tightening the twist of fabric around her nose, Neely reached out with her torch and whacked the bottom of the bag, which swung wildly at the end of its peg. With a yelp, she swung again, harder, losing her grip. The bag fell to the sewer floor, and the torch flew from her grasp and descended in an arc before landing in the deep water with a sickening plop. The beam of light spun like a cry for help before the waste flow carried it away toward the east. And it may have been the stench, or it may have been the flash of knowledge that hit Neely as the light finally failed, that turned her stomach: *This is where it happened. This is where she died. And whoever did it knew enough to take her away from here.*

With the last scrap of illumination, Neely grabbed the bag and looped the strap around her neck. Sickening drips fell onto her coat, onto her thighs, down the gaping mouths of her wellies. Shrouded in total darkness, a kind she had never seen in London – not in the deepest nights inside her flat, never in the permanently neon-lit Harrow Road – Neely turned around and felt along the wall the way she had come, listening to the roar of the interceptor line fade. She had begun to cry, and she didn't know why. She knew she was safe. She knew exactly where she was going, even though she couldn't see the way. She knew that so long as she kept one mucky boot in front of the other, she would get right back to the start.

She stubbed her toes and stumbled forward at the staircase, catching herself before her teeth would have shattered against concrete. Neely pulled herself up the ladder back toward Harrow Road, her head light, her feet leaden. At street level she sucked fresh air and let snow hit the tears on her face. Snot streamed from her nose. Sobs, desperate and alien noises, burst from her mouth into the empty road. Then headlights briefly lit up her face and a shriek of brakes matched the tone of her voice. Neely ducked back into the hole and the walls of the passageway shook as metal and motor hit the Westway overpass.

She knew she was not dead, that she had not been touched, but she screamed anyway, her voice echoing through the tunnel. Her body shook uncontrollably as the sounds of the crash and of herself faded back into silence. With a final burst of strength, Neely hauled herself up, dragged herself from the hole and lay on her belly on the pavement. Twenty feet away, a mangled driver's-side door opened with a crunch. Neely saw the electric pink coat. The driver stumbled out, spun, and stared at Neely with animal eyes.

'Michelle!'

The eyes stared harder and their owner stepped tentatively in Neely's direction. The bad skin, the gnawed fingers. An incredulous face that shifted into utter contempt.

'Michelle?'

'Who the fuck are you?'

Neely spotted a stirring in the passenger side of the wreck. The door opened slowly and a scarf fluttered out ahead of its owner. Neely thought of Isadora Duncan, done in by her own flowing silk scarf. She had found people knew of the death, but forgot the name. Well, she knew the name. Isadora Duncan. It had come up in the last pub quiz at the Hope and Anchor, the very last one they did together. Name of the American modern dancer killed when her scarf became entangled in a car wheel and snapped her neck. Thin Quizzy and Alan Partridge in a Pear Tree hadn't given an answer. Quizlamic Jihad called her Isabella Douglas. But Neely and Angela, Neely specifically, got it right to send Tequila Mockingbirds rocketing into second place overall behind Please Evacuate the Pub Right Now This is Not a Drill. Fantastic night, that. But Isadora Duncan at least went out in a posh car, not a Ford Fiesta in the shadow of the Westway.

Neely exhaled a mouthful of steam. 'You're Michelle, yeah? It's Neely, from Stevenage. Tasha? Is that Tasha?'

'What?'

'Where is he? Where's Brian?'

'Who the *fuck* are you?'

Cold, wet snow seeped through the knees of Neely's jeans and bit her skin. Unsteadily, she stood. 'Nobody,' she hollered, shocked by the strength in her own voice. 'Absolutely nobody!' Clumsily, she dusted clods of snow from her clothing and, head bent down against the blowing drifts, turned and walked west.

Neely shed her coat and wellies at the door to Flat C. The rest of her clothes came off just over the threshold. In the kitchen, watched by a collage of photographic memories stuck to a refrigerator door, she scrubbed up to her elbow in scalding water. She took a mouthful of Johnnie Walker, then another. Then, and only then, did she open the denim satchel.

She upended the bag and a mess of white pages, each one pencil-sketched, tumbled onto the lounge floor. Glossy photographic prints followed, home-developed black-and-whites of a woman Neely had never seen before, but whose cheekbones and jaw had surfaced in her girlfriend, and whose eyes had glared at her out of Andy Ormiston's face. The woman was naked, her swollen belly cradled in her long-fingered hands. The surroundings, the woodchip walls, the fluorescent lighting that couldn't be artfully restyled by the photograph's developer, seemed to scream the year of Angela's birth. The prints were topped by the thud of something more substantial. It was a small black volume, the same dimensions as the rainbow-striped journal. Neely opened to the centre: blank pages. She spun backward through the book: nothing whatsoever until she reached the first two pages. At the top, in Angela's clean hand, was the date. The 18th of December, the last day Neely had seen her alive.

So I was helping Dad sort through old photos a while back and I keep thinking of how he said all joking like, if you want to see Andy smiling as a kid you have to go back to primary. But it wasn't joking really cos it's true. She got ten years happy then ten miserable, ten happy again with her man and still going I hope. I found her school portrait from year 1 and I put it next to Jack's and he's got her face 100%. And if you want to see her smile again then you need to wait until the pictures where he's born. Then it's like someone switched from black and white to colour film. The lights came on when she had her kids.

Thinking of this because I'm thinking of Neely. I think it will happen for her, too. She and Andy are so alike. This is the one thing I can do for Neely and even if she hates me when she finds out, she won't hate me forever, because I know this kid is for the good. No doubting myself now. End of.

Neely, bless her. Her life has been so easy, she has to try to make it hard. Spends all her time worrying that her life isn't throwing her enough trouble – yeah, she hates her job, but it's a job with more money than I'll ever get. I know she hates living in this bit of town but it's not that bad to me. Maybe she's only with me because she thinks I'm such a sad case that I make her feel better about herself. But I can't hate that about her. She's just the greatest because she doesn't try to help. She's the most clever person I've ever met and she doesn't try to help because deep down she knows she can't. She's clever enough to know what she doesn't know. And she's clever enough to find out everything she needs, eventually. And one day she'll be tested and she'll come out top. But she can't do anything to change my life. And it's not a sad thing.

I'm alright with that. With having that knowledge. Because at least I know, y'know?

The one thing I can do right, that she can't do for me, to make everything better, is this kid. And it's going to be a good thing. It has to be. We could talk about it like normal people but we're not everyone else. No, it's just something I need to do. She'll be angry, yeah, but she'll come around. Andy always did.

The other thing I need to do is start cutting strings. I mean like everybody around here. We're going to move house. Neely wants to anyway. We need a clean break and that. Say goodbye to everybody I know, talk to them one last time, let them know I'm out of here for good. And then Neely and I can just build up a new life. What Neely made me realise is this city is so fucking huge and it's criminal that I've barely been out of this one bit. That's going to change now. It's all a good thing. Already.

I'm off the tablets. I'm trying not to drink. I fucked up at the weekend though. Better not do that again.

She will be okay. I know she will be okay. She always knows what to do. And maybe I do too.

Neely awoke on the floor hours later, her neck stiff, the journal beneath one elbow, graphite staining one cheek. With a start, she jumped up to draw the lounge blinds, but across the Harrow Road there was nobody awake to watch.

Twenty-One

Neely was hung over, again, with a bruise in the shape of a hardback book forming on the side of her arm.

Phone.

Sam.

'Neels.'

'Sam? I don't want to talk. Please.' It wasn't that she held a grudge; rather she didn't have the energy to consider whether it would help her to act like she did.

'Neels. No. Wait. Listen.'

'What.' Not a question.

'Bury the hatchet.' Not a request.

'You what?'

'Come over here. Please.'

'No, Sam. I'm not going all the way to Hackney. Say whatever you need to say.'

'Please, Neels. I'm asking you really, really nicely. Come over to mine.'

'And I'm telling you really, really blatantly, fuck off. Are you drunk? Did what's-her-name leave you? Is that it? It's the season for people leaving each other.'

'It's about Angela. It's something of hers. You need to see it.'

'Can't you just tell me now?'

'Nah. I did one better.'

'You what?'

'I just did one better. For Angela. And for you too.'

'I'm lost.'

'You won't believe me. Come around. I'll be home.' And then he hung up on her.

Westbourne Park to King's Cross. King's Cross to Highbury & Islington. Then Dalston Junction. Then up the road, up the stairs, face-first into where she thought she'd never stand again.

'Sam.' She knocked, no response. 'Sam. Let me in.'

Nobody opened the door for her, so she let herself in.

'Sam. You've got five minutes. What the hell do you have to show me?'

The smell in the flat was a fistful of pennies; of her younger hands after she had picked through her uncle Roger's box of miscellaneous foreign coins looking for ones with holes in the middle that she could thread onto a string and wear around her neck, and then the smell would follow her there, too.

'Sam?'

'Neels. Knew you'd come.' He sounded elsewhere, further away than the next room.

She held her breath and followed the voice and the smell into the lounge. He'd done some rearranging, or maybe it was his woman, his new woman, his nice woman who would want there to be a proper table in front of the TV for tea in proper matching mugs. She would be the one responsible for straightening the picture frames, alphabetising his records and adding hers to the shelves. But whoever this cow was, this Sophia, she would not be responsible for the sharp metallic smell, the one coming from the blood, the blood having come from the body on the floor, the body that was lying face down between Sam's discarded trainers and the television remote control.

The television remote control, and the Ikea catalogue.

And the nearly empty bottle of vodka. Smirnoff. The red labelling.

And the claw hammer.

Brian, too.

There were bits of Brian Powell on the claw hammer.

Brain from Brian.

'Don't cry, Neels. Don't. It's OK.'

'I know who he is. He's been round my flat.'

'Neels, it's alright.'

'He did it, didn't he?'

'It's alright.'

Her breath came ragged as she struggled to get enough in to yell back at him. 'This is not fucking alright!' The room spun, and black spots covered bits of the wall, the picture frames, one of Sam's trainers, Brian's good shoes, the television, the hair drenched in blood and the shattered bits of bone.

'It is. *It is.* You'd have done it yourself. You know it. It's a good thing. We've done a good thing.'

'We?'

'You and me and Angela. It's alright, it's done.'

'*Nothing's done.* Oh my god. Sam, Sam, *no.*'

She sat down on the couch with its familiar sag, staring at the unfamiliar addition to the flat. As in life, Brian's body didn't look quite real, all elongated limbs and awkward proportions, angles where they didn't belong, twists and turns when a straight course would have done just fine. There was something safe about him now, lying wrecked and still: the inside matched the outside, and it was perfectly fine for him to be unbelievable, dead on the carpet of Sam Wylie's rented flat in Hackney.

Sam whispered, 'It was so easy.'

'*Fuck.*'

'Neels.'

'You're a fucking murderer.'

'*He's* a murderer. I'm a fixer. I'm the repairman. It's all better now. Good as new.'

'No it's not. Where's Angela if everything's good as new? Eh? Where the fuck's Angela? Fucksake!'

'I did it for her and I did it for you so it's *good enough.*'

Sam squatted before her. Kissed her. Kissed her again: hard. This time, his eyes focused. Neely had never seen them steadier, never seen so much of the grey against the black.

'Neels.'

'*What?*'

'What happens next?'

She breathed deep and kept her voice steady. 'A wardrobe box.'

'You what?'

'Wardrobe boxes. For when you move house. They're big. You can put everything in your wardrobe in them without folding the clothes flat. It'll be the right size. Just wrap and wrap and wrap it up with duct tape with him inside. Weight him down. In the canal. In the Lea. He'll sink.' She heard her voice accelerating, picking up the sound of certainty the less she felt it herself. 'Who do you know with a van? Anybody? Any of those bands?

They've got to have vans. If they're already dirty, really minging inside, that's the best.'

'Neely, slow down.'

'No, Sam. You have to move him quick. What are you going to do about the blood? Rip up the carpet? Your landlord won't have it. Where can you go to burn it? Can you get out to the marshes? And the walls, you can't just paint them, you need to paper them over, too.'

'I don't know what to do.'

'You should have thought of that before you fucking killed him!'

You, killed, him. The words, simple and short as they were, felt foreign in her mouth. Sam killed him. Sam Wylie took a hammer and killed a person who was alive and now is dead. Little Sam Wylie, he's not that big except in his head, Sam Wylie took a hammer and killed the man who killed Angela Archer. She knew it now. Sam had to have known something Neely didn't. And Neely didn't like the idea of Sam Wylie, little Sam Wylie, that little alcoholic Manc waster Sam Wylie, knowing anything she didn't. It wasn't right. It wasn't natural. It wasn't the proper order of things. Neely thought she should be able to figure it out. She had the definite facts: body, brain, floor, hammer. Sam. She had the probable causes: Angela, journal, West London, three boys on Wormwood Scrubs years ago. Angela ruining her life however she saw fit.

Neely stared at the still and bled body and heard one of those sayings, one of those trite American sayings from an American politician, about how you should recognise there are known knowns and known unknowns and unknown unknowns, and Neely thought it was stupid, you shouldn't accept categories like that, you should figure out how you're going to know everything about everybody or else shut yourself up for good like Brian had shut up Angela and Sam had shut up Brian. Neely knew now. She was brighter than most. And everybody always knew she was brighter than most because even when she was little, before she could place Hackney on a map or work out Westbourne Park to Dalston Junction, she was always asking questions.

'Sam. How'd you get him here?'

'Knew him. He lives – he lived in Richmond Road.'

'Did you know what he did to Angela?'

'Then or now?'

'Both.'

'Yeah. Made him tell me.' He jutted his chin towards the hammer. 'Wasn't too difficult.'

'How'd you know him?'

'Oh, Neely,' Sam moaned, sitting beside her, pulling at the roots of his hair. 'Neely, it's shit, it's so fucking shit…'

'Tell me. How did you know Brian Powell when I barely knew Brian Powell?'

'Neels,' he sighed. 'I bought from him. Everyone around here did. He could get you anything cheap. Good Es. He wasn't big time, he was just some jumped-up shit who took as much as he sold and then he'd get stupid and run his mouth. And he ran it too far. You're not the only clever person. I put two and two together.'

'You didn't have to put them together like *this*.'

'Yes I did. He took Angela and he took my kid. He… he was saying he wanted things to be like before. Him and her. When they were kids. Bollocks like that. He kept saying he just wanted things to be the way they used to be. Kept giving me this shit about how he was dying and she had led him on and he loved her and that. But then she ended up going with girls instead. Kept showing off. Kept showing off *you* and all. He wouldn't shut up so I hit him again and again and I couldn't exactly stop and then he finally quit…'

'Fuck, Sam –'

'Don't blame me for any of this shit, Neely Sharpe. Don't you fucking blame me for this.'

'Then who do you suggest I fucking blame?'

'It's *your* fault. He couldn't stand the two of you… *flaunting* your nice little life together. Down Harrow Road. Down the pubs. The way you made her. He noticed.'

'I didn't make her any – she was *happy*. She was just happy. Why the fuck would there be something wrong with that?' The sight and smell of all that blood hadn't turned her stomach, folding it right over and shoving it where it didn't belong, but now this realisation did the job: her girlfriend had been murdered for the offence of happiness with Neely Sharpe, for those nights curled into each other's limbs, for parks in summer and on the sofa in front of the heater when it got cold, with any one of those stolen CDs blaring long-dead voices into a room where two women had never felt more alive; for lips that might find each other on the threshold of their one-bedroom, or in their grand union along the canal, or over one shared pint in full view of anybody who might not realise there was love in their road, in their borough, in their cold and electric city. There was love, and they'd had it, and they'd worn it like sequinned dresses sparkling under spotlights. And there had been hope, Neely knew. For herself, that maybe one person could make an entire life make sense. She just hadn't known what it was for Angela, then: that perhaps the ties that bound wouldn't become the ties that choked.

Sam didn't seem to hear her, but more likely he didn't care. 'You made her want more when she didn't have a chance of getting out of that shithole. You were making her your little middle-class zombie wifey thing.'

'Did *he* say that? Fucksake. Where are you getting that? She wasn't some moron, Sam. She lived her own life. In case you forgot, remember who *wasn't* with us last time I woke up here?'

'Whatever, Neely. You knew what you were doing.'

'You're high right now. You're fucking high. He was at my flat two nights after I last saw her and he didn't say anything about Angela. How the hell could he have killed her anyway? *Look* at him. She could have fought *him* off.' She pointed at the skinny and still wrists. 'Only way he could kill anybody is if they let him. Don't be stupid.'

'He did it. *He told me.*'

'Then he lied.'

'Yeah? You think? After he told me he tried to apologise to her – apologise about what he did when they were kids?'

'Raping her. Say the word.'

'Oh my god, just *shut up* for once. He said he tried to apologise and she wouldn't have it. Said she laughed at him. She said he wasn't important enough for it to have mattered what he did to her, because she was still there, living in that road, she hadn't become a basket case, she didn't let him and the other boys drive her from her home like her dad and her sister. She said she had a good life now and he was too meaningless to even have a *chance* of ruining it and she kept laughing at him. And then he lost it. Knowing he wasn't anything to her. That's what he told me. He went ballistic on her because she *laughed*. He wasn't making that up.'

Neely knew that laugh. Her eyes welled as she remembered it pealing through the Porchester Centre that first time, and she stared at the body. It wasn't just his head Sam had seen to properly. Dark blood stained the fingers she could see.

'And he would have died soon, anyway,' Sam spat. 'He had a disease, he was born with it. He *was* going to die. I did him a *favour*. Angela told me all about him.'

'Why didn't she tell *me?*'

Sam shook his head and smiled, hopelessly, a smile that knew any chance to make anything better, or even just OK, had left long ago on its cheap day return with no plans to ever visit again. 'Neely. You would have just tried to make a better world.' He stared into the middle distance, at his wall of records. 'And here you are. Look at you now.'

Neither spoke after that. Sam rose first and walked into the kitchen. Neely heard the sound of the tap, of the kettle. A cupboard opened and shut; two mugs clinked against the countertop. He returned and set the tea down on that table, the table he had picked out with his new woman, and he sat down beside Neely, the last he had left of Angela Archer.

Neely held her mug tight. *It's either going to burn my hands or it's going to burn my mouth,* she thought. *And I'm going to need my mouth.*

She thought of a river that became a sewer and promptly made herself stop. No, she would not poison Angela's only sacred ground. She would not let anybody else in to that revolting, foul, and utterly perfect place unless they bloody well found it themselves. And she remembered Angela's words in black ink on white paper: *She will be okay. She always knows what to do.*

She would make it OK. For herself, and only herself.

They sat, sipped, stared. Slowly, she relaxed, and Neely noticed the blood where no blood had been before: the drops on the wall, on the hi-fi. She tried to remember secondary-school physics. How had Sam swung to get that spatter on the window? She craned her neck to see around the dark mass of what had been the back of Brian's head. The eye she could see was still open, so she stared back.

Sam began rambling but Neely didn't hear a word. She thought of how she hadn't been allowed to touch Angela, to even see her one last time – she hadn't even been allowed to make the formal identification. That was for family and she didn't count. She'd seen no more than a blur of coat in the distant undergrowth. Gingerly, she crept off the couch and her hand reached for the closer leg before her brain knew what it was doing. He didn't feel as cold and stiff as she expected. She spread out her fingers, hovering over his neck, looking at her skin over his. Her hand shook but she didn't move away.

'Neels, what the fuck are you doing?' She sprang back into her seat.

'I don't know.'

He sat down beside Neely and threw his arms around her: not protectively, or at least not of her. She felt the flutter of his heart again, faster than before, and only then understood Sam was terrified at his own strength. He'd go along with whatever she said if she could only stay calm enough when she said it. It wasn't love, this strange embrace. Neely froze against him: was he asking to be held back? For an affirmation? A pat on the head? A simple, *You did the right thing?*

She would give him more than that. Just the one more time. Whether he wanted it or not. For gratitude, for absolution. And for her last act of sheer recklessness, the last one she would allow herself, ever, in this city where she thought everything would finally make sense, would finally fall into her lap, perfectly formed and polished, because she had already done enough.

'I'm sorry, Neels. I'm so, so fucking sorry.'

'You said it was a good thing.'

'No, like, I'm sorry for you.'

'Don't be.'

'I'm...'

'Shut up.'

She stood, suddenly; black spots danced in front of her eyes from the shift.

'You're leaving? Is that it?'

Neely shook her head. 'No. Come here.' She grabbed Sam's arm – it was colder than she had expected in the artificial heat of the flat – and pulled him toward the bedroom.

'Nah, Neels, this is weird, this is really, really wrong.'

'If this is more wrong than what you've done, then you're a fucking psychopath.'

'Both wrong. Just – Neels, no, this isn't a good idea.'

'Shut up. Undress me.'

She took a perverse pride in how his hands shook, how he fumbled with her button-front shirt. His fingernails, cut to the quick, looked particularly pale and pathetic. Neely smiled at him. He stared back blankly, pausing momentarily at the task at hand.

'I'll do it,' Neely hissed, unfastening the final button and wiggling out of the top. She unfastened Sam's belt while he took care of his own T-shirt. 'On the floor.'

'No. Neely. No way.'

She conceded. Her skin carpet-burned into the flat wouldn't do her any favours when it came time for evidence.

'Shut the door,' he whispered.

Neely scoffed. 'He's not watching, Sam. It's a bit late for that.'

He lay back on the bed and she took him in her hand. Nothing at all. Again. She nearly laughed – so much had changed, but some things never would, between them.

'Sam,' she hissed. 'You fucking want this. You want this so bad, and you're never going to get it again. Ever.'

He didn't reply. She slid down the bed, held her breath, and began sucking him off. Neely hated this, no matter who it was; hated the assault on her senses that came from putting her mouth where it had no business. She coached herself in her mind, urging herself on with encouragement she would never get elsewhere: *You're OK, girl. This is it. Just one time. This is all that's left, then you're done. Forever.* She thought of Angela and wondered how much of that short life had been spent engaged in this indignity, maybe in the same bed, on the same sheets. And she hadn't even wanted it. She couldn't have. Angela knew who she was and what she wanted and it wasn't Sam Wylie, it wasn't any man, but she had done it anyway, she had done a hell of a lot more than Neely had. And then she'd had the strength to say it meant nothing.

She felt him getting harder against her tongue, and impulsively she stifled a gag, *Jesus Christ, how could he, this is wrong* but Sam had his hands in her hair and they had both reached a point of no return, so she shut her eyes and imagined elsewhere. And another time. A happy girl, on the train into King's Cross, heading into a future she so naively believed would simply fall into her lap, and into her hands. *She will be okay*. Neely was not in a flat in Hackney, she was not in Harrow Road, she was still in a London she dreamed of on the way in from Stevenage. In those dreams the streets were nameless and the people had no faces except for her own. If she could draw like Angela could draw, then she could sketch features onto each passer-by, one at a time, building their identities with lines and curves, making an entire city in her image. And Neely once thought she could. Make yourself a place, she had thought, and you will own a scrap of the world. In her head, she recited the mantra, all the stations in order: *Stevenage, Knebworth, Welwyn North, Welwyn Garden City, Hatfield*. All those times the future she had been all but promised, the one she had expected to arrive at her door like a parcel delivery, had seemed within her grasp, right there at the end of the line. *Welham Green, Brookmans Park, Potters Bar*. And the line was right there. It was drawn on maps. It was drilled into the landscape. *Hadley Wood, New Barnet*. It didn't change, hadn't changed. Not in her lifetime. And it probably never would. *Oakleigh Park, New Southgate, Alexandra Palace*. And now, twenty-seven years and some matter of months, Neely lay in a bed that was not hers, sucking off a man who was not hers, in Hackney, thinking *Hornsey, Harringay, Finsbury Park, King's Cross where this train terminates*, and wondered how she had possibly got there.

When she had brought him almost to the brink but not quite, he had tears in his eyes. Hers were already sliding down her face.

'We shouldn't, Neels.'

'Yes, we should.' She pushed him back, her palm on his chest, and lowered herself on top of him, not caring if he saw her wince. Eyes closed, she didn't see anything. Sam came too soon, and with a shudder; this time, when they collapsed together, their sweat felt cold.

'Neels.'

'What?'

'You shouldn't stay here.'

'I know.'

Neely stared at the ceiling and listened to the heartbeat slowing, steadying itself. He slid out of her. Unprotected. So much for not leaving any trace at the scene. Relatively speaking, it didn't matter. Absolutely speaking, it probably meant even less.

Slowly, Neely pulled herself upright. Let her legs dangle off the side of the bed. She didn't even smell the air any more, the air and the blood.

'Neels.'

'WHAT?'

'I don't know what I'm going to do.'

She shrugged, and she sighed. 'I told you. Wrap him up. Dump him in the canal. Throw him away like her threw her.' She bent down to retrieve her shirt, and his; she moved slowly, pitying him, letting him have a long last look at her arse. 'But do it yourself. Not my problem. See this? See this nose? It's well out of it. Figure it out yourself. I'm not your designated thinker.'

'Neels. There's nobody else who can deal with this.'

'I know.'

'Please don't fuck this up.'

'I won't.'

'Promise.'

'I won't.'

'That's all you can say?'

'Something wrong with that?'

'You usually have all the answers.'

She laughed despite herself, and shook her head. 'No I don't,' Neely scoffed. 'No, I abso-fucking-lutely do not. Never have, never will.' She slid one foot into a boot, then the other. 'But, my god, it felt really, really good to know somebody thought I did.'

Neely stuck out her arm to hail the bus, and wormed her way through the Friday afternoon crush up to the stairs, up to the upper deck. One seat was vacant: front row, far left, best view of Dalston for the price of one ride. She stepped over the spread legs of the young man occupying its neighbour. She landed on the upholstery with a thud. *That's all*, she thought. *I am completely and utterly alone in this city*. Neely closed her eyes and listened to the rumble of the tyres on the road, and she smiled. She was free, and she knew what to do: get out of it completely.

She owed Brian Powell nothing. She owed Sam barely more. But neither of them factored into the decision she had made and solidified as soon as she got to the Overground station: she wouldn't tell anybody what she had seen, what had been done. That would only drag her deeper into this mess, enmesh her further into something that had never been in those grand plans for life and how London would give it to her. She owed it to herself to only think of Angela now.

Dalston Junction to Highbury & Islington. To King's Cross. To Westbourne Park. Out of the station and up the road. Past the Hope and Anchor where, through cloudy glass, Mel was wiping down tables with her arse stuck out for emphasis. *I should get a drink*, Neely thought. One last pint there. An alibi. And then it's straight home and onto the computer to clear the history and find another fucking place to live. Not West. Not East. North would do. A shared house in zone 3 with a few self-important media types who like their banter and like their barbecues in the summer, in their postage stamp of a back garden. *Little patch of earth for herbs, and I'll learn to cook, I'll learn to make the best Sunday roast in North London. We'll talk about the TV, we'll talk about books, we'll bitch about the authors. They'll be people we know. That will do nicely.* She closed her eyes again and pictured the map. Wood Green, maybe. It wasn't posh, but it seemed aspirational, right there at the foot of the hill, looking up at Alexandra Palace instead of down at Harrow Road. It's what she would have liked, before she had a life.

She showered, cold this time. Any blood on her had to be her own.

Neely twisted her hair atop her head, tied on the fluffy red bath robe – still fluffy, even after a wash – and pulled her mobile out from her handbag. Touched *CONTACTS*. Angela. A photograph of a blonde girl in a black hat, a fedora or a trilby or whatever it's called, with a bottle of Heineken in her slim fingers. Always summer in that photograph, the brief and beautiful London summer pixellated into memory.

Her fingers moving without her, Neely deleted the entry.

Then she touched the spot on the screen marked *RECENT*, and touched the number she had been trying so hard to memorise.

One ring. Two.

'Rachel Martin.'

'It's Neely Sharpe.'

'Oh, hello, Neely. How are you?'

'I've got your story.'

Twenty-Two

Age sixteen. Autumn now. Marianthi gone to Wood Green, Angela finished with school forever. Chioma Acholonu had wished her good luck before she left on the last day, and Angela had stood, blankly, wondering why she would need it.

Packing up the flat, packing up their lives. Angela stacked her father's framed photographs in cardboard boxes dragged home from Sainsbury's, sheets of newspaper between them. She smiled despite herself at the portraits encased in their temporary tomb, disguised as Walkers salt and vinegar packs of six. The landscapes were All-Bran, some miscellany turned into Ambrosia Devon Custard.

There was little left in the fridge now, awaiting moving day, and Angela felt like chips. She picked out enough in coins from a mess on the kitchen table and set out for the café beneath the Trellick Tower. She could do this walk blindfolded, but she knew there wouldn't be too many of these times left to attempt it. East Acton would be different. It was just down the road, yeah, but it was far enough. She'd have more people to talk to, and new streets to be seen, when they found that paradise southwest of Kensal Green.

She closed her eyes and felt her way down the corridor, down the stairs. The change in the breeze told her when she'd made it to the street. Angela followed the familiar curve of Hazelwood Crescent and allowed herself a peek when she stepped into Golborne Road – just in time to spring back and avoid the fast turn of a Ford Mondeo.

'Fuck,' she heard, a familiar voice she'd successfully avoided for several months, until then, until there. 'Trying to get yourself killed?'

Angela opened her eyes to see him standing across the street. Like nothing had happened, like any day in Kensal Town. Like shared jokes and confidences. Like something sure. Funny how something as immeasurably tiny as a feeling could gain the power to erase entire expanses of time. Funny how it could knock away ancient dirt, bulldoze all that elm and lime and London plane. She looked both ways this time. Forgot about any hunger, any fire in her belly. After all, she knew he didn't have much time. He smiled and for a moment she forgot. Silently, she shifted course. She followed the shape and its long, slim shadow across, down, through St Ervans Road.

'Go on,' Charlie told Angela, as Brian sparked up in the corner. 'Touch it.'

She'd never seen a gun before, not a real one. Only in films and on television, where nobody ever seemed to need to ask how to get one, and rarely did anybody hesitate or mull over the consequences of a pulled trigger. They were decisive, they were bold.

'You can pick it up,' Mo added. 'It's not loaded.'

'Why not?'

'Because I haven't fucking loaded it yet.'

She knew better to ask where it had come from, or where it was going.

'Go on. Pick it up.'

Angela reached out tentatively, as if not to disturb a sleeping creature. The gun was a dull, matt black. Smaller than she had usually imagined them, on the rare occasions she'd had reason to do just that. She had expected metal cold to the touch, but this felt as natural and normal as the tins she stacked at Sainsbury's. The weight satisfied; the angles fitted perfectly into her palm and fingers. She raised it slowly, reverently. Strange how something so small could be so powerful. So decisive.

Charlie burst into laughter.

'You mong! You fucking mong!'

'What?' Angela lowered the gun, the scene ruined, the image shattered. She spotted a clump of cat hair matted into the carpet just to the side of her knee.

He was crying with laughter now, actual tears glistening in the corners of his eyes. 'Oh my god, fuck, you're so easy. That's your fingerprints all over it now.'

Impulsively, she dropped the gun. It looked silly now, like a toy. 'How do you mean?'

'I fucking mean,' he started, gasping in his own laughter, raising his voice to talk over Mo's, 'That you're the last person who touched this gun and that's all I need.'

'What?'

'How fucking stupid *are* you? Do you just do anything people tell you?'

'Brian, what did you do?' But again, he had nothing to say, just a silence he punctuated by standing and leaving his bedroom. She thought she heard the turn of the lock in the toilet after he shut the door, but she couldn't be sure.

She lunged for the gun, but Charlie swept it out of her way with his foot, and stuffed it back in his bag with a sock over one hand. And that was the one time Angela really felt as stupid as everybody said she was – the time she thought, for a second time, that she might actually get an answer.

'You know what I said about it not being loaded?' Charlie said, back to serious, back to sure. 'Lied to you. So you're going to leave right now and be a good girl and not say one word, yeah? Are those short enough words for you? Do you need it in sign language? Big print?'

She ran.

She ran through all the streets she knew, and that she would remember: Golborne Road, Portobello Road and the market and who the fuck cared that she looked like she'd stolen something, Ladbroke Grove, the posh bit of Lancaster Road, the less posh bit, the crap bit, through the estate car parks and all who occupied them staring at her, the canyon in the tower blocks, the concrete and the brick, to Andy on her high perch.

Andy dried her tears. Yelled her out of her hysterics. Gave her a gulp of her vodka even though it wasn't a good idea, definitely not a good idea with her fits, but fuck what was a good idea for her fits. Andy told her to stay there, stay safe ten storeys up looking down at the motorway and the Tube, pretending it was all a big computer game, the movement of the city and the consequences therein, just stay right there while Andy smashed it all better.

And Angela did as she was told, for a bit. She wandered the small confines of her sister's flat, ran her fingertips over the furniture, snooped through her cupboards (ugh, all that Pot Noodle), tried on new-looking dresses that hung off her like tarps. She flicked on the television but found herself drawn to the window, where she curled into the frame. The cars all looked alike from up there, just identical boxes, moving together, shifting in time.

Then she locked up and walked – slowly this time – to what was still home.

Her carefully packed boxes were toppled, the photographs strewn across the carpet. A tornado had torn through the family home and taken the remains of the family with it. For a fraction of a second, Angela misinterpreted the scene in front of her. A completely understandable mistake, with all those curves and angles. It could have looked like love, then: Andy on top – as if she'd be anywhere else – with a knee planted on each side of Brian Powell, all her weight upon him, one hand around one skinny wrist. No gun. Just a knife, the fuck-off serrated bread knife the Archers never needed to use, pressed to his neck. He wasn't even fighting.

'You wouldn't look out for her,' Andy hissed. 'I will.'

From the door, unseen, Angela saw her raise the knife. And then Andy laughed. Angela remembered it because she couldn't remember the last time she'd heard it: genuine joy from her sister. Angela had looked away, awaiting the inevitable, but she couldn't help smiling to herself: *I want to laugh that laugh.*

'There's no point. You're already dead,' Angela heard her sister say, and when she looked back, there was no bloodbath, just a thin red curve blooming slowly, elegantly, along the line of his jaw.

Then, to her sister: 'Where's your schoolbag?'

Andy walked her to the Harrow Road, under the Westway. The roar of traffic overhead made talking pointless. Angela had never seen her sister with such calm focus, such assurance. For once, she looked satisfied in her own skin. She tried to match Andy's stride, tried to keep up.

Beneath them, in the wide open cut of the railway, the faint announcement from the Tube station: *This is Royal Oak.* The two moved faster through the treeless concrete landscape, picking up speed to match the Great Western train heading in the opposite direction, out of the city, wiping its path clean.

Then they stopped. Andy scuffed the toes of her boots – impressive heels, dangerous points to the tips, miraculously unscratched, not at all like those she'd worn growing up in Kensal Town – against the pavement. With one toe, she pointed to the kerb, to a bit of grate. Angela had never noticed it before. She had never needed to.

'Angela.'

'Yeah?'

'You should always know exactly where you don't want to go.'

Without even scanning her surroundings, she reached into Angela's denim satchel and dropped the knife down the grate. Andy didn't bother watching it land. She was looking up at the motorway, staring at the sky.

The posters came down where they could, frayed and rotted where they couldn't. Angela Archer, still blonde with dark roots, still wearing those gold hoops that were just a little too big and a little too trashy for the right kind of missing young white woman, still stared out at West London here and there. But outside Royal Oak Tube she lost one of those eyes and one of those earrings, and the snow come the end of February stained her face until it bled through to the club poster beneath her, and nobody who ever knew Angela Archer, or thought they did, could recognise her.

'I don't trust the police,' Neely had whimpered over the phone, listening to the journalist typing up her words. 'And I don't want – I don't want them slagging her off, yeah? When she isn't here to defend herself. But I trust you. And I want there to be something... nice written about Angela. So that she's not just a victim.'

It was in her journal, Neely said. Angela was scared of him. Always had been, ever since they were kids. He'd never let her go. He'd been stalking her. Following her home from work all the time. Saying *awful* things, *absolutely dreadful* things, that if he couldn't have her, nobody could, and terrifying her with guilt, saying he would kill himself, maybe drown himself in the canal, maybe jump out a window, maybe crash a motorbike. And the last entry Angela had ever made – well, off the record, entirely off the record, don't want him coming after me next – there was an address, Richmond Road in Hackney, maybe it's his, maybe someone should go round and check. His name's Brian

Powell. Somebody should really look into him. Go knock on some doors. In case he was serious.

Neely had surprised herself with how quickly the lies had rolled off her tongue, and how easy it had been to unleash them. This Rachel Martin, *Evening Standard*, all earnest voice and eagerness to make a name for herself, just like Neely had been those short years ago before aspiration became a different country, had lapped it up. The promised puff piece, the tribute, had gone straight from Neely's lips into reality: *We were going to run away to Brighton and get married on New Year's Day. Nobody knew. Brighton was special to Angela. It was the long lanes, the smell of the sea.* Neely said it and she didn't know why, but it flew from her mouth and onto paper and pixel, and it might as well have been real because there was nobody to tell her otherwise. Once she began, she couldn't stop, and the further it went, the better she felt. Andy had been right: memory was only going to drag her down. And Sam had been right, too: she only wanted to make another world. And she could.

There on the *Evening Standard*'s front page, a slightly blurry snapshot from an old night out: a blonde girl with dark roots with her arm around a skinny little thing in platform shoes bringing her up to average height, because somehow average became good enough. GIRLFRIEND'S TRUTH ABOUT TRAGIC ANGELA, the headline read. Angela Archer and Neely Sharpe, captured last summer at the Electric Ballroom in Camden Town, stared out at all of London on this one day, looking them in the eye with their smiles and their make-up on. Everyone would know, Neely thought, and everyone should bloody well know it was her who put together the pieces. Somebody should notice she is brighter than most.

'Angela was haunted,' Sharpe explains, sitting up straight on the couch in the flat they once shared. Reminders of the life that has gone adorn the walls: a black-and-white photograph of a young Angela on a riverbank and a summer festival snap of the two young women together. 'The police did nothing, nobody did anything. She felt that nobody was really looking out for her, and that nobody could ever help her deal with all the sadness she had inside. But nobody deserves sadness.'

To herself, she had thought: *Least of all me.*

'She'd come into some money a few years back and was saving it up.

Nobody was supposed to know. We were going to travel everywhere – that's what we were going to do. Leave our jobs, leave everyone, not tell a soul. Go to Morocco, go to Tenerife. It sounds so silly saying it out loud, but that's what she really wanted to do. She'd sell her artwork on the street, and we'd only come back when all the money had run out. Angela and I never told anybody this, but she really felt she could just leave tomorrow without a second thought. She had this thing she'd always say: we would go off to paradise by way of Kensal Green. Drive down the Harrow Road and not tell a soul and not care what anybody thought of us.'

Tears well in the petite office manager's eyes as she pages through her late girlfriend's journal. A faint smile appears on her face as she lingers on a line drawing of Kensal House in Ladbroke Grove, near where Angela Archer lived as a child.

'She could have done so much with her life. Look at these drawings – they're fantastic. I'm looking for a publisher who'll do a book of them. It's a very 'specific piece of West London at a very specific time, and one that's disappearing. She was part of it.'

'Everybody knows her as some girl who worked at the leisure centre, but Angela had a fire inside, and that's what I want everybody to know. We were each the only person the other had ever loved. Ever. I think there's more to Angela than any of us will ever know. I think she's left some more for us to find.'

An hour after the journalist and the photographer left 490 Harrow Road, so did Neely. She walked to the newsagents, a stack of photocopies under her arms. Words and pictures. Blown up from the A5 journal pages and extracted from their colourful binding. She stuck them up, hoping Angela's handwriting would be clear enough for all the local barely-literates to read: *Mo Zubairi was the worst. Because I thought he was better than this. But when he had a go I know he didn't enjoy it. God knows how he got hard enough. But he did it anyway. Rape the lezzer to prove you're not gay? I honestly don't think he's clever enough to have come up with that one by himself, but I thought he would be kind enough to not do it. I guess he knows his secret's safe with me.* Angela's portrait of him was particularly accurate, especially enlarged to life size. And Neely had extras from a time when she had hope, a time that seemed so long ago: MISSING – ANGELA ARCHER – 24 YEARS OLD – 5'9" TALL, BLONDE HAIR, GREEN EYES, FROM HARROW ROAD. WEARING LONG BLACK COAT, SHORT RED BOOTS, BLACK HANDBAG. DISAPPEARANCE OUT OF CHARACTER. Wide eyes and big goldish hoops. The next morning, Neely didn't walk by the shop to gauge the owner's reaction. And she knew there would be a reaction. If not from him, then from the passers-by on this sad and busy strip of West London. After all, superglue is a bastard to remove.

Neely crossed the street and walked past the Hope and Anchor, where the doors were shut and the lights were off. Head down, she didn't spot the signs written in Mel's sloppy hand and Sellotaped up with her fingerprints: closed until further notice. Further notice meant forever.

The bailiffs parked outside ate their sandwiches and waited for the locksmiths. Shithole, one said to the other. No money in pubs any more, the other said to the one. Plenty of money being made on the drugs, sure, but they don't sell those behind the bar and the dealers don't give a cut to the landlord. But maybe they should. Good old-fashioned partnership. It might save a couple of these places.

The first squinted through the darkened pub window and reiterated: shithole. And the other didn't argue. He turned to his copy of the *Standard* and dropped a dollop of tuna mayo down Angela Archer's top. He paused before popping it back into his mouth, but not for too long. He looked out the other side of the van, but not for long enough. Was that her, here, this bit of the Harrow Road? Nah. No way. And then he flipped the paper over for the football.

There was no exasperation for too much time off thrown at the skinny little thing from the photo when she went back to work one Monday. There was something worse. Pity. Endless looks of concern, the constant requests to know if she was alright, if she *really really was alright*, because *it's OK to cry, to let it all out*, as if Neely didn't know that already, as if she would possibly want to do such a thing in front of the graduate scheme cohort who had blogged and Facebooked and tweeted that they knew the girl who loved the girl who died. There were pats on the back, there were hugs she hated because they hurt the little knobbly bones of her spine, there were declarations that she was so brave and that they all admired her having the guts to speak up. She wanted to tell them, *no*. No, fuck you, you haven't the foggiest, it didn't take bravery to sell her story to the papers. After all, she got paid for that. She got paid enough to go all the places she'd lied about planning to go with Angela, and then some. But she didn't spit that out; she let the words unspoken roll around in her mouth until she swallowed them in one gulp. They were bitter. She let them harden deep inside her, let them be burnt and pressed into a diamond. She refused the offer of more time off. She put her head down and got back to work. She smiled, and she made the tea. She Googled coroner's inquests again to see what would be expected of her. And she checked every news outlet morning and evening with a thoroughness approaching obsession, but nothing of a body discovered in Hackney, in the canal or otherwise; nothing of an arrest of a Sam Wylie. She'd heard nothing from Sam, and silently to herself, she thanked him: he'd paid attention to her words. He'd left her out of it, whatever 'it' was now. Whatever might come of her saying Brian Powell's name, Brian Powell's street, to Rachel the journalist – it wouldn't be her fault. It would be someone else's triumph, and someone else's problem.

And then she lost it. No, not exactly then, but about a week later, boiling pasta in her kitchen. She reached for the salt shaker, and something, maybe muscle memory or maybe just a vicious kick of history, reminded her of reaching for something else: the days of the week, so certain to follow each other the way they had always been arranged, until one day they had stopped. She knocked the salt onto the floor, and then the tears just wouldn't stop coming. She shot off a sloppy, misspelled email to her manager and said she needed another week. No need to explain why. They'd all read it in clinical detail. She packed one bag, stumbled down the stairs even with the brand-new light bulb showing her the way, and got on a train back to Mum and Dad and her old bedroom from years before Angela Archer and Harrow Road and the *Evening Standard*. She watched London melt away into greens and browns and an overflowing ashtray of a sky. She had stepped off this train at this station hundreds of times – her teenage shopping trips and gigs in the capital, coming home to her mum or her brother waiting in the car – but this time was different, this time her stomach dropped right to her feet and stayed there. It was the feeling from childhood, of letting the ribbon of a helium balloon slip from her fingers, and the instant she realised what was gone would never, ever come back. It was hers, it was precious, maybe it even had her name on it. But now it was gone, and it was not her fault, but it was her business.

In her dreams, Neely is a fish. She is swimming, not at the Porchester Centre, where Angela Archer's work clothes are still entombed in her old locker, but in a leisure centre in Stevenage, somewhere on the edge of the new town where she grew up. She cuts effortlessly through the blue water, tapping at the wall and shooting back across, over and over without a pause. Well, not until she hears the voice – and she doesn't know whose voice, just some disembodied call: *There's someone who wants to see you outside.*

She hoists herself up out of the pool. She shoves her feet into the old sandals. She wraps herself in a towel, walks back to the lockers, gives herself a quick wash under the shower and wrings out her hair. She strips in the empty room, then jumps into her trackie bottoms and pulls on the same old blue sweatshirt and trades her sandals for trainers. She retrieves her pound coin from the back of the locker door – even in her dreams, Neely never forgets the pound coin. She runs her thumb over the serrated edge and its letters. *Decus Et Tutamen.* An ornament and a safeguard. She's read somewhere or other, because she's the kind to read these things, that one in fifty pound coins are counterfeit. But it means nothing to her life. Neely drops it into her pocket and walks out, past the front desk, out into the lazy winter sunshine where her breath makes thin white puffs around her head.

Angela is there. Angela Archer is there in her *long black coat, wool, size twelve*; in her *distinctive red ankle boots, New Look, size six,* carrying her *black leather-look handbag* which presumably contains her *wallet and mobile phone.* Bruises ring her neck, her hair is matted and her face is death-white where it isn't blackening. But it is Angela Archer, alive and smiling at Neely.

'I forgot your Christmas pressie,' Angela says.

'What? You didn't have to get me anything.'

'I'm really sorry. I forgot your Christmas present,' she repeats.

'Angela, don't be silly.' And she takes the blonde girl in her arms, the blonde girl who is now just bones and ash, who feels like nothing but bones under that bloody black coat. There is a dead leaf stuck in her hair. Neely picks it out and holds it up for a better look.

Angela Archer takes it from her hand and flicks it away. Then she links her arm in Neely's, like they used to on the canal towpath, when Angela would pile her hair under a newsboy's cap with the brim sloppily askew and speak of magic, and all of it in one place. Angela takes Neely down the road, down to her old street. Neely wonders, but not for particularly long, how Angela knew the way. At the corner stand her parents and Mr Archer with his photographs, talking business; outside the neighbour's house her big brother is leaning against their red Renault, joking with their son. Andrea and Alex Archer are on the other side of the street, staring. A car passes just before they cross: Marianthi Adamou in the driver's seat, waving, still looking a bit like that singer. Neely catches a quick glimpse of the young man from the Harrow Road newsagents, the one who wouldn't let one particular photocopied face darken his window, as Angela takes her to the front door of the home where she grew up. She could have sworn she caught sight of Rob darting out of the garden. *You don't have to go,* she wants to call to him. *You're fine where you are. There's absolutely nothing wrong with where you are.*

Neely tries the door. It opens. Angela drops her arm.

'Are you coming in?'

Angela shakes her head.

'Why not?'

She shakes her head again. 'That's me off.'

'Where are you going?'

Angela doesn't answer. She turns to leave and there is a gash down the back of her head, one Neely hadn't seen before.

'Angela, come on, wait!'

The girl stops and looks at her curiously, her eyes prompting, *So, what?*

'Did it hurt? Or was it, you know… was it quick?' *Did you suffer*, she means. *Did you fight? Did you give in? Would you tell if you did?*

Angela looks down at the pebble-dashed driveway. Smiles just the slightest bit. 'You know how lads tell you that maybe all you need is a good cock and then you'll change?'

And then they laugh – not girly giggles, but loud belly laughs and ear-splitting shrieks. Their parents and siblings creep over to in front of the Sharpes' home and peer through the hedges, over the wall, curiosity on their faces, wondering just what is so very funny. But even if they wanted to, the girls couldn't tell them. They gasp for breath, then lose it again in hysterics. Angela plops down into the grass, tears streaming from her eyes as she laughs the laugh that Neely never quite learned, but not for lack of trying. Neely feels the doorknob in her back, hits it with her head on the way to the ground, and laughs harder for the stupidity in it. By the time she recovers enough to open her eyes and stand up straight, the blonde bloodied girl is gone.

Angela Archer was 24 years old, five foot nine inches tall and of proportionate build, with green eyes. She had dyed blonde hair, and at the time she disappeared she had medium brown roots showing. She failed to return to her flat in Harrow Road. Her disappearance was completely out of character and her family and friends believed she did not leave voluntarily. Angela was wearing a long black coat and distinctive red ankle boots and carrying a black leather-look handbag believed to contain her wallet and mobile phone. She was last seen on the 18th of December in the Harrow Road. And that's it.

The dream is better. And Neely is just about ready to admit it.

Because the dream is almost always more interesting than the truth, and it's never the truth that makes a story. Truth happens every minute of every day, on every street, from Hazelwood Crescent in Kensal Town to the poshest corner of Kensington proper. It shoots down railways from new towns and old roads, and back up them again. Truth is waiting on Wormwood Scrubs and rippling along the canal, water like black binbags at night, reflecting up blank faces and rainbow slicks of oil in those rare moments of sun. The faces change and the chemical swirls shift but, once they're seen, they're never really gone. Somebody remembers they were there. Somebody watches and somebody waits.

Sometimes somebody writes. And it is a December evening not long before Christmas when Angela Archer's mobile buzzes with a text from a number so old she has it memorised, not saved in her contacts. *Party tonight. You coming?*

She smiles alone in her flat. *Yeah of course. After work*, she shoots back, and straightens her collar. Porchester Centre, it reads over her heart. She bundles herself into the black coat, the one Neely thinks looks so smart even though Angela thinks it has never really felt quite right on her bones. Feet slide into the red ankle boots. Size 6, the last pair of size 6 at New Look. *Your feet look gorgeous*, it says in silvery script on the insoles. Angela smiles. She always changes into the trainers she keeps in her work locker, but for the journey there, and the journey she intends to take back, she wants to take a little pride. That's all she ever wanted. Head held high, feet placed surely one in front of the other.

Through to the kitchen. Quick drink of water. She hesitates, and then she takes the tablet from the little box marked FRIDAY. But she doesn't pop it into her mouth and swallow. Angela holds it between thumb and forefinger as she gathers her few odds and ends – mobile, wallet, keys, things that could belong to anybody but this time they belong to Angela. They're souvenirs of a life, telling anybody who might bother to look that she has lived: she has friends, though few of them call any more now that she and her girlfriend have shacked up; she has a bit of cash, though it's never enough and never as much as Neely has; and she has a place to live, albeit on the street that always made her mother feel so poor and foreign and sad and sick. Angela cups the tiny tablet in her palm as she locks the door and feels her way down the darkened stairs. It's growing soft and sweaty by the time she steps out onto Harrow Road.

She flicks the tiny yellow lozenge out onto the road. It bounces on the pavement, catching street light, before rolling over the kerb and down into the gutter. *I don't need it*, Angela thinks. *I won't need it at all.* She's looking forward to seeing him. She's looking forward to tonight. Odds and ends that could be anybody's, but tonight, they're hers. For old time's sake. The way they used to be. She smiles and looks up at the rapidly darkening sky, feeling the fingers of the chill combing through her curls. She thinks of Neely, a girl so sad and strange and looking for a place in this world to match, and how her beloved Neely has a word for everything, an explanation for everything, all that trivia in her head – she could tell you the opening day of Westbourne Park Station but if she only knew about this – nah, it would blow her mind. She doesn't need to know. She'll never need to know. He can't hurt me, she reminds herself. He never has and he never will. He can't. Now I am fucking invincible. Because maybe I am an angel. Maybe I am already a ghost. And I will never, ever, ever die again.

Acknowledgements

I would like to thank the team at Unbound, particularly Kwaku Osei-Afrifa, Cressida Downing, Andrew Chapman, Xander Cansell, and Mark Ecob, for making this something you can have and hold.

The Columbia Fiction Foundry is where a project turned into a publishable book, and I thank every member of the workshop for their critiques and encouragement. A special thank you to Ralph White, Richard Hensley, Jen Kitses, David Gulley, and Will Hughes for their extensive feedback. The late Leslie Woodard, also at Columbia University, gave me the tough love every writer needs.

In London, gratitude to Tara Allen, Matthew Ames, Dimos Christodoulakis, and Peter Hicks for lending a place to stay when I felt pulled back across the sea. To Ben Ellis, Sean McGhee, and Andrew Montgomery for tales from the creative trenches. To Kayley Kravitz, for being the greatest friend imaginable and offering endless patience and optimism.

Finally, to my family – Steven, Catherine, and David Kite – for their belief in me, and in the possibilities of all those endless hours I spent behind notebook and keyboard. To my beloved Hal Laidlaw, the future and all it holds.

Patrons

Cordelia Bailey
Alistair Bell
Sharon Benjamin
Susan Braver
Joe Bryan
Wendy Grutterink-van Loon
Chris Hampson
Rita & Jim Heinsimer
Rachel Hensel
Harry Howard
Emma Jones
Peter Kaufman
Beezly Kiernan
Matthew Kroneberger
Grace Laidlaw
Doug Lindner
Richard Lombard
Kyle Lukoff
Bill Marden
Ellen McDermott
Denise Milstein
Ivy Moya
Young Musicians
Kasia Nikhamina
Dave O'Brien
Adam Sacarny
Dan Schinleber
Rabia Syed
Valerie Taylor
Tra Vu
Paul Walters
Ralph White

Monica White
David Winner
Rob Wolf
Tamar Zeffren